thrall

A NOVEL BY

REBECCA MAHONEY

HYPERION AVENUE
LOS ANGELES NEW YORK

First Paperback Edition, April 2026
10 9 8 7 6 5 4 3 2
FAC-004510-26163
Printed in the United States of America

Designed by Amy C. King
Art by © Adobe Stock and Shutterstock

Library of Congress Control Number for Paperback Edition: 2025947052
ISBN 978-1-368-11381-6

The authorized representative in the EU for product safety and compliance is Disney Trading B.V., Asterweg 15S, 1031 HL, Amsterdam, The Netherlands
email: DCP.DL-EU.bookscontact@disney.com

www.HyperionAvenueBooks.com

SUSTAINABLE FORESTRY INITIATIVE Certified Sourcing
www.forests.org
SFI-01681

Logo Applies to Text Stock Only

To BLCZ House, my roommates and friends.

Wherever we go, I'll always invite you in.

TRANSCRIPT OF ROLLINS UNIVERSITY STUDENT RADIO STATION WVBS ("PALLAS RADIO")

Broadcast number: Not yet assigned

UNKNOWN SPEAKER: My mother always said I'd get eaten alive, out here in the world.

Of course, every time she said it, "the world" meant a different thing. The bus stop. The crosswalk. College, eventually. When I was little, I always thought reassuring her was just a matter of proving that I was capable of navigating the wicked snares of the grocery store parking lot. But what my mother was holding on to was deeper, like it so often is. What she was afraid of was never bus stops, or crosswalks, or campuses. To her, they were all the same: a lottery wheel, always turning. And every time she or I left the house, it turned again and again.

I was never afraid of the wheel. Maybe it was the fact that she'd raised me in a layer of Bubble Wrap, but I've always found it romantic that there's no real life without chance. And if all the terrible things waiting for me—in the grocery store, at the crosswalk, or here, on our campus—if all of them came down to bad luck, then that was more comforting than scary. There's no real malice in that. Whatever could happen to me, it would never be personal.

I tried to tell her that, once. But that was never how she saw it. To her, the wheel had intention. It had teeth.

Maybe you're thinking, *Bet you wish you'd listened to her now*. But I think we were both right. There was something waiting for me, out here in the world. It *was* by chance. It wasn't my fault. And it was never personal.

But it had teeth all the same.

One

Lucy Easting, once again, took a slightly incorrect step. Her new roommate hadn't yet requested that Lucy avoid every one of the particularly noisy floorboards in their ancient dorm room. But judging by the way she arched her shoulders like an unhappy cat, it would, at the very least, be a future suggestion.

"Sorry," Lucy said.

Whitney Fielding took a carefully controlled breath. "It's fine," she said.

Lucy focused on the task at hand. She had to laugh. There she was, standing in her college dorm, the very first place she had ever lived without her mother. And yet getting ready for a night out still had the same furtive feeling as it had on nights when she literally had to sneak out under Jillian's nose.

But Lucy kept the smile on her face, even as she caught the wrinkle in Whitney's brow deepening. She had a plan. A whole host of plans, in fact—and staying civil with Whitney for the next ten months and change was one of them. Which meant that if Whitney was trying to cook up some Noble Academic vs. Frivolous Party Girl dichotomy, it was going to fall to Lucy to gracefully sidestep it.

Whitney kept her back turned, facing her computer. "You're not coming back late, right?" she asked. "I'm a light sleeper."

Lucy tied off the bust of her sunshine-yellow romper, then moved the important things from her purse to a small, light wristlet. Lipstick, pepper spray, keys. Insurance card and ID, because even if she and Whitney were in the midst of a cold war, she was still Jillian's daughter. In the Easting house, whenever you stepped out the front door, you always made the basic preparations to be hit by a bus.

"I'll be quiet," Lucy said, not committing either way. She could respect Whitney's laser focus on her thesis, even if it seemed a bit early in the year to be so intense about it. But her arrival at Rollins University was the result of five years of working, careful planning, and an explosive, bridge-burning exit from the place she'd called home her entire life. She wasn't looking to reinstate a curfew her first week of college.

It had been a tremendous relief for Lucy to hear that she was being placed in a senior dorm. At twenty-three years old, she had little to no chance to blend in with the freshmen.

And Whitney didn't seem to care that she was two years younger than Lucy. If anything, she seemed to think that she was the older of the two, saddled with some callow, directionless youth.

"If you want my advice," Whitney said, "you should let your first few weeks here set the tone. Do you really want your college career to be about your social life?"

"I don't have any pre-reading for my classes," Lucy said, which felt like a nicer answer than *Yeah, a little*. Classes also wouldn't start for another two days. Though that didn't feel like the kind of argument Whitney would be sympathetic to.

Whitney glanced over her shoulder, a rare departure from her screen, and gave Lucy a rather pointed once-over. On one hand, after a five-year taste of grim adulthood, it was a novelty to be treated like a rebelling teen. On the other hand, Lucy had wavy pale blond hair that fluffed in the humidity, and was perhaps at its peak fluffiness on this late-summer Tennessee night. Her voice was a little high and a little loud in a way she knew sounded affected, though it wasn't. She had a stick-and-poke tattoo of an asterisk on her wrist, something her high school classmate had given her at a graduation party while tipsily monologuing that it symbolized her as a "work in progress." She recognized the look of someone who wasn't taking her seriously.

"If you wait for someone to tell you how to prepare, you're already behind," Whitney finally said. "Like they tell you in college coaching."

Lucy paused in the middle of zipping up her wristlet. "There's coaching?"

Whitney's mouth thinned, as if unsurprised that Lucy didn't know there was coaching. "Just be careful," she said.

"It's a big campus. You can get turned around at night."

Lucy zipped her wristlet the rest of the way and accepted the kindness. Rollins itself was about as small a world as one could get at a university. The grounds, spread across a plateau on the Tennessee side of the Appalachians, may have been sprawling, but the community was tight-knit and self-contained. Lucy had to take a plane, two buses, and a college-provided shuttle to get here. That shuttle went down to the nearest town a couple times a week, and on a regular schedule on weekends. Otherwise, the students, faculty, and staff never seemed to look far beyond the boundaries of campus.

But the nights were dark up there on the mountain. The woods surrounding the Rollins grounds stretched for miles. Jillian's fears had always revolved around cities and civilization—never the wilderness. Though, as she looked out the window in that moment, Lucy had a feeling her mother would find more than a few things to fear out there in the trees.

And speak of the devil. When Lucy picked up her phone, there was a new text from her mother on the screen.

Can we please talk?

Lucy allowed herself one short, painful breath. One last quick squeeze of filial duty. Then she slid her phone into her pocket. She hadn't been the one who decided they weren't talking.

"Good luck with your writing," she said to Whitney, who had already turned back to her laptop screen.

"I don't need luck," Whitney said airily. "I have an outline."

Lucy opened the door and stepped into the fluorescent-lit corridors of Quincey Hall. The hinge creaked behind her. The stairwell glowed ahead. Jillian's wheel silently, feverishly spun.

And beyond all of it, the night waited.

Lucy had never known how deep night could get until she came to Rollins. The dark was so complete, up there on the mountain: a thick country dark, heavy with mosquitoes and cicadas and a wind that never stopped fluttering. There were plenty of lampposts to guide the way, of course. But they never seemed to stretch very far down the path.

She had never seen real mountains before coming to Rollins. Had never been farther north than South Carolina, really. But her orientation leader had taken great pains to remind them all that when they walked the rocky trails surrounding campus, they were standing on something ancient. It had seemed like a weird digression in their course catalog tutorial, but she understood it now. These woods were prehistoric. And when it was this quiet, she felt it.

As she neared the bus shelter for the campus shuttle stop, she sidestepped what appeared to be a pile of leaves—only to realize with a jolt that it was a crumpled, dead rabbit. She looked away quickly from its matted fur, dotted red at its throat, and swallowed a wave of nausea before she tucked herself into the bus shelter. They'd been assured that any animals on campus would be much more scared of the students than the students were of them. She chose to believe that was true.

Falls Quad was nearly a mile walk from Lucy's dorm. She wouldn't have minded—after five years of standing at a cash register by day and emceeing *Wheel of Fortune* marathons with her grandfather by night, she was looking forward to seeing actual scenery again, even if that scenery did hold the occasional dead rabbit. But tonight, at least, she'd take Whitney's advice to heart.

A gust of wind rattled a line of flyers taped to the plexiglass, and Lucy absently read them as they settled. Most of them were the same neon-pink poster with bold black lettering. *Pallas 87.1,* they read. *Independent campus radio for the nocturnal among us. Airs nightly, 9 p.m.–2 a.m.* Which was a nice idea—kind of cool and old-fashioned, like a cassette mixtape. Although much like a cassette mixtape, Lucy wasn't sure *how* anyone actually listened to radio anymore.

Someone had scrawled *CRINGE* across the bottom of the flyer closest to her. Which seemed a bit harsh. Lucy raised her hand to it with the absent, sympathetic instinct to smudge the letters, but they were pretty well carved into the paper.

She didn't see the plain, faded flyer at first, haloed by the Pallas Radio advertisements. Though once she did, the first thing she noticed was the way the Pallas flyers gave this one a respectful berth. Most of the pink flyers overlapped edges with the older flyers around them, or covered them altogether. But this one had been avoided. It remained prominent, despite its age. And though it was faded, it was still legible.

MISSING
HAVE YOU HEARD FROM SADIE GRAINGER?

Last seen 9/22 Holmwood Hall. If you are in contact with Sadie, PLEASE ask her to reach out. We're not angry. We just want to know she's safe.

To send tips, please take contact info below.

The tabs at the bottom of the poster had all been ripped off. And in the center, there was a black-and-white picture of Sadie's face, largely faded except for dark eyes and a smiling mouth. Maybe it was the printer quality, but Lucy also thought she could make out a smattering of freckles.

Lucy smoothed the poster. Rollins had looked idyllic in the brochures, of course: hiking trails full of steep hills and clear waterfalls, lush gothic architecture, gushing testimonials from the student population of ambitious misfits. But it was the moment she saw it as a cold, impersonal dot on Google Maps that made her realize it was where she was meant to be. It wasn't as far as she could get from Jacksonville, distance-wise. But it was far from civilization. As far as she could imagine from the life she'd lived until then.

That isolation didn't suit everyone, though. She knew, from all her late nights reading everything she could find about the school, that the first-year dropout rate was unusually high. The student newspaper frequently published lengthy interviews with the campus mental health team, or homesickness-busting tips. Even the very bus shelter she was standing in had at least two posters reminding her to practice mindfulness.

Lucy's hand lingered on the missing poster for a moment. Her grandmother had always taught her to imagine stress like the pressure gauges they sold at their family's hardware store: You equalize, or you explode. *Little escapes,* she'd said. *That's the key. You've gotta come up for air every so often, or you drown.*

So she was great at little escapes. Long sprawls under the stars. Dancing at clubs that had been lenient with her fake ID. Stick-and-poke asterisk tattoos with dubious symbolic significance. It was a fine-tuned equation. Take on pressure, let off steam. Find an equilibrium until the bigger release could come.

Poor Sadie. Rollins was Lucy's goal. Her big release. If Sadie hadn't wanted to be there—Lucy could only imagine how claustrophobic the sprawling campus could become. It was difficult, under the poster's crinkled stare, to imagine anything but the worst. But hopefully Sadie just needed a little escape of her own. Hopefully she'd reach out when she was ready.

The campus shuttle rumbled up to the shelter. Lucy checked her destination one last time before she climbed aboard, and Sadie's black-and-white face whipped out of view as the bus pulled out into the loop road.

Falls Quad was a cluster of junior and senior dorms along the opposite edge of campus. Lucy had her phone out to check the suite number as she stepped onto the wet grass. Though, as it turned out, she didn't need to. A few feet away, there were people spilling through an open door into the quad, laughing almost too hard to stand up straight. Behind them, the heavy bass beats of "Tainted Love" thumped like a heart. It was extremely clear where the party was.

And if it hadn't been, the sign out front reading ALL ARE WELCOME! GET IN HERE!! would have given it away.

As Lucy crossed the lawn, she could see curtains fluttering in the other dorms. She couldn't tell if the eyes beyond were curious or glaring, but either way, she waved sheepishly and kept walking. She grew up in a tightly packed housing complex. She'd been the one glaring on the other side of the window her fair share of times.

She sidled around a group in the doorway. They barely shifted to let her pass—a curtain of body heat closed around her as she disappeared into the suite.

The way ahead was lit by two rotating globe lanterns with

aqua light and star-shaped cutouts, and the galaxies spun across the walls as Lucy made her way deeper. The swirls of light glanced across dancing figures, the effect twisting the room like curtains in a gale.

Lucy didn't notice that one of those figures had broken away to bound toward her until there was an arm slung around the back of her neck.

"There's my *girl*!" someone hollered in her ear. "Ready to start your Rollins life off right?"

Lucy huffed a startled laugh, and staggered around to face junior Natalie Baker, the party's host. She was beaming at her like they'd known each other for years, instead of for roughly thirty cumulative minutes. Though Lucy could already tell that that was probably just how Natalie was with everyone.

She'd first crossed paths with Natalie the day before, when Natalie gave Lucy's orientation group a library tour. They'd only exchanged a few words then, but Lucy had been able to see immediately why she'd been tapped to lead tours—she had an enviably smooth way of keeping a conversation going, even to a group too shy to laugh at most of her jokes. She had hennaed burgundy hair and a perpetually all-knowing grin, and she was built just like Lucy, short with rounded hips and a soft, prominent stomach. She'd been wearing the kind of rib-knit bodycon dress that Lucy's mother would have told her *wasn't suited for a pear shape*, and she made it look confident and effortless. So much so that Lucy had realized, with a jolt, that she could dress however she wanted now.

In any case, Natalie had stood out to Lucy. And apparently, Lucy had stood out to Natalie, too. Enough that Natalie had recognized her when they'd crossed paths at the campus pool earlier.

Lucy had been on her way to swim a few laps, blow off some steam, when a text from her mother buzzed in. Lucy understood that they were fighting, of course. Jillian had made that quite clear. But she hadn't expected the kind of low blow that had popped up on her phone screen this afternoon.

Then she'd looked up from that text and seen Natalie's smiling face waving her down. She'd burst into tears on the spot.

Which was probably what Natalie was thinking about now as she gave Lucy a once-over. Lucy grimaced, and strained to pitch her voice over the music. "I'm sorry again for earlier!"

Natalie vigorously shook her head. A few strands of hair got caught in her glow-in-the-dark lipstick. "I love a good cry!" she bellowed. "Wish my skin looked as good afterward as yours does! I'd have been pink and blotchy all day!"

Lucy laughed through the twist of embarrassment. But embarrassment didn't seem like an emotion Natalie Baker spent much time entertaining. Back at the pool, she'd sat Lucy down on one of the hard-backed plastic chairs, gotten her a glass of water, and let her cry it out. And when Lucy managed a few wobbly excuses about "family drama," she didn't pry.

Instead, she'd gently put both of her hands on both of Lucy's. *I don't know you,* she'd said. *And please tell me to fuck off if I'm overstepping. But you strike me as . . . someone who has not enjoyed herself recently.*

So there Lucy was, at the first campus rager of the year. Ready for one last little release so that the Big Release could begin in earnest.

But before that. "Hey," she said, "I saw a 'missing' poster at the shuttle stop?"

"Oh, shit, that." Natalie squeezed her arm. "Sorry, that's pretty jarring, right? That's why they warn you about the drop-out rate during orientation week! Not everyone's a good fit for the mountain!"

"Yeah," Lucy said. It was the same thing she'd thought, after all. But still. "It's not *common*, though, right?"

"Oh God, no!" Natalie said. "When people go, they go home! Or to like, LA or New York or something! But all the more reason not to let things get to you in a place like this, right? When you gaze into the abyss, the abyss gazes back into you, and all that."

Lucy laughed, and allowed her unease to be mollified. It was hard to dwell on much of anything in the face of someone who could quote Nietzsche in glow-in-the-dark lipstick. "True enough!" she said. "I'd love a drink."

"There's a table to your right!" Natalie planted a neon-pink kiss on Lucy's cheek. "And then I'd better see you dancing!"

Lucy shouted her thanks. When she rubbed the lipstick from her cheek, it came away as a smear of light against her hand.

She weaved her way across the room, dodging elbows here and there, and she watched the whirlwind of outfits go by as she scanned the wall for the drinks table. The dress code was delightfully non-uniform: There were some dressed in light summer-wear like Lucy, a cluster of goths jingling cheerily as they danced, and at least two people in full-latex clubwear. The girl Lucy had to weave around when she reached the drinks table was wearing a T-shirt with a sequined rendition of a movie poster for *The Exorcist.*

Sequin Girl, it seemed, had been waiting for someone to cross into her orbit—she happily spun to Lucy as she scoured the table for a single seltzer, chatting as though it didn't bother her that Lucy's answers were barely audible over the bass beat. Lucy noted, with a poorly suppressed smile, that it seemed to be a Rollins-wide habit to ask about someone's major before getting their name.

"No major yet!" Lucy said. "I'm actually a first-year." At Sequin Girl's raised eyebrow, she reluctantly, for ease of explanation, used her least favorite euphemism. "Nontraditional student. I worked for a couple years after high school."

"Oh!" Sequin Girl beamed brighter than her shirt. "You're going to *love* it here. They let you study whatever you want, as long as you have a good plan."

"Really!" Lucy said. "What's *your* major, then?"

"Theater and anthro!" Sequin Girl said. "I'm working on my joint thesis now. I already know what I'm going to title it.

'Playing Dead: A Comparative Study of Theatricality in Modern Death Rituals.'"

Lucy cackled. Sequin Girl's obvious delight was infectious. "That fucking rules!"

"You think so?" Sequin Girl turned a little, swatting in the direction of another girl with her back turned to them. The girl, deep in conversation with the barely visible outline of a man, didn't seem to notice. "Alicia thinks I shouldn't use a pun! She says it's disrespectful to the dead!"

"I've planned two Catholic funerals," Lucy said with a demonstrative shrug. "There's no getting through one of those without some disrespect to the dead!"

Sequin Girl's eyes glittered as brightly as her T-shirt. Holding out her phone, she asked, "Could I interview you? I don't have any Catholics yet!"

Lucy dutifully typed her number into the phone. She didn't plan to talk about all that very much, not here. But she could make an exception for science. "Hey, have you seen any seltzers?"

"I saw a case in the kitchen!" Sequin Girl said. "That's smart. Go slow and all that."

"I'm allergic to alcohol!" Lucy said.

"Ohhh," Sequin Girl said. "Sorry for that loss too, then." Lucy threw her head back and laughed again as she pushed through the crowd to find the kitchen.

If there was one thing Lucy had learned about Rollins already, it was that people like Sequin Girl were far from a rarity. The students here had interests that Lucy couldn't have dreamed up if she tried—and even after a few days at Rollins, she wasn't yet tired of hearing of them. Quite the opposite, actually. It made her happy, listening to them gush, watching the moment the fire hit their eyes. It was too bad Whitney had decided she was some sort of troglodyte. It would have made Lucy happy to hear about her thesis, too.

It was fun. But it was also valuable information. Lucy had no idea what her major was going to be. Hadn't even considered it until she was well into packing to leave. There'd never been enough oxygen in Lucy's home to keep a fire going. She'd only ever wanted one thing—and getting to Rollins had been the full extent of her plan.

The acoustics of these old buildings are strange, Lucy thought as she slipped into the kitchen. The music should have been just as loud in the kitchen, but everything went muffled when she rounded the corner, like she'd dunked her head underwater. The aqua stars from the globe lamp skimmed the backs of her ankles as she crossed the threshold. Then she left them behind altogether.

The overhead fluorescents were switched off in favor of a small, yellow-tinged light over the stove. There was just one person in the kitchen with her, standing at the sink with his back turned to the rest of the room. Against his broad outline, Lucy could see the edge of the box of seltzers. She murmured an apology as she slid alongside him.

He was quiet as Lucy worked a lukewarm can out of the

box. Quiet enough that she laughed and said, "Pretty loud in there."

She cracked the seltzer open and took a sip. Somewhere in that moment, she saw his mouth move. But whatever he said was lost in the swish of raspberry-lime bubbles against her jaw. "Sorry," she said. "What?"

He turned, and for the first time, she saw his face. She would never remember how he looked at her in that moment. Only that it was the last thing she remembered seeing.

"Hold still," he said. And then nothing.

Two

The night had a pulse. It always had. The mountain around her was teeming with life: She could hear it in the air above and the dirt below. Lucy couldn't understand why, in all her years slipping in and out of the dark, she had never noticed it before. It was a wonder that anyone ever slept through this at all.

She laughed. Around her, the crickets sang. The grass bunched and scattered and whipped in the whispery breeze, and the stars whirled against the black above as if projected from Natalie's cutout lanterns.

And beyond its disparate parts, the night itself watched her.

Something buzzed against her thigh. Lucy frowned, grasped for it. Jillian was texting her—texting a few things, too quick and too blurry to make out. It was hard to focus on the new words. Her eyes kept drifting up to the old ones. To the words sent at 3:21 p.m., just a moment before Natalie Baker had called out to her.

I can't help but feel like you're relieved he's gone.

Even then, in the giddy haze of that beautiful night, it burned to read. He was her grandfather. She loved him. And of course she was relieved he was dead. Who wouldn't be relieved that someone they cared for was no longer in agony? All the IVs and catheters and injections, all the nights tossing and turning in his hospice bed, all the mornings he shouted himself awake from the pain—he had been so ready for it to be over. Everyone had seen it except his own daughter.

But death was never over in the Easting house, even after the dead themselves were gone.

"Why is it my responsibility to make her happy?" Lucy mumbled to the night. "Nothing makes her happy. Maybe if we'd crawled into his casket togeth—"

Shh, the night said.

"Okay," Lucy whispered obediently. She understood. That kind of talk didn't belong here.

Something within the trees shifted. And now that she was paying proper attention, she could see that the night had faces.

It had two faces, at least. One of them she couldn't quite see. The other was a girl's, peeking out from the edge of the tree line's curtain. Her skin was yellowed gray, crinkled like faded paper. As indistinct as she was, Lucy could make out freckles across her cheeks.

The girl smiled. Closed-mouthed, at first. And then her lips widened, and split open.

And then it was daylight, and Lucy was gasping for air.

She scrambled upright, and immediately regretted it. There was an ache in the base of her skull, sharp as a fireplace poker, and between the movement and the searing daylight, it surged. After an overcast couple of days, the sun had unfortunately found its way back to the mountain. It painted her dorm's white walls an eye-watering gold.

"You talk in your sleep," someone said.

Lucy rubbed at her temples. Whitney. For a dizzy second, she'd expected— Well. She wasn't sure, now that she thought about it. In her dream, she'd been talking to someone else.

"Sorry," she said automatically. She didn't talk in her sleep. She never had. But she'd save any arguments for when her head wasn't about to crack open. "How did I get home last night?"

When she chanced a look up, Whitney was looking at her from her desk chair, a crease between her eyebrows. "You got in around three. *Loudly*."

Lucy looked down then. She was still fully dressed—she could feel her bra's underwire. Her shoes were off, along with one sock. Otherwise, it looked like she'd walked in last night and collapsed.

Lucy had gotten to the party at nine. She'd greeted Natalie, then talked to Sequin Girl for maybe five, ten minutes. She walked into the kitchen, picked up a seltzer. Turned to the guy standing next to her. And—

And then what?

Whitney's ever-present stoneface softened an inch. "Are you okay, or . . . ?"

"Fine," Lucy said. Though even as she spoke, she was feeling for her phone. She found it under her pillow, neatly plugged in.

Five texts from her mother, which—she would give herself the gift of looking at those later. She turned first to the volley of texts from an unknown number.

The first was time-stamped at 9:51pm:

> Hey babe! It's Natalie!! Hope you're feeling a little better. Can you text me once you get back to your dorm? I know you're in the capable hands of the campus shuttle, but you know.

The second, time-stamped at 1:15 a.m, read:

> Okay, assuming you got back and crashed? Give me a call tomorrow morning when you read this? Just want to make sure you're okay. Party was a success . . . got a couple hours of scrubbing ahead of me tho 😩

Lucy cupped the phone in her hands and took a deep, somewhat shaky breath. If she was reading these right, she left the party before ten. The party was *over* by 1:15.

But according to Whitney, she hadn't made it home until three.

Her fingers trembled a little as she tapped out her reply.

> Hey, sorry I didn't see this until now.

Natalie's response popped in almost instantly.

Morning sunshine!!

Are you okay? How are you feeling?

I'm okay, Lucy typed automatically. And then deleted it. Natalie was a good person. She seemed like one, anyway. Either way, this felt like the kind of thing she should tell someone.

A little confused, I don't really remember last night.

Natalie's response took a bit longer that time.

You were pretty out of it.

I followed you into the kitchen and found this guy picking you up off the floor. Apparently you passed out?

The words blurred a little as Lucy read them.

That's what he told you?

Natalie replied.

Babe, that's what YOU told me.

You said you were a little overheated, and it happens to you all the time. I asked if you wanted to sit down and have some water, but you said you'd be fine after some sleep. I walked you to the campus shuttle after that.

Lucy wondered how much more she should share. She didn't want to scare this kind stranger who had already taken pity on her once this week. Not when this wasn't her problem.

She tapped the next sentence out anyway.

That's never happened to me before. I don't know why I would say that.

There was a lengthy pause before Natalie started typing again.

Okay

Okay, well, don't panic

Maybe the guy knows more than I do?

Did you end up getting his number?

Which guy? The guy who'd been standing at the sink?

What do you mean?

Natalie typed.

I mean, you were giving him these HUGE EYES the whole time we were bringing you around.

So I assumed whatever conversation you were having had been going well.

Lucy frowned down at her phone.

I'm a lesbian.

There was another lengthy pause.

Oh.

You're like, 100% sure you're not bi?

That startled a laugh out of Lucy. Though she wasn't feeling like very much was funny right about now.

I seemed into him?

There was definitely a vibe.

But maybe I misread what it was.

Lucy had just enough time to start overthinking that before Natalie's next message.

If it helps, though, he seemed chill enough? And I kept an eye on him to make sure he didn't follow you or anything. He was there til the party ended. And he must have been alone with you for like, less than 2-3 minutes total.

And then, after one more pause,

Did you drink anything?

Lucy took another breath. She could tell that Natalie was trying to dance around saying the words.

Two to three minutes. Two to three minutes wasn't a lot of time for someone to hurt her. And though the moments before she'd blacked out were still a bit muddy, she vaguely remembered the seltzer.

Just a sip of seltzer

She was about to add that it tasted fine, but—she was suddenly unsure whether she could trust that or not.

I opened it myself

. . .

There were a few more deliberative seconds of nothing before Natalie started typing again.

Okay, I'm sure nothing happened. But the guy said he came with my friend David. I can call Dave, ask what his deal is.

Lucy was already shaking her head down at her phone. She didn't know Natalie well, but she didn't seem like the type to pull her punches when sizing someone up. If the guy didn't ring any alarm bells for her, he probably *was* just a normal person. And as for the rest of it . . . well, Lucy had never passed out before. Maybe it was normal to say strange things afterward.

No, that's okay

Thank you so much for checking on me.

Natalie replied.

That's what I'm here for, baby!! Rest up today, and let me know if you need anything!

Eventually, Lucy made her cautious, squeaky way off the bed and onto the floor. Her headache was starting to recede, at least, but her legs felt wobbly under her. She needed to drink some water, probably. And maybe splash some on her face for good measure.

She felt a bit better by the time she reached the bathroom, but she still had to brace herself against the sink as she tied back her hair. She turned on the faucet and gingerly eased herself down to cup the water in her hands, exhaling through her open mouth as she brought it to her face.

She straightened. That was when she saw it.

There, just below her jaw on the right side of her neck, sat a deep, mottled bruise, a vibrant purple against the peach of her skin. Automatically, her hand rose to it. It wasn't painful, exactly. It was more of a heat under her fingertips.

It wasn't as if Lucy had never been afraid. But she spent much more time resenting fear than experiencing it herself. It was an all-encompassing, illogical force that had governed half her life. And almost none of that fear had been her own.

But in that moment, she wondered if it had been unfair of her to ever expect logic out of fear. There was nothing logical to be found in this feeling. The world shrank and sharpened to only the three most necessary points. The mirror. Her neck. And the bruise, glinting in the bathroom light.

Natalie.

It took her far too long just to type out her name.

I think we need to ask about that guy after all.

Lucy made a mental to-do list. She didn't think it would really help. But it felt like it would help, which was almost as good.

She stripped off last night's clothes and put on the first thing she could stand to wear: a light, comfortable dress that barely touched her hypervigilant skin. She emptied her clutch back into her regular purse, folding her ID and her insurance card back into her wallet. Then she mapped out, in her head, the rough path to the health center. If there really had been something in her seltzer, maybe they could run some kind of test.

It seemed like a tall order for a campus health center. But every bit of the practicality she usually had in an emergency had abandoned her. By the end of her grandfather's hospice care, she'd been very good with emergencies. But Pop had been dying, and there was one cold comfort when someone was dying: that no matter what happened, it was predictable. The ending, at least, was always certain.

She made her way down the three flights of stairs and stepped into the path of the floor-to-ceiling windows of the Quincey Hall lobby.

Her headache burst open like an overripe fruit.

Lucy staggered into the shadow between windows. Ducking out of the light helped, a little: Her stomach stopped surging, the vise around her temples slackened. She lowered herself to the nearest couch, the muscles of her legs twitching from the sheer effort of moving. Her cousin had migraines. Maybe that was what this was, though she'd never had one before.

Just like she'd never passed out before.

She tucked her head against her knees and, breathing raggedly, waited for it to pass. The campus shuttle stop was just out the door and around the corner. If she could make it there, then she could make it to the health center.

Just as her own shaking slowed, something quivered against the side of her hip. It took her a moment to recognize that it wasn't her own body this time. Inside her purse pocket, her phone was ringing.

Her mother was calling.

Lucy squeezed her eyes shut. Granted, her priorities had been suddenly, violently reshuffled after last night. But one thing hadn't changed. When Jillian called, she had to answer.

"Hello?" Lucy nearly winced at how rough her voice sounded. It was never a good idea to start a conversation with Jillian while on your back foot.

"*There* you are." It was only her opener, and she was already revved up. She said it like she'd been calling for hours—and it was only then that Lucy remembered the five unread texts from that morning. "What's going on? Are you hurt? Did something happen?"

Maybe, and maybe. Though how her mother had divined that, she had no idea. Her sixth sense for disaster was strong, but not *that* strong.

"Nothing's going on," she finally managed. "Sorry, I didn't get to read your messages yet. Is everything okay?"

"You haven't—" Jillian cut herself off. Lucy heard her take a breath. "Is that all you have to say for yourself? Lucy, I didn't sleep a *wink*. Why did you text me all that last night?"

Last night. Lucy's stomach dropped as she toggled over to her texts, scrolling back past the missed messages she hadn't read yet. Sure enough, there was a string of texts from her to her mother, too. Time-stamped just after one a.m.

mama

the night is alive

Either Jillian had already been awake, or the messages had woken her. Her own message was stamped just a few seconds later.

????

Lucy's reply came a minute after that.

natalie sent me home,

but I didn't want to sleep.

Jillian replied.

Lucy where are you?

Are you safe???

Then after that, the last message from Lucy:

sadie's calling.

Lucy lifted the phone back to her ear. Her own face felt clammy against her fingers. She didn't have time to take any of that in. Her first order of business had to be what it always had been: to calm Jillian down.

"I'm—sorry, Mom," she said haltingly. "I . . . think I might have been sleepwalking last night. I don't actually remember sending these. I don't know a Sadie."

"I don't care about Sadie," Jillian said brittlely. "I don't need to know all your little friends."

Lucy swallowed back a rush of poorly timed anger. Jillian had never liked any of Lucy's friends growing up. But whether or not she liked them was beyond the point, seeing as Lucy had barely spoken to any of them since graduation.

In any case, this wasn't the time to relitigate a five-year-old fight.

"Anyway," Lucy said, "I'll call you back later, if you want? I'm not feeling very well, so I'm going to the health center."

It was the wrong thing to say. Then again, when Jillian got fired up, there were very few right things to say. "Have you been drinking?"

"You know I'm allergic, Mom," Lucy said.

"Well," Jillian said. "You don't always make the best choices for yourself, sweetheart."

Oh. Lucy did not have the energy for the rush of rage that washed over her then. "Why don't I just text later?" she said. "I don't think this is the best time for us to talk about this."

"Are you upset about what I said?" Jillian said. "I'm not saying you didn't care about your grandfather. I'm just trying to explain how I feel. If you want to punish me for that—"

Well. As long as a fight was inevitable, why not? "I told you, I'm *sick,*" Lucy said. "I'm sorry I scared you. But I didn't do it to punish you. I don't do anything to punish you."

"Then you could have waited," she snapped. "Two weeks after his death, and you tell me you're leaving?"

Lucy rubbed at her temple with a shaking finger. She could have told Jillian the full truth. That she started the application when she knew he was close to the end. That she told herself she'd defer for a year if he hung in there a little longer. Or maybe even the worst part: that even if he had hung on longer, when Rollins said yes, she might not have had it in her to say no.

But she'd never have to find out what she would have done. And she already felt close enough to throwing up. No need to push it further. "They had an acceptance deadline," she finally said. "I waited as long as I could."

"And why not apply anywhere else?" Jillian plowed on like Lucy hadn't spoken. "I know how long you've waited to go to college. You think I don't understand, but I do. But we could have talked about it. You could have applied somewhere where I'd be close by, where *anyone* we know would be close by. How am I not supposed to worry?"

"I didn't come here to make you worry, Mom," Lucy shot back. "I never want to make you worry. That's the entire problem."

It was another mistake in a conversation of mistakes. The silence that followed was electric. "What's the entire problem?" Jillian asked.

Lucy froze, her knuckles painful around the phone. For the past year, she'd been on the precipice of understanding all the age-old forces that had shaped her relationship with her mother. But it was still a raw, fresh understanding. Barely a real feeling, let alone something she'd been able to put into words. And even if she did find the words one day, she had decided that Jillian never needed to know what they were.

It was sitting there, with that wordless understanding at the tip of her tongue, that she heard movement from the hall behind her. And then, a voice.

"You want me to take that?"

Lucy, her phone still pressed to her ear, swiveled around. The source of the voice stood at the mouth of the hallway leading to the first-floor dorms, her considering gaze drifting first to Lucy and then to the phone itself. She was tall, white, and lean. Her shoulder-length hair framed her face in soft, deep brown waves.

She crossed the lobby with a catlike silence, held out her hand, and then lifted a pointed eyebrow at the hand Lucy held to her ear.

Lucy was miles away from anyone who would know this about her, but there was nothing that could stun her into compliance quite like a beautiful girl wielding a certain, effortless competence. She had, rather famously, fallen for her ex after listening to her order a sandwich.

She wordlessly handed the phone over. The girl brushed her hair aside from her ear—her hair was so fine that a few strands immediately slipped back against her cheek—and cradled Lucy's phone against her face. "Hello?"

Lucy didn't hear what Jillian said in response, but she heard the pitch of it. The girl seemed unfazed. "Yes, this is—" The girl paused, then mouthed, *Name?*

Lucy felt dizzy. It was, at the very least, a completely different kind of dizziness than she'd been feeling before. "Lucy," she whispered, too baffled to do anything but play along.

"I'm Lucy's friend," the girl said. Another pause. "No, she can't, she's throwing up. Ah, no, I don't know how long she's been sick. You know, college campuses. We basically invent new diseases here."

Lucy grimaced. By the sound of the tinny little voice on the phone, Jillian reacted exactly as anticipated, but the girl smoothly went on. "I'm sure it's just one of those twenty-four-hour things. We were actually just in the middle of getting her to the health center. Maybe she could call you back later?"

This time, Lucy heard Jillian's voice a bit more clearly—"Let me talk to her." The girl turned and shot her the same questioning look as before, and Lucy knew she should at least make an attempt to salvage the situation.

But an exhaustion unlike anything she'd ever felt had settled over her. And for the first time in her life, Lucy couldn't make herself talk to her mother. She could barely bring herself to shake her own head.

Without missing a beat, the girl said, "She just started throwing up again, actually. Is there anything you want me to— Yes, I'll make sure she gets to the health center. Yes, I'll ask her to give you a call back. Nice talking to y—"

There was a beat. And then the girl ended the call, and handed the phone back to Lucy with a rueful little shrug. "She hung up."

Lucy attempted to arrange her face into an expression

other than *gaping*. She'd never had a rescue unfold quite that spontaneously before. Though when she thought about it, she wasn't sure she'd ever been rescued like this at all. "Thank you," she said.

The girl grinned. "Kinda seemed like you were struggling."

She knew that sympathetic look. She got a lot of them when it came to Jillian—from teachers and classmates, from customers at the hardware store, even from strangers. It made her want to stick up for her mother, or at the very least, contextualize things a bit. But *She lost her father* was enough of a damper on polite conversation. *She lost her father, and her mother a few years before that, and my father when I was a kid* was a cold bucket of water.

So she kept things light. "Do you make a habit of saving people from awkward phone calls?"

"Well, I saw you looking distressed. And then heard you say 'Mom,'" the girl said. "And not to brag, but I'm an expert at managing helicopter parents. They can't resist my No-Nonsense RA charms."

Lucy laughed for real that time. The girl was the building's residence assistant—that made sense. Her air of confidence didn't seem easily shakable. At least, not by anxious mothers.

"I don't think we've met yet," the RA said. "Big campus, I know, but still. Are you a junior or a senior? I'm a junior, but don't tell the other residents. Some of the seniors think I'm a grad student, I want to see how long I can keep that going."

Lucy kept smiling, but abruptly realized she was a bit too

queasy to launch into even the abridged version of her life story. "I'm neither, actually."

"Oh, are you our first-year resident? I was going to stop by and introduce myself this afternoon. Good timing, I guess." The RA leaned a little closer to look her over. Lucy couldn't help but feel a bit—sized up. "Well, I'm guessing you weren't lying to your mom about going to the health center. You look, well, very nice—love the dress—but a little gray in the face, there."

Lucy wasn't going to be gray for very long if the RA kept leaning in like that. Not a single thing within her at that moment felt particularly up to flirting. But she was ill, not dead.

"So what's going on?" the RA continued. "Your orientation group hasn't been trying to scare you off, have they? I promise you do not need a fourth major. You don't even need two."

Lucy laughed, though she was aware how flat it sounded. She'd intended to make her excuses and continue on her slow, queasy way. But under the RA's searching look, something in her crumbled.

"It's not stress, I don't think," she said. "I don't even know what I want my first major to be. I'm not one of those . . . genius multitasking poet laureate types they usually let in here."

It was far more honest an answer than she meant for it to be. But the RA, for her part, looked unruffled. "That's okay," she said. "I'm not a genius multitasking poet laureate, either. Plenty of us aren't. I love and cherish every single turbo child prodigy at this school, but we don't all have to be them, you know? Figuring out what you want is what you're here for."

That would have felt nice to hear yesterday. It still felt nice. Even if it wasn't Lucy's primary concern right then. "Do you think . . ." She stopped herself, at first. But the RA's steady, patient face didn't waver. It made Lucy want to keep talking.

"Do you think the health center could help?" she said. "If I . . . don't know. Took something?"

It felt like a bombshell, but the RA still didn't look rattled. "Depends, I think," she said. "What did you take?"

"Hah. That's the question." Lucy rubbed at her temples, suddenly unable to meet that unruffled gaze anymore. "I know I should call campus police. I should, but . . ."

But explaining herself to them would have been only slightly less intolerable than explaining herself to Jillian.

But her skin might crawl right off her body if she had more than one pair of eyes on her right now.

But they'd probably be politely useless at best and actively hostile at worst.

All of the above.

Thankfully, the RA didn't seem to need her to finish that sentence.

She sat down on the couch beside her then. "If you don't want campus police called, I'm not going to be the one calling them. Generally, I think the thing you 'should' do in any given situation is the thing you feel ready to do." She took a breath. Lucy could sense the caveat coming. "But before you say anything else, you should know that if someone hurt you, and you tell me about it, I'm obligated to report it to the university."

"Oh," Lucy said quickly, automatically. "It's not that serious, I . . ."

The RA's eyebrows rose, just a little, and Lucy wondered if she could hear the uncertainty in her words. Lucy herself had no idea how serious it was, after all. As Natalie had said, there hadn't been a lot of time for someone to—hurt her. At least, "hurt her" in most of the ways she could conceive of.

But that didn't mean that nothing had happened. If nothing had happened, she wouldn't feel like this, would she?

"Hey," the RA said. "If something happened that you didn't want to happen, even if you feel like it was just a little thing, it's serious. That doesn't mean you have to do anything about it if you don't want to—not with the police, not with anyone. But the 'serious' part isn't in question. Not to me, anyway. Okay?"

Lucy wasn't sure why she laughed again. None of this was funny. Maybe it was the no-nonsense tone, jarring but not unpleasant after the distant, dreamy haze of the night before. Maybe this was how divers felt, surfacing too quickly. "If I did tell you," she asked, "what would happen?"

The RA shrugged. From her, it seemed like a thoughtful gesture. "I'd put you in touch with someone from the Title IX office. Which I realize sounds like bureaucratic bullshit, but I know a few of the staff, and they're good people. They wouldn't make you do anything you don't want. If you want to talk to campus counseling, they'd help you get an appointment. If you change your mind about the cops, they'd help you make a statement. Or if you tell them you want to do none of those things, they'd respect that, too. Whatever you want, they'd follow your lead.

"But I know even that's too much sometimes," the RA said. "So before you say anything, I wanted to warn you. Give you a chance to decide what you *do* want to do right now. And if you need to think about that for a second, you're not keeping me waiting. It's a comfortable couch."

Lucy swallowed, and sat back. She could see why anxious parents folded in the face of the RA's calm competence. She had to be a few years younger than Lucy, if she was a junior. But for all the Big Decisions Lucy had had to make over the last several years, she wasn't sure she'd ever spoken with the kind of confidence and certainty she could hear in the RA's voice. This was someone who didn't seem to spend much time flinching. Lucy might have been envious if she weren't a little enthralled.

So Lucy tried to allow some of that certainty to rub off on her. "I don't know that somebody hurt me, exactly," she said. She was fairly sure they had—the bruise on her neck was proof enough. But she didn't want to report that to anyone, not yet. Not until she knew more. "I think I took something without knowing it. But I don't know what it was."

The RA inclined her head and took that in. "Health center, then. Did your orientation group show you where that was?" Lucy nodded, and the RA nodded back. "Great. The campus shuttle is easiest. Do you feel up to walking? Can you make it there?"

Ah, Lucy realized. Those really were two very different

questions. She almost lied. But in the face of the RA's straightforwardness, she found she wanted to respond in kind. "I can walk," she said. "But I think I'm having some kind of . . . migraine, or reaction to whatever I took. It's like everything feels . . . too bright, right now."

For a moment, Lucy thought she saw a ripple across the placid surface of the RA's face. But she only nodded again, slower this time. Her lower lip slid thoughtfully between her teeth. And then, standing, she took off her bottle-green cardigan.

In her sweater, everything about the RA had looked soft, from the curled ends of her hair to the flush of the warm mid-morning against her cheeks. But Cute RA wasn't just cute—she was *ripped.* Sitting there in her tank top and jeans, all the hard edges of her were on display: the curves of her biceps and her broad, lightly freckled shoulders, the strong and confident lines of her forearms. She held herself like an athlete at rest. Not tense, but ready.

"Well," Lucy mumbled. "You haven't been skipping arm day."

The RA arched both eyebrows. "Sorry?"

Lucy's mouth snapped shut. It was good to know that even now, of all times, she was still capable of being entirely too forward with a beautiful girl. "No, um—I'm sorry. I didn't mean for that to be, like . . . a line." Though she couldn't deny that any other time, it would have been.

"Hey, you're not wrong. I *have* been known to skip leg day, though." The RA gently draped her cardigan over Lucy's head. Her fingertip brushed Lucy's shoulder as she pulled it back. "Okay. This is a bit of a DIY solution, but—does that give you a bit more shade?"

If Lucy swallowed audibly, it was hardly her fault. "I," she said. "Actually, yes." Because as hot as her face still felt, the dizziness was receding. When she eased herself to her feet, she wobbled but held firm.

The RA's hand had slipped under her elbow, and the sudden warmth at her arm startled her. For a touch that was barely there, it was the steadiest thing she'd felt all morning. "I have a quad staff meeting in ten minutes," she said, apologetically. "But I have time to walk you to the shuttle stop. Would that help?"

Lucy smiled, and allowed herself a moment to imagine her arm was being held for nicer reasons. "That'd help a lot."

So they started to walk. And while Lucy's stomach still pulsed unhappily every time she tried to look up, the cardigan's thin protection was just enough to keep her going.

The shuttle was pulling up to the stop by the time they made their slow way out front, and the RA motioned for it to wait as she eased back from Lucy. "Do me a favor," she said. "Will you shoot me a text later, just so I know you're okay?"

It was, once again, a question that Lucy wished she was hearing under better circumstances. But even if Lucy was the older one, this girl was still her RA. She probably wasn't allowed to date residents. "Oh—sure."

Lucy started to dig for her phone, but the RA quickly motioned for her to stop. "My cell number's on your welcome sheet," she said. "Under the name Mila Rostova. Or just swing by at some point. It's the room closest to the front doors, you can't miss it."

"Got it." Lucy let her arms fall awkwardly to her sides. "Thank you, Mila." She turned toward the bus, then paused. "Wait, your sweater."

Mila shook her head. "Bring it back later," she said. "It looks better on you anyway."

Lucy managed one final smile, then ducked into the shuttle, where at least she could bury her face in her hands without an audience. The driver barely looked twice at her cardigan hood. Lucy figured he had seen significantly stranger things.

The bottom of her purse buzzed, and sinking into a seat, Lucy fished out her phone. It was Natalie again.

Lucy,

Her stomach curled. Any news that started with her first name was rarely good.

I just talked to my friend David. Before I explain, just try to stay calm, okay? We're going to figure this out.

It was long past time for Lucy to stay calm. But whether she was ready for this news or not, she needed to hear it.

What did he say?

She didn't need to ask, exactly. She could guess, just from that message, what David had said.

He came to the party alone.

The world went gray. Lucy took a breath, and she could have sworn she felt the mechanics of it. Felt the fragile tissue of her own lungs fluttering.

Thank you for letting me know.

For the rest of the ride, she didn't look at her phone again.

A nurse called Lucy's name within fifteen minutes, and she drifted to the back, still clutching Mila's cardigan. She hoped Mila wasn't cold back at Quincey. Then again, maybe all that muscle kept her warm.

"Hop right up here, honey." The nurse was distracted, but efficient, strapping a blood pressure cuff and oxygen monitor into place before Lucy was fully settled. "What seems to be the problem?"

Good fucking question. And if Mila had to report an assault to the university—Lucy's brain balked at the word *assault*, but determinedly continued the thought—the nurse probably did, too. So for a lack of a good answer, Lucy went for a simple one. "I went to a party last night," she said. "And I didn't drink anything but seltzer, but I woke up feeling really, really sick. I think I took something without realizing it."

The nurse's expression barely twitched at that. "Did you leave your drink unattended? Maybe pick up a cup that might not have been yours?" When Lucy shook her head, the nurse said, "Then you're sure it was straight seltzer? Some of those boozy drinks don't have the clearest labels."

"It was definitely seltzer," Lucy said. She didn't remember much. But she remembered the generic label from the local store. "And I opened it myself."

Once again, the nurse didn't seem fazed. It wasn't the same easy calm that Mila projected, but she operated like she already understood the situation. Even though Lucy wasn't entirely sure that she did.

"Well," she said cheerfully, "let's check you out just in case."

It was harder to sit still than she expected. The sights and sounds of an exam room should have been intimately familiar to her by then: She'd fallen asleep so many nights with the smell of antiseptic still in her nose. Maybe she'd gotten out of practice since her grandfather died. Or maybe she just wasn't used to being the patient.

She wasn't squeamish, at least. She'd done enough caretaking for each of her grandparents that squeamishness had fallen by the wayside a long time ago. But it was surprisingly difficult to tolerate the feel of any touch, any external pressure at all. Maybe it was the mounting pressure of the bruise, which had started to ache.

The nurse took her oxygen—"Normal"—and her temperature—"97.5, a little chilly, but everyone's baseline is different." Lucy checked the wall clock at least twice as the nurse pumped the blood pressure cuff along her arm. She didn't object, just gritted her teeth and waited.

And finally, the nurse did something Lucy both expected and hoped she wouldn't do. She started paying attention.

"Eighty over fifty," she said.

Lucy watched the nurse's mouth, a rapidly thinning line. "That's bad?"

"It's . . . a little low." Another pause. Another thinning of her lips. "What did you say your other symptoms were?"

Lucy repeated them. The nurse nodded through her litany, her forehead crinkling above her brows. As much as Lucy had wanted her full attention just a few minutes ago, it was hard to feel particularly grateful for it now.

Finally, the nurse said, "Tell you what. I'm going to take a little blood for some labs. And then I suggest you go back to your dorm and get some real rest. If you need to sit out the first day of classes, I'll write you a note."

Lucy nodded, automatically extending her arm and shutting her eyes. Needles usually weren't a problem for her, either. And maybe the sick coil of nausea running through her had nothing to do with the needle, but even so, she didn't really want to look at it.

As the nurse gently pulled her skin taut, wrapping the latex tourniquet just above her elbow, Lucy let her thoughts flood with whatever was in reach, whatever could distract her from what the nurse was doing. Natalie's neon-pink lipstick in the dark. Mila, holding Lucy's cell phone. A broad back in a dimly lit kitchen, the blurred face turned toward the sink.

It was surreal how vivid the memory was. The blackness that would follow just a few moments later was so absolute. But this, she remembered: a whorl at the back of his sandy-blond hair. The creased edges of his shirt. A hand a shade paler than her own. When she stepped next to him, she could remember how his shoulder felt, inches from hers. Not warmth. Just presence.

The needle touched her skin. And maybe it was her nerves, but even with her eyes closed, Lucy felt the blood draw as if in slow motion. The pressure, then the puncture. The queasy shift of fluid in her veins.

But it wasn't that feeling that sharpened her nausea to a point.

It was the smell.

Lucy trembled as she suppressed a gag.

"Hold still," the nurse murmured.

"Okay," Lucy gasped. She breathed shallowly through her mouth, but that just meant tasting it instead. It was a dull, metallic slide down her throat. Like the taste of a penny, but sharper.

Lucy thought she knew what fear felt like. More than most people her age, at least. Growing up with Jillian, she'd become acquainted with its sounds, its colors, its smells. But she had never been this afraid before. She had never once tasted this.

And when the nurse withdrew the needle, pressed the cotton ball to the tiny drop of blood, the smell was snuffed like a candle.

The dorm was empty when Lucy returned.

As the door swung open, the shadows bent, long and jagged, around the light from the hallway. Lucy checked twice for signs of life, for a lump under the quilt or a missing shower caddy. But for the first time since Lucy moved in, Whitney wasn't there.

Maybe she'd decided to go for a walk. Or maybe she was at the library. Lucy seemed to recall Whitney saying, at some point, that the library was too noisy to get any *real* work done. Maybe she'd decided to try anyway?

Either way. It should have been a relief to Lucy, to catch her breath in private. But standing there in the quiet, it didn't feel like much of a relief.

She scrubbed at her face and let her bag slip off her shoulder. Getting herself to the health center had been the one thing keeping her more or less upright. Now that it was over, the last of her reserves were bleeding out. Maybe she could at least take advantage of the relative peace and lie down.

Lucy tugged off her dress, crawled into an oversized shirt. She folded herself onto her creaky, extra-long twin mattress.

And she balled Mila's cardigan up underneath her chin. She'd have to return it later. For now, the acrylic felt cool and soft between her fingers.

She didn't have to close her eyes. They pulled shut slowly, like weighted shades. The sun was a deep, insistent gold behind the blinds. She wasn't sure she'd ever slept this early. For a second, she wasn't sure she could.

But another wave of exhaustion landed hard, tugging at her ankles. This time, she let it take her under.

Four hours later, something that was not Lucy Easting sat up in her bed.

Three

Lucy woke like she was surfacing from water.

The air was thick and damp when she gasped it in. But there was a breeze moving on her skin, lukewarm as breath. There was a chorus of frog song overhead. And a few feet away, the tree line sat patiently.

She was standing outside, in the field across from her dorm. In her pajamas, without shoes. And the low afternoon light she had fallen asleep to was long, long gone. The night was deep around her. So deep that the pond in the center of the field looked like a hole in the earth.

The sidewalk lights whirled as she spun around. There was no one with her in the quad that she could see—and she could see surprisingly well, despite the dark. Most of the lights in the windows were off.

And yet something about the dark felt very . . . full. As she stood, scrambling for her bearings, she found her eyes drawn once, then twice, to the same corner of the woods.

I don't want to be here. It was a hilariously inadequate thought. But her whole body screamed it.

Between the low light and the surge of adrenaline, all four buildings looked the same. She darted to the wrong dorm first. And once she correctly located Quincey's front entrance, she realized, with a jolt, that she didn't have her ID for the card swipe. She knocked softly, at first. Then, when she remembered that the RA's dorm was a ways down the hall, she pounded with both fists.

She forgot, until she saw the rumpled figure emerge, exactly who the building's RA was. But making a better second impression wasn't her first priority at the moment.

Lucy? Mila mouthed, her brown eyes narrowed in sleepy confusion. She padded across the hall and, with a *click,* pulled open the heavy outer door. "What's wrong?" she rasped. "Are you okay?"

"Sorry." Lucy's own voice startled her: It was a cracked whisper even rougher than Mila's. Her throat felt sore. "I think I was sleepwalking."

Mila's brow smoothed out, softening the rest of her face. She moved to the side of the door's threshold, motioning for Lucy to come in.

"You're certainly having a day, aren't you?" she muttered. "Is your room unlocked, you think? Or is your roommate there to let us in?"

"I . . ." Lucy blinked, hard. Had Whitney come home? She was usually a light sleeper, so she didn't think she'd missed it.

Though she usually wouldn't sleep through climbing out of bed, descending a flight of stairs, and walking outside, either. "I'm not sure."

"I'll get my keys and walk you up," Mila said. "Wait here a second?"

Lucy watched Mila disappear around the corner toward her room, then slumped back against the textured cool of the concrete of the wall.

She could feel one last bead of sweat slipping down her neck—a slow, lukewarm slide. Absently, she reached up to swipe it away with two fingers.

They came away red.

And for the second time that day, she smelled it. That bright metallic tang.

It was standing there, with blood on her fingers and that smell coating the back of her throat, that the word finally swam through her consciousness. It was such a full, immediate understanding that it must have crossed her mind, if only subconsciously, before that moment. Maybe in the health center. Or maybe the moment she'd spotted the bruise on her neck.

"Mila?" Her voice sounded so quiet next to the blare of her thoughts. The useless cries of a door alarm for an intruder who was long gone. "I'm just gonna use the bathroom for a second."

"Huh?" came Mila's faint voice in reply. "Sure. Take your time."

Lucy slipped through the nearby door and flicked on the overhead fluorescent lights. She didn't run. It didn't seem like there was much point anymore.

Her perpetually pink complexion was a sallow gray in the bathroom light. Her pale blond hair was a ghostly cloud from the humidity. When she swept it back from her neck, it felt damp under her fingertips.

She didn't have to look. She could have left her hair right where it was, followed Mila back to her dorm. She could probably still pretend, if she tried hard enough, that none of this was really happening. But it would still be right there against her skin.

So she moved her hair clear. And she could see now exactly what was bleeding. Mixed among the mottled blue and purple in the center of the bruise, there were two deliberate punctures along the curve of her neck.

There was no such thing as vampires.

But if there wasn't—then what was this?

It was a little past four a.m. when Mila let Lucy back into her dorm, but Whitney's bed was still untouched. Lucy didn't have long to worry, though—when she picked up her phone, she saw that Whitney had texted her earlier, while she'd been asleep.

Visiting my parents for the day. Won't be back till late—don't lock the deadbolt.

She pursed her lips and put her phone aside. She would have welcomed the clacking of Whitney's keyboard. Or the light of the laptop, or even just the sound of someone else's breathing. In the dark and the quiet of the dorm, even lying there awake felt indistinguishable from sleep. And sleep didn't exactly feel safe at the moment.

So she curled sideways onto the bed and watched the door. It wasn't until the dorm walls were washed with early-morning light that she allowed herself the luxury of shutting her eyes.

She jerked awake a few hours later with a gasp. No one was there to shush her for it.

She hadn't meant to doze off, but she had to admit that it had done her good. Her head was less tight, her body less heavy. The overcast light still made her eyes water, but it wasn't quite as painful to look at anymore. It was more like trying to read very small text: a strain, but a doable one.

Lucy draped an arm over her eyes. She could barricade her door, pull the covers over her head, and wait for Whitney or for Monday morning, whichever came first. It would be the easiest thing to do. Maybe even the most logical. But for the first time since the party, she had a clear head. She wasn't sure she could afford to waste that.

As it turned out, Natalie wasn't about to waste any time, either. By the time Lucy picked up her phone to text her, Natalie had already texted her twice.

Found someone who talked to Kitchen Guy at the party! We're meeting at the Falls Quad Café at 2:30.

And then after that, time-stamped a few minutes later:

Do you want to be there? Totally understand if it's too much, I can handle it myself if you need me to.

Lucy ran a thumb across her phone. If she made it through the next few days, she owed Natalie about five times over.

I want to be there

Thank you so much for doing this.

Natalie replied quickly.

You've got it, babe

See you in a bit.

Lucy got dressed, forced herself through some plain instant grits, and took the shuttle ride to Falls Quad.

The courtyard was a very different place in the sleepy daylight. Even well into the afternoon, the quad was quiet: This time, when Lucy crossed the grass, no curtains fluttered to watch her. She moved quickly anyway.

The Falls Quad Café was markedly nicer than the mostly underground quick-service food court on the other side of campus—and while natural light wasn't Lucy's best friend at the moment, the café's bright airiness was a bit of a comfort. The lunch rush had passed, and most of the seats were empty. The café was liveliest by the door, where it looked like there was a small club fair going on. Lucy summoned a weak smile and politely demurred as several of them tried to pass her flyers.

A few of them had a surprisingly long reach. "Support independent campus radio?" asked the girl at the end of the table, extending her flyer into Lucy's path.

Lucy stumbled a little as she made eye contact with the speaker, a beautiful girl with thin, delicate braids down to her waist. PALLAS RADIO, read her placard, FOR THE NOCTURNAL AMONG US.

Even now, Lucy was not in the business of saying no to pretty girls. "Sure," she said. "Though I'm not feeling very nocturnal lately."

The girl offered a closed-lipped smile as Lucy took the flyer. "Check us out anyway," she said. "If you fall asleep, we won't be offended."

Lucy tucked the flyer into her purse and shuffled into line: For the first time since the party, she felt genuinely hungry, and something in the kitchen smelled amazing. There were sandwich and salad fixings, chicken fingers and greasy french fries, some kind of quiche. But whatever she smelled was deep and rich and meaty, with a hint of sweetness. Almost like Jillian's multi-hour, labor-of-love Guinness stew, if you drizzled a bit of honey across the top.

She stepped past the brownies, peered under the heat lamps—and there was no oven tray resting on the slats. The smell wasn't something being served. It was something wafting from the kitchen in the back.

Lucy peered through, and she caught the eye of one of the staff members working over something on the cutting board. He noticed her, winked. "This'll look a lot prettier by dinner," he said.

She glanced down, then, to the shape in his gloved hands. A slab of steak, glistening, marbled red, and raw. There was a light, watery sheen of blood against the butcher paper.

And her stomach roiled once again. Not with nausea, or disgust.

With hunger.

Her heart pattered unevenly as she stepped out of line and made her way towards a table by the back. She could eat later. Or maybe never again.

She sank into a chair and rubbed at her temples as she watched the door for Natalie. Though as hard as she massaged the side of her head, she couldn't quite dislodge the impossible word that was once again surfacing in her mind.

Natalie arrived just a few minutes later, with a girl that Lucy didn't recognize. She rose to her feet to greet them, welcoming the opportunity to put everything else aside. Natalie crossed the café in about four long strides, gathered Lucy into a tight hug, then drew back to appraise her.

Natalie's mouth narrowed. "How are you feeling?"

Lucy smiled. That felt like a very kind, concerned way of telling her she looked like shit. "I'll get back to you."

Natalie winced. "Here, sit. This is the friend I mentioned—Alicia, this is Lucy."

Alicia lightly perched on the chair opposite Lucy, like a bird alighting on water. She moved like a dancer. Though any dance instructor would have told her to fix that dour look on her face before going onstage. "I'm friends with your roommate," Alicia said. Lucy couldn't tell if the brittleness in her voice was directed at Whitney or at Lucy herself.

Probably me, Lucy reasoned. "Thank you for meeting us," she said anyway, though Alicia continued to look determinedly unhappy to be there. But that was fine. At least they were on the same page about that.

"Do we really have to sit in here?" Alicia said tightly. "That creepy LARPer is up front."

Alicia jerked her head. It seemed like she was indicating the tables by the door, where the nice Pallas Radio girl was. But Lucy didn't have time to ask. Natalie shot her a sharp look and said, "Be nice."

"You didn't have to bring your friend all the way here, by the way," Alicia said to Natalie. "I only talked to the guy for about ten minutes before he went to get a drink. Since he didn't come back, I figured he found what he was looking for elsewhere."

Lucy didn't miss the way Alicia's eyes flickered to her with a broad, assessing look. She opened her mouth. But Natalie cut her off.

"What the fuck, Alicia?" she said. "What's with your fucking tone? We think she might have been drugged."

It was hard to say who flinched harder, Lucy or Alicia. "Oh,"

Alicia said. Her face was flushed all the way down to her neck. "Whitney said her roommate came home wasted at like three a.m. I figured—"

"And you figured incorrectly," Natalie said viciously. "Found what he was looking for elsewhere? Apologize to her right now. Jesus Christ."

Alicia flinched back, and Natalie shifted her own chair, as if she'd move the entire table to put herself between Alicia and Lucy if she had to. The clenched fist in Lucy's throat unfurled. She'd liked Natalie the moment she met her, but she couldn't help but feel that she'd underestimated her a little, too.

"It's okay," Lucy said. It was definitely not okay, but she wasn't that interested in Alicia's apology, either. "If you could just tell me what you remember about him, that would be a huge help."

Eventually, Alicia brought herself to look Lucy in the eye again. "Honestly, not much," she admitted. "I was pretty wasted. Kinda weird, actually, I only had like two beers. Anyway, he was nice—cute, too. Light hair, blue eyes. Quiet, but not in that awkward way. He let me do the talking."

"What *did* you talk about?" Lucy asked.

"Mostly about me." Alicia grimaced. "But he did introduce himself. Luke, a fourth-year philosophy PhD student. Oh, and he did say this was the wildest party he'd seen since he bartended for a cruise liner. He'd just started to tell me a story when I saw him notice you walk into the kitchen. He said he was just going to get a drink of water, but. Well. When he didn't come back, it was pretty clear what had happened." At a particular narrow-eyed glance from Natalie, she added, "That's what I thought then, anyway."

Lucy waved away the attempt at an apology. She was far too busy processing what Alicia had just said. "You said *he* followed *me*."

"Uh," Alicia said. "Yeah?"

"You're sure about that," Lucy said. "It couldn't have been someone else?"

Alicia hesitated. But she sounded confident enough as she said, "No, I'm pretty sure it was you. I remember your hair. It was kind of glowy under the black light."

"What is it?" Natalie said.

Lucy shook her head a little. She couldn't be absolutely sure. Not when that night was so fuzzy. But when she closed her eyes, really tried to picture it, the man in the kitchen was already there when she walked in, standing at the far end by the sink. She didn't remember anyone following her. She remembered him *there*. "Natalie, is there another way into the kitchen?"

"Just the one," Natalie said. "Why?"

"I'm not sure," Lucy mumbled. It was hard to say how much of her own recollections she could trust, but this one felt particularly clear. "Alicia, did Luke tell you which cruise liner he worked for?"

"Like I said," Alicia started, "I was pretty . . ." But Lucy could see the moment something shifted loose in Alicia's mind. "Wait. Yes. Demeter Cruise Lines."

"You're sure?" Natalie asked.

"I'm a classics major," Alicia said dryly.

Lucy nodded slowly, only half taking that in. Processing could come later. Right then, she was pretty sure she needed to be out of this café.

"Thank you for your help, Alicia," she said mechanically. "Natalie—I think I'm gonna go."

"You can come back to my dorm," Natalie said quickly. "If you want company."

Lucy did want company, actually. She hadn't realized, until that moment, just how much she didn't want to go back to that empty dorm. But practically, she knew she needed a second to breathe. "Thank you," she said. "But I think I need to lie down."

Natalie hugged her again as they all departed the table. And as Lucy made her way back into the stinging light of the afternoon, she imagined the pale corridor of Natalie's kitchen one more time. As she'd come out from the dance floor the other night, it had looked like a little oasis in the dark. It had looked safe.

And by the sink—she blinked, and she could almost see it. The broad, straight back of the stranger. She closed her eyes. Tried to push her memory just a few steps farther. He had turned to her. He'd opened his mouth, told her something. This she was sure of.

But when she tried to imagine his face, she saw nothing.

Lucy's phone buzzed in her purse as she made her heavy way back up the path to Quincey. Another text. Her phone hadn't been this active since high school.

This time, though, it wasn't Natalie, or even her mother. It was a string of numbers with a local area code.

> Lucy, your bloodwork indicates a possible iron deficiency. We recommend a screening for anemia at your earliest convenience. I've included the number of a local clinic below.

She tucked her phone away again and fumbled with her ID card to swipe into the building. Anemia. That would be a nicer explanation than all the explanations that kept coming to mind. But it felt less like an answer and more like a marker on the road to the answer.

She shut the door behind her and blinked, hard. Even after all that sleep this morning, she was exhausted. But she still had work to do.

She checked her mail, found another handful of flyers for Pallas Radio—she faintly admired the hustle, but did have to wonder if this was why people didn't seem to like them. The recycling bin was stuffed completely full, so she absently shoved them into her tote bag to throw away later.

The room was still empty when Lucy returned, and she glanced again at Whitney's text. It was still the weekend—Whitney was probably still at her parents', or maybe on the road. But she'd feel better if she knew exactly where Whitney was. She typed a response to Whitney's last text.

When are you coming back?

When there was no immediate answer, she uneasily set her phone aside. Well. Maybe it was for the best, at least for a little while longer. According to Whitney, Lucy's typing was "too forceful."

Lucy booted up her computer and settled it on her lap. A Rollins PhD student named Luke, who had once worked at Demeter Cruise Lines. At least she had some specifics now.

For one brief, beautiful second, she thought it would be easy. The company was small enough: an Outer Banks–based liner that operated up and down the Carolinas, and the staff directory (complete with pictures) only listed about fifteen or so employees. But she didn't see any pale-eyed guys with sandy-blond hair. Plenty of women in varying shades of bottle blond and middle-aged men with sun-weathered skin and craggy smiles, but only a handful of younger people in general. There was *a* Luke, with dark hair and a grinning face. He looked the right age, at least, but—she found herself shaking her head. The silhouette was off.

She hit the back button, and her original search reloaded. It was only then that she caught the listing for the company on the sidebar, and the bolded subtitle. *Permanently closed.*

She flipped back to the website, an uneasy weightless

feeling in the pit of her stomach. There was nothing in the cheery blue font or the endearingly janky graphic design that indicated anything was "permanently closed." But Lucy noticed the social media feed a little down the page this time. The most recent post was time-stamped a little over three years prior.

In memoriam, it read. Followed by a link.

Lucy caught that scent again: that sharp penny tang. When her eyes darted down toward the source of it, she saw that she'd clenched her fists tight enough to draw blood.

She clicked the link. And those same fifteen or so faces from the staff directory smiled up at her.

She didn't let herself read each paragraph. Every accolade and anecdote, every list of surviving family—if she let herself stop and take it in, she didn't know what she would do. But she couldn't stop herself from finding Luke's grinning face halfway down the page, or reading the last few sentences under his name. *Luke Thompson was recently accepted into the prestigious philosophy graduate program at Rollins University.*

Numbly, Lucy tabbed away from the dead boy's face. And returning to her search, she clicked on the next link down the list. A news item.

TRAGEDY IN THE OUTER BANKS: 15 missing, presumed dead.

A stifled whimper broke the silence of the dorm. Even as Lucy felt it on her own lips, she couldn't quite believe that such a wounded, animal sound could live within her.

The search for the missing crew of the Outer Banks–based Demeter Cruise Lines has been called off, a representative from the Coast Guard announced this morning. One month after the company's flagship vessel was found abandoned near Bodie Island Lighthouse following an all-staff party, divers still report "no sign" of the attending employees. The vessel was discovered clean and intact, and police have not yet declared whether foul play is suspected.

The family of Demeter president and CEO Walter Rengrove issued a statement expressing "sorrow and solidarity" with the families of the missing. Rengrove, who is at this time the sole confirmed casualty of the group, was found in nearby waters one week after the ship's discovery. The cause of death was determined to be drowning, though local naturalists remain concerned by the unusual animal bite—

The screen blurred then. The sounds coming from outside faded, sinking into the hum of the computer and Lucy's own harsh breaths. She shut her laptop hard, pushing herself back across the bed and away from it.

But she already understood that there was no pushing this away. Didn't she? She couldn't push away something that was already underneath her skin.

Lucy curled up tight, burying her face in her pillow. And she cried until it hurt.

She lay wrapped in her blankets for a long time. Long

enough that she moved past crying, past anything except for short, ragged breaths. Her pillow was coarse against her face. Some cold water would have helped. But she didn't know how safe it was to unlock the door. How safe it was to be *anywhere.*

Her eyes slid shut, though she was far beyond sleep. But she was so tired. Tired enough that unlocking the door didn't sound so bad, when she imagined it. Lucy used to joke, when she had friends to joke with, that if the zombie apocalypse hit, she hoped she'd die immediately. Ideally before she knew what was going on, before she had time to be scared, because she sure as hell wasn't much of a runner *or* a fighter.

It was a joke. But it wasn't all that different from the way she felt at home sometimes. The way that she'd felt all those years, when it didn't seem like she was going anywhere except for maybe around the corner once in a while.

She wanted to have a real life. She wanted it so badly that all these years she had taken her living wherever she could get it: in fake IDs or in late-night walks or in ill-advised amateur tattoos.

But maybe she wasn't meant to be the kind of person who'd get to live. Lucy scrubbed at her face, as if with enough force she could scrub right at the thought.

No. No, that wasn't true. She'd already lived with death for this long. All those hours and all those years Jillian spent planning around and obsessing over and trying to avoid death, she made space for it in their home instead. It ate at their table every night. It slept with them in their beds.

If the zombie apocalypse came, if the boy who called himself Luke Thompson appeared at her door, if any one of the mundane horrors Jillian imagined manifested, maybe Lucy wouldn't be able to control what happened next. But she wouldn't welcome it in, either. She *would* fight, no matter how tired she was. She would outrun it the same way she'd outrun that house, the one that had kept her safe but had never made her feel all that alive. She hadn't made it all the way here just to stop running now.

Blearily, she checked her phone. It was much later than she realized, already a little past nine thirty. Whitney still wasn't back. And the sounds of life out in the hall had started to quiet down. In the absence of voices, she could hear the stirrings of the building itself. Breathing in and out with the movements of the earth below.

The walls felt so thin as they shuddered around her. Thin enough that they didn't seem like much of a match for a tall, sandy-haired stranger introducing himself with a dead boy's name.

Lucy swallowed. Her crying had wrung all the moisture out of her throat. That, at least, was a problem she could solve.

She reached for her nightstand. Her fingers brushed card-stock on the way to her water cup. The little stack of Pallas Radio advertisements, poking out of her tote bag.

Lucy gathered them up, slid forward on the mattress so she could reach the recycling bin at the end of her bed. She noticed the ink first. Fresh enough to come off a little on her thumb.

The flyers fanned out as she loosened her hold. And that was when she saw it, on the flyer closest to her hand, where her finger had smudged against neat, blocky handwriting, at the center side of the page:

Lucy—call us.

Her eyes scanned each of the flyers spread across the floor. Because the message wasn't just written on one of them. Each of the flyers had it written in the same exact spot. *Lucy—call us. Lucy—call us. Lucy—*

Jolting upright with the force of a sudden memory, she grabbed for her purse where it was drooping along the edge of her bed. The flyer she'd been handed in the café sat near the top, folded neatly behind her wallet. As she fumbled it open, the words were the first thing she saw:

Lucy—call us.

Her breath shook on the way in. *Maybe they do this for everyone,* she thought, without any real conviction. Even if anyone put that much effort into advertising their independent student radio show, stuffing mailboxes was one thing. The girl at the Pallas Radio booth this afternoon had put this flyer directly into Lucy's hand, at the café in a quad where Lucy didn't even live. Lucy was a stranger. There was no reason at all for that girl to know her name.

Pallas Radio: For the Nocturnal Among Us aired from 9:00 p.m. to 2:00 a.m., according to the card. It was 9:45 now. Lucy didn't have a radio, she doubted anyone had a radio anymore that wasn't inside a car. But it took her less than five minutes to find a radio app for her phone.

When she carefully tuned the app to 87.1, the signal was faint at first. The touch-screen slider wasn't exactly built for nuance. But when she tapped the bar backward one last time, the voice on the other end of the signal snapped into focus.

"We're about fifteen minutes from the hour now." The host had a steady contralto, smooth as water from a ladle. There was a smile in her voice. Not a broad one. The kind of thin, soft curve that hides all your teeth. "Once again, I'm your host, Pallas. Does waiting ever get easier, Rollins? Most of this job is waiting, but that hasn't made it much more bearable yet. It could be worse, though. I could be waiting without all of you here, waiting with me. So let's not wait in silence, shall we? First, a few updates.

"We'd like to thank last week's caller again for the invaluable information on Sadie Grainger's last whereabouts," Pallas said. "Sightings of our friend with the cold hands around Holmwood Hall that week remain unconfirmed. But caller number twenty-seven's description of Sadie's mental state is consistent with that of Addison Greene, our potential fall semester victim of two years ago. Stay safe out there, caller number twenty-seven."

Lucy sat up a little straighter in her bed. She remembered

the Sadie Grainger poster at the bus shelter, clearly something that had been put together by Sadie's parents. *We're not angry,* it had said. As if Sadie, or someone who knew her, was in a position to be coaxed back.

But that was not how Pallas spoke of her now.

"And speaking of Addison," Pallas said. "Let's not lose sight of her as the search for Sadie continues. As we all know, our friend with the cold hands is drawn to . . . isolated people. Sadie's family hasn't forgotten her. Addison hasn't been so lucky. It's a sobering reminder that not everyone comes to this campus with a family who has their back. We have to be Addison's family, Rollins. As always, if you have any information, you know where to find me."

She let that sit, for a moment. Her breathing echoed across the airwaves. Against it, Lucy could hear how fast her own breathing had become.

"We've also confirmed a credible sighting of our friend in the vicinity of Falls Quad on Friday night. Caller number five, it was good to hear from you again. We are still actively seeking information on the potential Friday incident, but—if you don't mind, we're asking that you hold that thought just a little while. For those of you just tuning in, we're keeping our phone lines clear tonight in the hopes that our special guest got the message. Caller number thirty-two, are you listening yet?"

Lucy froze. Something in the host's calming voice had shifted. Sharpened. Her attention narrowing from her faceless audience to just one person.

An invited special guest.

"I know you're scared, caller number thirty-two." It was almost soft enough to be inaudible. "I haven't been where you are. Not exactly. But I think I can imagine how it feels. I know you have no reason to believe me, but you *are* among friends here. And we can't help you until you pick up the phone."

Lucy swiped uselessly at the moisture slipping down her face. She hadn't thought she had any tears left in her. Then again, she hadn't thought she had the ability to trust strangers anymore, either.

That wasn't true, though. Was it? For every exhausted inch she'd crawled since the party, she'd done it because someone was helping her. Mila's cardigan was still crumpled on the corner of her bed. There was an unread text from Natalie sitting on her phone. Even Alicia, as unpleasant as she'd been, was the only reason Lucy knew as much as she did now. Strangers were the only reason she'd made it this far. What was one more?

She turned off the overhead lights. It wasn't going to do anything to hide her—the door was already shut and locked, the blinds drawn. It just felt safer somehow, making this call in the dark.

She closed the radio app. Pallas's voice, midsentence, was snuffed into silence. And, with shaking fingers, Lucy keyed in the number.

Four

The line at Pallas Radio rang just twice. The second ring had barely finished when the call was answered. When Pallas's calm, gentle radio voice emanated through her speakerphone, Lucy flinched.

"Well, Rollins. Our wait may be over." Pallas sounded so much closer on the other end of the line. Like she was sitting just on the end of the bed. "Welcome to the show, caller number thirty-two. Are you who I think you are?"

Lucy's lips had barely parted when Pallas added, "Now, before you answer that, just one thing. I meant what I said. You're among friends here. But we can't exactly control who's listening, either. If you're still listening to the show through your radio, you'll be able to hear that we've disguised your voice. While you're on the air, don't use your name. Answer with as little identifying information as you can."

A laugh bubbled up through Lucy's throat. "How do I know I'm the caller number thirty-two you were expecting?"

“I don’t go handing out invitations to just anyone, you know.” A hint of wryness crept into Pallas’s voice. “I asked one person to call tonight. Is that you?”

Lucy swallowed. The air felt cool and dusty in her throat. “Yes,” she said. Because there was no denying it now.

“Good,” Pallas said. “Now. We’ve got a lot to discuss. But why don’t you start us off? I’m sure you have questions.”

Lucy laughed again, intentionally this time. “I don’t think all my questions would fit into your time slot.”

“That’s fine,” Pallas said. “Let’s just go one at a time.”

For a long moment, Lucy just listened to the sounds of Pallas on the other line, waiting for her. But she couldn’t stall forever. So finally, she asked. “Do you know what happened to me at the party?”

“I do,” Pallas said. No hesitation.

“The person I’m looking for,” Lucy said. “Is he the . . . ‘friend with the cold hands’ you keep talking about?”

“He is,” Pallas said.

The next words closed tight around Lucy’s chest. “What is he?”

“You already know that, caller number thirty-two,” Pallas said. “Don’t you?”

All of a sudden, Lucy’s fingers itched to turn the light back on. It didn’t feel safe anymore—it just felt like one more extension of the night beyond.

“I do,” she whispered. Because she did. The sunlight. The

scent of blood. The two neat puncture marks. The simplest answer. And the correct one.

"It's okay to be scared," the host said.

Lucy shook her head tightly. "I can't afford to be scared."

"You can," Pallas said. "Listen to me. Fear is a good thing. Fear wants to keep you alive. You'll need it for what's to come."

"Am I . . ." Lucy thought she understood then why the host was using a euphemism on the air. The next words felt like tempting fate to say out loud. "Am I turning into a vampire?"

Pallas hummed, and it shivered through the airwaves. "The answer is complicated," she said. "But I don't think you are. Not yet. It's not so easy to turn someone into something that they're not. Like anything, there's a . . . process."

"Is that what he wants to do?" Lucy said. "Or does he just want to kill me?"

When Pallas spoke next, there was a terrible tenderness in her voice that Lucy wasn't sure she wanted. She was too young to remember her father dying. But she was there for every minute of her grandmother's hospice care, and then her grandfather's. She knew the voice for breaking inevitable news.

"I don't know what he wants," Pallas said. "But there's one thing I can tell you for sure. The fact that you walked away from that party Friday night? The fact that you're still here right now, speaking to me? That's not mercy, or carelessness. That is by design. Over the past three years, we've observed a specific pattern from our friend. He does not finish his chosen victims over the course of an evening. He allows them to run, and then he follows. For days, sometimes. Because he has the luxury of toying with you. Have you figured out why yet?"

Lucy pressed a hand to her mouth to stop the whimper in her throat. She hadn't figured it out. Not before now. But in the dark of the room, she could see the echo of it: his face, still blank in her memory, turning toward her. *Hold still.*

"Because I'll do whatever he says," she whispered.

"You will," Pallas said. "He has that power over us. But he especially has that power over you. Once he drinks from you—you are his to control. You could try to run. I'd help you, if I thought it would do any good. But all he'd have to do is crook a finger and you'd walk right back to him. He has a hold over you far stronger than your own free will. Stronger than most people's will, I'd think."

Pallas's voice went a little softer. "But here's the thing. Maybe I'm underestimating your will. Maybe he is, too."

Lucy squeezed her eyes shut. It didn't make much difference, here in the darkness. She could feel that bone-deep exhaustion at the edge of her awareness, threatening to tug her all the way down. Put down the phone, it said. Unlock the doors. Let whatever happens happen.

This time, though, she could track a softer, more insistent urge underneath. Like when she was twelve and home alone, and realized, in the midst of a dead sleep, that she'd left the door unlocked. She had almost dismissed the sense of wrongness then. Almost rolled over and gone back to sleep. The urge to wake up, to put a name to the wrongness, had been stronger.

But this particular wrongness was something different. It wasn't instinct. It wasn't her subconscious. The thoughts only felt like hers if she didn't look at them too closely. And now that she *was* looking at them closely, this urge to give up, to give herself over—it didn't match her voice. It was as if the font was different, the color was different. If her own thoughts were in prosaic black-and-white, these thoughts were red.

Hold still.

She pressed her nails into her palm. The bite of it was gentle, grounding. *I want to live,* she thought, louder than those red thoughts. It felt more impossible than it ever had. But it was still as true as it ever was.

"Will you help me?" Lucy said. It was smaller than she meant it to sound.

For the first time since Lucy turned on the broadcast, Pallas's voice faltered. "Before we go any further," she said, "you should know this. I can tell you what I know. I can tell you what I think will help you. But what we're fighting? It's already under your skin. I *will* help you, caller number thirty-two. It's just that my help means nothing if you don't fight back. Do you understand?"

Lucy laughed wetly. Fighting again. She was so tired of fighting.

But that had never stopped her before.

"Oh," she said. "I'm way ahead of you."

"We'll be in touch"????

Lucy sighed as she read Natalie's text, shifting a few times in the narrow chair/desk combo before coming to the conclusion that there was no comfortable way to sit in it.

That's what she said.

Natalie replied.

You're really going to tell someone they're turning into a vampire and then hit them with a "talk later"?

Lucy shot a furtive look to the front of the room. But the astronomy professor, a rail-thin man with a deeply stoned affect, was too busy trundling through the syllabus to pay her any mind. He had already assured them all that the class would be "chill," and that they were just there to "talk about stars." Reading ahead on the syllabus, though, there appeared to be a bit more physics than was strictly chill.

She blinked hard. Her eyes still felt dry and stiff. She'd tried to sleep a bit after the phone call with Pallas, impossible as that felt. But just when she'd started to drift off, she was catapulted awake again by someone banging on the door. If Whitney hadn't called out "It's me," Lucy's next stop would have been out the window.

Whitney looked miserable to be there, and even more miserable to see Lucy. She was glowering darkly when Lucy eased the door open, looking gray and tired under the hallway fluorescents. "Forgot my keys," she said, by way of explanation.

This time, though, it had been easy to forgive Whitney. Lucy had never been so happy to see such a dour face.

In any case. To Natalie's point, Lucy texted back,

Pallas said we can't talk over the radio. Can't be sure who's listening. She said she'd find us a place to meet, and she'd call me again today.

Natalie replied.

They really think a vampire is listening to student radio?

Lucy paused for a moment, before typing out a response.

Well, he used to be a person.

She meant to type something after that, but—she was no longer sure what she meant by it.

Or more accurately, she meant a few different things at once. He used to be a person, so he probably knew what a radio was. He used to be a person, so maybe he'd seen one of those dozens of Pallas Radio posters across the campus and had guessed what they were for. He used to be a person, so surely he knew the ways in which people warn each other when a fox reaches the henhouse.

But she couldn't decide which of those things she meant to type. So instead she said:

You really believe me?

There was a brief pause before Natalie's reply.

Why wouldn't I?

Lucy stifled a laugh. Because she hardly believed it herself, for one.

Because if you believe me, you should probably be scared of me.

Natalie's replied. No pause this time.

I'm not scared yet.

Lucy breathed in slowly. If she stopped to let the full force of her gratitude crash over her, she was pretty sure she was going to cry. She typed out a response before guilt or self-consciousness could stop her.

Can I text you later? When Pallas calls.

Natalie's reply seemed to hit instantaneously.

GIRL. If you DON'T text me I'm gonna be pissed.
Now pay attention to class!! I'll talk to you soon.

It was easier said than done. Now that she no longer had her phone to distract her, it was difficult to ignore the quiet but persistent cacophony of the classroom around her. The hair-raising scritch-scratch of pencils. The softer, mellower loops of ballpoint pens. One particularly emphatic mechanical pencil, which kept breaking under the force of its owner's press. *Snap. Snap. Snap.*

She bit back a wince. When she asked if she was becoming a vampire, Pallas said it was complicated. But the world hadn't been quite so loud just a few days ago. And maybe it was her potentially heightened senses, but as she fidgeted, she could feel the weight of someone's attention on her.

She carefully maneuvered herself out of the desk and to her feet. Someone probably *was* looking at her, with all her fidgeting. She needed to step out for a bit. Get some air. Splash some water on her face, maybe.

As she made her way to the back of the room, someone stuck a sheet of paper out in front of her. She glanced up to the dimly lit, closed-lipped smile of the boy holding it. "Attendance sheet," he whispered.

Lucy smiled quickly. "Thanks," she whispered back as she initialed her name. The boy nodded as she slipped out of the room.

The Goldwell building was part of an academic quad on one of the higher hills of Rollins. It was the smallest of the four buildings: just one floor aboveground and one below. The ground-floor atrium was lit with golden early-afternoon sun, and the full force of it felt slightly less oppressive than it had the day before. But Lucy couldn't deny that right now, she felt more comfortable in the dark.

As she crossed the hall to the basement stairwell, she

caught the sound of two voices. There were two students a little way down the hall, their heads bent together as they talked.

"—third one since I got here. I almost stepped on it." The first voice was brimming with revulsion. "I'm calling it into that radio show."

"Jesus, not you too," the second voice groaned. "Rabbits die all the time, Maria."

"It's weird!" Maria hissed back as her companion opened the side door back to the quad. "You can't tell me it's not weird! Whatever's killing them, how come it always leaves so much behind? Unless the meat isn't what it's really after."

Whatever Maria's friend had to say to that, Lucy didn't hear it. The door shut behind them, and they had officially passed out of Lucy's earshot.

Lucy opened the stairwell door and started down to the basement. She'd seen a dead rabbit too, now that she thought about it: on the way to the bus shelter, the night she was bitten. She hadn't made much of it then. Like Maria's friend said, rabbits die all the time.

But it seemed Pallas wasn't the only one to notice that there was something not quite right about the campus. For all its detractors, maybe her show gave some students exactly what it had given Lucy: the relief of clarity. Though maybe it gave the detractors that clarity, too. There were few things more annoying than a truth you didn't want to see.

The chill of the concrete steps bruised the soles of Lucy's

flats. The stairs were built for someone taller. She had to point her toes a little as she lowered herself from one to the next, the banister a cool slide along her palm.

It was disorienting, this sudden awareness of her own body. Lucy was young, and until now, she'd been healthy. For all her focus on living, she'd never thought very hard about the mechanics of being alive. Her body was something to look at, to twist, to study, to hide or not hide depending on the circumstances. It was a thing in motion, an object in space. It had never been a place where she lived. It had never been a house that could crumble.

She felt all of it now. The air rushing into her nose and seeping out of her mouth, the unsteady squirm of her pulse. It didn't feel like being alive, though. It didn't even feel like something that was wholly hers. It felt like unseen things wriggling under a rock.

Pallas had said it was complicated, what was happening to her. Lucy needed to know how complicated it was, exactly.

Not for the first time that day, Lucy wished that Mila were here with her. She could have used some of that cool, calm decisiveness right now. And if Mila wanted to let Lucy squeeze her hand until it hurt a little, that would have been fine, too.

She made her vague, meandering way toward the signs for the bathroom. There was a strange sound rumbling at the edges of her magnified hearing. Part of it was the rustling of the classroom above, though she wasn't quite sure if that was real or just an echo in her ears. But she was gradually becoming aware of something beyond it.

She slowed as she listened. And as she did, she felt a confident sort of understanding in the back of her mind. She was starting to recognize, as she had last night, which thoughts weren't quite her own. The thoughts that had a different color, a different pitch. The red voice.

The red voice heard the sound, and knew it. *Through that closed door,* it told her. *To your left.*

Lucy drew in a breath. Pallas had warned her that the vampire targeted students who were isolated. He was probably counting on her being alone and stupid.

But Pallas wasn't here yet. Mila wasn't here to walk her through her options. And in the absence of any new information, Lucy wanted to know what she was up against.

There was a gentle *pop* when she opened the door, like a wine cork giving way. And the first thing Lucy sensed, sticking her hand into the half-lit hallway beyond, was that it was a few degrees cooler than the hallway behind her. Not dramatically, but enough to raise the hair on her arms. The higher notes of the thrum were louder now, closer. *The water heater,* the red voice told her.

But beyond the water heater, there was something else. A sifting, grinding sound. And beneath that, a sound not unlike the sounds under Lucy's own skin. The squirm of something living.

The night is alive. That was what she texted her mother the night she was bitten. She still had no memory of sending it. But she must have heard something like this that night. The whole world shifting and breathing and decaying. Exactly what she heard from the hallway ahead.

She remembered, then, all those nights she'd spent googling Rollins. The campus ran on steam heat through the winter, which meant that there was a widespread system of steam tunnels across the mountain. She'd read that there were accessible entrances through a few different buildings, but that they were locked and alarmed. Students had been barred from entering them altogether after one too many hazing incidents.

But the hallway ahead hadn't been locked at all. Maybe the real entrance was a bit farther down.

Or maybe someone had left this door open.

Lucy stilled, and tried to remember that article. There wasn't a tunnel entrance in Quincey. She would have noticed by now if there was. But it seemed that the Goldwell building could be accessed from underground. It wouldn't have been difficult for someone to get in. To go upstairs to the ground floor, to delicately sidestep the sunlight streaming in through the front windows. To duck into the auditorium. To slide into a faceless crowd of students, like they belonged there.

The boy who had handed her the attendance sheet. She hadn't looked at him that closely, beyond his smile. Did he have light hair?

Lucy's purse buzzed against her leg, and she had to stifle a yelp into her hands.

She fished her phone out of her purse with shaking hands. Blocked number. Thank fucking Christ. It had only been a little more than half a day since Pallas of Pallas Radio said she'd be in touch, but it had been an extraordinarily long half a day.

Lucy slammed the door to the tunnels shut and beelined for the staircase to the ground floor as she cradled the phone against her ear. "Hello?"

There was a beat—not all that long in reality, but long enough that Lucy tightened her grip on the phone. And then finally, Pallas of Pallas Radio said, "Sorry to keep you waiting, Lucy."

The breath Lucy let out was much louder than she intended it to be. It didn't escape her notice that she was "Lucy" now instead of "caller number thirty-two." Wherever Pallas was, she didn't seem to think anyone was listening.

"Hang on," Lucy muttered. "Let me get outside."

She thought she'd said it calmly, but there must have been something in her tone that Pallas heard. "Are you safe?" she asked.

Lucy laughed darkly. "Good question."

She made her way back to the ground floor, tucking herself into a sunbathed corner. Instantly, the now-familiar headache started behind her eyes. "Okay, I'm good," she said. She hoped she was, anyway. "Pallas, you have to tell me what's going on."

"Soon." Pallas's off-air voice had the same calm, sonorous quality as her radio voice did. "I needed to find us a neutral place."

"I can't just come to you?" Lucy asked.

"Neutral place first," Pallas said. "For now."

Right, she thought. Pallas had told her the night before that the vampire had power over her. And whether or not that was true, Pallas probably didn't trust her. "I'm still in control," she said quickly.

The beat of silence *was* a long one this time. "Lucy," Pallas said. Her voice had gone gentle. "If you don't mind my saying so, that may be what he wants you to believe."

Lucy shivered. All right, then. Touché.

"Okay," she said. "Where's this neutral place?"

Pallas let out a slight hum. "Your tour would have taken you by the Interfaith Triangle. Do you remember it?"

"The place with all the yellow tape?" Lucy said.

"That's the one," Pallas said. "It's one of the safest places on campus. Meet me there at six, and I'll tell you why. And I'll tell you anything else I can, too.

"Oh, and Lucy?" Pallas said. "I understand you may not have much say in this. But try not to be followed."

"I feel like this is pushing it," Lucy said. "Semantically speaking."

"Semantically speaking, you're doing exactly what she told you to do," Natalie said. "She said 'Try not to be followed.' You're literally trying to stop me from following you. You can proceed guilt-free."

"I don't know if my guilt is what matters here," Lucy said.

Natalie offered one of her breezy shrugs. "Ms. Pallas Radio will survive. If she wanted me to trust her, she shouldn't have had you meet her all the way out here."

The Interfaith Triangle lay just ahead, a glittering arrangement of concrete and glass in the golden-hour sun. The structures, one Jewish, one Catholic, and one Protestant, were beautiful. But even from this distance, it was easy to tell that they were long empty. According to Lucy's orientation tour, various services were being held in the student center while each building was having its roof replaced, but it didn't appear to be much of a priority. The heavy machinery, parked by the drained reflecting pool, looked dusty. The fluttering NO ENTRY tape was flecked with dirt.

"You should keep your distance, in any case," Lucy whispered. "She seems—cautious."

"Well . . . I get that. But there's cautious, and there's cloak-and-dagger bullshit." Natalie slowed, turning toward a wide-trunked tree to their left. "I'll wait here out of sight. I should be close enough to see if anything goes wrong, but maybe we need a code word if something seems off."

"Natalie . . ." Lucy faltered. "You really don't have to do this."

Natalie blinked. Somehow, in all the chaos of the day, she'd had time to put on her false eyelashes. "This happened to you at my party," she said.

"That doesn't make it your responsibility," Lucy said.

"Oh, I know." Natalie offered one of her breezy shrugs. "But I feel like the Middle Ages had it right about hospitality. If someone eats your food, they should be safe in your home. Dorm, I guess." She paused. "If you really would rather go alone, though—"

"That's not it," Lucy said. She wasn't sure why she was getting flustered. It wasn't like she hadn't had friends in high school. But they'd been so young then. Young enough that it was still scary, the idea of having someone else rely on them.

However, Natalie wanted to be relied on. That much, in the past few days, had been made clear.

"I'm glad you're here," Lucy finally said.

"Well, good," Natalie said. "Because I'm here for whatever you need. Unless it's manual labor, obviously. This may shock you, but I don't lift." She cast a wary eye ahead, and added, "I'll hang back here. If something goes wrong, the code word is *Warsaw*. Or you could scream, I guess."

Lucy shot Natalie a look and did something with her lips, genuinely unsure if the end result was a smile or a grimace. And as she went on ahead, Natalie slid behind the tree and fully out of sight.

The NO ENTRY tape snapped in the breeze, a crooked finger.

"Okay," Lucy breathed, more to herself than anything. "Here goes nothing."

The walkway was cool. A little wet—Lucy could feel groundwater seeping through her shoes. The sun's curtain had slipped a little lower, but not low enough to worry just yet. Sunset was in about an hour. Plenty of time to talk.

If anyone was coming at all. It was 6:02 now, according to Lucy's watch. Not exactly late enough to worry. But if Lucy was worrying a little extra right now, she didn't think anyone could hold that against her.

There was a little shuffle then, behind the Protestant chapel. Almost imperceptible: the sound of shifting weight in the dirt. But the relief of the sound didn't last long. Whoever was there, they didn't keep walking. They stayed right where they were.

And Lucy, fully against her will, could hear the twitching animal of their heart.

All at once, she'd had enough of it. If this really was Pallas, Natalie was right: This was cloak-and-dagger bullshit. And if it wasn't Pallas—either way, Lucy was tired of waiting.

"Who's there?" she called.

In the beat that followed, Lucy heard someone draw in a slow breath. "Not yet." The voice was pleasant. Smooth, and low. But Lucy caught a dissonance in it. A strain. "We'll do introductions when Pallas arrives."

So it wasn't Pallas, but it was someone who was expecting her. It should have been a relief. But now that the anger had set in, it was putting down roots. "I understand that you don't trust me," she said. "But you can come out. We can at least talk normally while we're waiting."

"We can talk right here," the voice said. "You should be able to hear me very well, right?"

It was the casual understanding of it that sent Lucy's blood surging into her ears. The easy acknowledgment of what was happening to her, when Lucy barely knew the half of it herself. It didn't matter that Pallas had promised to tell her when she arrived. Right then, it only mattered that they'd kept it from her for this long.

"I'm on edge," Lucy snapped. "You're not helping."

"If you're on edge," they said, "seeing me won't help."

Lucy had no idea what that was supposed to mean. She wasn't in the mood to try to parse it, either. "I'm going to see you eventually," she said. "Might as well get it over with now, right?"

"Hmm," the voice said. Noncommittal. "Are you sure?"

"Yes," Lucy said. "I'm sure. Come out, please."

She heard a low breath, and then the rustle of the hedges behind the chapel. And slowly, Mila Rostova stepped fully into the light, grimaced, and shrugged.

Without that bottle-green cardigan, there was no veneer of softness. The casual tension of her posture that Lucy had noticed when they met—it didn't look all that casual anymore. And low at her side, like an extension of her arms, she held an entire fucking bow and arrow.

She raised it a little, but kept it pointed at nothing. The

arrow was only gently nocked, barely held in position. She wasn't poised to fire. But in a matter of seconds, she could be.

"Mila?" Lucy said.

The quiver of arrows at her hip jolted, just once, with the motion. "I tried to warn you."

TRANSCRIPT OF ROLLINS UNIVERSITY STUDENT RADIO STATION WVBS ("PALLAS RADIO")

Broadcast number: 445

CALLER #5: It's weird, right? But I don't know. I could be wrong. You know how some people have face blindness? I feel like I have that, but only for white men.

PALLAS (HOST): Then I suppose my question is this. Do you think you *are* wrong?

CALLER #5: I . . . Hah. No. I'm not. He was talking to my friend for a really long time. And then the next time I saw him, he was in the kitchen with the girl who passed out. When he was with my friend, he was behind me. He would have had to push me aside to get past. Do you think it was him?

PALLAS: That's what we'll need to find out. But thank you. This was more helpful than you know.

CALLER #5: I feel so stupid. I actually took down that girl's phone number, but somehow I didn't save it. I don't even remember what her name was.

PALLAS: You just focus on staying safe. We'll find her. [beat] Hey, before you go: How's that thesis coming along?

CALLER #5: Oh my God, *so* well. I decided to focus on performance in modern death ritual—

PALLAS: Ah ah ah. No identifying details on the air.

CALLER #5: Right. Fuck. Sorry.

PALLAS: Don't worry too much, caller number five. Even if our friend with the cold hands is listening—for better or worse, it sounds like someone else has already caught his eye.

Five

"What the fuck are you doing here?" Lucy said. "And what are you *holding*?"

Mila inclined her head, but otherwise didn't dignify that with a response. And it was then that Lucy understood the cool tension of her posture. It wasn't the stance of an athlete. It was the stance of a hunter.

Lucy's brain tripped uselessly over at least three or four half-formed questions. Her mind was a tangle—the same kind of tangle it had been just the other day in the Quincey lobby, when Mila had sat with her and helped her consider her options. The same Mila who was now giving her a long, evaluating stare.

"Pallas will be here soon," she said evenly. "Let's keep things civil."

"I'm not the one holding a weapon," Lucy said.

Mila delicately arched her eyebrows. "I have a weapon. And you could *be* a weapon. Feels pretty fair from how I see it."

"I'm not going to hurt you," Lucy said.

"Glad you feel that way. But you're just going to have to let me see that for myself."

In some ways, Mila wasn't talking to her any differently now: She still had that easy cadence, that same assessing gaze that had sized her up back at Quincey. But there had been a weight to that gaze that had soothed the deep, clawing feeling in Lucy. It made her feel like she was in safe hands.

That same weight was still there. But it wasn't so soothing now. Lucy felt pinned. Studied.

She held up both hands. "Fine," she said.

Mila adjusted her grip on her bow. Lucy's sight was growing sharper as the sky darkened: She could see the lines of tension in Mila's knuckles. "I get that this is hard," she said. "I'm not looking to make it harder. Let's just cooperate with each other for a few more minutes, okay?"

It wasn't much of a question. More than anything, Mila's tone suggested that it would *have* to be okay. But if nothing else, it was a stalemate.

That stalemate didn't last long, though. In her shock, Lucy had already forgotten: She hadn't come here alone.

"Hey!" Both Mila and Lucy whipped around just in time to see Natalie barreling across the grass. "Get away from her!"

Lucy caught her breath just in time to see Mila raise her bow. "That's a friend," she said quickly, "a *human* friend!"

Mila's eyes didn't soften much at the clarification. "You were supposed to come alone."

"I was asked not to be followed! Not to come alone!" Natalie's logic didn't sound nearly as confident coming out of Lucy's mouth. It didn't help that she was half convinced she was about to see Natalie get an arrow to the chest.

She moved between Natalie and Mila as Natalie closed the distance. She didn't think Mila would hurt a person—at least, a person who wasn't under the influence of a vampire. But she wasn't about to assume anything in that moment.

Natalie didn't seem interested in being protected. She side-stepped Lucy and got directly in Mila's face. "You've got some nerve telling her what she is *supposed* to do, by the way. Seeing as no one told her that you or your deadly weapon were going to be here."

"I don't know what you two think this is," Mila said. "But if you want our help—"

"Mila," called a now-very-familiar voice. "It's okay."

There was a clear shift in Mila's demeanor at the sound of Pallas's voice. Her back straightened. And when she stepped aside, clearing the path between Lucy and the direction of the voice, she stood taut, as if at attention.

From behind the middle chapel, Lucy heard someone gently but deliberately brush a branch out of the way. And then a figure stepped onto the pavement.

Pallas dressed like someone trying to blend in. She wore light-wash jeans, a plain black hoodie, and a pair of clean white sneakers. But she was so strikingly beautiful that she would stand out anywhere. She was tall and willowy, with delicate braids that cascaded down to her waist. Her skin was a deep brown, and her dark eyes were as watchful as Mila's, but softer. She moved across the pavement with long, soundless strides.

"I know you're upset," she said. "And that's my fault for running late. But if you don't keep your voice down, it won't just be our friend with the cold hands who hears us."

Lucy had to marvel, in the quiet that followed, at what her sharpened senses could pick up in the absence of other sound. She could hear the itch of everyone's heartbeats. Natalie's hard and loud. Mila's metronome beats. Pallas's much faster than she would have thought, looking at her placid face.

But despite the breathless patter of her pulse, she was smiling. "First things first," she said. "Why don't we all sit down. Relax, to the extent possible."

Sitting appeared to be the last thing Natalie and Mila wanted to do. But Mila was the first to obey, perching on the edge of the bench directly opposite Lucy with her bow resting neatly across her lap. Lucy quietly filed away the fact that despite all Mila's easy confidence, it seemed she deferred to Pallas. Even when she looked a bit reluctant to do so.

Lucy settled onto the bench closest to her. Natalie remained standing. "Natalie," Lucy murmured, lightly patting the spot next to her. "It's okay."

"We'll see about that," Natalie muttered. But eventually, she complied.

Resting her hands on her thighs, Pallas turned to Natalie.

"Why don't we start with your name? I think the rest of us have been introduced."

It wasn't admonishment, exactly, but Natalie squirmed at it anyway. "Natalie Baker."

"You hosted the party," Pallas said. This was, as Lucy noticed, a statement rather than a question.

Natalie seemed to notice that, too. Her uncharacteristic discomfort deepened. "I did," she said. "I don't like it when people hurt my friends. Particularly on my watch."

"It wasn't a person that hurt your friend," Mila said. At Natalie's curt nod, she added, "But you came anyway?"

"You know what hurt her," Natalie shot back. "And you still came, too."

Mila ran one absent finger down the curve of her bow. "I've considered what could happen to me," she said. "I don't know that you have."

Natalie looked unruffled. "My ex once said that I had a 'yes, and' mentality."

Mila laughed. It was a short, harsh sound. "I don't know that you can improv your way out of this one."

"Mila, she's already here," Pallas said. "We need all the help we can get."

Mila didn't seem entirely sure about that. But as before, she deferred to Pallas.

Another silence followed, this one much less deliberate than the last. As if they'd each realized, in roughly the same moment, that it was time to stop stalling.

"Lucy." Pallas turned. It was the first time, Lucy thought, that Pallas had looked at her dead-on since she arrived. "You don't have to be nervous."

Lucy laughed warily. "Just feeling a little—exposed."

Pallas nodded slowly. "Does it help if I tell you that this is one of the safest places on campus?"

Natalie perked up. "Because of the religious buildings?"

"Not exactly. Not for our friend, at least," Pallas said. "Turns out that horror stories are just as susceptible to church propaganda as anything else. Figures, right? The idea that religious objects are supposed to protect you—crosses, holy water—I'm not sure if that messaging came from the church itself, or if that was just the God-fearing public trying to self-soothe. But either way, it isn't true. As far as I've been able to tell from my research, Christian iconography only works if the vampire itself was a Christian in life. It's a placebo effect. If you think God can hurt you, then maybe He can.

"But when it comes to our friend—it doesn't seem like he was a believer." Something in Pallas's face clouded, then cleared. "Anyway. It's actually that 'no entry' tape doing the heavy lifting. Some of the lore is true: They *do* need to be invited in. And the university hung the tape. I still don't know if that means that President Ballard would have to extend the invitation, or the construction workers—but either way, it means we're safe here."

Lucy glanced over at the aforementioned, terrifyingly fragile tape. "That feels like a very narrow loophole."

"Oh, it works," Pallas said lightly. "Unfortunately, I've tested it in person. Completely by accident."

Lucy waited for her to continue. But Pallas didn't elaborate. And her silence had an expectant quality.

It was Lucy's turn to speak then.

"Have you seen him?" Lucy finally said. It felt like a hilariously inadequate way to ask what she was really asking.

"I did," Pallas said. "Two years ago."

Lucy sucked in a breath through her teeth. "Did he—"

"He didn't bite me," Pallas said. "I got very, very lucky that night. If I hadn't run through here completely by chance, I don't think I'd be talking to you right now."

Lucy could hear Pallas's quick rabbit heartbeats again in the silence that followed. "What does he look like?"

"You don't remember?" Pallas said.

"I don't remember anything," Lucy said.

Pallas nodded. "If he passed us now," she finally said, "you'd think he was anyone else. That's how he hunts. He just looks normal."

Lucy's own pulse fluttered loudly—loudly enough that it felt impossible that no one but she could hear it. He looked like a person. That was what she remembered, too. But in the days since, the thought of it no longer made sense to her. What kind of thing could upend her life—so many lives—so completely, and still look human?

"Why did you stay here, after?" Natalie said. "I think I would have transferred."

It was a bit blunter than Lucy would have put it, but Pallas didn't seem to mind the question. "That would have made sense, right?" she said. "I was like you, Lucy. I got here late. Did my first year at community college to save money, then transferred in starting my sophomore year. I was planning to wait until my junior year, actually. But my biology teacher at the community college sent one of my papers to the chair of the neuroscience department here at Rollins, and he recruited me. Got me a special scholarship, too."

That same clouded look passed over her face again. "Stubbornness really is a fatal flaw, isn't it? I guess I thought—why do I have to give this up, just for him?"

"You worked hard to get here," Lucy said. She couldn't say she didn't understand that.

"And it was more than that, too," Pallas said. "I had been here for just a few days when I was attacked, like you. There was no one I could talk to, except the campus police, and they didn't believe me. They thought it was one of the underground frats pulling a prank on some poor transfer student. No one looked into it. And I knew that if I didn't stay, no one ever would."

Pallas looked almost sheepish as she shrugged. "I guess I have something in common with Natalie, here. I don't like to see people hurt on my watch, either. But even after I started Pallas Radio, I was out of my depth. Addison disappeared right before winter break the same year I was attacked. Sadie disappeared almost a year ago, a few weeks after classes started. And it's not just Rollins students. If you know what to look for, you see signs of him in the news around here: hunting accidents, lost hikers, strange nursing home deaths, mauled rabbits."

"But Rollins students seem to have a special place in his heart," Mila said grimly. "He always comes back here. And when he finds a victim, he toys with them first. People have called into the show about Sadie and Addison. They say that they looked strange and sick in the days before they disappeared. So if we see a student acting erratically or looking ill, we keep an eye on them."

Pallas nodded. "Mila and I both took jobs on campus that would bring us into contact with as many students as possible. We have the show, of course. But Mila also has her RA work. I started peer counseling, volunteering with orientation groups. We had a lot of false alarms over the years. We missed Sadie completely. But thankfully Mila didn't miss you."

Reluctantly, Lucy turned her attention back to Mila, who was studying the weapon in her lap. "You knew right away," she said.

"About two seconds after we started talking," Mila said. "So I went and told the boss, here, and we tried to figure out how we could approach you without scaring you off. Guess we had some mixed success there."

"Well, now that you *have* found me . . . what do we do?" Lucy asked.

Pallas laughed. It was the most uncertain sound Lucy had heard from her so far. "The only thing we *can* do," she said. "We have to stop him from hurting you again. Which means we have to kill him."

Once again, Lucy was not a fan of this new, microscopic awareness of her body. When she swallowed, she could feel the movement of it all the way down. "I mean . . ." she said. "I'd be all for it. But aren't there like . . . professionals?"

"You'd think," Mila said. "But in the past three years, Pallas and I pulled together money to hire two people who turned out to be scammers, and one probably legit guy who fell down a steam tunnel halfway through the night and broke his ankle. If Buffy Summers exists, she's not making house calls. And when our only real resource is the internet, it's not that easy to tell who's real and who's role-playing."

Mila ran one careful finger down the loose arrow now resting at her side. It seemed that one more piece of vampire lore was true—and Mila expected to drive that arrow right through their "friend's" heart. "So if someone has to kill him," she continued, "I'm it."

"You will," Pallas said. "This is as close as we've ever been."

Mila straightened, and her face lost a little of its characteristic ease. Though her next words were addressed to Lucy, she was still looking at Pallas out of the corner of her eye. "I'm ready for whatever I need to do," she finally said. "The problem is, he's ready, too."

Lucy could feel Natalie trying to catch her eye, though she didn't dare return the gesture in front of their audience. But she noticed the same thread of tension that Natalie must have. It was the first time since Pallas arrived that Mila seemed just slightly out of step with her.

"All right . . ." Lucy said. "One more question. You said you don't think I'm turning into a vampire on the phone the other night. So what *is* happening to me?"

The tension in Pallas's face shifted. It was still uncertainty, but a kind she seemed more comfortable with. "It's hard to say this for sure," she said. "My sources are basically the weirdest self-published books on the internet and monsterfucker forums that may or may not be a lot of wishful thinking. If what I've read is true, the bite causes some kind of preliminary infection, something that primes your body for the transformation. But without the reciprocal consumption of blood, the transformation isn't complete. Basically, he can't just drink from you. You have to drink from him in return."

"And let's say I don't do that," Lucy pressed. "Does the infection go away?"

"I think so?" Pallas grimaced. "Again, I'm relying mostly on vampire dating forums, here. But I've seen more than one poster on those sites warning against letting your partner feed from you too much in a short period of time. The only one of them to elaborate just wrote that it made things, quote, 'weird.'"

"Weird how?" Lucy said.

Pallas's mouth thinned. "I found a thread where someone

asked exactly that," she said. "But they took it to DMs."

"Great." Lucy squeezed her eyes shut. "The one time you need someone to overshare on the internet."

Mila gently tugged at her bowstring. "I've seen a bit of what happens when he feeds from someone," she said. "All you need to know is that *weird* doesn't cover it."

Lucy decided against asking for clarification. "The other night, I woke up in my quad courtyard, and my neck was freshly bleeding. He may have fed on me twice already."

Pallas and Mila each had their own muted reaction to that. "All the more reason for us to take precautions," Pallas said. "Most importantly, no going out after sunset. If you have evening classes, drop them. If you have classes in buildings connected to steam tunnels, drop those too. You should be safe in Quincey Hall, for now. We just have to do our best to keep him from being invited in."

"I asked the other RAs to spread the word that one of the residents has a toxic ex," Mila said. "There's an email going out right now warning Quincey students not to let anyone in who doesn't already have card-swipe access. But overly helpful students aren't our biggest risk. That would be you."

"Because I'll supposedly let him in," Lucy said.

"Oh, you will," Mila said. "With a smile, too."

Lucy considered arguing. But it was hard not to think of her one clear memory of the other night. *Hold still.* Even before he'd fed from her, she'd obeyed him.

“Okay,” she said. “So if I’d let him in—how do we make sure I don’t?”

“If he’s going to draw you out, then there’s going to need to be someone there to pull you back,” Pallas said. “I know you may not like this, Lucy. But this is the best we can do to keep you—”

“Let’s at least try to give this a positive spin, boss.” Mila held up both her hands in a wry little *ta-da*. “I heard you’re not a fan of your roommate, Lucy. Want a new one?”

Six

"No," Lucy said.

"I don't love the idea myself," Mila said. "They don't exactly encourage me to have sleepovers with my residents, you know."

"Bet they don't encourage you to point weapons at your residents, either," Lucy snapped.

Mila exhaled. "And here I thought we'd moved past that."

"It won't be the most comfortable arrangement," Pallas said, with the polite desperation of a kindergarten teacher. "But, Lucy, our friend *will* come for you. And when he does, Mila is our best chance of protecting you."

The thought settled in Lucy's stomach like a stone.

"Listen," Mila said, "I know you're pissed that I lied to you. But if anyone's going to keep you alive, it's going to be me."

That was probably true. But Lucy felt distinctly unmoved nonetheless. First of all, she wasn't pissed that Mila lied to her. She was pissed that Mila had threatened to kill her. If that was unreasonable of her, so be it. "There's no one else who can do this?"

"Yeah, what about me?" Natalie said. "I've got plenty of room."

"Room, sure," Mila said dryly. "But how's your aim?"

"When he comes for Lucy, our hope is that he'll be fully focused on her. And that maybe that'll make him more vulnerable," Pallas said. "And Mila was a junior archery champion. She won't miss."

"So Lucy is bait," Natalie said.

Mila's smile went brittle. "Isn't that better than the alternative?"

"If this is going to be a debate, you should move it inside." The strain was a bit more evident in Pallas's voice now. "Sunset is in half an hour."

Lucy glanced up. A delicate orange had started to wash over the sky. There was plenty of light now, but she'd learned over the past week just how quickly night could fall on the mountain.

Mila stood up. "I can walk you to the shuttle, boss."

"No, that's okay. It's not far," Pallas said. "Natalie can walk with me. And you two can go right over the hill to Quincey. It seems like you have a lot to discuss."

Natalie caught Lucy's eye, clearly waiting to read her reaction. The problem was, Lucy wasn't sure her reaction was terribly rational. Pallas and Mila were right. Or more accurately, they had a plan, which was almost as good as being right. But that didn't mean Lucy wanted to spend the rest of the night looking at the cool appraisal in Mila's eyes, either.

"Lucy?" Natalie asked, finally. "I can go back with you, if you want."

Reluctantly, Lucy uncoiled. She didn't want to make Natalie worry. She was probably in good hands now—at least she hoped she was.

"I'm okay," she said. "You should go back. It's not safe for you out here, either."

"He may not be after you," Mila said as Natalie stood. "But you invited him into your suite at the party. You should barricade your door, if you can."

"Trust me," Natalie said tightly. "I'll be spending the night whittling something wooden and sharp. Once I figure out how to whittle."

"And, Lucy?" Pallas said. "The number I called from earlier was the station landline. This is my cell."

She tapped a few buttons on her phone, and within a few seconds, an incoming AirDrop popped up on Lucy's phone. It was a contact. *Athena Barnes.*

"Oh..." Lucy's fingers moved carefully over Pallas—Athena's name as she saved it to her phone. It felt oddly fragile in her hands. "I think you might have—"

"Don't worry. It wasn't an accident." Pallas's smile thinned, as if self-conscious. "I hear him calling my name, some nights. He doesn't try to get into the radio station anymore, not for a long time now. But he still calls me anyway. Like he thinks one day I'll get desperate enough to come out, just to make him stop."

She took a slow breath that eased the tremor out of her voice. "I came here intending for you to keep calling me Pallas. If this goes badly . . . I didn't want to hear you calling my name, too. But we're asking you to trust us. It's not fair if I don't give you some of my trust in return."

Athena smiled, and nodded, as if to wordlessly take her leave. Natalie exchanged brief, wide eye contact with Lucy as she passed. But she followed Athena just as silently.

"Be careful," Mila called out after them.

Athena turned just long enough for Lucy to see her smile twitch, then fade. With every step, her rabbit heartbeat grew just a little quieter. "You know me."

It was an excruciatingly quiet walk back to Quincey Hall.

Lucy scrambled in the wake of Mila's long strides. She knew she should probably say something. Technically speaking, they hadn't finished their argument yet. But her earlier anger was crystallizing into a brittle, embarrassing hurt that she didn't want to put on display.

She had nothing to be upset about. She and Natalie finally had help, from people who ostensibly knew what they were doing. And—well, it wasn't like Mila had truly betrayed her trust. They'd had two conversations. A conversation and a half, really. Lucy was acting like a child.

But still. During that conversation and a half, beneath Mila's easy confidence, there had been real warmth. Calm, unobtrusive reassurance, a steadiness that had kept Lucy on her feet. Sure, it had been nice to get a smile and a cardigan from a ridiculously beautiful girl at a moment when she'd never felt less pulled-together. But it went beyond that, too. Mila had looked at all her fear and uncertainty and hadn't flinched. Maybe it should have meant more that she hadn't flinched, knowing now that Mila had clocked what was happening to her from the very beginning.

Except that when Mila looked at her now, that warmth was gone. No understanding, pity, cruelty, anything. Just business.

And unfortunately, that hurt.

"You can say what you're thinking, you know," Mila finally said as they approached the Quincey front doors. "Might make you feel better."

Lucy's lips gave a bare, unamused twitch as she unlocked the door. "I don't think it'll make either of us feel better."

"True. But you could say it anyway."

When Lucy filed into the building and kept her mouth shut, Mila let out a breath. "Okay. We can save that for later, then. For now—you know you can't stay in that room, don't you? Your roommate—"

"I get it," Lucy said shortly. Mila didn't need to elaborate. She realized it the moment they started walking away from the Interfaith Triangle: that as much as she wanted to curl up in her own creaky, extra-long twin bed, away from Mila's assessing stare, that was impossible. If the vampire managed to get an invite into Quincey, Lucy wouldn't be the only one to get hurt. Whitney would be there, too.

So, reluctantly, she acknowledged that out loud. "I don't want to get anyone else involved, either. Just—give me a second to go get some stuff, and I'll meet you at your room."

"Oh." Judging by the look on Mila's face, she'd expected a bit more of a fight than that. "Um—you want me to come with you? I can help you carry stuff."

Lucy flinched. Mila probably meant it innocently, but—God, it brought her right back to that stupid line about arm day. On top of everything else, Mila was probably well aware that Lucy found her attractive. Lucy wasn't in the habit of hiding that kind of thing.

"I shouldn't have much to bring." She said it with her back turned, already halfway to the stairs. The last thing she wanted Mila to see was her face already starting to crumple. "This'll be over soon either way."

Lucy was around the corner and halfway up the stairs before she had to reach up to wipe her eyes. It was ridiculous. But apparently *this* was going to be the straw that broke her back.

When Lucy was younger, she used to spend a lot of time watching the faces people made when they looked at her. At the pharmacy, trying to work out prescriptions. Confirming instructions with doctors, haggling with insurance companies, picking out the caskets when Jillian decided it was more than she could bear. Even earlier than that, walking out of her first-grade classroom the day they'd told her that her father was dead, though that was less of a memory and more of a faint impression in her mind.

She used to be so sure of what they were thinking in those moments. *Look at her. Glad that isn't me.* She knew now they probably weren't thinking that at all. She understood, most days, that people weren't looking at *her*, even if they were looking in her direction. Most of the time, they were too wrapped up in their own problems to really see hers.

But Mila saw her. And whatever was happening to Lucy—to Mila, it was the worst possible outcome. Lucy felt very sure of that.

At the very least, her eyes were dry by the time she reached her door. Her face was probably a bit puffy. But thankfully Whitney, unlike Mila, was rarely all that interested in looking at her.

Lucy turned the key in the lock. And the door swung open into a darkened room.

She blinked. Her vision was much sharper in the dark after the bite—she supposed that was the infection, preparing her body for a transformation that would hopefully never come—but the sight startled her nonetheless. Whitney disliked the overhead fluorescents, but she had more floor and desk lamps than Lucy had ever seen one person fit into a small space. It didn't seem like her to hunch over her laptop in the dark like this.

"Whitney?" Lucy called. There was an odd stillness to the room, one that was rare with Lucy's newly sharpened hearing. If she hadn't been looking directly at Whitney sitting at the desk, she would have thought no one was there.

"What do you want?" Whitney said, without turning away from her laptop. "I'm busy."

Be nice, Lucy reminded herself. If she survived the next several days, she had big dreams of making it through the rest of the year without her or Whitney killing each other. "Got it," she said. "I just wanted to let you know that I'm staying with my friend for a couple days, so I'm going to pack a few things really quickly. You don't have to turn the light on or anything."

Whitney didn't seem to have any objections to that—which was good, because Lucy wasn't planning on honoring any. She sidled in between the bed and the makeshift closet, tossed her duffel bag on the bed, and started piling up any clothes within reach that looked comfortable. A few days' worth of clothes was probably enough. She could always come back for more if she lived longer than that.

She took stock of her packed bag. This was probably all she needed to do, for now. The fewer details she gave Whitney, the better—Mila would probably get in trouble if the school found out there was a first-year staying in her room. Even a first-year who was at least a year older than her.

Lucy snorted quietly. If Whitney thought she was a party girl now, Lucy wondered how she'd react to the idea of Lucy shacking up with an RA on the first day of classes.

“Shut the fuck up,” Whitney said under her breath.

Lucy’s whole spine stiffened. *Be nice,* she reminded herself again. Not to preserve her relationship with Whitney this time. But because her senses weren’t the only thing that had sharpened since the bite. Every feeling that used to be effortlessly swallowable now brimmed at the top of her throat. And of those newly crystallized feelings, the strongest was her anger.

“Whitney,” Lucy said. She thought it was remarkably calm, considering. “Don’t tell me to shut up.”

Whitney turned, just a fraction, in her chair. Her pupils were massive in the dark. “I don’t understand why you’re here,” she said tonelessly. “I told Res Life that I strongly preferred a single.”

Lucy blinked. “Yeah,” she said, “I think there’s a lottery, or—”

“Shut *up*!” Whitney said. “God! If you’re not talking, you’re moving. If you’re not moving, you’re breathing.”

Lucy stuck her toothbrush into her bag. More accurately, she slammed it. “Yeah, Whitney,” she said. “People need to breathe to live. You can put that in your thesis.”

Whitney’s fist came down onto her desk with a bang. A sharp groan and a caving sound, like a car wreck. And Lucy, who could now see in the dark more clearly than she’d ever seen in daylight, saw that the cheap metal and laminate had crumpled like paper around Whitney’s hand.

In the stillness that followed, Lucy could hear her own

body with perfect clarity. The dutiful passages of her blood. Her breath, growing shallower and faster. It was what fear sounded like. Her vitals setting a stage for those first gasps of fight or flight.

Across the room, Whitney's own body was silent. Lucy could have read it as absolute calm. But then she heard the noise in the pit of Whitney's chest. The low, guttural roll of a growl. And when it made its way to the top of her throat, Whitney's lips peeled back, showing all her teeth.

At the front of her mouth, two pointed canines glinted in the light of her laptop.

Lucy shook her head. She was barely conscious of doing it. "This isn't funny."

As if Whitney were the type to play jokes. As if there was any way Whitney could have known what had happened to Lucy last Friday.

"Maybe it is funny." The air whistled in Whitney's throat, like water filling a broken jar. "I've never been good at knowing what was funny."

A noise escaped Lucy, too small and smothered to even be called a whimper. Her mind whirred, piecing together the edges of the past weekend. That first text from Whitney. The one or two unanswered texts during her absence. The knock that had woken her last night, around three thirty a.m. The gray of Whitney's face when Lucy eased open the door.

Forgot my keys, she'd said.

And Lucy remembered how, half-asleep and already

preoccupied with her own relief, she had stepped aside. *Okay,* she'd said. *Well. Come in.*

Whitney hadn't been with family. She had never even left campus.

The strap of the duffel bag dropped from Lucy's fingers. When her foot slid back, it bumped one of the legs of her bed.

"It happened quick," Whitney said tonelessly. "He emailed me the day after your stupid party. Said he'd heard about my thesis from his advisor, thought we could collaborate on this paper he was working on. I didn't know why a philosophy grad student would have heard of my paper, let alone his advisor, but I thought—best-case scenario, a publication credit while I'm still an undergrad. And if he's full of shit, I'll walk away."

"Whitney," Lucy said, "listen to me. What's happening to you is happening to me, too."

"You have no idea what is happening to me." Whitney stumbled out of her chair, her long legs clumsy under her. "He told me he was so sorry he rushed me. He told me transformation should be beautiful. It wasn't beautiful. But he needed someone to watch you. He knew that girl on the radio would come for you, and he needed me to be here when that happened. You must know how much he wants you. But it's nothing compared to how much he wants her."

"Listen to me," Lucy said again. If only because it felt like Whitney couldn't exactly hear her right now. "There are people who are trying to find him. They said—they said that if we can stop him, I might go back to normal. Maybe you'll—"

"Do I look normal to you?" Whitney said. "Go on, listen. He told me you wouldn't notice. But if you really listen, you can hear it, right? Do I sound like how normal people sound?"

A slow, horrible understanding settled over Lucy. She'd noticed it when she walked in, hadn't she? This stillness. She thought it was odd, though she couldn't put her finger on why.

All day long, she'd been hearing signs of life from the people around her. Their breathing. The beating of their hearts.

Whitney's body didn't make any sound except for the thin vibrations of her vocal cords. When she was quiet, she didn't breathe. Her blood didn't hum. Her heart didn't beat.

She sounded dead.

And she was.

"It's your fault, you know," Whitney said. "You called out to him. You think you don't know what you want? You want everything. So much, so badly, he heard you over all that noise. He's gonna make our lives beautiful, Lucy. But first you need to lead him to that girl. You need to lead *me* to that girl."

There were tears rolling down Lucy's cheeks. She hadn't felt them until one hit her shoulder. "Whitney—"

"You can make this easier for both of us," Whitney said. "You just need to stop fighting him. I fought him. And now . . . now I need to earn his trust back."

Whitney took two staggering steps. It unbalanced her. She shifted her weight onto her left foot, leaving her right side unsteady. And behind Whitney's right side was the door.

"There's going to be a feast," Whitney whispered. "When I

give him what he wants. I'm supposed to save my appetite. But maybe just a little . . ."

Lucy could hear her own blood shift. Fuel for the engines of her potential energy. There was no doubt, from the way her eyes darkened, that Whitney heard it, too. There would be no element of surprise. But maybe Lucy could be fast enough.

She ran.

And Whitney lunged.

Seven

Maybe it was the infection. Or maybe it was just adrenaline that made the next moment seem impossibly slow. The options presented themselves to Lucy with surreal clarity. She could backpedal toward the window, a three-story drop she doubted she'd walk away from. She could fight, which she already knew was impossible—there was only one true vampire in that room. Lucy could feel her own legs, weak with lack of sleep and loss of blood, trembling under her.

Whitney's stance still slightly favored her left side. So Lucy dove once more for the right, *hard.* Adrenaline surged up in her, conferred a little borrowed strength, but next to Whitney's strength it was less than nothing. Whitney pivoted, slamming Lucy into the wall.

Her hands went for Lucy's neck. Lucy wedged her own fingers into Whitney's grip—she couldn't free herself, she didn't have the leverage, but the extra inch of air let her keep breathing. They locked eyes then. Whitney laughed the same splintered laugh. “Didn’t think you’d smell good,” she said. “You came home from that party smelling like sweat and dirt.”

Lucy felt a brief and entirely selfish flicker of regret that she’d never get to tell Whitney what a fucking asshole she was. Her mind stuttered on that thought, choked on it. Whitney was still here, still standing right in front of her, *still being an asshole.* She couldn’t be dead.

“Whitney, please,” Lucy gasped. “I want to help you.”

“I don’t want your help.” Whitney’s teeth glistened with saliva. “I want to rip your fucking throat out. Maybe then you’ll stop talking.”

Lucy looked around wildly. She couldn’t hold Whitney off forever. She wasn’t holding Whitney off *now*. There was nothing in reach, nothing to use as a weapon, except for Whitney’s MacBook on the desk to her right. Too light and sleek and modern to be much of a blunt object. But she realized, with a jolt, that it didn’t need to be.

She made a blind grab for the laptop. Her hand slipped off it the first time. But on the second grab, it snapped closed under her fingers.

Lucy pulled it to her chest like a shield. The effect was instant: Whitney’s grip dropped from her neck and she reared back as if she’d been burned. “Give that to me,” she said.

Lucy laughed, though it was the least funny anything had ever been. “Oh,” she said. “Is this still important to you?”

Whitney growled again, deeper this time. “Put that down. Give it back.”

"Sorry," Lucy said. "Not going to do either. I need you to focus, Whitney. This is what matters to you, isn't it? It matters more than whatever he asked you to do to that girl on the radio."

"Put it down!" Whitney said. "It's not finished!"

"You really think Rollins will let you finish this after you rip my fucking throat out?" Lucy said. "Just back off, and we can talk."

Whitney wasn't backing off, though. For a second, she looked almost—*annoyed.* Annoyed in that normal, Whitney way. But that familiar annoyance was rapidly contorting.

"I tried to be nice to you," she spat. "I tried to give you advice!"

Lucy's fingers trembled against the laptop. This seemed far from the ideal time to have this argument. But in an all-out fight against Whitney, she was going to lose. Here, at least, she had footing.

"And what did you tell your friend Alicia about me?" she said. "I met her the other day. Didn't seem like she had a very nice impression of me."

"I just told her you weren't *focused*!" There was something that could have been funny about the venom she poured over that word. It probably would have been, if Lucy wasn't more scared than she'd ever been in her life.

"You have no idea how focused I am," Lucy said. "You have no idea what my grades were, you have no idea how hard I did or didn't work. Just because I'm older than you, just because

I didn't go to college prep courses, you decided I was some burnout fuckup who needed your advice. And I don't even care about that anymore, by the way! But if you don't listen to me right now, you are going to die!"

"I'm already *dead,* Lucy!" Her mouth opened wide as she said it, showing all the ridges of her teeth. "If you really wanted to help me, you'd hold still!"

The light flicked on. Whitney jerked back, whipping around to face the now-fully-open door. Lucy followed suit. And she locked eyes with Mila Rostova, her hand hovering by the light switch.

Several things happened then, close enough to be nearly simultaneous. Mila reached for the quiver of arrows hidden just beneath the long edge of her coat. Whitney lunged for the window. And Lucy, with far more reflex than thought, hurled Whitney's laptop in Mila's direction. It didn't hit her. It landed exactly where it was meant to: in the path of the arrow that Mila had just nocked.

Mila cursed, scrambled to reposition the arrow. But by then, it was too late. Whitney had kicked out the screen and hurtled into the night.

Mila threw her bow on the ground, and the two of them tore across the room to the window. By the time they looked down to the ground, the only signs of disturbance were two firm footprints in the mud. Even from that height, Whitney had landed on her feet.

And as Lucy's heart slowed and the sweat across her face

cooled, it began to dawn on her what she'd just done.

She turned to face Mila, who was already facing her in return. The look in her eyes was—hard. Not angry. But it was close.

"You realize," Mila said, "she could be on her way to hurt someone else."

Lucy realized it then. So keenly that it rose like nausea in her stomach. But she hadn't thrown that laptop to spare a vampire. The only thing on her mind in that moment was the fact that she was about to see her asshole roommate skewered by a junior archery champion.

"We can't just kill her," Lucy said uselessly, and Mila's gaze didn't so much soften as shift. She didn't need to say it. Lucy knew it perfectly well. Whitney was already dead.

"Get your things," Mila finally said. "Before someone comes to see what's going on."

Numbly, Lucy picked up her bag and followed in Mila's long strides, stepping over Whitney's forgotten laptop on the way out. Lucy wondered if after all that, she'd broken it. Strangely, she hoped she hadn't.

Halfway into the hall, Mila stopped. "Wait," she said, easing Lucy's duffel bag off Lucy's shoulder and onto her own. *Full service,* Lucy thought dully. "My bow. I think it's behind the door. Grab it for me."

Lucy picked it up, draping Mila's green cardigan over the top to more or less conceal it. "You trust me to hold it?" she asked.

Mila's laugh was colorless. "I have the arrows."

They were almost to the stairs before Lucy could bring herself to ask. "You're her RA," she said. "What will you—do you have to report anything?"

Mila didn't answer, at first. She made sure the door was tightly closed. That the stairwell below them was empty. "I'll tell my supervisor that her roommate hasn't seen her since the weekend. It's the truth, more or less," she said. "If I can't tell her parents what happened, at least I can tell them that *something* did."

They shuffled down the first-floor hall, Lucy trying to hold Mila's bow in a manner that looked halfway inconspicuous. She didn't quite have that part down. Mila walked with it like it belonged in her hand. Lucy clutched it to her chest like the world's hardest and most angular security blanket. She needed something to clutch right then.

They slipped into Mila's room, and Lucy took a single bare second to acknowledge the utter strangeness of being there. Mila slid in behind Lucy, tapping the blue-and-gold mezuzah mounted to the doorframe, then locked them in.

She held out Lucy's bag. Lucy, in turn, handed the bow and the cardigan back to Mila with a mumbled "Tradesies." She didn't know where that came from. She wasn't sure she'd ever used the word *tradesies* in her life.

"Keep the sweater," Mila said, gently easing the bow out from under it. "You're shivering."

Lucy let out a soft noise of affirmation and tucked the

sweater against her chest. *Well.* Maybe chivalry wasn't dead.

She slipped into the bathroom and mechanically went through the process of getting ready for bed. Last time she'd spent the night with—well, anyone—was with her senior-year girlfriend, Jo, right after prom. Lucy faintly wished that looking cute was anywhere near her radar tonight. The ghost of the feeling hung just far enough away that Lucy could vaguely sense the inappropriate weight of it.

Whitney was dead in every way that mattered. Lucy herself might be dead in a matter of days. And in her knee-jerk instinct to protect Whitney, Lucy might have guaranteed the same end for someone else. However Mila wanted to treat her right now, it was probably far kinder than she deserved.

When she opened the door, Mila was still fully dressed. Her bow was in the kitchenette, out of her immediate reach, which Lucy thought was kind of a nice gesture.

"No one should bother us," Mila said. "I told my supervisor this morning that I had a family emergency and I won't be able to do night duty for a little while. I might get some residents knocking on my door, but I can send them to another floor."

"And that's okay?" Lucy said.

"It's what it is. My Resident Director wasn't *happy*, but if she fires me for it, that's one less job I have to do. Now," Mila said, "you should take the bed."

Lucy shook her head tightly. "I'm fine on the floor."

"I've slept lately," Mila said. "I don't think you have. His hold on you may be stronger if you're tired."

Well. If she put it that way.

Lucy crawled into the bed, which was marginally bigger than her own upstairs, and rolled to face the wall. Mila's sheets smelled a little like her sweater. Like unscented laundry detergent that nevertheless had a smell to it—a little clean, a little sweet.

Her eyes had been closed for about thirty seconds when Mila spoke to her again. "I'm sorry if I snapped at you upstairs."

"You didn't snap," Lucy said, without opening her eyes. Mila had been remarkably patient with her, all things considered. It was what was making this so much worse. "And it's not like you were wrong."

She kept her back turned to Mila, who was quiet for a moment. She didn't fidget, like Lucy did when she was stressed. Her breaths were still calm and measured.

"I understand that you have had a lot less time to adjust than we did. And don't get me wrong. You *need* to adjust, if you don't want to see anyone else hurt. But . . ." Mila took a deep breath. "She was your roommate. It's—normal, to try to protect her."

"I didn't even like her," Lucy mumbled. "She got upset if I moved around the room too much. She once implied that I breathed too loudly for attention. And I think she was kind of classist."

"Yeah, well." Mila sighed then. "It's also normal not to want terrible things to happen to people. Even when they suck."

Lucy didn't answer that. Even if she'd had the will to, she wasn't sure if she had the energy. Her shock and sadness and fear still curled heavy against her, but even those weren't as powerful as her own exhaustion.

"I'm going to try to sleep," she said.

"Go ahead," Mila said. Whatever ripples there had been in the evenness of her voice had long since smoothed. "I'll keep watch."

Lucy tucked her face into the pillow and breathed deep. Maybe it was her own keyed-up senses, but she thought she smelled something floral on the edge of the pillow. A smudge of lotion or perfume, maybe. It smelled like the night-blooming jasmine bush outside her bedroom window at home. It sent a softer, blurrier unease through her.

It should have been impossible to sleep through that unease, through the weight of Mila's eyes on her. But it was hardly the most impossible thing that had happened that week.

Two hours later, the thing that wasn't Lucy Easting pried her eyes open.

She didn't move, at first. Just marveled at the velvety warmth of the dark as it unfurled across the mountain. The night leached into Quincey Hall. Crooked its fingers at her. Said, Come here.

Lucy had been right, earlier that day. She had felt someone watching her. His smile was a faint curve against her mind. He smelled like fresh-turned dirt, and something sweet.

She sat up in bed. The motion rocked the mattress gently under her, and she pressed down a hand to still the juddering springs. They did not bother her. But Lucy moved her body cautiously, like a deer trying not to be seen.

"Lucy?" The hunter hadn't moved from where she sat cross-legged on the floor. In the dark, every cautious line of her face was sharply visible.

She could answer to that name, still, though it was incorrect. She could sound like that name, too. "I'm going to the bathroom," she said.

She stood, and it looked natural—she moved the way she was supposed to, slow and tired. But it was hard to move so slowly when the body was so much more responsive to her now. It was not as worn or as wrung out as Lucy believed it to be. If she treated it right, it would sing.

But that was for later. The hunter was still watching her. "Be my guest," she said.

The thing that was not Lucy Easting crossed the room, turned the corner. Eased the door closed behind her. And she waited until she felt the unseen pressure of the hunter's attention leave her before she flicked the light switch.

There was a window at the other end of the bathroom, its blinds partially closed. And as the lights extinguished themselves, the silhouette beyond the blinds snapped into focus. A head and shoulders and torso on the other side of the pane.

The heart in her chest quickened. Every nerve in her body prickled like hairs standing on end.

"I'm here," the thing whispered with Lucy's mouth.

Good, *the man in the night whispered back.* Are you afraid?

Her head shook. In the hazy bathwater warmth of the dark, not many of her feelings had names. But standing before the silhouette was no more frightening than standing at the edge of the ocean, or under the stars of an unpolluted sky. It was a comforting smallness, a helplessness. There was no more fighting here. There was nothing left to fight.

The gift you asked of me, *he said.* Are you ready to have it?

Two tears slipped out of Lucy Easting's eyes as the thing that was not Lucy closed the distance between herself and the window. She'd been ready for days. She'd been ready even as this body had rejected its own readiness. As she reached for the blinds, watched every line of the silhouette, she breathed in that scent in the air. It really was so, so sweet. Whatever it belonged to, maybe this visitor would let her taste it.

She opened her mouth as she drew open the blinds. There were two words that he needed to hear.

Something seized her by the waist and pulled her off her feet.

Eight

The thing that was not Lucy Easting dug her nails into the arm locked around her. Lucy might have felt like a prey animal, but she had never known less about her own body—she had fight in her, enough fight to claw through the walls.

"Fuck!" someone bit out. And then the world spun, and the thing that was not Lucy was thrown against the cold tile wall.

She scrambled for purchase, grasped for leverage, but she quickly lost it. The hunter was already on her again, an arm pressed like an iron bar against her collarbone. The thing that was not Lucy opened her mouth. He was still out there. If she called out for him just once—

"*Lucy!* Wake up!"

Lucy blinked and found herself pinned, Mila's panicked eyes inches from her own.

She gasped. Her head snapped to Mila's left, to the bathroom window. The blinds were drawn all the way to the top, and through the pane, she could see the faint lights of the quad beyond. No one was standing there. She had been positive that she was about to see someone standing there.

"Mila," she said. Her mouth felt cottony.

"You're hearing me? You're not about to do a swan-dive out the window?"

"Why would I dive out the window?" Lucy said helplessly.

"Because you were in the middle of doing that when I walked in!" Mila let go of Lucy's upper arm long enough to make a single, panicked gesture. The other arm remained in place, strapped across Lucy's upper chest. "He was fucking calling to you!"

"Calling to—" Lucy's eyes snapped to the window again. Still empty, but . . . "Was he there?"

"I didn't see him." Mila drew back to look at her more fully. "I was a little focused on your jailbreak."

Lucy felt clammy, almost feverish. When she reached up to rub her eyes, her fingers were trembling so hard that they were slightly blurred. "I'm not going anywhere now. You can let go."

"Yeah, well . . ." Mila exhaled. "You said a few minutes ago that you were just going to the bathroom, so excuse me if I've heard that one before."

Lucy rubbed at the arm Mila had been holding. It didn't hurt, but Mila's grip had left little dents in her skin. "I sounded normal?"

"Normal as I've heard so far," Mila said. "Though I haven't exactly gotten to know you in normal circumstances. Come on, back in the room. He could still be watching."

Mila took a slow step back to let Lucy move off the wall. She really did move like a cat—unhurried but watchful, ready to launch herself at Lucy if she had to. But even if Lucy still wanted to throw herself out the window and into the courtyard, she had never felt less equipped to do anything. Her legs shook as she stumbled out of the bathroom. Mila reached back to tug the blinds completely shut, then followed her.

Mila paced to the edge of the room, then back. "Well, now I know, right? You can go back to sleep, if you want. And if you try to go anywhere—"

Lucy laughed, a little rudely. "I am *not* going back to sleep tonight."

"Fair enough," Mila said. "But I can't exactly leave you awake on your own, so . . . let's sit, I guess."

"Oh. Good." Lucy eased herself to the floor next to the bed. "Quality time."

Mila snorted, and it sounded much more genuine than mocking. Then again, Mila hadn't actually mocked her, had she? It was Lucy's own embarrassment that colored it that way.

Lucy let her head drop back onto the mattress, then thought better of it. The urge to go back to sleep was nearly as strong as the urge to curl up on the floor and scream herself hoarse. "So," she said. "What do you want to talk about?"

"We don't have to talk if you don't want to," Mila said.

"If we sit in silence, I may lose my mind," Lucy said. "So I'd prefer talking, if that's okay."

Mila settled along the wall where she'd been sitting before.

Maybe it was Lucy's imagination, but for the first time since Lucy had met her, she looked a little uncomfortable. "Okay, then," Mila said. "Let's talk."

Lucy was suddenly no longer sure if she wanted to ask the first thing that had come to mind. But like Athena said, trust went both ways.

"I know why Athena is doing this," Lucy said. "But what about you?"

Predictably, Mila's expression darkened. "That's not really a soothing bedtime story," she said.

"I don't think I'm going to be soothed tonight." Lucy paused. "You don't have to go into details—"

"No. No, it's fine." Mila leaned more heavily against the wall and exhaled in a controlled burst, like she was letting out a puff of cigarette smoke. "You probably deserve the details."

The central air-conditioning kicked in overhead, and the blinds above Mila's bed swayed a little with the disturbance. Every time they clicked against the window, Lucy's eyes were drawn back to them again. But if anyone was still watching from outside the dorm, they were no longer visible.

"I wasn't going to apply to Rollins," Mila finally said. "I'm from Oregon. And I hate humidity. So Tennessee wasn't on my radar—never even thought of leaving the Pacific Northwest, honestly. I don't know if I would have heard of it if it wasn't my boyfriend's dream school. Jon wanted to go into neuroscience, just like Athena. Dreamed of working with the same professor who headhunted her. He probably would have hero-worshipped Athena, too. He loved listening to smart people talk."

She closed her eyes for a moment. The blinds kept tapping the glass like fingernails. "I tried not to apply here. I didn't want to go to the same school as Jon. I didn't want to get married right out of college. I didn't . . . want to be with him in the first place. But even if I didn't love him, I *loved* him, you know? He was my best friend, all my life. The only misunderstanding we ever had is that he thought we felt the same about each other.

"You might find this hard to believe, but I wasn't very good at being straightforward back then," Mila said. "The most I could make myself ask for was a little space. I told my parents and Jon that I was going to take a gap year, just to save a little money and get some work experience. And I thought, a year is a lot of time. Enough time to figure out how to tell Jon we weren't going to get married.

"So I drove him to the airport," Mila said. "I spent the drive home trying to figure out how the hell I was going to break his heart. And I let him come here alone."

Lucy pulled Mila's cardigan off the bed to wrap around herself. She felt the sudden, panicky impulse to cut Mila off. To tell her that whatever terrible thing happened next, Mila couldn't have seen it coming. It was like Mila had said earlier. Normal people responded in normal ways, expected normal things to happen. Whatever hunted on the Rollins campus was never something they were meant to cross paths with.

But there was something fragile in Mila's voice now.

Something that said that if Lucy opened her mouth, the story would end. And though Lucy wasn't sure now that she wanted to know, she needed to.

"I wish I could remember this next part more clearly. I was distracted that night, when he called me," she said. "But he told me he had a roommate change at the last minute, and that the guy was *so* cool. His parents were Russian, he grew up in Moscow. My parents are from Vladivostok, so Jon wanted us to talk sometime, when things were less hectic. He said the boy was named Vanya."

A faint, brittle smile flickered on Mila's face. "That's one of the only things Athena and I disagree on, by the way. She thinks Vanya is another alias. But as far as we can tell, Jon crossed paths with him right after he arrived at Rollins. I don't think he'd started giving out aliases yet. I think Jon asked his name, and he gave it honestly. One of the few times he's been honest on this campus."

Mila went quiet for a moment. Lucy didn't want to ask the question she'd been chewing on for the past several minutes. But it didn't escape her notice that when Mila talked about Jon, she used the past tense.

"How did it happen?"

"I can't tell you how much I wish I knew," Mila said. "By the time Jon's parents called me, it had been about a week since any of us had heard from him. What they told me at the time was that he had a psychotic break of some kind. Attacked a classmate, then a security guard who tried to break things up.

Jon was moved to a hospital in town, and his parents booked a red-eye that night. They asked me to come. They— Well, I think we all thought that my not being there was part of it. We'd never been apart for so long before."

Mila exhaled again. Lucy's sharpened senses heard it rattling through her chest. "By the time we landed in Nashville," she said, "Jon was dead."

Consciously, Lucy eased her grip on Mila's cardigan. Her fingers had gone so tight that it hurt. "How?"

"Jon's parents never gave me the details," Mila said. "Wanted to spare me, I think. The hospital they brought him to is so close to here. Sometimes I think it wouldn't be that hard to go down there, find a way to get the coroner's report. But however much I want to know—I really, really don't." She breathed out in a long, harsh rush. "He wasn't a vampire yet, Lucy. They took his vitals when he got to the hospital. He was alive, and then he wasn't. He had the same infection you have—and it killed him.

"Oh, and the kicker?" Mila added. "According to everyone I spoke to, Jon didn't have a roommate. His real roommate dropped out two weeks before move-in."

They sat in silence for a long moment. Outside, something moved, but even from the safety within Mila's dorm, Lucy could feel that whatever it was, it was something alive. Its blood hummed to her, tuneless and inviting. Or maybe not to her. It was the infection that could hear it. The infection currently simmering in her like water in a pot about to boil.

If Mila's timeline was correct, Jon had been alive for about a week after he was bitten.

So how long did Lucy have?

Lucy shook her head once, to herself. She didn't want to follow those thoughts any further. She wanted Mila to keep talking. "So you came here."

"Yeah, I can't exactly judge Athena, can I?" Mila said. "She may have stayed, but I had the chance to stay away to begin with. I took my gap year—it was too late not to, at that point—but as soon as they let me enroll, I made my plans to come. Athena was attacked the same semester I enrolled. She started Pallas Radio. Most of the students thought it was fiction, or bad taste, or both, but it started to resonate, too. It's impossible not to feel the wrongness of this place, when you live here. It's just that some people talk themselves out of feeling it."

She shrugged. "So I heard some goth kids talking about the show in class one day. I listened to enough to be sure it wasn't bullshit. I picked up the phone. And here we are."

There they were indeed. Lucy swallowed. "You said Jon attacked someone after he was bitten," she said. "Do you think that's what I'm going to do?"

"Trust me, I don't want to believe that." Mila's laugh was dark as she shook her head. "You seem nice, okay? And you seem like you went through a lot to get here. I wish I *could* just be your RA. But it was complete dumb luck that Jon didn't take anyone with him when he died. And that means I cannot let my guard down with you. Ever."

Lucy closed her eyes. For the first time since just before she'd seen Athena's note on the radio flyer, all of this almost felt like too much to bear. Those thoughts that weren't hers, the ones that told her to lie down and give up, surged at the edges of her mind. But those thoughts weren't thoughts at all. *Vanya,* she thought, because having a possible name for him was better than having none. He was calling to her, even now.

"And if you like me," she said, "it's harder to kill me, right?"

"Hell," Mila said, "you don't even like your roommate, and you didn't want to see her die, right? I'm sorry. But I have to—protect myself. I know it's cowardly."

"It's not cowardly," Lucy said. The small, hurt part of her from earlier in the evening didn't want to reassure Mila. Wanted to let her sit with that guilt. Though that part of her was quickly fading. "But maybe you could do one thing for me."

At Mila's affirmative sound, Lucy tentatively opened her eyes. Mila's eyebrows were raised, faintly confused, but she looked as patient and thoughtful as ever.

It didn't make what Lucy wanted to ask less embarrassing, but she had the feeling nothing would. So she took a breath, and she blurted out, "I just need you to be nice to me."

There was a pause, then a faint flicker of surprise across Mila's face. Her easy smile returned, a little startled this time. "Have I not been nice? You're sleeping in my bed. I let you touch my bow. I thought that was pretty nice."

"You've been *cordial.*" Lucy swallowed her bubbling frustration. You could be cordial to anything. You could be cordial to a spider right before crushing it. She needed Mila to understand the distinction. "If you really have to kill me, I don't want you to feel bad about it, either. Just—while I'm still alive, don't treat me like I'm already dead."

For the next few seconds, Lucy felt studied. "Is that what's been bothering you all night?" Mila said.

Lucy laughed once. "Sorry," she said. "I'm sensitive."

Mila gave a little bob of a nod, as if to say *Fair enough*. "All right," she said. "If it'll help, I'll be nicer. And if I start being . . . *cordial* to you again, you can tell me to knock it off.

"But," she added, "in return . . . whatever I have to do? Don't hold it against me."

Lucy swallowed, and again, she felt the bullet-time motion of it all the way to her belly. She didn't want to agree to it. Agreeing felt like tacit permission. It wasn't as if she wanted Mila to feel guilty. It was just that she didn't want to pretend that she was okay with dying, either.

But she'd let Whitney go earlier because she couldn't accept something terrible happening. That was a mistake she couldn't make again.

Lucy smiled. It didn't even tremble that much. "Shake on it?"

Mila's own smile was grim as she pushed herself across the floor. Her hand felt warm. Or maybe Lucy's hand was colder than she realized.

"Deal," Mila said.

TRANSCRIPT OF ROLLINS UNIVERSITY STUDENT RADIO STATION WVBS ("PALLAS RADIO")

Broadcast number: 34

CALLER #2: I'm really only your second caller?

PALLAS (HOST): Not literally. But second legitimate caller. I don't count the prank calls in my tally.

CALLER #2: Get a lot of those, huh? No offense, but you bring it on yourself with all those flyers.

PALLAS: All publicity is good publicity. Or so they tell me.

CALLER #2: I heard some kid the other day say that you have delusions of grandeur.

PALLAS: [laughter] Really? Wow. That might be the strongest review I've gotten so far.

CALLER #2: Yeah, well. Speaking of delusions. It seems like we share one.

PALLAS: That's not very nice.

CALLER #2: I've been listening to your show for the past week. You said it yourself. No one believed you when you were attacked. We've got that in common, too.

PALLAS: No, caller number two. I mean, that's not very nice to yourself. Just because they say it to you doesn't mean you have to repeat it.

[Pause.]

CALLER #2: I haven't seen him. Not like you have.

PALLAS: That's all right. If you're calling me, I assume you know his work.

CALLER #2: Not as well as I'd like to. But someone I care about . . . well. I think he got to know your friend's work extremely well.

PALLAS: So you have questions. And that person you care about . . . they aren't around to answer them, are they?

CALLER #2: Hah. I guess we do understand each other.

PALLAS: Well. First of all, caller number two. I'm so sorry for your loss.

And I'm sorry to all of our curious listeners—I'm sure you'd like to hear caller number two's questions as much as I do. But I think perhaps—we'd best take this conversation off the air. Don't you agree?

CALLER #2: All right, then. Your place or mine?

Nine

"Well," Natalie said. "I still don't like her."

Lucy wrapped her sweater tightly around her shoulders. The wind felt more like autumn than late August. The temperatures would soar back to the eighties later in the afternoon, but Lucy was finding that she didn't mind the frost-bitten mountain mornings. The clear air made for a clearer head. "I don't *have* to like her," she said. "If she keeps me from turning into a vampire, I'll kiss her on the mouth."

"Yes," Natalie said. "I can tell it would be a real hardship for you to kiss her on the mouth."

Lucy flipped her a double-middle-fingered salute. Clearly she was right. And clearly Lucy could stand to make more of a secret of that. But it wasn't worth thinking about Mila's steady confidence and tragically sculpted arms anymore. For one, Mila was at the ready to kill Lucy if things went south. Also, even if they weren't in this situation, it would have been doomed anyway, since Mila wasn't allowed to date a resident.

Although if they weren't in this situation, maybe Mila wouldn't have been an RA at all. Maybe she'd still be that long-ago people pleaser, trying to figure out how to break up with poor Jon. Maybe she wouldn't have come to Rollins to begin with.

Athena had been a transfer student in her sophomore year. Jon had been hundreds of miles away from the girl he thought he'd be with forever. Even without knowing Addison's or Sadie's circumstances, Lucy thought she was starting to understand how Vanya operated. That he gravitated toward those on the edges of the crowd.

In any case. She put Mila, who was back at her dorm catching up on sleep, out of her mind for now. She'd been left in Natalie and Athena's custody for the morning.

She glanced back to Natalie, who was warily looking at the path ahead. "So Athena's sure that the campus radio station is safe?"

"I don't think Athena goes anywhere she's *not* sure is safe," Lucy said. Although Athena seemed to have a more optimistic view of Lucy's chances than Mila did, Athena struck Lucy as the more cautious of the two. Which was saying something, given how cautious Mila was. "The steam tunnels don't pass under the studio. And also . . ."

As they approached the gray, vaguely Brutalist multimedia center, Lucy stepped past Natalie and withdrew her ID card. She tapped it to the card reader, waited for the "click" of the lock, and then eased open the heavy door.

"... we've been added to the guest list," Lucy finished. "Athena said everyone who uses the multimedia center gets a similar message to the one they sent to Quincey residents about an abusive ex on the loose."

Natalie gave the card reader an unusually intense once-over as they passed. Lucy made a questioning noise. "Oh, nothing," Natalie said. "I was just thinking... the vampire had some power over you even before he bit you, right? He told you to hold still, and you did. Telling people not to invite anyone in is one thing, but—"

"But what if he just tells them to do it," Lucy mumbled. "Good question." And one she was sure Athena and Mila would have thought of before. Vanya had been stalking Athena for years now. He was desperate enough to get to her that he had, apparently impulsively, turned Whitney. Thinking of all that he'd done so far, the radio station's modest protections didn't seem like much of a barrier.

Maybe there were limits to his power. That would be nice, if that was true.

Or he had patience. Which was a much less promising thought. But the more Lucy thought about it, the harder it was to shake the thought that Athena had been unreasonably lucky so far. Maybe unrealistically lucky.

The two fell quiet as they made their way to the corridor of soundproof suites that housed Pallas Radio. Lucy could see other occupants through the tiny windows—one student practicing trombone, another recording some kind of video essay—but the thick walls did their job. The hallway was silent. Without Lucy's unnaturally sharpened hearing, she might not have caught the muffled conversation coming through the cracked-open door of suite number thirty-two.

"—give me a minute?" Athena's voice, first. But it was neither her Pallas Radio voice, nor the soft, even tone with which she spoke to Lucy. It was a voice Lucy knew intimately after her many years behind the counter of the hardware store. The customer service voice. "I think I actually have a call coming in."

"You can let it go to voicemail." The other voice was older. And as they drew closer to the door, Lucy caught sight of Athena's conversation partner: an older white woman in a navy-blue blazer-and-skirt set. "Athena . . . it's not as if we don't appreciate your creativity here. But after three years of this, are you sure you don't want to pivot this project at all? The Campus Community-Building Grant wasn't really intended for—works of fiction."

"Pivoting would defeat the purpose, ma'am," Athena said. "The committee was very enthusiastic about the concept of building community through audience participation in an immersive narrative. It doesn't work if I switch gears in the middle of the story."

Natalie let out a little hum under her breath, presumably at that very smoothly delivered bit of bullshit. The navy woman flashed a sucked-lemon smile back. "And . . . you have an ending for that narrative in mind?"

"I hope so," Athena said. "But we'll see."

There was a beat of silence. The tension roiled like a summer storm. At length, the navy woman said, "Just take care to devote as much time to your own studies. Dr. Conners said it's not too late if you'd like to rethink taking on a senior project."

Something shifted in Athena's polite, closed-lipped smile. It looked more genuine, but not more friendly. The smile, maybe, of someone who knew she'd won.

"Thank you, Dr. Horne," she said. "But I think my schedule is all set this year."

Dr. Horne turned slightly toward the door. She didn't look at Lucy or Natalie fully, but she clocked, at least, that she was being watched. That seemed to be enough to force her surrender.

"I'm always here if you need to talk," she said.

Athena's pleasant front didn't waver. "Of course, ma'am."

Dr. Horne squeezed Athena's shoulder just a touch too forcefully—muscle tension apparently had a sound, and it scraped unpleasantly at Lucy's ears. Maybe Lucy didn't manage to hide her grimace quickly enough when Dr. Horne swept out of the room. When her gaze flicked to Lucy and Natalie, her own nose was crinkled with slight distaste. She clicked briskly down the hall in her heels, and eventually out of sight.

Athena didn't look very pleased herself as Lucy and Natalie stepped into the suite. There was an uncharacteristic sharpness when she spoke. "Dammit," she said. "She made me miss a call."

Natalie glanced around as Athena strode over to the phone, as if there might be someone else hiding in the room that they could have missed. She shut the door before she asked, "Who was that?"

"Dr. Horne. The Vice Provost of Student Events and Activities." Lucy wouldn't have thought that Athena's gentle voice was suited to sarcasm, but the title dripped with it. "Even though I have this grant now, she's still here every other week trying to find some new way to derail me."

"How is that her business?" Lucy said.

"She thinks I'm using fiction to run away from the trauma of my attack. Which, even if I was, would *still* be none of her business. I thought getting my own funding would help. The grant is through a campus life nonprofit. But the money gets sent to me through the student activities office. Which means I have to smile and nod every time she decides she wants to climb up my ass." Athena audibly took a deep breath to steady herself. "Sorry, Lucy. Can I listen to this voicemail really quick? I'll be with you in a second."

"Take your time," Lucy said. Athena looked like she wanted to seethe for a few seconds longer. And as someone who'd spent most of her life keeping a lid on her frustration, Lucy recognized one of her own.

Athena took another beat before keying in the PIN on the ancient campus landline. There was a brief silence as the message loaded. And then there was a cheery voice, a little tinny through the speakers.

"Ms. Pallas Radio!" said a lovely, lilting voice. It was a man's voice: probably older than an undergraduate, but not too old. A graduate student, maybe. "Sorry I missed you. I should probably know better than to call the nocturnal among us during the day, right? I know you've told us not to mention names on the air, but I wanted to run one by you. I don't really have anything definitive to report, but the guy really had a *vibe,* you know? Kind of spooky. And it was near Falls Quad on Friday night. That was where that party was, right?

"Anyway: the name. The guy introduced himself to me as Ivan Volkov. V-o-l-k-o-v. Sorry I don't have more than that, but I hope that's of some help. You stay safe out there, Ms. Pallas. Bye."

Athena let out another breath as the message shifted. This time, it sounded far more tired than tense. "Well, I'm glad Dr. Horne didn't overhear that," she said. "The last thing I need is for her to think I'm about to whip up an angry mob on a man with *spooky vibes*."

"You don't think it's real?" Lucy said.

"I get a lot of pranks," Athena said with a shrug. "It was a calculated risk, setting up the show as a piece of fiction. I needed campus resources, and the admins needed to think that I wasn't having a break with reality. But I've never said on the air that the show isn't real. The people who don't know, or don't believe, can assume that I don't break character, or whatever else makes sense to them. And the people who need the show find it. Just like you."

"This one might be real, though," Natalie chimed in. "Vanya is a nickname for Ivan, right? I took a year of Russian."

"Don't get me wrong, I'll look into it," Athena said. "But even if it *is* legitimate, all this tells us is that our friend was in the vicinity of Falls Quad on Friday, possibly using an alias that he's used before. Helpful confirmation, if it's true. But unfortunately not any information that we didn't already have."

Lucy watched as Athena flipped open a notebook on the desk, logging the call before casually flipping the pages closed. Mila was right: Athena didn't seem at all convinced that the Vanya identity was any closer to the truth than the philosophy PhD student lost at sea. Or maybe the truth of who the vampire was didn't matter all that much to Athena to begin with.

What would change just by having his name? What was his name other than a person he once was, but wasn't anymore?

Lucy understood all that. It didn't stop her from wanting to know anyway.

"Nice security out there, by the way," Natalie said.

Athena shrugged a little sheepishly. "I told the building admins that I've been getting harassed since my attack," she said. "It's close enough to the truth, anyway. And the university's given me accommodations. My dorm is unlisted, though I don't go there anyway. The residence staff are under strict instructions not to tell anyone that I live there. I know half of them think I'm neurotic. But they can think whatever they want as long as it keeps me alive.

"Now," Athena said. The single word seemed to shift the tenor of the conversation. They were no longer talking to Athena—they were talking to the voice of Pallas Radio. "Sit. Why don't you tell me what you can remember about last night?"

A little awkwardly, Lucy folded herself downward. There were a few thick cushions on the wood-paneled floor, as well as a longer one in the corner, twin mattress–sized and outfitted with a pillow and blankets. That must have been where Athena slept.

"Not much," Lucy said. "I know I must have walked into the bathroom, but from my perspective, one minute I was falling asleep and the next minute Mila was holding me down. She even said I *spoke* to her, but . . ."

The spot between Lucy's brows throbbed. She ground a thumb against it. "I think I'm being terrible bait."

Athena's solemnity broke a little. Her lips twitched as she sat opposite Lucy, forgoing one of the cushions in favor of the cool floor. "I don't know that 'good bait' is something you should aspire to."

"Manageable bait, at least," Lucy said. "How is Mila supposed to kill this thing if I'm trying to give her the slip?"

"Let's not jump to despair just yet," Athena said. "Last night happened, whether we wanted it to or not. Why don't we see if we can get some information from it?"

Lucy sat up a little straighter on her cushion. "How so?"

Athena leaned back against the wall. "After my attack," she said, "the university referred me to a counselor. It was inevitable. Even the ones who believed I was telling the truth thought I was jumping at shadows. The counselor diagnosed me with PTSD, which—is not really accurate if the traumatic event is still happening. And therapy can only help so much if you have to keep lying about what happened to you.

"But sometimes it was helpful," she continued. "My therapist understood that I'm pragmatic, and that I like data. She taught me how to make an honest assessment of my safety in a given situation, though I'm sure her goal there was to prove to me that I *was* safe. And when there was more fear than I could manage, she taught me how to slow down and sort through it. I'd like to try that with you right now, if that's okay."

Lucy perked up. "Try what?"

"Nothing groundbreaking," Athena said. "Just a bit of guided meditation. I was thinking . . . our friend is trying to take control away from you. He wants to disconnect you from your own instincts, your own body. Maybe we can try to reconnect you."

Athena had begun to look uncertain, as if hearing the idea out loud made it less plausible to her. Anything was worth trying. And if nothing else, she didn't want to be discouraging. Lucy was the first living victim of a vampire that Athena had ever met. There must have been things, all these years, that even Mila couldn't understand.

Lucy understood the feeling. Though she didn't quite share

it. Athena knew so much more than she did in so many ways. But the only people who understood exactly what Lucy was going through were probably already dead.

"Let's do it," Lucy said.

Athena gathered up a few cushions to pile around Lucy: one behind her back, one under her legs, and one for her head. She motioned for Lucy to lie back, and when Lucy did, she had to admit that it was somewhat comfortable. She would have been able to fall asleep right there without much trouble—though after last night, she was still inclined to stay awake as long as she could manage.

"I should warn you," Lucy said, closing her eyes. "My classmate hypnotized me once and nothing happened. I just pretended to be under so that she wouldn't feel bad."

"I'm not exactly hypnotizing you here." She could hear Athena's smile. "I'm just going to take you through some exercises. Don't pressure yourself to relax. Nothing less relaxing than that."

"Which is fucked up, by the way," Lucy mumbled, but otherwise settled in. Jillian had taken her to yoga with her grief support group once, which had been nice enough. But this had been Lucy's least favorite part: the end bit, savasana, when they were all lying on the floor in silence. When she stopped moving, there was nothing to do but think.

But Athena's voice was louder and clearer than her own thoughts. She focused on that instead.

"I want you to start by counting your breaths," Athena said.

"You don't need to count them out loud. Breathe in for seven seconds, hold your breath for two, breathe out for eleven. Try not to think. But if you have to think anything, tell yourself, *This body is mine.*"

It was hard to think of anything *but* the counting at first. But after the first round, she relied on the counting much less. She had the rhythm of it, and she had to admit, that rhythm was making a difference. Every exhale felt like a ladle gently passing through the tension in her, bailing it out of her abdomen bit by bit.

Okay, she thought. *This body is mine, I guess.* And then, deciding to commit: *This body is mine.*

"Now," Athena said. "One by one, tense up each of your muscles for about five seconds, then release them. Start with your toes and work your way up to your scalp. Take your time. Let me know when you're done."

Lucy did as she was told. She started with her toes, worked her way up her legs, her core, her shoulders and chest. Some of her muscles clenched and released easily. Some of them couldn't manage much more than a confused twitch, unused to much conscious movement on Lucy's part. They still responded to her, though, even if she couldn't hold them for very long.

This body is mine.

This body is mine.

She squeezed her eyes shut tightly, tensing her scalp, and then let everything sink a little more deeply into the cushions. It wasn't until Athena called her name, some time later, that

Lucy realized she'd been lying in silence for a while.

Right. She was supposed to let Athena know when she was done. Though she had the faint sense that if she formed words right now, the fragile thread of calm she'd managed might fray. She hummed, and hoped that was enough.

"You can let your mind wander, if you want," said Athena's voice, softer now. "You probably haven't let your mind wander much lately. People aren't built to be in fight-or-flight all the time, Lucy. This room is safe. I've made sure of that. When you're here, you can let go."

Lucy exhaled again, and tried to trust that they really were alone. She only felt two sets of eyes on her here: Athena's, and Natalie's. But the more she relaxed, the more that the constant awareness that had been with her since the bite started to blur.

There were no windows here, but she could feel humidity's late-summer curtain fall over her, stronger than the air-conditioning vents. It didn't feel as if she was inside, there in that hazy in-between. It felt as if she were sprawled across roots and hard-packed dirt.

Her head spun, more vertigo than dizziness. She pried her eyes open to orient herself.

She was no longer in the studio at all. She was lying on dirt, breathing in the thick and wet mountain air. And far overhead, a startlingly vast blanket of stars shivered against the sky.

Lucy sat up. The sharp movement wasn't enough to jar her out of her trance, or whatever this was. She could hear murmuring in her ear: Athena's tone and cadence, the words inaudible. She clutched a nearby root, as if without it she'd go spinning right off the side of the earth, and strained her heightened hearing until she could make something out.

"It's all right, Lucy," Athena was saying. *"Keep breathing."*

Lucy made herself breathe deep. She was dreaming—or something like it, anyway. She'd never had a dream look so vivid before.

Cautiously, Lucy got her legs under herself and pushed herself up. That ever-present spatial awareness had started to seep in again, even in the probably unreal landscape around her. It noted each sound and sensation. The cresting of the wind. The blades of grass against her bare ankles. The crunch of the dirt.

It felt real. As real as the cushions and wood paneling of the studio had felt just seconds ago. But already she'd been on the Rollins campus enough nights, with or without the vampire's infection, to know that something important was missing. The nights here on the mountain were alive: with frog and cicada song, with the crawling crackle of ticks and ants through the dirt, with the rustle of nocturnal animals picking their way through the leaves. The sounds of the living were absent here. As far as Lucy could tell, the only living thing in earshot was herself.

"Athena?" she said.

"Right here." It was a soft, barely audible murmur in her ear. *"Are you all right?"*

Lucy's eyes snapped to the direction of the voice, though she already knew there was no one there. It did sound as if it was coming from the direction where Athena had been sitting when she closed her eyes. She wasn't here on the mountain, though. She was back there, lying on the floor of the recording studio, with Natalie standing protectively at the door.

She hoped that was the case, anyway.

"I'm okay," she said into the quiet. "I think."

She turned in a slow circle. And she realized then that, like a slowly loading video game, the empty landscape around her was gradually filling itself in. The longer she looked, the more the faint shadows in the dark gained definition. The concrete rectangle of Quincey Hall in the distance. The tree line, directly ahead of her, leaves undulating in a wind she could neither hear nor feel. And directly beside her—

"Jesus," Lucy blurted out. Because when she turned, she saw herself, just inches away from her own face. But it wasn't a mirror image of her. It was a Lucy with fresh, red blood dotting the curve of her neck. A single trickle had slid down, staining the collar of her sunshine-yellow romper. The outfit she'd worn the night of the party.

Lucy shifted to look at herself, though she was hesitant to get too close. The other Lucy's face was perfectly slack. Her pupils were flat, dull coins, blown wide in the dark. She might have been on her feet, but she didn't look conscious. She didn't really look alive.

That silent wind seemed to stop. The leaves stilled; the grass stopped rippling. And then, beyond the tree line, barely audible, Lucy did hear something.

Lucy, something whispered.

Every hair on Lucy's arms pricked straight up. It was a gut-dropping chill, the kind of purely animal fear she was becoming more and more familiar with now. But if Lucy had learned anything in the past several days, it was that she had no more time to freeze in the face of that fear. However overpowering it felt, that terror was information. It meant that she was looking in the right direction.

So she shifted. She looked past the trees and into the woods. And she found two gleaming pairs of eyes nestled in the leaves. Eyes that were wholly focused on the Lucy in yellow.

Those eyes belonged to two girls. At least, they looked like girls. The one nearest to Lucy was even taller than Athena—her jeans weren't quite long enough on her, stopping just above the ankle. Her hair was fine and straight and sleek, the kind of hair Lucy used to wish she had. When that intangible wind picked up again, her hair rocked around her like an empty swing.

And next to her, a little more nestled in the trees, was a girl who was keenly, maddeningly familiar, though Lucy was sure she didn't know her. It wasn't the face Lucy recognized, or the curly hair. It was the freckles. They were scattered across her broad face and her smile lines as wildly as the stars that scraped the sky above them. They were the only parts of her with any real color. The rest of her was pale and crinkled, somehow. Like a crumpled poster.

"Sadie," Lucy whispered.

Neither of the girls moved. But both pairs of eyes smoothly, silently shifted from one Lucy to the other. And with a steady glide, like two swimmers in tandem, they opened their mouths.

Lucy gasped and stumbled, but there was nowhere to go. There was firm pressure at her back, like a wall. She twisted against it, tried to open her mouth, tried to move *anywhere*. But as she grasped for purchase, someone took her arm and held it down.

"Lucy," Athena said. The voice was right in her ear now. "Can you hear me? You're in the studio. We're alone here. You're safe."

Lucy blinked furiously. The stars had gone white-hot above her and melted together, coalescing into a single painfully bright light. It took her a full moment of squinting against it to realize they were no longer stars at all. She was looking up into the fluorescent light of the Pallas Radio recording studio. She couldn't back away because she was still lying on the floor. As she'd suspected, she'd never left the studio at all.

And above her, where she'd always been, was Athena. She sat back, carefully removing her grip on Lucy's arm, though her hand hovered at the ready. "Lucy?" she said. "What happened just now?"

Lucy rubbed her eyes with a shaking hand. And behind her eyelids, she could still see those two girls. Their tandem movements. Their pointed teeth.

"Addison and Sadie," she said. "They're not dead. They're vampires."

Ten

There was a strange, rote choreography to being hunted by a vampire. Not half an hour after learning that Sadie Grainger and Addison Greene were still somewhere on the Rollins campus, Lucy was frowning down at her class schedule on her phone. Her after-dark fencing class would obviously need to be dropped, which was too bad—a fencing foil wouldn't do much harm to Vanya, but it would be nice to be the one pointing a weapon at someone, for once.

The trickiest obstacle to avoid was any buildings with access to the steam tunnels. Astronomy was out for that reason. The same was true for Horror Literature, though she'd move to a safe building if she switched to the nine a.m. section. It was, in Lucy's opinion, a disgusting time of day to attempt to learn anything. But it felt worth it to keep at least part of her class schedule intact.

Thankfully, her next destination that day was also free of any doors to the tunnels. Which was a particular relief. There wasn't much point to being a college student if you couldn't get into the library.

Johnson Library was a largely subterranean specimen: It went two floors up and many, many more floors down. Lucy's orientation group hadn't descended all the way to the bottom during their tour, but if she recalled correctly, the lowest floor was B6 or B7.

She could feel it as soon as she walked in, even surrounded by all the light and bustle of the ground floor. There was a chill coming up from the tile floor, and from the mouth of the concrete stairwell. She could smell the must and age of the contents below. And just as she had in the basement of the Goldwell building, she could hear the sounds of living things crawling in the earth. They were faint sounds, all the way up here. But still present.

Lucy glanced over furtively. She was back in Mila's custody; her newly revised schedule was clear for the afternoon, which left her little to do except go wherever Mila needed to go. "You're sure there's no tunnels through here?"

Mila raised an eyebrow. "Positive. Why?"

"Just checking," Lucy demurred. She wouldn't go into it. There was never a good time to explain that she could hear the worms underneath her.

They moved through the entryway and main foyer, turning off into a study room. "Sorry that you have to wait around for me," Mila said. "You can only watch movies from the library *in* the library, for some reason. It's an intranet thing."

"It's fine," Lucy said neutrally, though the ever-watchful Mila probably caught the way Lucy was studying her. Mila had had a strange look on her face ever since Athena caught her up on what they'd discovered. Every so often, it looked like she was going to explain herself—but she hadn't yet.

Finally, as they sat down, Lucy cracked. "Okay," she said. "What's that look?"

"What look?" Mila said.

"Your forehead's been all crinkled since we left the studio," Lucy said. "Is this about Sadie and Addison?"

The crease in Mila's brow deepened then. It could only be about Sadie and Addison. But Lucy still didn't expect what Mila said next.

"We never thought there was more than one," Mila said.

"Hmm?" Lucy said.

"We've been keeping close track of all the deaths in the area." Mila was facing Lucy, but her focus was on some vague, invisible point in space. "Roughly one missing student per year, of course. Deaths at nursing homes, missing hunters. So-called animal attacks all across the mountain. It's not as if we know how much vampires eat. But for three vampires, now four? It seems—"

"Too few," Lucy murmured. Three vampires on a bustling, isolated college campus? It should have been like unleashing a cat colony on a bird sanctuary. "What about the dead rabbits?"

"Could be," Mila said. "But then I guess my question is still the same. Why the restraint? They could turn this campus into an all-you-can-eat buffet any time they wanted to. For some reason, they haven't yet. And it's not because they're scared of anything we could do to them."

It was a question Lucy didn't particularly want to consider. But she'd wondered the same thing back in the studio, hadn't she? Athena was smart. She was cautious. She'd devoted her entire college life to staying alive, to keeping as many other people alive as she could.

And yet. What was all that to something that could hijack free will with a wave of his hand?

"Whitney told me she was supposed to save her appetite for a feast," Lucy mused. It wasn't an answer so much as another part of the question. For whatever reason, they *were* holding back. Maybe for the same reason that Lucy herself had survived so far.

Everything Lucy was feeling rippled across Mila's face. "Well," she said. "Let's try to make sure she doesn't get it."

"No argument there," Lucy said softly.

Mila rubbed at the bridge of her nose, hard enough to look like it hurt. "Sorry," she said again, needlessly. Lucy really needed to tell her later that being nice to her didn't need to involve quite so many apologies. "I should start this stupid movie so we can both get out of here."

Lucy made a short, noncommittal sound. She wouldn't mind getting out of the library and away from its wet, underground smell. But it didn't make too much of a difference where they were on campus. No place felt completely safe to her now.

"What's the class?" Lucy asked.

"It's a class on adaptations," Mila said. "We read a book, we watch the movie it was based on, and then we analyze how the story changes to suit the format. It's an English class, so. Lots of talk of narrative devices."

"Are you an English major?" Lucy said.

Mila shrugged. "Nominally, yeah," she said, as if there was some distinction between being an English major and an English major in name only. "I finished most of my requirements already, so now I'm mostly just filling time with elective credits. I like books. I like movies. And the professor is the most beautiful woman I've ever seen in my life. I've taken classes for less."

Lucy carefully did not react to that last bullet point. Her budding crush on Mila had already passed through an assembly line of life-shattering, boner-killing revelations in the past twenty-four hours: There was no more reason for her to get excited that Mila was into women. She quietly noted it anyway. It was data. There was nothing wrong with collecting a little data about the person who was meant to keep her alive.

"That's not very Rollins of you" was all she said. "Where are the five majors plus an internship?"

"I did tell you that not all of us are turbo-child prodigies here, didn't I?" Mila flashed her wry, closed-lipped smile. "It's the same as Athena. Hard to have time to find anything else to get interested in, you know? Unfortunately, we ended up majoring in trying to find needles in haystacks."

Lucy was quiet for a moment. Mila was still going through the motions of setting up her computer, pulling up the movie—she didn't seem to realize that she'd just said something crushingly sad. Then again, Lucy had said the same thing about herself, hadn't she? It was hard to be interested in much of anything when you were keeping your head above water.

"I'm gonna start this," Mila said. "Did you bring your own work, or—"

"It's the second day of my freshman year," Lucy said dryly. "I haven't learned shit yet."

That drew a quiet laugh from Mila. One that parted her mouth wide open. "Okay, well. Entertain yourself somehow, then."

Mila slipped on her headphones, and Lucy was officially alone with her thoughts.

She sighed and tipped her head back. This was almost certainly better than sitting back in Mila's dorm room with the windows drawn, listening to every little creak in the walls. But Mila's movie was 105 minutes long, and that was a lot of minutes to kill. She hadn't brought her laptop, but there was a free library desktop down the table.

She slid over into the next chair and logged in with her Rollins email. She briefly considered tying her ankle to the chair leg for security—but she only went wandering when she fell asleep, and it wasn't as if she had any rope. She did, however, tuck that idea into her back pocket for later.

The Rollins Library Catalog and Information Services

home page blinked cheerily at her, its margins decked with clip art of books, magnifying glasses, and a strangely suggestive image of a finger pressed to a pair of lips in a shushing gesture. The page header framed a search bar, captioned with the words *What do you want to know?*

Lucy laughed. Everything she wanted to know at that moment would have filled 105 minutes and then some.

With no real expectations, she typed *vampire* and pressed the search button with a flourish. It didn't take her long to see why Athena had given up on the internet: The first few search pages offered her a wealth of books and articles, all predicated on the completely understandable idea that vampires didn't exist. *How vampire traditions developed around the world,* the summaries read. *The origins of a legend. A tongue-in-cheek look at vampire myths, from medieval to modern.* It wasn't as if she expected academia to have any particular ideas for her. But it was sobering to see real, living proof of how few people would believe her.

She scrolled aimlessly for three pages before she was too depressed to keep going. She wasn't going to find anything useful this way. Nothing that Athena hadn't already dug up.

That said. Now that she thought about it—there was one thing she knew now that Athena wouldn't look into very closely.

Ivan Volkov, she typed into the search bar. Her expectations hadn't gotten much higher. But the name on the screen sent a cold prickle up her arms.

There were a lot of Ivan Volkovs. It felt silly, in retrospect, to assume there wouldn't be. There was a poet, a biochemist, a literary critic. Lucy was nearly six pages into the results before she'd moved past the texts authored by Ivan Volkovs and into the texts *about* Ivan Volkovs. She ran each results page through a Google Translate filter, hoping the long list of Russian and Bulgarian article names would yield some clue. Instead, she got things like *Victory of the Kolkhoz Construction Workers in the Belarusian SSR. Hammurabi, King of Babylonia. Mass Development of Old and Abandoned Lands.*

She had just begun to feel very, very naive for having any hope when her eyes skimmed the translated title at the bottom of the page:

The Mountain Villa Massacre: The Strange Case of the Volkov Family.

Lucy's cursor paused. The result was probably just pulled in by the matching last name—at least, that was what she thought at first. But the small gray text at the bottom of the search entry read *contains: 'ivan volkov.'*

She clicked. And despite the library's ancient Wi-Fi, the next page loaded as quickly as a slap in the face. *You've taken a wrong turn!* read the cheery Comic Sans text. *Redirecting . . .*

With a short, frustrated sound, Lucy tried the link again. She could have sworn she was redirected back even quicker the next time.

Dead end confirmed.

She leaned back in her chair, and all the largely useless text on-screen blurred. Maybe this Mountain Villa Massacre was just as useless. If there was anything she'd learned from the last several pages, it was that there were a lot of Ivan Volkovs in the world. But she had an hour and a half left to kill.

"Mila," she whispered, leaning around the computer. "Do you mind if I—"

She clipped her question off halfway. Sometime in the past ten minutes, Mila had pushed her laptop back in order to pillow her head in her arms. Her back was rising and falling in a steady pace, and the fringe of her bangs partially, but didn't quite, conceal a closed eye. When Lucy carefully pushed her chair back and stood, Mila didn't even flinch.

Lucy laughed softly. She figured that Mila's two to three hours of sleep that morning hadn't been sufficient, no matter how many times Mila tried to convince the both of them that it was. But still. It was a little surprising to see exhaustion get the better of her. Not many things seemed to get the better of Mila Rostova.

Her hand hovered above Mila's shoulder. It would be sensible to wake her up and tell her where she was going. But she doubted that either of them would have a quiet night ahead. It couldn't be a bad thing to let her rest a little while longer.

Carefully withdrawing a notebook and pen from her bag, she started to write on a fresh page. *DON'T PANIC!* she wrote first, in all caps. *Going downstairs to reference librarian. If I'm not here when you wake up, the desk is on floor B2. Sleep well.*

She backed away carefully, as if slipping around a sleeping

lion. Hopefully Mila would see that before she armed herself in the middle of a crowded library. The black bow was safely in its bag at her feet. Ideally it would stay that way.

Lucy made her way out of the study room and back across the main floor. She had a faint memory of where the reference librarian's desk was from the library tour, but Natalie hadn't taken them all the way there. *He's cranky,* she'd said, which was fine with Lucy. With any luck, he could help her find the article quickly, and she'd be in and out.

She crossed out of the sunlight as she moved into the stairwell. She still wasn't used to the instant relief, like laying a cold washcloth on a headache. Of course, she hoped she wouldn't have a chance to get used to it at all. She'd envisioned so many sunny walks across campus during her orientation tour. So many hikes to nearby caves and waterfalls. Now it felt as if she belonged down here, in the dark, with the worms.

Her grandmother used to tell her nothing was permanent: no circumstance, no feeling, no bad day. It was something Lucy had repeated to herself over and over since she was young. But that was far more comforting when the worst that could happen to her was living out a long, cramped life in Jacksonville, Florida. There was a whole different kind of powerlessness in her potential future now.

She rubbed at her temples with a wince. The relief of the shade hadn't lasted long. There was a different pressure taking its place now. Not the feeling of eyes on her, like she'd felt in Goldwell. Not the intrusive creep of sounds and sensations, like she'd felt in the classroom. This pressure didn't quite have direction. It was a wall over her head, steadily pressing downward. Like the pressure shift of a summer storm.

Lucy realized then that her hand was quivering over the banister. She was shaking. She was shaking like a Chihuahua, actually—she could feel it in her whole body. Was there actually a storm brewing outside? Her childhood cat used to crouch low to the ground when she felt them coming. Maybe her own heightened senses could feel some of it, too?

She rounded the stairwell, past the B1 sign, and pressed on to B2. And the wall, steadily and gradually, pressed harder.

"What the hell," she whispered. She could feel sweat springing up across the back of her neck. Her scalp prickled, tickling the crown of her head. This wasn't fear. This wasn't a feeling so much as an instinct. Lucy had enough trouble reading her own human instincts, sometimes. To read the instincts of the infection felt like a world beyond.

She took a breath and got a grip. There were no steam tunnels in the library. She wouldn't be here unless Mila was completely sure of that. Which meant she was almost certainly alone in that stairwell, psyching herself out.

She wasn't alone for long, though. There were a few bare signs of life as she stepped into floor B2. There was definitely a small crowd in the first reading room she passed: No one was talking, but she could hear the faint scratches of their heartbeats through the door. There was a set of stacks ahead in the main room, and at the very back, a horseshoe-shaped desk.

Lucy could make out a blond figure behind it, leaning over a book.

She'd made it. It should have been a relief. But as she approached, her legs gradually shook harder. Until it was almost too difficult to move.

He heard her coming. And he lifted his head.

His eyes, a pale and indifferent blue, met hers. And like lightning passing over her head, every nerve in her body rippled with electricity. The feeling of his attention was beyond weight. It was its own force of gravity. Even as she reeled under the force of it, she couldn't help but come closer.

Vanya, she thought, at first. But even without knowing what Vanya looked like, the person at the desk could never be mistaken for the hazy impression of him in her mind. He was tall and long-limbed, his hair more yellow-gold than sandy, handsome but etched with lines around his mouth and forehead. When he looked at her, it wasn't appraising. It radiated sourness. It was like the atmosphere itself curling a lip in disgust.

And unlike Vanya, he was not young. *Young* was not a word Lucy had associated with Vanya until this moment. But as this man looked at her, Lucy felt sure that she'd never met anything older. Not even the mountains around them.

He closed his book. And a single lifeless blue vein jumped against his delicate jaw.

"Oh, no," said the ancient creature at the Johnson Library reference desk. "Absolutely not."

Eleven

"You're—" Lucy blurted out.

"Be quiet," he snapped. "Unless you'd like to announce to the whole of the floor what we are."

"We," Lucy echoed. Her thoughts were firing nearly as fast as the patter of her heart—her words couldn't keep up. "So you're—"

"Yes, dear," said the ancient creature—the vampire—with an elegant wave of his hand. "We're in the same club. Though"—his eyes swept the length of her body once, cursorily—"you don't appear to be a full member of that club *just* yet."

Lucy's throat closed, even as her mouth hung open. The vampire regarded her with impatience—if she couldn't see it in his face, she would have felt it in the weight of his presence. But before Lucy had been a not-human not-vampire, she had been a cashier. She knew how to gauge whether or not someone would cause trouble. And while the reference librarian wasn't happy, he wasn't tensed to strike. He was angry, but it wasn't an anger with heat. It felt more like jaw-clenched resignation.

"You're not going to hurt me," she said slowly. It felt like wishful thinking to say out loud. But she knew as soon as she said it that it was also true. She'd been surrounded by hunters, of one kind or another, all week. His was a completely different energy.

The vampire huffed. Since he didn't need to breathe, she assumed it was for emphasis. "Obviously I'm not going to hurt you," he said. "I don't eat from others' plates. Please do give the little prince my very best. Or better yet, don't tell him that you saw me at all."

Her heart rate picked up, fast enough to make her nauseous. "You know him."

"Every farmer knows the local wolf," the vampire said, regarding her again. "And its pups, I suppose."

"I'm not his pup," Lucy said.

"You're worse," the vampire said. "You're his thrall."

"And what's that?"

"Tomorrow's meal," he said darkly. "Listen, girl. I sympathize. But you should go enjoy what's left of your mortal life. All that brat wants is attention. You don't have to give it to him while you're still alive."

He moved to turn his back to her. That strange pressure gave her a little push as he moved away. As if the air itself were gently trying to turn her around and walk her back where she came from.

Lucy was not going to be walked back where she came

from, though. Not yet. She lunged forward and locked both hands around one of his wrists.

She could feel the shift in the atmosphere as he rounded on her. That crackling summer storm feeling. But it no longer mattered to Lucy that she was talking to something several times older than electricity. She'd come here for an article. As far as she was concerned, she'd found something better.

"Even as you are now," he said, his eyes unblinking, "you must be able to feel a fraction of what I am. Don't you?"

Lucy's grip slackened. This was instinct, too. She forced herself to ignore it. This was what Jillian had been preparing her for all her life, wasn't it? To turn some unfortunate corner and find Death waiting there for her. She wondered if she'd live long enough to tell her mother that Death was a librarian.

Lucy took a breath, shifted her stance, and held on to his wrist, which looked deceptively thin and delicate in her own hands. He wasn't going to hurt her. Though he wanted her to know that he could.

"You *are* the reference librarian, right?" she said. "I'm trying to look up an article. If you can help me find it, I won't bother you anymore."

There was no way to make that request sound casual. The vampire certainly didn't seem to think it was. "We've got a lovely catalog you can browse," he said. "Very intuitive search engine."

"It wouldn't load. So I came to ask you." Lucy chose her next words carefully: Even if this vampire truly wasn't dangerous, that didn't mean telling him everything was wise. "Someone called into a campus radio station with what they claimed was Vanya's full name. Ivan Volkov. If you don't want to get involved, I can leave right now. No matter what happens to me, I won't tell him that I saw you. But there are people who are helping me. Even if I don't survive, I want to give them their best chance. I just want to see if this article tells me something they can use."

The vampire's cold, flat look shifted. "Someone called Pallas Radio. With his full name."

Lucy tried not to look surprised. If she were a vampire on a college campus, she probably would have been very aware of the local vampire-hunting radio show, too. "That's right."

Another prickle of indignation made its way through the air. But at the very least, this time it didn't seem to be directed at Lucy.

"The person who left the message," he said. "Did his voice have the cadence of poetry?"

"I . . . don't know that I could tell you what that sounds like," Lucy said. But after a few more seconds of thought, she added, "I guess there was something a bit musical about it?"

"Of course," the vampire said, matter-of-factly. "Right, then. You wait here a moment. I'll just need to kill him."

And with that, the vampire swung elegantly on his heel and made a beeline for the closed door at the back of the stacks. His long legs took him all the way across the room in just a few soundless strides.

Lucy faltered. It was probably best to do what he said. Waiting at the desk did seem like the safest bet. But there was a boldness coursing through her that she knew she couldn't afford to lose. Maybe it was all the time with Natalie. She was getting pretty good at the *yes, and* mentality herself.

She took off following him across the library floor. As she slipped through the door at the back of the room, she caught sight of the nameplate nailed to it:

L. ROMAN

REFERENCE LIBRARIAN

L. Roman, who barely acknowledged her presence this time, reached over her to shut the door. And then he hissed, in the direction of the corner, "Hiro. Are you using fucking *court whispers* at my place of employment?"

Lucy noticed only then that the office wasn't empty. Curled up in an armchair in the corner, buried in a book despite the low light, was an East Asian man in a light blue button-down and loose, flowing slacks. He had a thick-knitted cardigan draped over the back of the chair, and his black hair was pulled back at the nape of his neck. He looked soft, approachable. But it didn't take long for Lucy to guess why the storm-cloud sensation was even heavier here. She was no longer in the presence of just one vampire.

"*Our* place of employment," Hiro said, as if by reflex. He lowered the book, his face slipping between pleasantness and confusion as he spotted Lucy. "Hello. Hi. Welcome to the reference floor. What court whispers?"

"Oh, I don't know," said L. Roman, brushing his hand through his elegant hair. "Maybe something to do with your call to Pallas goddamned Radio?"

Hiro blinked, nonplussed in the face of L. Roman's mounting rage. But as he looked back to Lucy, he sat up so quickly that his cardigan slipped to the floor.

"Oh my," he said. "Caller number thirty-two?"

Lucy waved weakly. "Hi there."

Hiro leapt from his chair to grasp one of her hands in both of his. "I am such a fan," he said. "When you said, 'Oh, I'm way ahead of you'? Chills, my dear, chills!"

L. Roman's delicate hand landed hard against the wall. Lucy heard a distinct *crunch*. "I thought we agreed—"

"Not to get involved with the radio children," Hiro finished, almost dutifully. "But they were stuck. They needed a little push. How was I supposed to know she'd show up here? You're the first one to say that the children don't utilize their library resources enough."

L. Roman looked as displeased as Lucy had ever seen anyone look. "You agreed to start wrapping up your affairs here."

"Which I have been doing, as requested," Hiro said. "But if we're leaving anyway, why not give the radio children a helping hand on the way out?"

"A helping hand straight into that brat's jaws?" L. Roman said.

"Well," Hiro said, "that's some kind of conclusion, isn't it?"

"I'm not joking," L. Roman said.

"Neither am I." And abruptly, Hiro really wasn't joking anymore. For the first time, Lucy saw a shadow cross his youthful face. The barest hint of his age. "At least they'll go with eyes open. Isn't that better than those poor girls got?"

The silent standoff that followed went on long enough that Lucy's back foot slid a little closer to the door. She still felt reasonably sure that no one here wanted to hurt her—but she didn't want to be here if they decided to hurt each other, either. Finally, Hiro uncoiled.

"I didn't mean to go behind your back." He really did have a poetic lilt to his voice. "But this place has been good to me. I wanted to leave it with a farewell gift, of sorts."

L. Roman's anger shifted into something remarkably sulky. Hiro laughed. "Goodness, what a spectacle. Have you at least introduced yourself to our new friend, or have we given her a preview of our dinner table conversations before we even shared basic pleasantries?"

"She's not a friend," L. Roman said. "She's the little prince's next meal."

"With that attitude, she will be." Hiro's smile gentled as he turned back to Lucy. "Forgive our manners, dear. Hiromasa Minamoto. The disagreeable one is Laurentius of Rome. And I assume you don't go by caller number thirty-two?"

"I . . . Lucy," she managed. Her brain was moving at a crawl, and her tongue was moving even slower. "And by 'Rome,' you mean—"

"Laurentius of the Roman Empire, to be more exact," Hiro said. "Had you guessed already, with that ridiculous alias of his? 'L. Roman.' You won't be surprised to hear that he's not a man of much flair."

"I thought we weren't subjecting her to our dinner table conversations," Laurentius of Rome said moodily.

Lucy shifted her weight under the renewed force of Laurentius's annoyance. Hiro lightly patted her shoulder. "Oh, don't worry, he's not as threatening as he feels. When you're as old as he is, every baby vampire in a five-mile radius can sense you coming—I'm not surprised that even a thrall can feel it. He won't actually do anything with all that displeasure. He'll just glower about it."

Lucy smiled weakly, and didn't point out that Hiro felt nearly as old. "So you two . . . work here."

"That's my name on the door, isn't it?" Laurentius said.

"She didn't mean any offense, beloved," Hiro said. "This time last week, she didn't believe vampires were real. Now there's six of them on one campus. That's what you meant, right, Lucy?"

". . . Yes," Lucy said, taken aback. Actually, it had been what she was thinking almost word for word.

"Ah, sorry about that," Hiro said. "You have particularly loud thoughts, no offense. But anyway—there's a bit of a location bias here, believe it or not. College campuses have lots of dark offices and windowless rooms. Usually some kind of subterranean system for steam heating. No one's terribly interested in what you do outside of academia. And you can usually count on employment records to switch to a new system every few decades. Laurentius here is about to celebrate his tenth work anniversary—for the third time. It's not the worst place for our kind to be."

Lucy nodded, taking everything in. *Trying* to take everything in, anyway. "So you were here before Vanya."

"Correct," Laurentius said, biting hard against the *t*. "And it should have been very clear to him that this campus was already spoken for. But Ivan is a child. And he has a child's appetite."

"Quite the old-fashioned appetite, too," Hiro said. "You don't usually see someone so young hunting out in the open like this."

"You don't?" Lucy said. It seemed to Lucy to be one of the few things one could count on, where a vampire was concerned.

"Hunting is fun, if you're into that sort of thing," Hiro said. "But it's messy. It creates a paper trail, especially in this lovely little surveillance age we've found ourselves in. And why go out and hustle for your next meal when there's a whole world on the internet full of fantasists dying to be bitten by a vampire? Kids these days will pay *you* to feed from them. Why risk getting caught?"

"And not that he cares," Laurentius added. "But when you share your territory with others, hunting puts a target on their backs as well. I've survived four angry mobs in my lifetime. I'm not anxious to summon a fifth. That's why we're leaving, as soon as the semester is over. He's getting bolder. And we don't want to suffer the consequences alongside him."

"But this is your territory, isn't it?" Lucy said. "You're older than him. You can't chase him off?"

"My feelings exactly." Hiro's laugh wasn't so musical that time. "It *is* our territory. I'm not keen to give it up to some gluttonous child. But brute strength is the province of young men, even for vampires. My beloved here wouldn't be a match for him. Not with his old vegetarian bones."

"A vampire of my age doesn't have much of an appetite," Laurentius said, as if to head off any accusations of altruism. "Rabbits suit my purposes fine. Significantly less small talk involved than with Hiro's customers."

The rabbit corpses were his. One question mark explained, at least. "So you feed from humans?" Lucy said to Hiro. "Can't you stop him?"

"Oh, I'm a lover, not a fighter," Hiro said. "Even becoming nature's perfect killing machine didn't change that."

"Even if we were a match for him, it wouldn't be within our power to evict him. Bureaucratically speaking, that is," Laurentius said tartly. "Our boy has an advocate."

Lucy's mind stuttered. "What do you mean, 'advocate'?" she said. "Someone here? At Rollins?"

"In the upper administration, to be exact," Laurentius said. "Someone has enabled him to make his home here. Someone who has smoothed things over with those two missing kids. I don't know the details, but he is being protected. Which means that *you* aren't."

For such simple sentences, they didn't gel. Not when she thought about Sadie's face on those missing posters, or Addison, standing in the trees, with her long straight hair and vacant smile.

It was the thought of Whitney's empty desk, never to be occupied again, that finally drove Laurentius's words home. Someone was protecting Vanya here. Which meant that someone had served up those girls on a silver platter.

"It would hardly be the first time," Hiro said, responding to her thoughts once more. "That's America, isn't it? A few bodies are the cost of doing business."

"Which is why," Laurentius said, with the cadence of an oft-repeated line, "we are *not* staying."

"You never said I couldn't try one last thing," Hiro said. "This is our home."

"And here I thought you were helping out of the goodness of your heart," Laurentius said acidly.

"We're not leaving yet. We can wait to see how this plays out," Hiro said. "The radio children have a plan. Or they must, if they reached out to Lucy, here."

"Which is proof enough that any plan they have isn't very good," Laurentius said. "They've invited a thrall into their inner circle. One snap of the brat's fingers and she'll turn them all over as an appetizer. And now she can tell him that *you're* scheming against him, too."

"So tell me what to do, then." The words were out of Lucy's mouth before she could think better of them. But she no longer had the energy to think better of anything. Her eyes hurt. Her shoulders hurt. The bruise on her neck was throbbing. And she was abruptly sick of people and vampires alike talking over her head. "Go on. Maybe you can't beat Ivan Volkov into a pulp, but you must know something we foolish little radio children don't, right? I'm not a vampire, but it's been made very clear to me that I'm not totally human anymore, either. Tell me something I can do. Tell me how to keep him out of my head."

Hiro turned, obscuring his face, and seemed to share a long look with Laurentius. Laurentius's face remained fully visible to Lucy, but his blank look betrayed nothing. "Love," Hiro finally said. "Why don't you go make us some tea?"

Laurentius's shoulders sank like a pricked balloon. "No, you go," he said. "I'll talk to her. No need for you to dig us deeper into this mess."

"Ah. I see." Hiro sighed and stretched, as if under the weight of the same tired limbs and creaky joints as a mortal. Lucy knew that he wasn't, of course. His lifeless body crossed the room like a fish through water: smoothly, with barely a sound. "Don't be afraid, Lucy. He's all talk."

And, with a smile, he swept from the room. Laurentius stared after him with enough exasperation to burn a hole in the wall.

It seemed that if there was to be any talking, Lucy needed to go first. "Are you two married?"

"That's right," Laurentius said. "My own personal saboteur for over one thousand years."

Lucy swallowed. She'd already approximated the math, but it was another thing to hear out loud. "Mazel tov."

"He was a courtier," Laurentius said. "In Kyoto's Heian court. It's why he can't help but meddle. It was his full-time job when he was alive."

"He wants Vanya gone," Lucy said. "Don't you?"

"I think you know the answer to that question perfectly well," Laurentius said. "I suppose I sounded flip, earlier. But I don't like wandering. I don't have a taste for it anymore. You cannot fathom how much I would prefer for him to go and for us to stay." He paused, laughed once. "Well. I suppose you can. You've met him."

"I don't remember him," she said. "But I can imagine."

"Ah," he said. Lucy wondered if she imagined the slight note of solemnity there. "Of course. His specialty."

"If you don't want to get involved, I don't care," Lucy said. "It's not like it changes anything for us. We weren't planning to have help to begin with. But we don't know anything about vampires. Nothing definitive. If you could just give us something to work with—"

"I wouldn't have lived this long if I made a habit of handing over our weaknesses to strangers," Laurentius said. But there was no real conviction behind it. "Listen. You wanted honesty, so I'll give it to you. You're still human, for the most part. You will be until the moment you drink his blood in return.

But until the infection fades, you'll be at the mercy of your instincts. You'll have all of a vampire's weaknesses and none of its strengths. You can barely fight yourself, let alone him."

Lucy wasn't fazed. She didn't have time to be. "But the infection *does* fade."

"As far as I know," Laurentius said. "I haven't fed from humans for years, but Hiro does. His clients might crave rare meat for a few weeks, or miss out on a few opportunities to tan, but they're back to normal by the end of the month. You've been bitten twice. His hold on you could last far longer. Much longer, I'm sure, than he plans to leave you alive. Frightened creatures have a taste—too acidic for my palate, but I know the brat loves it. He's building that fear in you now. Seasoning to taste, if you will. When he's satisfied it's enough, it's going to be over for you. I really do take no pleasure in telling you this, but at this moment, your best chance of escaping him is to accept what he's offering. Allow him to turn you. You'll have a better chance of outrunning him as a vampire than as a thrall."

"No one has outrun him yet. He's got Sadie Grainger and Addison Greene doing his bidding," Lucy said. "Do you think they're here because they want to be? Or because for some reason, they can't leave?"

His mouth shifted then. She wanted to believe he was thinking, as she was, of those two girls. But she was looking at something that hadn't been human in thousands of years. Maybe he didn't feel that kind of empathy anymore. Maybe Lucy wouldn't have, either.

She sank into the chair vacated by Hiro, suddenly shaky. It creaked under her weight as she and Laurentius of Rome stared each other down.

"Can you read my mind?" she finally asked.

He snorted. It was almost a laugh. "A little. It's more Hiro's gift than mine."

"A little is probably enough," Lucy said. Vanya had felt it all the way across a crowded room, after all. Her stupid, loud thoughts. "Maybe you can tell that I already spent my whole life with someone who thought she could control everything that happened to me. She did that because she loves me. She loves me so much, she thought she could spend her entire existence standing at my door and deciding what was allowed in. And I left her. It broke her heart. It broke *mine*. And I left her anyway. Can you feel me remembering all of that right now?"

It was quiet for a moment, under Laurentius's watchful eye. He didn't study her with Mila's careful appraisal, or Athena's threat assessment, or Vanya's cold, predatory weight. His gaze suggested he hadn't made up his mind about her yet.

But he finally said, "Yes. I do see that."

"So," she said. "If I won't be controlled by the person who loves me most in this world, then why do you think I would let Ivan Volkov do it for even one day?"

When Laurentius wasn't moving, or speaking, the stillness of his body was especially apparent. Now that she'd grown a bit used to his outsized presence, she could understand how unassuming he might look if you didn't know what he was. How he might have slipped by, unnoticed, over all these years.

"I'm sorry," he said, "but I truly don't know how to help you. Hiro is the only vampire I have ever made. I know how I would keep Ivan out of my mind. I know how I would tell Hiro to do it. I have no idea what to tell a thrall."

Lucy rubbed at her face. Letting her feelings out in front of an audience had given her an odd sense of calm. What did it matter if he could help or not? She wouldn't be any better or worse off than she'd been before. "Okay," she said.

He didn't have anything to say to that. Not at first. But then, quietly, he added, "I could keep thinking."

Lucy's resigned sense of serenity fled her in an instant.

"So you think there's something I could do," she said.

"I think that there is an infinitesimal chance that there is some way you can prolong your mortal life, at least for a week or two," Laurentius said. "And I think even that is very unlikely, by the way. But I didn't just take this position for the sunless ambiance. I'm very good at what I do. So on the slim chance that I find something . . . I will pass it along."

Hope and suspicion were a heady mix. Lucy breathed both of them in. "I thought you didn't want to help me."

"I'm a realist. And I did not live this long by underestimating anyone's capabilities, let alone those of a young, careless hunter." Laurentius pressed a thumb to the bridge of his nose. "But we're leaving anyway. Perhaps this will give Hiro some closure on the way out."

"Well . . . thank you," Lucy said softly.

Laurentius's eyebrows furrowed. "I've just told you that this is a fool's errand that has very little to do with you. There's no need to thank me."

"Oh, I know," Lucy said. Though it was sort of shocking to her, too, how little she cared about how noble the vampire's intentions might be. Athena and Mila genuinely wanted to help her—and were also planning to kill her, if they had to. Help was help. "But thank you anyway."

A light knock at the door startled her. Hiro eased it open, carrying a hot beverage in a paper cup and wearing a Cheshire cat smile. "Sorry to interrupt," he said, in his lilting voice. "I come bearing tea. And someone looking for you, Lucy."

The door opened a little farther, wide enough that Lucy could see Mila beyond Hiro's shoulder. "Sorry to interrupt," Mila said. She had her RA voice on—the one she'd used on the phone with Jillian. But Lucy's magnified hearing picked up the slight strain behind it. "She was gone for long enough that I thought she'd gotten eaten down here."

Lucy didn't wince, but she was close. She'd been gone long enough to make Mila worry. And Mila didn't know the half of it yet. But they couldn't exactly discuss it here. Just because she was ready to conditionally trust Laurentius and Hiro didn't mean she was ready for them to know who was behind Pallas Radio.

"I prepared your tea to go," Hiro said brightly, handing it over. "Sounds like you've got a tight schedule upstairs."

"Thanks," Lucy said. "Ah, sorry, Mila. I just need to ask Mr. Roman one more thing."

Mila seemed to take that in stride. Very cautious stride, but stride nonetheless. "I'll wait for you at the reference desk."

Hiro waited until Mila's footsteps had fully receded before he said, "Nice kid." His tone all but confirmed that he, with his courtier instincts and his tendency to pluck loud thoughts out of people's heads, already understood far more about Mila than Lucy wanted him to. "Are you going to tell her whom she was just speaking to?"

"We're not a threat to you," Lucy said quickly.

"Oh, I know. It's not the threat to us that I'm worried about." As Hiro resettled in his chair, he reached out and moved one of Laurentius's slim hands to his shoulder. Laurentius sighed but allowed it. "You should remember this, Lucy," Hiro went on. "Your new friends genuinely wish to help you. But they have also spent the better part of three years believing, more or less correctly, that creatures like us are the enemy. Their trust in you is a resource. You should take care not to waste that resource."

Lucy smiled, though she was well aware of how queasy it must look. She knew all of that already. She understood it far more keenly than she wanted to. Athena, unable to pursue the degree she'd been recruited for. Mila, forever unable to break the heart of the boy she treasured but didn't love. It wasn't exactly trust they had in Lucy, who now had so much in common with the monsters that altered the courses of their lives. They were gambling on her.

No matter how genteel the two vampires in front of her looked, no matter how quietly they lived their lives, they were still vampires. Something that Athena and Mila would never gamble on.

"If they don't trust me," Lucy finally said, "then I think maybe that's wise."

It seemed they had nothing to say to that. But as she stepped through the door, she heard Hiro call out to her one last time. "Oh, and, Lucy? That article you wanted? Check your email."

Twelve

"There he is. L. Roman, library staff." Mila paused her cursor over the blank spot where the headshot would be. "No picture. I guess we still don't know if they show up in them, come to think of it. Maybe you should take a selfie with him next time, test it out."

"We still haven't decided if there should be a next time," Athena said tightly.

Mila's grin, which had already been strained, dropped. "Sorry, boss," she said. "I was joking."

It hadn't been a real choice whether to tell them about the library vampires: Regardless of how they'd react, Lucy couldn't afford to pass up a real lead just because Athena and Mila wouldn't trust it. But that, of course, didn't change the fact that they didn't trust it. Lucy had been politely trying to ignore the speed of Athena's heartbeat since the words came out of her mouth.

She hadn't even broached the subject of the article

currently sitting in her inbox. But given how much she'd already rocked the boat today, it was probably best to read it before making a big deal out of anything.

"Maybe we shouldn't stay here." Athena pulled open a desk drawer, sending a whittled stake rolling to the front. "The younger vampire could read your thoughts. He probably knows what suite we're in."

"Boss, nothing's changed," Mila said. "This building is still the safest place on campus. Even if they know where you are, they haven't tried to get to you before now."

"I really don't think they're a threat to us." Lucy tried not to take it personally when Athena shot her an annoyed look. "Which is not to say they have our best interests at heart or anything. But you said it yourself, Mila: There have been five, now six, vampires on this campus, and surprisingly few victims. And I believe that Laurentius and Hiro want Vanya gone as much as we do."

"It does explain the dead rabbits," Mila said. "I don't know about Sadie and Addison, but our friend doesn't strike me as someone who'd settle for animals."

Athena had stopped pacing, stopped fiddling with her belongings like she was thinking of throwing them into a box. But her gaze was still hard as she looked at them.

"Okay, then," she finally said. "Let's say they come back to you tomorrow, Lucy. Let's say that they tell you they've figured out a way to help you. What do you propose we do, if that happens?"

"I mean . . ." Lucy faltered, aware she was about to say the last thing that Athena wanted to hear. "I think we have to take them up on it, don't we?"

"I agree," Mila said, which was somehow even more shocking than the fact that there were vampires in the library. "But I don't think you should see them again without me, Lucy. You never should have been alone with them in the first place. Just because they don't feel like a threat doesn't mean that they aren't." She turned to Athena then. Ever deferential. "Does that seem reasonable?"

Athena still didn't seem to think any of this was reasonable. But she exhaled slowly, and then said, "Okay. And, Lucy? If Mila doesn't think it's safe, promise me that you'll respect that."

Lucy nodded, and tried her best not to look sullen about it. She wished Natalie were there and not in class. Natalie would have backed her 100 percent. Natalie would already be at the library getting a warm oolong tea and the good gossip from Hiro Minamoto.

"All right, then," Mila said. "If we're all agreed on that, then we should head out, Lucy. The boss has a show to prepare for. And we should get some dinner before it gets dark."

They were quiet for a while after Athena saw them out. Lucy waited until they'd put a fair distance between themselves and the studio. It was her own strange deference to Athena. It didn't feel quite right to talk about her too close to her sanctuary.

"Thank you for backing me up," she said.

“Strictly speaking,” Mila said, “I backed both of you up.”

“Oh, yeah, I know. I didn’t mean to . . .” Lucy paused to collect her thoughts. The daylight was a bit more bearable with every passing day, but it still muddled her head a bit sometimes. “I know Athena’s right. But . . . still.”

Mila moved a pace or two ahead of her. When she spoke, she addressed the words to the path ahead. “You know,” she said, “by the time I met Athena, it was a few months after she’d been attacked. Even after I discovered the radio show, it took me a while to call in. I thought she’d laugh at me, I guess, or pity me. I was pretty sure by that point that the show wasn’t fiction. But I was still ready for her to tell me I was delusional. Pretty much everyone else had, even when they didn’t use that word.

“But from the first few seconds I talked to her . . . I mean, you know how she is,” Mila went on. “She knew exactly what I meant even when *I* didn’t know what I meant. She listens to people when they talk. Really pays attention, like what you’re saying is the most important thing anyone’s ever said. I don’t think anyone listened to her like that, after she was attacked. I think that’s why it’s so important to her to give that to other people.”

She slowed a little as they started down the steep hill, allowing Lucy to catch up. “She hates being afraid, you know,” Mila said. “She hates knowing that her fear could get in the way of what she needs to do. She hates that she’ll never really know if every precaution she’s taken is enough. And she hates that all of that scares her even more. She’s so, so scared every single day, it's like the fear is just another presence in the room with her. So if there's anything you can ever do to be a little more cautious—you should do it. I think we owe her that."

Lucy hummed, but didn't say anything yet. Fear did get in the way. Fear could run a household, if you let it. If she were Athena, she would hate that she was afraid, too. For her own part, all she'd been trying to do since the bite was keep her own fear in check.

But she and Athena weren't the same. However much trouble Lucy was in, she would never know what it was like to be hunted for years. To have her name called out, over and over, in the night. Mila might have been there during the day, but every night in that recording suite, Athena was alone with her own fear. It was her first and most devoted listener.

Jillian's wide, hurt eyes flitted across Lucy's mind. She tried not to think any more about her mother, now alone with her own fear, too.

"She's lucky to have a friend like you," Lucy finally said.

"Well. I hope we're friends," Mila said. "I guess we're best friends. Though I don't know if she'd see it that way."

Lucy nodded. Her thoughts had already drifted back to the two vampires in the library. "You're really willing to let me see those vampires again? You have as little reason to trust them as Athena does."

"Oh, *trust* is a very strong word," Mila said. "But this is the best lead we've gotten so far. And. Well. I'd love not to kill you."

Lucy wondered if her bar for compliments had just gotten

very low, or if that was the nicest thing anyone had said to her in the past several days. "Thanks," she said. "I'd love not to die."

Mila cleared her throat and looked up at the sky, which had started to take on the orange of late afternoon. "Let's get you some food," she said. "I think we're in for another long night."

"Oh—I almost forgot," Lucy said. She'd had an idea back in the library, before she met the vampires. And she was pretty sure Mila was going to like this one. "I think I know how to make that long night a bit easier."

Surprisingly, Mila did not like the idea.

"I don't get you," Lucy said. "I thought you'd like some help making sure I stay put."

"I would," Mila said, from her spot on the bed. She had, reluctantly, agreed to Lucy's plan. She'd been buried in instructional YouTube videos since they arrived back at the dorm. "But this is a first for me, as you might imagine. I'd like to make sure I don't cut off the circulation in both of your wrists in the process."

"I don't imagine anything," Lucy said honestly. "For all I know, you've got people tied up in here all the time." Or maybe not all the time, but at least once or twice.

Then again, as far as she knew, Mila had only had two long-term relationships: a doomed childhood romance, and a lengthy commitment with Revenge. Neither left much time for tying anybody up anywhere.

With a loud exhale, Mila set about tying the restraints to her headboard. Lucy frowned over her shoulder. "Are those neckties? I thought we'd be using ropes."

"Ropes chafe, Marquis de Sade," Mila said. "I'm trying to keep you from leaping out the window, not trying to peel all the skin off your wrists. You're lucky that I have about a thousand thrift-store ties from my sophomore-year suit phase."

"Technically in this situation, you're the Marquis de Sade," Lucy said, allowing herself a brief moment to picture Mila's suit phase. "It's getting dark. Should you lock me in now? It might take time."

"Dude." Mila tied off the burgundy tie on the left to match the navy on the right. "If I promise to tie you up ten minutes before sunset, will you sit still and eat something? I'm just going to watch one more video."

Lucy handed Mila the vegetarian burrito that she'd picked up for her before turning to her own double-steak. True to her word, Mila had returned her focus to her phone, but she looked up at Lucy periodically to make sure she was doing as she was told. Lucy bit back a sigh, and tucked into her burrito. She hadn't eaten since breakfast.

She'd been hungry when she ordered it—at least she thought she'd been hungry. But now that she was eating it, it felt gristly and overcooked against her teeth. The muscle fibers felt like rubber. She would have eaten around the meat, but the sour cream, the lettuce, the cheese—it mostly just tasted cold. Only the steak, unpleasant as it was, had any real flavor.

She grimaced. Laurentius had said something back at the library, something about Hiro's groupies craving rare meat for a few weeks. Was real food going to be this unpleasant until she rode the infection out?

Well. Not all real food was unpleasant. She could think of one thing that could make her mouth water. That thick, marbled, raw filet at Falls Quad Café the other day. And the faint sheen of red against the white butcher paper.

Lucy put her half-eaten meal back in the bag and withdrew her phone. That was enough eating for the night. It was time to turn her attention to something marginally more pleasant: the article Hiro had shared that was currently waiting in her inbox.

The Mountain Villa Massacre:
The Strange Case of the Volkov Family.

Do you like true crime?

If so, you're not alone. Open your podcast app, and you'll find dozens of murders and mysteries awaiting you, from polished prestige media outlets and wide-eyed amateurs alike. You might be forgiven for assuming this boom is a recent development. But long before there were podcasts, humanity was captivated by the macabre. In the Christmas season of 1916, less than one year before the Bolsheviks would change the future of Russia forever, one such case captivated Russia's upper class.

The story is this: A few days after Christmas, 1916, the corpses of the Volkov family were discovered in their winter home. The father, Andrei. The mother, Anna. The daughter, Sofiya. The eldest son, Alexei. Their injuries, of course, were strangely minimal, given the condition of their bodies. They lay neatly and calmly at the nearly bloodless scene. If not for the two small punctures at their necks, they would not have looked injured at all.

It was a fascination for the aristocracy, for a while. The Volkovs had a profile just high enough to cause panic. But what fascinated everyone most was the missing son, Ivan. He had been twenty-five years old, fit and strong, a loyal advocate for his father and brother. No one wanted to believe he had done it. Though if he hadn't, where had he gone?

But the case never entered the annals of history's great unsolved mysteries. In November 1917, the Bolshevik Revolution blanketed the aristocracy in fresh blood. No one remembered the Volkovs by the time everything was scrubbed clean. And Ivan never returned to remind them.

Lucy closed the tab. So perhaps a vampire had come to the Volkovs' mountain villa that night, had turned Vanya and killed the rest. Or maybe Vanya had already been turned elsewhere. Perhaps he was the stranger in the villa, making sure none of his family would outlive him.

And yet the people who had known Ivan Volkov didn't want

to believe he'd done it. Maybe the vampire wasn't anything like the man. Maybe in life, Vanya really had been the loyal brother and son everyone thought he was. Or maybe he'd never been that man at all. He died young and handsome. People never look at young and handsome men and correctly imagine what they can do.

"All right. Fifteen minutes until sunset, if you want to get set up over here," Mila said. "You really don't have to do this. I'll be up all night watching you. I won't let you go anywhere."

Lucy set her phone down and decided not to say anything about the article for now. She wasn't sure if she had gained any new information, really—just more questions.

"I trust you," she said. "But I want you to be able to, like... blink. Or get a glass of water. And I'll sleep better if I know I'm not about to climb out a window."

Mila looked supremely unconvinced, but she gestured for Lucy to come over to the bed. "Okay. But if you ask to be untied for any reason, I'm going to untie you. I'm not running a Chamber of Torment in here."

Lucy laughed, and lay down. "As long as you keep an eye on me."

"Oh, I will. Fool me once, et cetera." Mila bent over her, pulling the cuffs of Lucy's pajama shirt over her wrists. As Lucy strained to get a look at what she was doing, Mila said, "I don't want to tie these over your bare skin. Let me know if I've got your arms too far back, here."

Lucy held still and let her work. Maybe Mila would be a fast learner at the whole Chamber of Torment thing. Her grip was smooth and no-nonsense as she gently moved Lucy's right arm into position.

"You know . . ." Mila's face bent mostly out of Lucy's field of vision as she slipped the red tie around her wrist. "I wouldn't have expected you to be so gung-ho about this. Especially just after telling me to be nicer to you."

Lucy grinned as she closed her eyes. She was making herself dizzy trying to watch. "I try to hype myself up every time I have to do something unpleasant. Apparently it comes off as a little intense. When my grandmother went into hospice care, I had to learn all the emergency stuff to do if no one was there—how to get her into her wheelchair, change her catheter, all that. I had this friend who got *so* upset when I was telling her about it. She thought I wasn't taking it seriously."

Mila let out a short, unimpressed noise. "It was *your* dying grandmother. What did it matter to her how seriously you were taking it?"

"Things could get a little dark at home," Lucy said. "So sometimes the things I talked about could get a little dark, too. Not everyone wanted to go there. *I* didn't always want to go there. But then they'd see me getting out, having fun, and they couldn't quite understand that, either. It was how I balanced the pressure. Fake it till you make it and all that. I guess it looked a little flippant, though, if you didn't know where it was coming from."

A soft, satiny knot closed around Lucy's right wrist. Despite

Mila's worries, it didn't pinch. It was secure, but not tight.

"They were your friends," Mila finally said. "It should have been obvious that you were just trying to stay afloat."

"Well," Lucy said as Mila moved to the other side of the bed. "I was an idiot teenager. Maybe I didn't make it that obvious that I was struggling."

"Maybe not," Mila said as she pulled another tie around Lucy's left wrist. "But if you explained it then anything like you're explaining it to me now, she should have been able to tell. I've never heard anyone sound so solemn about having fun."

Lucy sat up just enough that it jolted the right bedpost. "What do you mean by that?"

"I mean that I've known you for less than a week, and you're talking about going to The Club like you were drafted for war," Mila said. "If I were your friend, I think I'd be able to hear that in your voice."

"I—'drafted'?" Lucy said. "It wasn't like that."

"I am so sorry to break this to you," Mila said. "You sound like my great-grandpa reminiscing about the shores of Normandy."

Lucy might have swatted at Mila's arm, if she had the free hands to do so. Mila laughed, as if she'd seen the urge flitting across Lucy's face. "It wasn't like I was miserable," she said. "I just never knew how long my family was going to need me. So I wanted to experience however much I was allowed to experience."

Mila tied off the left knot. "And then you got to leave home after all?"

"And then I got to leave home after all," Lucy echoed. And there she was, sporting two puncture marks on her neck and tied to an almost-stranger's bed.

Mila moved Lucy's arm in the binding, as if testing that she had enough slack, and Lucy blinked heavily. "What time is it?"

"A little after eight," Mila said.

"Hah," Lucy said. She was starting to feel it again, that bleeding-out kind of tired. "Going to sleep at eight p.m. was not really what I pictured from my college life."

"You got maybe two or three hours last night," Mila said. "And who knows how much the night before. Go to sleep."

Lucy blinked. Her eyes were slow to open again. "You'll wake me up if something seems wrong?"

"Trust me. If anything happens, you will be getting woken up." Mila was quiet long enough that Lucy had started to drift off by the time she spoke again. "Is he out there?"

"Hmm?" Lucy's eyes didn't quite open that time.

"You said that when you met the library vampires, it was like you could feel them. Is it like that for him?"

Lucy tipped her head back. The box spring was so stiff under her, even with a memory foam pallet nestled under the fitted sheet. But she was so powerfully exhausted, it felt as if every breath sank her deeper and deeper down.

She couldn't know for sure if there was a feeling. She had been in Vanya's company three times now, and she remembered almost none of it. It probably didn't feel the same. Laurentius and Hiro's presence felt like history, like the mountains themselves, but Vanya was so much younger.

However, there was a different kind of weight she'd come to know over the past few days. That unmistakable feeling of attention. Like someone's eyes when you cross a room. Since the bite, that feeling hadn't stopped.

"I don't know," Lucy finally said. "I think I feel him all the time."

She wasn't sure if Mila had anything else to say to that. Lucy thought she heard her mumble something, after a long period of silence. But by then, Lucy was already nearly asleep.

Thirteen

Lucy was awake, but she didn't want to be. It was still dark behind her eyelids, she miraculously didn't need to pee that badly, and she was tired enough that the creaky extra-long twin felt deliriously comfortable underneath her. She could be asleep again in moments, if she let herself. If she opened her eyes, she risked breaking the spell.

She allowed herself the small luxury of shifting on the pillow.

Both of her arms went along with her, with no resistance.

She lurched upright. She wasn't only untied—the restraints were gone altogether. "Mila," she said, her tongue thick. "Why did you—"

But when she turned to the corner where Mila had been the night before, she found it empty. The same was true for the little table near the kitchenette, and the shitty overstuffed armchair by the window. It was dark in the dorm: The only lights came from outside, through the blinds, from the lampposts and the blue glow of the emergency phone a few feet away.

And Mila wasn't there.

Lucy's feet shook a little as she swung them around to the floor. Maybe she was dreaming again. Her body didn't hurt the way it had when she'd crawled into bed that night. She didn't hear the sounds of footsteps in the room next door, or voices and muffled music in the hallways. But if it was a dream, it was a vivid one. The room wasn't fuzzy the way the forest had been in Athena's guided meditation. The details weren't flattened. It didn't feel as if she'd gone anywhere. It was just that everything was quiet, and she was alone.

A shadow passed across the blinds. For a moment, the blue emergency phone light had been occluded. Blocked by something with shoulders, a torso, a head.

She peeled two of the blinds apart, but barely. Just enough to look.

The light from the phone was visible. The shape of it wasn't. There was a viscous fog rolling into the quad courtyard, in thick, tangible coils. It moved like dry ice, blanketing as it spread. If she opened the window and reached down to the ground, she could scoop it up in handfuls.

But as quiet as it was, the night outside didn't feel watchful. Not watchful like she'd tried to describe to Mila in those moments before she fell asleep.

"Nope." Lucy shook her head as she released the blinds. The back-and-forth swish of her hair felt uncomfortably real against her chin. "Not tonight." It had to be a dream. The alternative was that Mila was gone, and something was moving outside. She slid back under the covers and yanked them up to her chin. She wasn't here. Or rather, she was in another version of "here," a real one, still tied to the bed under Mila's watchful eye. Maybe she just needed to be still long enough to let this dream end.

She waited for exhaustion to overcome her. But she was still wide awake when she heard the sound.

Click-click.

She sprang out of bed. The dorm had grown darker. Like a hole punched in the world.

But darkness was nothing to Lucy anymore. So, when she heard the *click-click* a second time, she saw exactly where it came from. She saw the slow, gentle turn of the doorknob leading to the hall.

It turned without resistance. It was unlocked.

Lucy's ankles nearly buckled as she scrambled to the other side of the room. She didn't have far to go. Just a few feet. But by the time she reached the door, it was already slightly wedged open.

She hit it with all her weight. She'd surprised whoever was coming—she felt the opposing force falter, then redouble. But her shaking hands had found their target, and she pressed the lock shut with her thumb, hard. She grabbed for the deadbolt next. Her fingers, slick with sweat, nearly fumbled it. The door rattled again, hard, as she snapped it closed. But it held. It bowed a little with the force of another push, maybe a shoulder driven into the wood. And then it wasn't pushed again.

"Who's there?" Lucy's voice was so guttural that it startled her.

She staggered back, and for a moment, no one answered her. Until someone called out, "A bit of a pathetic showing. Sorry to say."

Lucy's chest heaved as she struggled to catch her breath. That . . . was a very strange thing for someone to say after trying to break in. And it didn't quite sound like the vague impression of Vanya in her mind. It didn't sound like *Hold still.* But she knew the voice, nonetheless.

She raised herself onto her tiptoes to look through the peep hole.

Laurentius of Rome, the reference librarian, stared balefully back at her.

"Are you going to open the door?" he said. "Or are we going to talk like this?"

Another night, Lucy might have thought better of opening Mila's door to nature's perfect predator, even one she had conditionally decided to trust. But in her adrenaline-fueled anger, she would have opened the door to anyone. She would have let Dracula himself through if it gave her a better vantage point to yell at him.

"What the fuck," she rasped, as she wrenched the door open, "are you *doing* here?"

"Watching you lie in bed and wait to die, apparently." Laurentius moved into the room, delicately sidestepping her. "What was that pace? If I hadn't turned that knob one fraction at a time, you never would have kept me out."

"Not an answer," Lucy snapped. "Why were you trying to get in to begin with? And—how did you just walk in without an invitation?"

"Because none of this is real, of course," he said, with the enunciation of someone stating the obvious. "Everyone else has been in your head. Why shouldn't I be?"

She took several breaths, and reminded herself that throttling Laurentius of Rome would do absolutely nothing for her. He'd probably catch her in one hand, with ease. "Okay. Then maybe we can start with what you're doing in my head."

"It wasn't my idea," he said. And now that the rage-haze was clearing, that made sense. She'd known Hiro Minamoto for a cumulative five minutes, and she could still guess that this had him and his court whispers written all over it. "I didn't create the scenario, either. We used one of your memories as a base."

"My memory?" Lucy echoed. This was the second night she'd spent in Mila's dorm. She hadn't had a lot of time to make memories there.

"The situation, if not the setting, then," he said. When

Lucy's stare stayed blank, he added, "You were a teenager. Your mother was away for the evening, with your grandmother at the hospital. And you woke up in the night and remembered—"

"That I hadn't locked the door," Lucy realized out loud. *Of course.* She'd been in bed, mostly asleep, and she'd dreamed she heard someone walk into the apartment. It had started the same way, too. With the *click-click* of the turning knob.

"You think of that moment often, when you're feeling vulnerable," Laurentius said. "You thought of it just the other night, when you realized that your thoughts weren't entirely your own."

Lucy sank into one of Mila's kitchenette chairs. It felt very solid for something in her head. "You told me that you didn't know how to help me," she said slowly. "A few hours ago, you said that. And now your husband is giving you detailed reports of the goings-on in my head?"

"Don't mistake me. I still don't know how to help you," he said. "But Hiro thought it might help if you visualized the issue in a way you'd understand."

As Lucy looked up at him, she noticed, for the first time, how wide his pupils were in the dark. Hers must have looked the same to him. Nearly black. "The 'issue' being that Vanya is breaking into my mind?"

"To be a vampire is to constantly take inventory of what you control," Laurentius said. "You control your territory—or ideally you do, barring some ravenous young upstart moving in.

You control your hunger, whether you sate it with convenience or with violence. You control your mind, fortify its defenses against the rest of your kind, keep bad actors and curious busybodies from reading your thoughts. To be human is to control nothing. You make choices, here and there. You change your clothes and rearrange your furniture. But you spend most of your lives allowing things to happen.

"But," he said, biting down on the *t*. "Even if you're not a true vampire, perhaps you can still guard your own mind, to a degree. And whatever other skills you lack, what's easier than locking a door?"

Lucy leaned back against the hard chair, suddenly dizzy. "So if I visualize locking a door, I could lock him out of my head?"

"*Could* being the key word," he said. "And if you'd like this to have any chance of working, I'd suggest you be much quicker next time."

Lucy felt the chair back vanish behind her. She yelped as she fell, braced for impact, but she didn't hit the ground. She hit something nearly as unforgiving, though. Mila's extra-long twin mattress.

There was a *click-click* around the corner. And then the slow sound of scraping metal.

"Fuck!" Lucy jumped out of the bed, the rush of vertigo threatening to toss her off her feet. But she gained her bearings, and by the time she reached the door, she'd built enough speed that she felt real impact when she hit the wood. She could feel the pressure of Laurentius's push against the door, but this time, she was faster. She clicked the lock, flipped the deadbolt, and slumped forward to hold it shut.

She had a few seconds to catch her breath again. Then Laurentius's muffled voice called, "That was an improvement."

She took her sweet time opening the door. "You're an asshole, by the way."

"Yes, well." He stepped through the door once more. "I'd like to see you live thousands of years and remain chipper."

She settled back into the kitchen chair. Lucy wasn't exactly sure why this conversation had gotten so under her skin. Except, perhaps, that she'd never really liked people who were certain of everything. Even if those people were as old as the rise and fall of several civilizations. "Hiro doesn't want to leave, does he? That's why he's making you help me."

Lucy had meant it to antagonize him. But Laurentius looked thoughtful, if irritably so. "Getting involved may benefit me as well," he said.

"How so?" Lucy said.

"Because maybe he'll finally understand that it's hopeless," he said, "when he sees how this goes for you."

Lucy suppressed her shudder. It was a reminder not to forget what he was, no matter how relatively harmless she had determined him to be. She had lived a fraction of his life. Whether she died tomorrow or decades from now, it was not going to make a difference to him.

"I'm surprised it's not him here, then," she said. "Since he's the one who reads minds."

"He's better at explaining his own foolish plans, too," Laurentius said. "But he thought I could speak to something that he couldn't."

"Which is what?" Lucy said.

His mouth folded into a grim line. Somehow, it was the most human he'd looked thus far. "I spent my mortal life trying to grasp control where there was none," he said. "A long time ago, of course. But he thought I could—relate."

He paused, and didn't quite meet her eye. That rueful human grimace had faded, leaving his face smooth and empty. By the light of the moon, and by the blue glow of the emergency phone outside, his stillness made him look like something carved out of stone, or marble. He didn't look like something that had ever been living. Let alone something Lucy could relate to.

Then again. He probably looked at her and felt the same.

Laurentius raised his head. And all that smooth blankness in his face suddenly sharpened to a point. His gaze snapped, catlike, to the window. As if following movement.

"You should wake up now," he said, calmly. "You're not alone."

And then Lucy was flat on her back, tied to Mila's bed.

She blinked. This time, the room was as she had left it. The light was switched on in Mila's kitchenette, casting a low yellow glow in the room. When she turned her head, Mila herself was back in the corner, her eyes closed and head tilted against the wall. But Lucy could tell by her breathing that she wasn't fully asleep.

And that watchful feeling, fully absent from the dream, came rushing back. It felt closer than it had been when she'd fallen asleep. So close that it felt as if he was just outside.

She took a breath. Slowly, so as not to alert Mila that anything was wrong. Laurentius must have sensed him from inside the dream. But she'd felt Vanya's attention long enough that she noticed gradations to it now. It wasn't like the night before, when she'd felt him outside the window. She didn't hear the *click-click* of the doorknob, the sound of her mind being opened. He wasn't trying to call out, or get in. It was as if he just wanted to stand close enough to be known.

Once again, she remembered what Laurentius had said about the taste of a person's fear. Strong and sharp, tinged with vinegar and acid. Vanya's favorite. It was difficult, knowing that now, to see any of her small victories against Vanya as victories. If he didn't try to reach her tonight, it wasn't because they'd done anything right. It was because she was still being seasoned.

Motherfucker, she thought. She hoped he heard her. *I'll make you choke.*

Technically, Lucy had finally gotten some sleep. But it seemed hosting Laurentius of Rome in her mind hadn't been particularly restful. She was still exhausted. She knew she looked it, too: Mila had offered to watch over her a little longer, sans restraints, if she wanted to sleep in.

As kind as the offer was, Lucy declined it. For one, she wasn't sure how to explain why she was so tired in the first place, when she had just promised not to go back to the library vampires without Mila. Sure, she hadn't *meant* to break that promise when she went to sleep. But she hadn't tried very hard to wake up, either.

She would tell them what she found out, of course. She just needed to think hard about how to present that information. Laurentius had been right. It would be all too easy for Lucy to lose Athena and Mila's trust.

She adjusted her backpack as she swiped into the multimedia center, with Natalie on her heels. Lucy had finally gotten to spend the morning in one of her classes, though her Horror Literature course hadn't done much to get her mind off things. The only thing she'd written down from the lecture was *Unfinished business is a Western construct*. And, more relevantly, *Death is inevitable.*

She rounded the corner and slipped through the open door of Athena's studio. But even as Natalie closed the door behind them, Athena and Mila barely looked up. They were standing by the desk, heads bent over a piece of paper.

"What's that?" Natalie said.

"Oh no." Lucy's stomach dropped. "Is someone else missing?"

"Not yet," Athena said. Which was not the kind of denial that Lucy had been hoping to hear. "Come look at this. It was taped to the front door when Mila got here."

Lucy sidled alongside them and followed their gazes down to the kind of cheery, inexpertly designed flyer that littered every spare wall of the campus. There was nothing alarming, upon the first read, about the text on its own:

Looking for answers?

Well, we don't have them, either. (But let's find them together!)

Join our philosophy department info session and mixer this Wednesday, 3 p.m., Lower Alton Hall #105. Meet our majors and graduate students, have some pizza, and maybe get some answers to your burning questions (but then again, maybe not). See you there!

"I don't get it," Lucy said. "What am I looking at?"

"Oh, wait. Remember that fake identity Vanya used at the party, with Alicia?" Natalie said. "He was going by the name of that philosophy PhD student he killed on the cruise line."

So much had happened since they spoke to Alicia that Lucy had almost forgotten about Demeter Cruise Lines and Luke Thompson's smiling face on the In Memoriam page. But now that she thought about it, Alicia wasn't the only person who had mentioned a philosophy PhD student in the past few days. Whitney had, too.

"He could be using this Luke Thompson alias regularly," Athena said. "The library vampires told you that he's got protection from someone higher up, right? If that's true, he could have some kind of excuse to be on campus."

It sounded disturbingly possible. How much did Vanya need, after all, except for a little plausible deniability? With a student ID card and a good excuse, that would open more than enough doors for him. Maybe Luke Thompson had given Vanya more than a meal back on Demeter Cruise Lines. Maybe he'd given him an identity to assume. And a new hunting ground to call his own.

"I assume Lower Alton has a steam tunnel entrance?" Lucy said.

"Give the lady a prize," Mila said faintly.

"But the party is at three p.m.," Natalie said. "And Lower Alton's a pretty new building. Lots of windows."

"What better way to tell us we're not in control than to threaten us in the middle of the day?" Athena said. "He left Lucy alone last night, and now he invites us somewhere in the middle of the afternoon? He wants us to know that we can't predict him. And he's right, isn't he?"

Lucy could feel what Mila had spoken of yesterday: Athena's fear, in the room with them like a presence. *She hates that she'll never really know if every precaution she's taken is enough,* Mila had said. But looking at Athena now, Lucy couldn't help but feel like that wasn't it. Lucy would have recognized the fear of uncertainty. It was her mother's constant companion, after all.

This felt like the opposite. A fear that came from understanding. Because Athena knew Vanya better than anyone else alive. She *knew* that no precaution could truly be enough. The moment Vanya wanted this to be over, he would end it.

"I'll go," Mila said. "Maybe I can lure him out."

"The hell you will," Athena snapped. "This is a trap, Mila."

"Then we should see what happens when I set that trap off." It was the strongest disagreement Lucy had ever heard out of Mila, at least where Athena was concerned. "I'm sorry, boss. But he clearly knows we're trying to lure him in. If he's not going to let that happen, then I have to go to him."

The flinch was only visible in Athena's eyes. "Mila," she said. "You promised me no more of this."

"I know. And I really am sorry about that." Mila took a breath before she spoke again. "But I don't know how much longer we can stay in this holding pattern. I don't know how much longer—" The sentence ended in a vague gesture. But it was hard not to notice how carefully Mila avoided looking at Lucy.

Mila didn't know how much more Lucy could take. And Lucy couldn't help but think, with a rush of cold down her chest, that she was right to wonder.

“I’ll come with you,” Natalie said.

“Natalie—” Mila said.

“No, I’m going,” Natalie said. “I’m the one who invited that thing into my dorm in the first place. I’m sick of sitting around waiting to see which of us he’s going to hurt next.”

“Natalie.” Lucy was the one to say it this time. “It’s not your—”

“Babe,” Natalie said, “I love you to pieces, but if you say it’s not my fault one more time, I’ll bite you myself. I know it’s not my fault. And I know I’m not a junior archery champion. But I’ll bet you could use me for something. If Mila’s going, I’ll go, too.”

Lucy let out a breath. What she was about to say was not going to go over well with any of them. But if Mila and Natalie were going, she wasn’t going to sit in the studio and wait by the phone. “I’ll go with you.”

The uproar started almost instantly. Lucy raised her voice over them before the protests could gain steam. “You said it yourselves,” she said. “My role here is to be bait. So . . . I should go be bait, shouldn’t I?”

“Lucy.” Athena’s voice, always calm no matter how fast her heart was beating, had started to tremble. “I know the waiting is hard. Believe me, I know. But this isn’t the way.”

Her eyes fell back to the flyer, as if by scanning the cheery font one last time, they’d find something useful. But there was no more information they were going to find that would change anything, just like there wasn’t going to be an article about what happened after the Mountain Villa Massacre. No web search or book was going to be able to tell them what Vanya had done once his family was dead. What he planned to do now. What he hungered for.

This was no longer a hunt. It was a siege. He had surrounded them, and now he was trying to smoke them out. And if anyone could survive that siege, it was Athena. He was never going to bait her into leaving this fortress that she'd built. She could outlast him. She probably would, in the end.

That would never be true for Lucy. No matter how many doors she put between them. No matter how many times she practiced locking them. Sooner or later, she would walk out into the night.

"I'm sorry" was what she finally said. "But I'm tired of waiting, too."

TRANSCRIPT OF ROLLINS UNIVERSITY STUDENT RADIO STATION WVBS ("PALLAS RADIO")

Broadcast number: 62

CALLER #6: I . . . Sorry. [laughter] I don't know why I'm so nervous.

PALLAS (HOST): Take your time. We're in no rush.

[Pause.]

CALLER #6: It's just that . . . the v—the friend with the cold hands. You said he had light hair. Blue eyes. Average height. Right?

PALLAS: Yes, that's correct.

CALLER #6: By average . . . How tall is that exactly? Like, five foot eight? Five foot nine?

PALLAS: I—don't think I could say. Caller number six, are you calling to report a sighting?

CALLER #6: Oh! [laughter] Oh my God, sorry. Nothing like that. I'm just like, you know. I'm a tall girlie, so I didn't want it to be awkward for him to reach my neck. But people were shorter back in his time, right? I'll make it work.

[A longer pause.]

PALLAS: Caller number six, you should know that I have an immediate hang-up policy for prank calls.

CALLER #6: Who said this is a prank? I'm shooting my shot here. [raising her voice] Uh, hey, Rollins vampire? Do you listen to this show? If you're into *consensual* biting, you can find me at—

[CALLER #6's line cuts out. Rustling noises. Then a long exhalation.]

PALLAS: Well, Rollins. You'll recall that I told you that we create this show together, you and I. Whether you're a caller or a listener, this show is whatever we need it to be, from hour to hour. I didn't set out to put limitations on that. But to be fair, I didn't think that I needed to.

That said. On the off chance that tonight's call was in earnest, I hope you'll allow me a caveat. Pallas Radio is for the nocturnal among us. That much will always be true.

But if you're looking to become a creature of the night yourself? With all the respect in my heart: Do that shit on your own time.

Fourteen

For a clandestine mission, the setup was relatively low-tech. Athena would call Lucy. Lucy would keep a single earbud nestled in her ear. And the call would remain open the entire time so that Athena could listen in. Ostensibly so that she'd know if they needed help. Though, of course, if they needed help, who was there for Athena to call?

Athena looked miserable. Miserable that she would be stuck at the studio, miserable that they hadn't listened to her, probably miserable wondering if this would be the last time she saw any of them. She apologized that she wasn't going with them, though to Lucy, that was a given from the start. The last thing she wanted was to put Athena in Vanya's reach.

Well. Maybe putting *herself* within Vanya's reach was the last thing. But next to Athena, Lucy had the dubious honor of being a secondary consideration. She was an appetizer. She wasn't the prize. And if Vanya wanted to use her to lure Athena out, maybe he had some slight use for her alive.

They said goodbye to Athena, and started the call. "I'm sorry," Athena said again as she saw them out the door.

"You can avenge us if we all get eaten," Natalie said.

"Don't joke," Athena said.

"Who's joking?" Natalie said. "I'm contingency-planning."

Mila was the last out the door. And watching her, Lucy really felt the limitations of her new senses. She could feel the tension in Mila's jaw, in her shoulders. She could hear her heartbeat, nearly as quick as Athena's now. She could read feelings, or at least, she could read how they manifested themselves physically. But she wasn't Hiro, and she definitely wasn't Vanya. The thoughts behind those heartbeats were as unreadable as they'd always been.

"Don't worry," Mila finally said.

Athena attempted a smile then. "Too late."

She hovered by the door as they started down the hill to lower campus. When Lucy glanced back, she was still there, as if she were watching a doomed voyage depart from the dock.

Lucy met Natalie's eyes. They didn't say anything, not with Athena on the phone in Lucy's ear. But they exchanged uneasy grimaces.

Mila adjusted her bow's carry bag across her shoulders. Natalie looked relieved to find something else to occupy her attention. "No quiver?" she said. "Oh—are you going to decapitate him with the bowstring or something?"

It was enough to jar Mila out of her silent misery. "How strong do you think bowstrings are, exactly?"

"How can I know when I haven't seen you in action yet?" Natalie said.

It actually jarred a laugh out of Mila. "The quiver would be kind of conspicuous at a department mixer," she said. "But I always keep an arrow or two in the bow's bag in case of emergencies."

Lucy surveyed the bag. It did look pretty unassuming; she doubted any present or future philosophers would notice that one of the attendees was toting a deadly weapon around the drinks table. Except perhaps one. If Vanya had spent all these years watching Athena, she doubted that Mila had gone unnoticed.

As they neared the building, Mila said, "All right." And with just those words, she was the hunter again. "Natalie—when we get in, I want you to stay by the door."

"Hell no," Natalie said. "I came here to help."

"And you *can* help if one of us gets in trouble," Mila said. "Lucy will need to be in the middle of things to try to lure him out. I'll need to stay by Lucy, but not too close. So if something goes wrong, I want you near the sunlight where he can't get you. If anything happens to us, get back to Athena as fast as you can."

Natalie looked dubious but didn't argue. "What about the other students? If things go wrong, should I try to get everyone out?"

"I don't think he'll risk a scene," Lucy said. As strong as Vanya was, he didn't chase groups. He got people alone.

Which meant even he was conscious of being outnumbered.

"But by all means," Mila said, "if you see blood, pull the fire alarm."

Natalie shrugged blithely. "That's generally my philosophy anyway."

Despite the obvious wear and tear on the walls and fixtures, Lower Alton was a bright, airy space, full of sunlight and floor-to-ceiling windows. There was a door leading straight into room number 105 from the outside, and it was not hard to spot the philosophy majors, clustered up ahead around some pizza. This was a decidedly medium-sized event, taking up less than half of the atrium ahead. The scene couldn't have been further from the dark neon crush of Natalie's party. It wasn't a group large enough to hide anyone, let alone Vanya.

Even so. Standing a ways back from the other students, Lucy couldn't help but think of Natalie's kitchen, the party behind her and the turned back of Ivan Volkov ahead. She hadn't been expecting him then. She was expecting him now.

"I'll be here," Natalie said under her breath.

Lucy attempted a smile. "We'll be back, hopefully." And then she fell into step with Mila, and left Natalie behind.

Mila leaned in as they approached the table. "Let's chat with them for a bit," she said. "Get the lay of the land. Make sure to keep me in your sight. And this probably goes without saying, but don't get anywhere near the basement stairs."

Mila had been right. That went without saying. "Oh, hey,"

Lucy muttered, as they passed the cheese and fruit table. "Garlic crostini."

"Pocket one to throw at him," Mila said. "You never know."

They fell silent as a girl with a blazer and a crisp smile spotted them coming. She hurried over to shake hands, like they were at some kind of business meeting. "Come on in, grab some pizza," she said. "Ah, you two don't look like first-years—are you thinking of changing your major? Or are you prospective minors?"

"She's a first-year, actually," Mila said, as smooth as ever. "I'm just along for the ride."

Lucy felt a little pang, looking into Blazer Girl's bright, enthusiastic face. It hadn't been that long ago that Lucy would have happily listened to her talk about her hyperspecialized thesis or self-designed major. The question of Lucy's future major had seemed so overwhelming, just a few days ago. It would have been nice if that were still her biggest problem.

"I was talking to one of your grad students the other day, actually. He got me really interested in the program," Lucy said. "Do you know Luke Thompson? He said he'd be here."

"Whoa," said a curly-haired man over Blazer Girl's shoulder. He looked older than her, maybe grad-student age himself. "You actually saw Luke? Like, in the flesh? He's been in his dissertation cave for so long, I was kind of worried that he died in there."

"Oh!" Lucy said, as if her stomach hadn't just crawled into her throat. "Do you know him?"

"Only a bit," the man said. "He started his PhD at a smaller university that shuttered its program, and one of his advisors got him transferred here. Super nice guy. But by the time he got here he was already done with coursework, so we don't get to see him much."

Lucy carefully avoided Mila's eye. Athena had been right. Vanya did have an identity here—one he had designed well. A graduate student in the midst of his dissertation: Who would notice if he kept odd hours, or didn't socialize? What student would second-guess him if he reached out, hoping to collaborate? Lucy thought of Whitney, of all the weird, passionate people of Rollins University, and felt sick. She had to protect them. She had to try, anyway.

But what Blazer Girl said next knocked every other thought out of Lucy's head. "Isn't he coming today?"

"Is he?" Lucy said. It was a miracle she got the words out of her mouth without throwing up. "I was really hoping I could talk to him again."

"I mean, I don't know if he's here *now*," Blazer Girl said. "But he definitely registered for the event. I printed a name tag for him."

"If you're talking about Luke, he's definitely here." Another girl leaned over. "I saw him in the seminar room earlier. Scared the hell out of me, actually! I didn't hear him come in at all."

Somehow, Lucy summoned a polite smile. "I'll check there for him, then," she heard herself say. "Thank you so much."

"We'll be here if you have any other questions," Blazer

Girl said. And then she turned back to a clutch of impossibly young-looking undergrads, leaving Lucy and Mila facing the door her classmate had indicated, in the corner of the room.

Lucy took a step closer to the seminar room. It looked dark and still. Like no one was in there at all. "I'll be right back," she said faintly over her shoulder, in case any of the others could still hear them. "I just need to make a quick call."

"Do you want me to go with you?" Mila said.

More than anything. But good bait didn't bring company. "No," Lucy said. "I should only be a minute." She hoped she'd only be a minute, anyway.

As she stepped away from the crowd, the sound of breathing in her ear startled her. She'd almost forgotten that Athena was listening in. "Lucy?" she asked.

"Still here," Lucy whispered. *For now.*

She drew closer to the dark seminar room. She could feel Mila behind her, trying to stay close but far enough away. The way they were moving was all wrong, she thought. Predators cornered prey, not the other way around. But there weren't many examples in nature of what they were trying to do, were there? Survival so often depended on evasion. Being poisonous, or being hidden, or being able to run.

Unfortunately, Lucy had already decided that she was sick of evading. And steps from the seminar room door, there wasn't anywhere else to go.

She crossed the threshold. And there she found herself standing at the mouth of an empty room. There were a few jackets and bags scattered around, probably dropped here by students at the event. But as always, she could see very clearly in the dark. There were no signs of life ahead. Or undeath, for that matter.

She turned back to the atrium. Mila, dropping all pretense, crossed the room to meet her. "He's not in there," Lucy said.

Mila exhaled through her teeth. "How would he have gotten in and out? This room is wall-to-wall west-facing windows. Do you feel him here?"

"No more so than usual," Lucy muttered. The heaviness of his attention was there, but it felt like it had the night before: just close enough to raise the hair on her arms. He was somewhere nearby, but he wasn't in the room with them. "And I haven't heard—"

She faltered. She'd almost forgotten that in all the chaos of the day, she hadn't told anyone about Laurentius yet, about the *click-click* of the doorknob turning.

"Heard what?" Mila asked.

Lucy shook her head. She did need to tell them. But she needed to tell them later. "Maybe he's deeper in the building."

"I'll check the hall," Mila said. "Stay here in the light."

"Neither of you should be leaving the light," said Athena's voice in Lucy's ear.

"You shouldn't go alone," Lucy said. "I'll come with you."

"What did I just say?" Athena said. "Lucy, I don't like this. Tell Mila you need to withdraw."

Athena's tinny voice was apparently audible to Mila, too.

"Tell her we're not withdrawing yet," Mila said. "I won't be gone long. I just want to take a look around."

Lucy winced. This was rapidly becoming overwhelming. To Athena, she said, "We're okay. We're just figuring out what to do." Then, to Mila, she said, "If you don't want to take me, take Natalie. Just because I'm the one he's after doesn't mean he hasn't recognized you as a thr—"

Click-click.

The sound of the turning knob came from just over Lucy's shoulder. She started to rush toward it before she'd fully recognized what it was. And before she could do anything—visualize the door, press the lock, slide the deadbolt—there came another sound. A pop, then a creak. Something opening.

In the pin drop of a moment that followed, Lucy had just enough time to lock eyes with Mila. What an impossible thing they were all asking of her. To expect her to juggle both this creature she would have to kill, and this near-stranger she had to try to keep alive. It was so much to ask of this girl who looked so calm and in control that Lucy kept forgetting she was a regular person, too. Lucy wished she'd gotten to apologize for that.

But then nothing happened. The sun kept shining through the windows. The red voice didn't flood her mind. She still felt Vanya's presence, but at a distance. Nothing had changed. She was still in control.

"What?" Mila said.

"I don't know." Lucy turned in one direction, then the

other. Where had that come from? It couldn't have been a normal door. It was too loud. "I thought—"

It wasn't until Lucy's gaze landed at the front of the atrium, where they'd entered, that she saw what was missing.

Natalie wasn't where they'd left her.

"Mila." The name came out like a punch in the stomach. "Where's Natalie?"

It was horrible, hearing the blood drain from Mila's face. "She was just there," Mila said. "Wasn't she?"

"Lucy," said Athena in her ear. "What's wrong with Natalie?"

"Just a minute," Lucy said. Then, to Mila, she said, "The hall." Natalie wasn't in the crowd, and she wouldn't have just left. That meant there was only one place she could have gone.

Mila nodded tightly, and reaching down, she took Lucy's hand. Athena was still in Lucy's ear, still asking what was happening, but Lucy didn't have answers for her yet. They passed by the edge of the crowd, heard a snatch of conversation. And then that overrode everything else.

"—had a really weird moment setting up earlier," someone was saying. "I thought I saw *Addison Greene*."

"Well, that's impossible, right?" another voice said.

"Yeah," said the first voice. "Probably just someone who looked like her. That was so weird, though. I haven't thought of her in ages. . . ."

It wasn't clear to Lucy who broke into a run first: her or Mila. But Mila, with her long strides, pulled ahead fast. If not for their linked hands, she would have left Lucy far behind her.

They stumbled through the side door together, into a narrow, harshly lit corridor. Most of the sunlight was safely contained in room number 105: There was one window in the hall, somewhere behind them, but everything else was fluorescents. They'd left the crowd fully behind. The only person with them in the hall was the figure at the opposite end, facing a pair of double doors.

"Natalie!" Lucy said. But Natalie's attention remained ahead, leaving only her side profile visible. Her face was calm and slack. The one blue eye Lucy could see was flat and dull, like an old penny.

With a smooth, steady hand, she opened the door. And two sets of hands tugged her into the darkness.

Somehow, Lucy outpaced Mila to the end of the hall. It wasn't something she thought she would have been able to do. But she was the first one to Natalie, the first to throw both arms around her shoulders. The opposing force from the basement pulled hard, like a wave being sucked back from the shore, and for a terrifying moment, Lucy's weak grip was the only thing keeping Natalie on her feet. Then she felt the weight of Mila reaching them. One arm locked around Lucy's waist, the other gripped for Natalie.

"Lucy?" Athena's voice was high-pitched in her ear. "What's going on?" But even if Lucy had had the breath to answer, she didn't know. She didn't know until she found the strength to raise her head.

It was only then, with nowhere to look but forward, that she saw the three sets of eyes gleaming in the dark. The first was familiar to Lucy, even though she'd had just a handful of days to get used to it: Whitney, wrapped around Natalie's left forearm. Natalie's right arm was in the grip of a taller girl, with pale green eyes and sleek auburn-red hair. She had a calm, closed-lipped smile on her face, like she was looking out upon a beautiful piece of scenery. It was Addison Greene.

The third girl wasn't smiling. She wasn't holding on to Natalie, but she was fully focused on her, as if she didn't see Mila and Lucy at all.

Sadie Grainger carefully brushed aside Natalie's hair as she leaned in. "It's all right, Natalie," she whispered. "That was just the wind. Let's keep walking."

"Lucy!" Athena said. "Answer me!"

Lucy couldn't. She couldn't even find enough breath to call Natalie's name. It was all she could do to hold on, but even then, she knew Mila must have been doing most of the work to hold them both down. But Mila couldn't hold them down *and* reach her bow.

Lucy could hear the strain in Mila's muscles, the tremor of bones as she started to shake. All of the weaknesses, none of the strengths. She could hear Mila's strength flagging, but she couldn't do a fucking thing about it.

"It's all right, Luce," Natalie said tonelessly. Her body was so relaxed in Lucy's grip. So completely free of resistance.

Without Lucy and Mila's combined weight, she would have been gone. "They're going to help you. We just need to go downstairs."

Addison still had that beatific smile across her face as she regarded the scene. She showed none of the strain Lucy could hear from Mila. She looked serene. Like she was waiting for something wonderful.

Sadie's expression betrayed nothing. Even as she whispered, nonstop, into Natalie's ear, her eye was now on Lucy, as if waiting to see how she would react.

And something rose up in Lucy in response. The thrill of absolute familiarity. *This is your sister*, the red voice told her. *Why are you fighting your sister?*

Lucy bit down on her tongue. It was the only thing she could think to do, with her hands full. If anyone was her sister here, it was Natalie. She wasn't letting go.

"Is he there?" Athena sounded ragged. "Is he with you right now?"

Then Lucy heard the tremor of muscles. Someone else was shaking—someone who wasn't Mila. And looking at the vampires, it wasn't hard to guess who. Whitney was the only one visibly straining. There were lines of exertion etched into her face. Now that Lucy was focused on her, she could feel that the pull on Whitney's side was weaker than the pull on Addison's. It was probably the only reason they hadn't lost their grip on Natalie already.

I'm supposed to save my appetite, Whitney had said, back at the dorm. She said there was going to be a feast when they had Athena. They didn't have Athena yet.

The weakness in her grip—was it hunger?

Lucy sized up her plan of action fast. Whitney was on Natalie's left, which meant that Lucy would need to direct her to the right, outside her immediate grip. It would happen quickly. Lucy remembered exactly how fast Whitney could move when she was closing in on a meal.

"Mila," Lucy managed. "Hold on as hard as you can."

She didn't give Mila time to answer. But she didn't doubt that she'd been heard. If there was one thing she knew Mila could do, it was react with just a second's notice.

Lucy shifted her grip to free one of her arms. And then she dug her nails into Natalie's arm until she smelled blood.

The pressure vanished from Whitney's side. Whitney had let go, had realized her path to Natalie's blood wasn't clear—she tried to dart around, behind her sisters.

Addison's saintlike smile melted off her face, and she grabbed Whitney by the back of the neck like she was a kitten. "Whitney," she snapped. "Together, or not at al—"

Whitney and Addison's combined strength was too much. But Lucy and Mila against one distracted half of Addison's strength was just enough. One more wrench with all they had, and they tore Natalie out of Addison's grip. Lucy nearly fell back under Natalie's deadweight before she realized: Mila was no longer helping her. Mila had ripped the bag off her back, unzipping it in one downward strike.

But however fast Mila was, the vampires were still faster. One look at the curve of the bow, and they scattered like moths into the dark of the basement. Mila started after them.

"No," Lucy rasped.

Mila barely looked at her. "They're getting away," she said.

"They could come back!" Lucy said. She no longer cared what they came here for. Natalie had gone frighteningly limp in her grip. "Mila, please. Help me get her into the light."

Mila's attention never fully left the door. But she did return to Lucy, then, did help her drag Natalie to the opposite end of the hall. They didn't stop until Natalie lay directly under the single pathetic sunbeam within their reach.

"Natalie," Lucy said as she dropped to her knees again. "Natalie, can you hear me?"

Natalie's blank stare was fixed on the ceiling. If not for the sleeplike cadence of her breaths, she would have looked dead, lying there. The only thing that moved in response to Lucy's voice was a single bead of blood that slipped down her arm.

Lucy anxiously rubbed it dry. The nauseating, mouth-watering smell of it crested in the air. "I'm sorry," she mumbled. "I hurt you, I'm sorry." She was supposed to be the bait. She was supposed to be hurt, if anyone. Natalie wasn't the sort of person these things were supposed to touch. Lucy had never really considered that anything would reach her. Naive, selfish, self-serving—Lucy should have told her from the start not to get involved, she should have screamed it if that's what it—

"Lucy!" Athena's voice was loud enough to hurt. "Please answer me!"

Not now was what Lucy had meant to say. Or *One minute*, or *Let me think*, or any of the other proto-sentences that had bubbled up as she clutched at her ear in pain. But what came out of her mouth wasn't words. It was something much deeper in her throat than that. It was a roll of low, guttural thunder. A growl.

Everything froze. Lucy, Mila, and the breaths from the other end of the line.

And then Natalie sat half upright and gasped for air.

"Natalie." Lucy scrambled to get her hands on Natalie's shoulders for support. She was staring straight ahead, her eyes focused now, her pupils narrowed to pinpricks. "Can you hear me?"

"Yeah. Yeah." Something like a laugh escaped Natalie as she nodded. "What was I . . ."

"Can you stand?" When Lucy looked back to Mila, her face was shuttered. "We need to leave."

"Hah. Yeah." She wiped at her face, but not before Lucy saw a tear slip out of each eye. "Don't have to tell me twice."

Lucy clambered to her feet to help Mila lift, then ducked under one of Natalie's arms to support her weight. Natalie walked with them easily enough, though she was stiff in their grip, as if the last thing she wanted right then was either of them touching her. Lucy could still hear Athena, breathing on the other end of the line. But for the time being, she was silent, too.

Lucy had never been so grateful for the spike of pain the sunlight brought. And as she and Mila maneuvered Natalie into it, Lucy turned to shut the door.

For just a moment, as the door's window caught the late-afternoon glare, it looked like a lone figure was watching them from the stairwell entrance. Where they'd been just moments ago.

But by the time the door closed, there was no one there.

Fifteen

"Do you need anything else?" Lucy knew that she was hovering. She also knew that it was only making everyone feel worse. Natalie had managed to wrestle a smile back onto her face, but the longer Lucy stood there in the recording studio doorway, the more strained it looked. "I probably have time to make another trip to your dorm."

"No, no. Don't you dare. It'll be dark soon." Natalie squeezed her elbow—such a sweet, automatic Natalie gesture that it twisted the knife deeper. Even now, she was trying to comfort Lucy. "Athena's got enough bedding here for me, and I can always pick up some more stuff if I want to stay longer."

How was Natalie so good at this? All this time, she'd been there for Lucy like it was nothing. It was horribly apparent now that that wasn't such an easy thing to do. Mila had steered them all back to the studio with ruthless efficiency. Athena had brewed the tea that was currently nestled in Natalie's shaking fingers. But all Lucy had been able to do was stand there and watch. It was all she had done since she got to Rollins.

Over Natalie's shoulder, Athena wasn't looking at them, but Lucy could tell she was listening nonetheless. She hadn't said much since they'd come back. A few hushed words of comfort to Natalie, a few equally quiet but much more businesslike words to Mila.

But there was no *I told you so*. There was no pointing out that they'd been impatient, and that it had nearly gotten them all killed. She was fully focused on her equipment for tonight.

If Lucy hadn't had a few days' worth of experience reading Athena's microexpressions, the look on her face would have seemed neutral. She did have that experience, though. She saw the wariness behind the placid exterior.

She touched the hollow of her own throat. Wariness was the least of what she deserved.

"Hey." Natalie set her mug down and wrapped her arms around Lucy. Her pulse pattered against the side of Lucy's neck. "I'll be okay. I just need some sleep and a good cry. But not too loud of a good cry, because I don't want tonight's callers to ask who that wailing woman behind Pallas is."

Lucy squeezed her tighter. "Call me if you can't sleep."

"Sure. But if you pick up, I'm going to be so mad." When Natalie pulled back, her eyes were wet. She laughed ruefully as she scrubbed at them. "Okay, shoo. Go get some rest."

A hand came to rest on Lucy's shoulder from behind. It was Mila, drawing her back into the hall. "I'll call you later to debrief," Mila said over Lucy's head.

Athena nodded as she straightened. Any wariness, or anger, or whatever else she was feeling slipped neatly behind her mask. “Be careful getting back.”

Once again, they started down the hill. This time to the dining hall—though Lucy wasn’t sure she’d ever felt less like eating in her life. They were nearly halfway there by the time Mila finally spoke.

“It’s not your fault,” she said.

“You’re only saying that because you think it’s your fault,” Lucy mumbled.

“Is it not?” Mila said. “Because I very clearly started it.”

“And we both agreed to go,” Lucy said. Her stomach felt sour just thinking about it. “But I knew what I was getting into. Natalie didn’t. Not really.”

“Don’t let her hear you say that,” Mila said.

“It’s the truth, isn’t it?” Lucy said. “She was the only one of us who hadn’t seen a vampire firsthand, until today.”

“Well, true,” Mila said. “But until I came face-to-face with your vampire roommate the other night, I’d never seen one up close, either. I’d never seen Vanya—still haven’t. I’ve just seen the chaos he leaves in his wake. So I get Natalie. Once you see what he does to people, it’s hard to let it go.”

Lucy folded her arms tight as she walked, as if to hold herself in place. “What did Athena mean earlier, by the way? When she said that ‘you promised’?”

“Oh, nothing that complicated. I just promised not to do shit like this anymore.” She laughed darkly. “I’m such a hypocrite, right? Telling you not to worry her when historically, I'm the biggest offender. I tried to become more patient when I met her. I used to tell her all the time that I didn't know if I could. That I failed the marshmallow test as a kid, twice. And then she would remind me that the marshmallow test was a sham and was not a predictor of adult success."

She chewed on her next words for a moment. "She did teach me caution eventually. I know that it saved my life. When I got here, the only strategy I had was to stick my neck out and see if that'd get his attention. If I hadn't called her show that night, maybe he would have taken me one of those nights, instead of Sadie or Addison. I never could have killed him on my own. He *relies* on people being alone. All I was really doing was serving myself up."

Lucy watched her carefully as they made the turn into the quad. "But you don't feel that way anymore."

"Feel what way?" Mila said.

"Like being cautious will keep us alive," Lucy said.

"Oh, I think it might keep *me* alive." As they reached a bit of uneven path, Mila reached for Lucy's hand to steady her. Lucy smiled to herself as she took it. Chivalry wasn't dead after all. "I just don't know if it'll keep you alive."

Lucy had the impulse to squeeze Mila's hand before letting go. She ignored it. "Because we don't know how long I can hold out?"

Mila didn't answer that. Probably because she didn't need to, not out loud. They both knew that she was thinking of Jon.

Even if they could wait Vanya out until they all graduated, the fact was that Jon had died from the infection alone. Which meant that there was something they didn't understand about how it worked.

Mila was right. This was a race between Vanya and his bite as to which would kill her first. There was no third competitor.

So there wasn't anything reassuring she could say in this particular moment. But at the very least, they could be miserable together. "It's kinda humbling," Lucy said dryly. "I've probably only lasted this long because I'm not his first priority."

"Hah," Mila said. "Don't take it personally. I'm sure he wouldn't remember who I am, or Jon. And I'm sure he barely noticed Natalie today. There's only one person who's ever had his interest."

They were quiet for a while. It wasn't until they were close to the dining halls that Mila turned back to her. "Hey, wait," she said. "What did *you* mean earlier, when you said you couldn't 'hear' Vanya?"

Ah, Lucy thought, *shit.* In all the chaos, she still hadn't said anything. "If I tell you," she said, "will you promise not to react until I'm done explaining?"

With a now-familiar sharpness, Mila gestured for them to step aside to a nearby bench. Apparently they weren't eating until this conversation was done. "That will depend on what you're asking me not to react to."

Lucy winced. Fair enough. "Laurentius of Rome was in my head last night."

"Okay," Mila said. "I'm reacting."

"I didn't mean to go behind anyone's back," Lucy said. "I thought it was a dream at first, and by the time I realized it wasn't, he said what he was doing would help, and I figured I should probably hear him out. He was trying to teach me how to recognize when Vanya's entering my thoughts. I haven't had a chance to test it out yet, but back at Lower Alton, I think I heard the moment Sadie took control of Natalie."

Mila's brow furrowed. She looked angry, but Lucy didn't hear anger in her heartbeat. "What does it sound like?"

Lucy let out some of the breath she'd been reserving for a fight. "The sound of a hand on a doorknob," she said. "You know how sometimes you can hear right before someone turns it? That *click-click* as they take it in their hand."

"And what do you do, when you hear that?" Mila said.

"Well. Lock it," Lucy said. "Or imagine myself locking it, anyway."

Now Mila looked far more exhausted than angry. But her voice was still calm when she spoke. "All right," she said. "How about you let me be the one to explain to Athena how this happened? We don't want her thinking that the library vampires have corrupted you behind her back."

"Probably wise," Lucy said. Though now that she was thinking about it, she had an idea. "And while you're doing that—can you ask her if the two of us can go see them tomorrow?" At

Mila's arched eyebrows, she quickly added, "Those were the terms of the agreement, right? If I go, you go to keep an eye on me."

"Just what I want to bring to the boss after a day like this," Mila said dryly. "The terms of an agreement."

"I know she's not going to want to take more risks after today," Lucy said. "But you said it yourself: We need to take at least a few. And when it comes to risks, I think this is one of the smaller ones. I think she'd hear that. At least, she'd hear it from you."

Mila rubbed both hands over her face. Hard enough that it seemed, for a moment, like she was trying to erase herself directly from the conversation.

But when she dropped her hands, she looked resigned. "I know I said I'd do the talking," she said. "But I think you should throw in a bit of groveling when you see her tomorrow, too. For diplomacy's sake."

Lucy laughed. "All right," she said. "Deal."

No one came to Lucy that night. Not Laurentius, not Vanya. But it was not a restful night. Mila had gotten a call from her *other* boss, the building's Resident Director, just as she finished securing Lucy to the headboard. The call was to inform her that one of their Quincey Hall residents hadn't been seen or heard from in a few days, and her parents were getting concerned.

Mila had taken the call in the bathroom. It was probably easier to lie when she didn't have to look at the thrall she had tied to her bed. But even then, Lucy didn't know how she got through it. How could she pretend that they hadn't seen Whitney just hours ago, fighting her would-be sisters to taste a single drop of blood?

The call couldn't have lasted that long. But Mila was still in the bathroom by the time Lucy slipped into an uneasy sleep. She could hear Mila's muffled voice in the dream, somewhere at the end of a hallway that kept growing longer.

Lucy crawled into wakefulness a little after sunrise, feeling even worse than she had the night before. But she woke to a bit of good news, at least. When Mila saw that her eyes were open, she flashed a deeply subdued thumbs-up.

"Library vampires are a go," she said. So Lucy pried herself out of bed and prepared for yet another day of trying to keep herself alive.

Lucy must have looked as rough as she felt, because as soon as they arrived at L. Roman's office on B2, Hiro bundled her into Laurentius's nice chair and furnished her with a hot cup of sencha tea. Lucy sleepily allowed it. She was so far beyond having too much pride to be fussed over.

"You poor thing," he crooned. "Just relax. Take a moment to catch your breath." He paused a moment before turning his sunny smile toward the other side of the room. "Can I get you something, too?"

Mila had positioned herself in a chair by the open door, her bow perched on her lap. She had once again left her quiver at home. Though in exchange, she'd fished one of her spare arrows from her bag to place onto the chair next to her.

"No thanks," Mila said. "Caffeine makes me jittery."

"Fair enough," Hiro said. "Wouldn't want *those* hands shaking."

Laurentius watched them with his usual withering eye. "If everyone is settled," he said, "then I suppose we should get to the point. You said you've come to practice?"

"I mean . . . I get what you showed me the other night," Lucy said. "Obviously I know how to lock a door. But maybe it would be good to try it a few more times. Just to make sure I'm fast enough."

Laurentius, as always, had a look like she was wasting his precious eternal life. Though now that they were meeting for the third time, Lucy was beginning to suspect that his face was just like that. Sitting next to him, she felt oddly at ease. His presence was comfortable in the same way that watching the river on a winter day was comfortable. There was something soothing about keeping company with something that *could* kill you but wouldn't.

"Close your eyes, then," Laurentius said. "Deep breaths. I can't enter your dreams this time, but maybe a relaxed state will do."

"You're going into her mind?" Mila said. Lucy didn't miss the shift in her voice.

"Mila," Lucy said. She hoped that she sounded comforting. "It's okay. If I need help, I'll tell you."

She closed her eyes. Even as the office slipped away from her, she could hear Mila, muttering on the other side of the room. "If you need help, you'd better scream at the top of your lungs."

Though she was awake this time, when she opened her eyes, the scenery was just as it was the last time Laurentius had entered her mind. She was lying on Mila's bed, unbound, in the blue-lit darkness of the dorm. When she sat up, Laurentius and Hiro were watching her from the little kitchenette table.

Lucy blinked into the dark. "I thought you were going to try to break in."

"Well, about that." Even in her mind, Hiro had somehow procured a pot of tea. "We actually thought you'd be better served by a bit of a breather."

Laurentius ran one pale finger around the edge of his mug. It was one from Mila's cupboard. A party favor from a family reunion. "You don't need any more practice. You understand exactly what you need to do. But your body and mind are both under tremendous stress. The infection is demanding all your resources."

Lucy bristled. *Now* Laurentius cared about her resources? He hadn't seemed to care that much when he'd cost her a night of sleep. "You think I can't manage it?"

"*Obviously* I think you can't manage it," Laurentius said. "You were never managing it."

"Lucy," Hiro said, "I'd say you were running on fumes, but I think you spent the fumes days ago. If you don't slow down, you'll end up like that poor sweet boy your friend back there came here to avenge."

"Don't get in her head," Lucy snapped.

"Frankly, I don't need to," Hiro said. "It's pouring out of her every time she looks at you. She thinks that this is how he must have looked before he died. And she's probably right."

"You need to stop attending classes, at the very least," Laurentius said. "They're an unnecessary drain on your energy."

"I'm not doing that," Lucy said. "If I survive this, I'm going to end up weeks behind."

"And if you don't survive this, you'll never attend classes again," Laurentius said. "Seems like simple math to me."

"I came here to go to *college,*" she shot back. "If I don't actually get to go to college, all of this would have been for nothing."

"That's a patently ridiculous thing to say," said Laurentius. "You came here because you wanted to live your life, correct? As of now, your classes are a risk to your survival. Why not cut them out?"

"Dear," Hiro said gently. "Perhaps this is one of those things we no longer understand. Obsession is a very human foible, isn't it?"

The word stopped Lucy short. "I'm not obsessed."

"Oh, child." Hiro's sympathy had shifted over into pity. Lucy had much preferred the sympathy. "Your leader has devoted three years to chasing Vanya's shadow. Your archer still half believes she should trade her life for the one she lost. And you've traveled all this way, far from your only family, because your own home felt like rot and decay to you. Even your friend, the one who got hurt yesterday, would risk her life for the kind of loyalty I doubt many of her peers would give her in turn. Obsession is the mortal's bread and butter. Even little Vanya still carries his grudges from life."

Lucy sat back on the bed. The fight, for the time being, had gone out of her. "You know what he was like when he was alive?"

"I only know what he told us, back when we were on better terms," Hiro said. "You read that article I sent you, didn't you?"

Lucy nodded. "He was a Russian aristocrat."

"And as he tells it, he was the darling of the old empire," Hiro said with a grand wave of a hand. "A prodigious fighter, a talented musician. A playmate of Tsar Nicholas's little daughters. And in the years leading up to his death, a loyal soldier to his honored father and brother." He took a sip of his tea. Lucy wondered if it tasted like anything. "Bullshit, of course. His thoughts are almost as open as a mortal man's. He was a second son. He's never gotten over being a second son. He died like a second son, cowering under a table and watching his parents beg for the life of his brother. And worse, it was some passing monster that brought his family to its end. If the Bolsheviks had gotten them months later—well, at least that would have been a story."

"He's not what I'd call a complicated specimen," Laurentius said. "People like Ivan Volkov fall into two molds. They enjoy their neglect, or they come to resent it. I don't think you have to guess which type our boy falls into. He was never given the keys to the kingdom, so he decided he had to create one."

"Three college students aren't a kingdom," Lucy said.

"You assume he's in a hurry," Laurentius said. "And if he gets his way, it won't be three for much longer."

Lucy's head swam, her mind full enough to burst. Hiro rose gracefully to his feet and crossed the room to squeeze her shoulder.

"I should go entertain your lovely bodyguard before she shoots us both," he said. "Why don't you and Laurentius stay and chat for a while longer?"

Apparently, it wasn't a difficult process, leaving someone's mind. In the space of a blink, Hiro was there, and then gone.

She lifted her attention to Laurentius's clouded face. "I apologize if he seemed flippant," he finally said. "Human nature was of interest to him in life. It has remained so in his undeath. I suppose to humans, it sounds insensitive."

Lucy summoned a smile. *God.* She really was tired. "Don't worry," she said. "He's not as insensitive as you."

Laurentius actually laughed. Just once, but he made no attempt to hide it. "Yes," he said, "that's true."

The silence that followed was expectant. Lucy had the feeling that she was being invited to explain why she was here. But she waited until Laurentius put the question into words.

"You didn't really come here to practice something you already know, did you? Are you doubting your human friends?"

"Not doubting . . . exactly," Lucy said. *Doubt* made it seem like it was their fault, somehow. It was the furthest thing from their fault. But still. "We took a risk, and Natalie paid for it. If we take more risks, we'll probably keep on paying for it. But . . . if we keep playing it safe. If we keep waiting for him to make a stupid mistake. Then Mila thinks I might not last."

She confessed the next part much more quietly. "And I think she's right."

Laurentius's ever-present look of consternation had faded into the background again. His moments of blankness no longer scared Lucy. But they did mean he was thinking of something that he didn't want her to read.

"Those aren't your only options," he said.

Lucy straightened. Even in her mind, Mila's twin bed creaked. "I'm listening."

But Laurentius didn't have the face of someone who was presenting a solution. His scowl carved deep lines across his handsome face. "It's not a cure-all," he said. "And in some respects, it presents more problems than solutions. We'd obviously have to move up our departure timeline—none of us will want to be on this campus when he finds out. But in many ways, we've just been dragging our feet, anyway. It will be good to leave. And we don't have much to carry—not much that matters."

"Laurentius," Lucy said. It wasn't like him to dance around the point. "What are you saying?"

Laurentius pinched the bridge of his nose, and paused a second longer. It was comforting to know that even centuries-old vampires couldn't help but delay the inevitable.

"Hiro is the only vampire I have ever made," he said. "I intended for that to be true forever. But immortal life is interminably long. I've already broken most of the promises I've ever made to myself. What's one more?"

Ah, Jillian would have said, in a moment like this. *The penny dropped.* It certainly felt as if something dropped. Lucy barely heard her next words over the ringing in her own ears.

"You're offering to turn me into a vampire," she said.

"Don't say it out loud. I'm already running the risk of rethinking it." Laurentius scrubbed violently at his brow. "Fucking Hiro. Had me playing messenger at every turn, probably knowing from the start that I'd give in. He'd turn you in a second, by the way. He'd be delighted to. But my blood is older. It would snuff out any of Ivan's influence on you. And whatever my other failings, I would not be any risk to your free will. I'm far too busy to command any baby vampires."

All Lucy could do was stare. On some level, Laurentius's words weren't quite gelling. And on another level, she heard them more clearly than she'd heard anything in days.

"Well?" he said. "I'm offering you a way out, here. Are you going to say anything?"

"I don't know what to say," Lucy said, completely honestly. "Or, um... I'm not really sure I understand. Why would you offer me this? You never really wanted to help me. You made that completely clear."

Annoyance creased Laurentius's face. It almost made Lucy laugh. Out of all the questions she could have asked him, was he not expecting her to ask why? But his scowl faded. And as he sank back into the chair, he looked thoughtful.

"If Hiro were here, offering to be your sire," Laurentius said, "he would have painted you a beautiful picture. Eternal time, finally yours to use as you choose. It's the picture I have endeavored to keep intact for him across these years. But he was a poet, in life. He used to write about how human life was beautiful because it ends. Even in this second life, with everything he wants—his art, his cadre of beautiful blood donors, me—I know he wonders if this unending life is still beautiful. The long nights weigh on him more than they used to.

"As for me . . . I'm making you this offer with the understanding that life grows colorless, after a time. This existence can be drudgery. Treading carefully to hide your tracks, or relying on the generosity of humans who cater to you for a chance at a colorless long life of their own. Your community will be tiresome old men like me, or murderous little brats like Ivan, and you will have no choice but to share a polite meal with them from time to time, because you are one of a shrinking few. And no matter how tedious the company, it will be necessary. It will become such a rare thing for you, to be understood.

"But," he said. "I was a servant to a patrician when I was

alive. I didn't have the build for physical labor. So my master kept me in the house. He let his sons throw stones at me by day to see how fast I could run. By night, I sang for his guests on bleeding feet. My sire was a traveler. A stranger. He didn't offer to turn me out of altruism. He recognized the rage in me. Wanted to see what I would do with it once I had power. But whatever his motives, he gave me a life within my control."

His eyes unfocused. Settled on a fixed point in the distance, far away in time. "I don't regret accepting that life," he said. "I don't think you would, either. That's why."

He didn't rush her to speak. She didn't think she would have been able to, in that moment. She felt everything she would have expected to feel at the idea—the horror, the anger, the revulsion. She'd only ever lightly sketched her life beyond college. A house, if she could ever afford one. A smart and funny wife. A job she didn't really care about, some travel, a quiet death in old age. She hadn't even figured out what she wanted to major in yet. To go with Laurentius would be to write all of that off.

But horror and anger and revulsion were not the only things within her. There was something else. Something that did not have a name so much as a temperature. It was a red-hot spark in the pit of her stomach. Not the kind that hurt. The kind that lit her up.

Her grandfather had died when the cancer had metastasized to his brain. He'd been hallucinating for days by the time he passed. Her grandmother had gone much quicker, though it hadn't felt that way to anyone in the room. Her lungs were full of fluid. She had drowned on dry land.

And her father? The reason Jillian saw muggers and murderers and speeding cars around Lucy's every corner? It wasn't foul play, or a freak accident. It had been a pulmonary embolism. Jillian had studiously turned all that grief and fear outward, toward the world, but it had been his body that betrayed all of them. One clot, moving in the wrong direction, and he was gone.

Lucy knew better than most: There was no such thing as a quiet death.

Laurentius was still watching her, with as much patience as she'd ever seen from him. And even if he wasn't as perceptive as Hiro, he *was* in her mind. Surely he could feel some of what she was feeling.

"I . . ." Lucy swallowed. Her throat was bone dry. "I need to think about it." She needed air. She needed to lie down. She needed to sleep, though that seemed less and less likely.

"You may," he said. "Though I don't think I need to remind you that you don't have much time left to think."

Lucy nodded. And for a second, that spark surged again. The lure of so much time.

But for the time being, she snuffed it out.

It was nearly impossible to get anything past Mila. But somehow, Lucy managed it. She'd left the library quiet, distracted, and more than a little woozy. But she had more than enough reasons to be all those things, so she'd more or less managed to play it off.

Though with Mila, one could never completely play anything off for long. So it was a relief to see her off to class and to excuse herself, once again, to Athena's studio. She needed to think about something other than Laurentius's offer for an hour or two. It was time to turn to a question that was nearly as difficult: what to say to Athena.

She supposed it wasn't *that* difficult, in the end. *Sorry for growling at you, it just kind of happened.* But now that she was on her way, the apology felt particularly insincere. She was, after all, considering something that would scare Athena far more than a growl.

Her stomach roiled as she walked. She didn't think Athena was afraid of her now, but when she thought about it, what reason did Athena have *not* to be afraid? Lucy was starting to regret asking Mila to do the convincing for their visit to the library. Laurentius and Hiro had warned her that first day that their involvement might sow mistrust. Lucy had always thought that Mila would be the one she needed to worry about.

But that had never been true, had it? No matter how kind Athena was, no matter how genuine her desire to help, there had only ever been one safe person for her, and it was Mila. Lucy and Natalie were already interlopers. Lucy was already a threat. Athena didn't have room in her calculations for another.

Lucy swiped into the radio station and fervently wished

she could text Natalie. But she'd gone back to her dorm when the sun rose, and she hadn't answered Lucy's check-in text from that morning, so she was likely getting some real rest. Lucy couldn't help but wonder if Natalie had done the smart thing and cut them all off.

She slipped into the station and made the usual turns down the hall, still faintly rehearsing what she would say. It occupied enough of her attention that she didn't notice the sound of hushed conversation from Athena's suite until she was at the door.

"Athena?" Lucy knocked first—then, thinking better of that, opened the door. "Are you . . ."

But as she entered the room, Athena wasn't the first person she saw. That honor went to an older blond woman in a navy blazer-and-skirt set whose gaze was now firmly fixed on Lucy. It took Lucy a moment to remember her. Dr. Horne, the Vice Provost of Student Events and Activities.

"Good," Dr. Horne said, in a high, clipped voice. "You're here, too."

"I'm . . . sorry," Lucy said, glancing from Dr. Horne to Athena's shuttered face. This was the woman who had come to ask Athena about her thesis, right? "I don't think we've—"

"Let's skip the formalities, I've got a very full schedule today," Dr. Horne said. "And shut the door behind you. We need to have a serious talk about our friend with the cold hands."

Sixteen

The name hit the room like a thunderclap. Lucy looked to Athena. The shock didn't show on her face. But as always, her heartbeat betrayed her.

"Dr. Horne," she said tightly. "Here I thought you didn't listen to the show."

"A tremendous waste of my time, by the way," Dr. Horne said. "But Ivan insisted that I keep listening, just to keep an eye on you. I don't know which of you is more obsessed with the other."

Lucy stared, still not quite comprehending what was happening. Dr. Horne's own heartbeat pattered irritably. Air whistled in and out of her mouth. She shifted her weight, and the sunlight through the blinds glinted through her bob. "You're not a vampire," Lucy said.

"Oh, for goodness' sake," Dr. Horne snapped. "Of course I'm not a vampire, you idiot."

It sank in, then. Laurentius did say the first time they met: that Vanya was being enabled to be at Rollins. Which meant that someone from the administration had to be involved.

Dr. Horne arranged her shoulders like an offended bird might ruffle its wings. "If we're going to have a conversation, Ms. Barnes, I'm going to ask that you take a step back from your recording equipment."

Athena's heartbeat picked up, and her fists were faintly shaking at her sides. She didn't look scared anymore—she looked deeply, profoundly furious. Lucy's heightened senses felt it like a charge in the atmosphere.

"So that's why you've always been so fixated on my show," Athena said. "You don't care whether I do a thesis. You've been trying to protect him this whole time."

"I care about both, to be clear," Dr. Horne said. "Your advisors think you have quite a bit of promise, you know. You're going to reflect very well on Rollins one day. Why do you think I've asked Ivan to stay away from you?"

Lucy saw the moment that landed in Athena's eyes. The answer to her burning question, the thing that scared her the most. It really wasn't all her planning, or all her precautions that had been protecting her. It was someone who thought she would be useful to Rollins one day.

But it was beside the point. "He *hasn't* stayed away from her," Lucy said. "He's been tormenting her since the moment he saw her. He's never stopped."

Dr. Horne shifted her attention back to Lucy. And Lucy could see, in that moment, just how different they were in her eyes. Athena was a necessary annoyance. A bureaucratic hiccup. But Lucy was nothing.

"You must be aware by now how difficult it is to make a vampire do anything," she said. "I've done my best, haven't I? He has agreed to conditions to be here. He—limits his hunting on the Rollins campus. He likes to tease Ms. Barnes, that's all. It's his old-fashioned sense of humor. All she ever had to do was ignore him."

"Sounds like a lot of trouble," Athena said, taking a carefully controlled breath. Lucy didn't need Hiro's gift for mind reading to guess that Athena had recognized an opportunity to gather information. "Surely your job would be easier if you didn't have to cover for the disappearances of new students every year."

Dr. Horne seemed to understand exactly what was happening. It didn't stop her from answering. "Oh, sure," she said. "There are a lot of things that would make my job easier. But do you have any idea of the state of our endowment? Do you know how difficult it to raise money when half of your student body is devoted to inventing new fields of study? No one's going to fund a research project on the Eurocentric bias in the written history of the clarinet. It looks nice on the brochures, but it doesn't keep the lights on. Our award-winning starving-artist alumni aren't donating buildings. Our funds have to come from somewhere."

Lucy's stomach churned. Dr. Horne wasn't there to hurt them. Lucy felt sure of that now. But she also didn't seem to expect any consequences from telling them all of this. "He's *donating to the school*?"

"He's got plenty to burn." Dr. Horne flashed a queasy smile. "He's old money, if you'll pardon the joke."

Athena clearly did not pardon the joke. "So he's paying you. You're literally taking bribes to look the other way while he hunts your students."

Ms. Horne looked unmoved. "You pay tuition to be here. Is that a bribe? I gather he learns some philosophy, from time to time. It sounds as if you learned that yesterday evening as well."

"If you know that we went to that party," Lucy said, "then you know what happened there. He tried to murder our friend. Aren't you supposed to be limiting his hunting?"

"As of now," Dr. Horne said, "Mr. Volkov has not violated the rules I've set out for him. I suppose I never told him he couldn't sample more than one student before making his choice."

"Sample?" Athena spat out. "You're disgusti—"

"You didn't let me finish," Dr. Horne continued. "There *was* someone who may have violated a rule this week. And that was you, Ms. Barnes."

Athena's stare could have melted iron. "And what rule is that?"

Dr. Horne glanced toward the answering machine on Athena's desk. Then, very carefully, she withdrew a folded piece of paper from the inside of her blazer. "I reviewed the funding terms you agreed to for your . . . radio show, here," she said. "I specifically recall a member of your committee sharing his concern that real students would be named in your fictional project. You've agreed to avoid doing so in your contract here. 'The contents of Pallas Radio shall be entirely fictional. No students, faculty, staff, or departments will be named or featured on Pallas Radio without written consent of the contributor.'"

Athena stiffened. "I've never used real names on my show," she said.

With a sigh, Dr. Horne withdrew her phone from her pocket and loaded the Voice Memos app on her phone. "And the names of real departments?"

As she clicked play, Athena's breathless voice cut in almost instantly. *"—one is okay, physically, at least,"* she said. *"But we can no longer ignore that our friend with the cold hands has grown significantly bolder. A student's life was threatened, in broad daylight. I could easily be reporting another disappearance to you today. Thankfully I'm not. Instead, I come to you with a warning. I encourage all of you to exercise extreme caution at philosophy department events. And to all philosophy students, please watch your backs. It's not always so easy to know who your classmates are."*

Dr. Horne had a wry look on her face as she stopped the

playback. "The philosophy chair is very curious to know why you're using a community-building grant to defame his department."

Her hard, birdlike eyes watched Athena closely, as if waiting for her to be ashamed. It seemed Athena wasn't going to give her the satisfaction. "And did you remind Professor Baek that this is a work of fiction?" Athena said.

"Hmm. Well," Dr. Horne said. "We'll leave it to the grant committee to decide how far 'fiction' is permitted to go. But that kind of review will take time. And I'm sure you'll understand that we can't let you keep going with the show for the time being."

Lucy stepped forward. Out of the corner of her eye, she saw Athena grab for her hand, but she sidestepped it. She wasn't going to hurt Dr. Horne. No matter how much she wanted to.

"He'll get bored with you one day, too," Lucy said. "And when he does, I hope you feel every bit as helpless as those kids you served up to him."

Dr. Horne's lip curled. But the words landed. Lucy heard it in her heartbeat. "You're going to be a delight to deal with for the next four years, aren't you. Maybe he'll drain you dry and spare me the trouble for once."

"That's not going to happen," Lucy said.

"Sometimes life goes in a different direction than we anticipate, Ms. Easting. It's not as if I expected any of this when I earned my PhD," Dr. Horne said. "Let me tell you this. Ivan

Volkov doesn't particularly like me. The feeling is mutual. But he's never going to get bored, as you say. Whatever his flaws, he's a man who understands the convenience of doing business."

She turned neatly to Athena, her heart rate back in perfect rhythm. "I'll deliver the committee's decision in due course," she said. "But as you know, they're busy people. They may need to review past broadcasts, and you're quite the . . . *prolific creator*. It will take time. Possibly through the end of the academic year."

"When I graduate," Athena said.

"Goodness," Dr. Horne said. "You say that like that's my intention."

"I notice that you're not denying it, though," Lucy said.

"No point in that, is there?" Dr. Horne made her brisk way across the room. When she reached the door, she paused. "I'll leave you with a word of comfort, if I may. You might think I'm a monster. But I don't disagree with you on everything. It's unseemly, the way he drags these things on. It's cruel." And with that, she was gone.

Athena watched the empty space she'd left for a long time. When she spoke again, her back was still turned to Lucy. "For a second, I thought you were going to hurt her."

"I wasn't going to," Lucy said. She didn't love hearing that uncertain note in her own voice.

Athena's face was darkly wry when she finally turned. "I'm starting to wish you had."

Lucy laughed. Suddenly exhausted, she positioned herself next to one of Athena's floor cushions and folded herself onto it. Athena hesitated before perching opposite her.

"It was stupid of me," Athena said quietly. "The broadcast. But after what happened to Natalie—I don't think we can trust that you and I are the only ones he's after anymore."

"No, I'm glad you did it," Lucy said. It was kind of funny, imagining what all those nice, normal philosophy students would think when they heard it. "And maybe they'll still let you back on the air."

"I'm not sure they will. I think Dr. Horne will see to that." Athena attempted a smile, but it quickly failed. "She's been looking for an excuse since I started Pallas Radio. . . . I guess now I know why. And if something else happens . . ."

Something else. Lucy wondered if she meant someone else getting attacked. Or maybe she was talking about what would happen when Vanya moved on to someone else. When Lucy was already dead.

"You'll find another way to warn everyone," Lucy said.

"Until I graduate," Athena said somberly.

"Then maybe someone else can take up the mantle," Lucy said. "Mila could host a show. Or Natalie. Can you picture Natalie's Pallas Radio? That would be a vibe shift."

It was supposed to make them both laugh. But Lucy's stomach curdled again at the thought of Natalie, and Athena looked similarly somber. "Have you . . ." Lucy had to swallow to wet her throat. "Have you heard from her yet today?"

"Not since she went back to her dorm." Athena studied her for a moment, then added, "She stayed up most of the night while she was here. She's probably just resting. She'll be in touch when she's ready."

"She probably shouldn't be in touch at all," Lucy said.

"Probably not," Athena said. "But let her decide." With a sigh, she unfurled her long legs in front of her. There was still something coiled about the way she sat, though. She never left herself completely exposed. "You know," she went on, "I thought your library vampires were trying to scare you when they said our friend was enabled to be here. I could understand no one believing me, even if it was negligent. But to know what's happening and let it happen . . ."

"Laurentius told me something," Lucy said. "About vampires needing to rely on the 'generosity of humans' to survive. He was talking about people who hoped to become vampires themselves. But I guess there's more than one way that a human can benefit."

Athena's gaze remained neutral, but by now, Lucy was good at catching those moments when her eyes sharpened. She and Mila were alike in that way. "So your meeting today was productive. That's good."

"I'm sorry." The apology came straight from Lucy's gut. "I should have talked to you about it myself. But I know I scared you yesterday, and I thought maybe if Mila was the one to explain—"

"Lucy, I promise, I'm not upset." And she didn't sound

upset anymore, really. Not her voice, and not her body. Her breaths, the delicate pumping of her blood, it all sounded as exhausted as Lucy felt. "At the beginning—my only concern was finding you. Helping you however I could. I knew you were going to have questions I didn't have answers to. But I didn't realize I was going to be so . . . ill-equipped, I guess. I know the vampires can explain things to you that I couldn't even begin to understand.

"And I understand why you didn't want to talk to me," Athena added. "I know you're well aware that it scares me. I know you probably don't want me to be scared of you, too." She took a deep breath. Lucy heard the way that it caught. "I wish I could say there was something you could do to make me less afraid. But . . . yeah."

"Yeah," Lucy echoed, her heart plummeting like a stone. Of course she'd known that. Of course. Athena was too smart. And being afraid of Lucy was the smart thing to do.

At least Vanya was predictable. No one could say for sure what Lucy was going to do. Least of all Lucy herself.

"I understand. You're probably right to be afraid of me," Lucy said. "But I really don't think the library vampires have any interest in hurting you. And if nothing can be done for me, then—then I really think you should go to them for help."

Athena was quiet for a while. Once again, Lucy had to marvel at the utter uselessness of her heightened senses sometimes. She could hear that Athena's breathing had changed. She could hear that her heartbeat had quickened. But she had no access to what had just crossed Athena's mind. Like any human, she could only guess.

"I came here to be a neuroscience major," Athena finally said. "That doesn't really mean as much to me as it used to. But it still informs the way I see the world, in a lot of ways. Habits. Instincts. Associations. The brain is such a complex thing. But no matter how complicated a living thing can be, any higher thoughts or higher reasonings can be overridden by a few simple biological imperatives. Thirst. Fear. Hunger.

"I knew that from the beginning. But I still wanted to believe there was something human about vampires, at first," she said. "They looked human. They *were* human. I thought, *Maybe at least part of them still thinks like a person thinks*. But there's no human framework for the life they live. Humans are omnivores. Humans rely on community for survival. But the vampire needs just one thing to live: life itself. And once your community is the food source you need to survive, how can you possibly view them the same as you did before?"

"But they *do* have other ways they can live," Lucy said. "Hiro—one of the library vampires—he told me there are people who will pay vampires to feed on them."

"And I'm glad that works for him. But I wonder—if you asked him, do you think he would say that satisfies him?" Athena said. "That night, when I was hiding behind that caution tape. Our friend with the cold hands figured out fast that he wasn't going to get in. If he was just hungry, he could've found other food, couldn't he? But he waited. All night, he tried to manipulate me into leaving. The things that he said . . ."

She squeezed her eyes shut. "I don't call him Vanya. I've never thought of him as Vanya. I think you're all probably right, that it was his name once. But I'll never know Ivan Volkov the person. All I know is the thing that lives in his body now. The thing that chased me half a mile and has chased me ever since. It's not just that they need our blood to live. It's that he needs the *hunt*. Maybe that's not true of your library vampires, but it's true of him."

Lucy pulled her legs a little closer to her. She was getting cold, here on the floor.

"Maybe that is true," Lucy said, thinking of what Hiro said back in the library. "Or maybe the cruelty was always there, and what he became was just an opportunity."

Athena's smile was tired. "And maybe you're right," she said. "But I don't know. I'll probably never know for sure. All I can say is that if I'm right? I don't think vampire Lucy would be capable of seeing me as her friend anymore. Just something she could choose to eat, or not eat. I'm not sure either of us can afford to forget that."

All Lucy could do was nod. Not a nod yes, exactly. Just a confirmation that she'd heard.

She thought of Laurentius's face as he offered to turn Lucy into what Athena feared most in this world. He hadn't looked at her with disdain, or like something he was deciding whether or not to eat. He looked at her with understanding.

But she also remembered the red-hot spark his words had

lit. The one that sat waiting for her decision, even now. It would have scared Athena to know about it. Maybe it should have scared Lucy, too.

"Do you want me to stay away from you?" was the only thing Lucy could think to say.

"Don't you dare," Athena said. "I said I'd help you, and that's what I'm going to do. Being afraid is one thing. But I can't let it make me run."

Lucy squeezed her hand and bit back a laugh. They had just agreed, moments ago, that Natalie should run. They'd probably agree that Mila should run, too. And while Athena hadn't let herself leave back then, she still could. Maybe, if she went far enough, he'd never even find her.

But she was a scientist. And Lucy didn't have to be one herself to see why *maybe* wasn't enough.

"Well. I'm with you, for now." Lucy smiled shakily. "Lucy Easting the *person* isn't dead yet."

There was a glint of ferocity in Athena's usual calm. "And I'll do everything in my power to keep it that way."

Seventeen

Lucy's mind felt uncomfortably full by the time she returned to Quincey Hall that night. With sunset quickly approaching, she knew that she needed to use the brief pocket of calm to sort through her thoughts. She certainly had enough of them to put in order. And probably not a lot of time left to do so.

But her head was aching. Her brain itself felt sore, too stretched to be of much good. Thankfully, there were few things as strangely clarifying as an argument with Mila Rostova.

"I'm not saying you can't do it," Mila was saying as Lucy swung open the bathroom door. "I'm just saying that you're cutting it close."

"I'm not cutting it that close," Lucy said. "It's not even sunset. It's barely pre-sunset."

"Maybe," Mila said. "But we can't be completely sure what Vanya's timing is. Like, does he need to wait until the last rays of light have left the sky, or can he start to move when it gets even a little bit dark?"

Lucy was going to take Mila by her beautiful shoulders and shake her. "I will be done well before it starts to get dark at all," she said. "It's a shower. I'll be quick."

"I don't understand why it's desperately urgent for you to wash your hair," Mila said.

"Because I *need* to wash my hair," Lucy said. "After the day I've had, I deserve to wash my hair. Would you like me to tell you about the day I've had again?"

Mila looked appallingly unmoved. Maybe it was because Lucy could only tell Mila about roughly half of the day she'd had. She had to excise any parts about Laurentius's offer. But even leaving all that out, she'd been through more than enough to warrant the hottest shower known to man. She had fully sweated through her pajamas tossing and turning the night before. She had barely managed to take three bites of even the rarest meat they were able to find in the dining hall. And she still hadn't heard from Natalie.

Mila raked her hands through her hair. "Okay, okay, fine. Stop looking at me like that," she said. "But I have a safeguard in mind. It's just not going to be very comfortable."

"I'm okay with that," Lucy said. What had been comfortable about the past week? "I feel like dirty laundry. I probably *look* like dirty laundry. I'll do anything."

"You do not look like dirty laundry," Mila said.

"Next to you I do," Lucy said. "Everyone's probably looking at us like, what is that beautiful Amazonian goddess doing with that sentient dumpster?"

Mila didn't laugh. Which seemed fair enough to Lucy, at first—her sense of humor was among the many things that had suffered over the past week. But just as she was going to ask about this uncomfortable safeguard, Mila said, "Beautiful Amazonian goddess?"

"Well . . . yeah?" Lucy said. "Sorry. I could probably come up with a better descriptor if my hair was clean. About that safeguard—"

"Why would you say that?" Mila blurted out.

Lucy reeled back. She read Mila's tone as anger, at first. But as they locked eyes, she recognized the look on Mila's face. Total bafflement.

"No," Mila added quickly. "Sorry. You need to shower."

"Well, no. Now I have follow-up questions," Lucy said, against her better judgment. "Are you actually embarrassed that I'm calling you beautiful?"

"I'm not embarrassed," Mila said, which was a bold thing to say when she'd gone so uncharacteristically pink. "I'm just—surprised."

"Surprised?" Lucy felt like she was having a stroke. "I thought I was being obvious."

"Obvious when?" Mila said helplessly. "We've known each other for a week. You've been mad at me for half of it."

"When we first met," Lucy said, as if she could somehow jog Mila's memory. "I blatantly hit on you."

Mila looked at her like she was speaking French. "You were traumatized."

"I was traumatized," Lucy agreed. She could hear a warmth in her own voice that she would have thought she was too tired for. "And I was also hitting on you."

Mila looked so utterly lost that it was Lucy's turn to go pink. She'd been so humiliated that night, when Mila had stepped out from behind the chapel. So sure that she'd made a complete fool of herself, making eyes at someone who was eventually going to have to kill her. And now it seemed as if Mila just . . . hadn't noticed?

She needed to mercy-kill this conversation. Before they both dug themselves into respectively deeper holes. "I should, um, shower. What's this safeguard?"

"Right. Fuck. We're wasting time." Mila whipped out a pair of handcuffs from behind her back.

"Mila!" Lucy said.

"I told you it would be uncomfortable!" Mila said. "But if I'm going to leave you alone next to a window, we should restrain you with something stronger than cloth."

"Okay, sure! Understandable!" Lucy said. "But you couldn't whip out the handcuffs before I started calling you beautiful?"

"Well, sorry! I'm clearly not familiar with handcuff etiquette!" Mila looked as if she wanted to melt into the bathroom tile. "And if you're going to beat the sunset, you're going to need to hurry."

Lucy groaned. "Okay, yes," she said. "Give them to me."

Mila hesitated in the midst of passing them to her. "Do

you want help putting them on? You'll probably have to get undressed first, though."

Lucy wasn't usually one to kick someone when they were down. But in this scenario, she didn't think a light prod would go amiss. "I've just told you that I think you're beautiful," she said, "and now you'd like me to strip naked so you can handcuff me?"

The handcuffs were deposited in Lucy's hands faster than she could blink. "I'll leave so you can put them on."

"That's probably wise," Lucy said, not unkindly. "We'll figure out the most dignified way for you to let me out once I'm done. Now—if you wouldn't mind leaving, that would be great."

"Right. Yes. I'm gone." Mila made for the door like the hounds of hell were after her.

Though, halfway out the door, she paused.

"You—don't have to worry about looking good, by the way," she said stiffly. "You always look good."

And then she shut the door behind her, long before Lucy could decide how to react.

"Well," Lucy said, to no one at all. Maybe an argument with Mila wasn't so clarifying after all. She'd already guessed that Mila had never dated anyone besides Jon, but she had no idea the situation was this dire. Her poor head had progressed from full to bursting. As much as she wanted to analyze Mila's parting words within an inch of their life, it was, unfortunately, the least urgent thing she needed to think through.

She turned on the shower—the pipes in Quincey always

took their sweet time to warm up—and allowed herself a minute to splash some water on her face. A brief glimpse in the mirror showed absolutely nothing that "looked good."

She straightened. Before she found a place to cuff herself, she should probably close the blinds. Didn't need anyone asking about that.

She looked up, her hand already halfway to the window. And through the glass, she met a pair of eyes, half hidden by a dark hood.

Lucy may have been exhausted, but days of hypervigilance had quickened her reflexes. She seized the cuffs from the bathroom counter and locked one around her wrist, then turned sharply to find someplace to anchor them. The shower rod was too high, the towel rack was too fragile. But the radiator was sturdy, and the right height. She clicked the other cuff into place around one of its accordion-shaped pipes, and when she tugged, it held.

"Are you *handcuffing* yourself?" said the voice at the window.

Lucy froze, her heart hammering. It was not a voice that could have belonged to Vanya. It was crisp, judgmental—and entirely familiar.

Slowly, she looked up. And this time, she got a good look at the face on the other side of the glass, nearly concealed by the raincoat draped over her head.

"Please don't scream for your bodyguard, either." Whitney's voice sounded strained. And Lucy could guess why.

The light of the sunset was barely low enough to skim the trees. "I'm here to talk."

Lucy faltered. Yelling for Mila would have been the smart thing to do. But like Athena with Dr. Horne, Lucy recognized an opportunity to gather information when she saw it. She reached over to the shower and gave the dial another nudge, turning up the water pressure. Hopefully it would be enough to drown their voices out.

"Okay," she said. "But the handcuffs stay on. I don't want your sire commanding me outside. Unless whatever's left of Sadie Grainger is taking point on that these days?"

Whitney's eyes had a yellow sheen to them, like a nocturnal animal. Lucy supposed that was what she was now. "It wasn't my idea to attack your friend."

"I didn't think it was," Lucy said. Whatever else was true, none of this was Whitney's fault. "But I assume that's not what you're here to talk about. How are you here, anyway? It's not dark yet."

"Oh, I've noticed," Whitney bit out. "You can't imagine how much it hurts just to be standing here. It feels like the worst flu of my life. But the only time he's not watching is when he's sleeping."

Completely unwillingly, Lucy wavered. This was not the time for softness. But there was a desperation in Whitney's eyes that stuck in her heart.

The night of Natalie's party, Whitney had told her not to get lost in the dark. She hadn't exactly been a pleasant person when she was alive. She was rude. Judgmental. Possibly a little classist. Even still, she cared whether or not Lucy made it home safe.

Maybe Athena was right. Maybe it changed a person irrevocably when every living thing around them became their natural prey. Maybe all Whitney could see, looking through this window, was something to eat or not eat. Maybe the Whitney Fielding who had been her roommate no longer existed.

All those things could easily be true. *But please,* Lucy thought. *Just this once, let Athena be wrong.*

"Whitney," Lucy said. "You could run right now, if you wanted. He's probably still sleeping, right?"

"I'd never get off the mountain before he found me," Whitney said. "He told me that if I brought him that radio girl, we could go wherever I wanted. He said he'd fly me to the Sorbonne, or the Bodleian. But all we do all day is sit in those tunnels and eat rats. He says we eat together or not at all, but I know he's feeding when we're not there. And the worst part is, he lied to me. He never expected that I'd be able to bring him that girl. He only wanted me to scare her. He's not even allowed to kill her until she graduates."

Lucy inhaled sharply. So Dr. Horne, unsurprisingly, overestimated her own power on Vanya. He had no plans to spare Athena, to let her reflect well on Rollins as a graduate. He was going to kill her the moment she was no longer a student. And what could Dr. Horne do to stop it? Lucy doubted she'd even object if the next donation was big enough.

She looked back up to Whitney. She did look noticeably more gaunt than she had just a few nights ago. She and Mila had been so close to the truth the other day, wondering at the number of victims. It hadn't seemed like enough because Vanya was starving those girls.

"What about your sisters?" Lucy said. It made her nauseous, how easily the word rolled off her tongue. But that was what they were. She herself had felt that pull to them. "Do you think they'd come after you?"

"Don't know." Whitney hissed with pain and adjusted her hood. The sun had lowered in the sky, but it still looked excruciating. "Addie's strange but nice. All she talks about is how happy she is that I'm here, and that we're all together. Sadie . . . I don't know. She looks out for us. She catches rats for me when I'm too tired. But she doesn't talk much. And when she does, it's to make people do what he wants. She's good at it. Even better than he is."

Whitney glanced over her shoulder, as if expecting to see something there. Lucy couldn't hear anyone nearby. But Lucy was a thrall, and Whitney was the real thing. Maybe she sensed something Lucy didn't.

"You said the other night that you'd help me," Whitney said. "Were you just saying that so I wouldn't kill you?"

Despite herself, Lucy laughed. "A little. But I do want to help you. I just—we can't turn you back to what you were. You already know that, right?"

"I do," Whitney said. Though Lucy could tell that it was

another thing, hearing it out loud. "God, why did I even come here? You can't help me. You can't even help yourself."

Lucy winced. That was fair. "Maybe not. But there are other vampires on campus. Vampires who are planning to leave here, to get away from Vanya. If I can get you to them, maybe they'll take you with them."

But Whitney's scowl only deepened. "He's told me about your friends already. The fossil, the bunny eater. I'm not going vegetarian. I never want to touch another rodent again."

"It doesn't have to be that way," Lucy pressed. "You can feed from people. They'll even pay you to do it—there's a whole vampire gig economy or something, I don't know. They can explain it better than I can. But you *would* get to leave here. You could have an actual life."

The darker it grew outside, the more striking the shift of Whitney's eyes was. They looked more silver than yellow now. "A life," she said. "I'd still be a vampire. People would notice that I don't eat. Or go out in the daytime. If I stayed around my family long enough, they would notice that I didn't age. And if I got hungry around them . . ." Her hands had come up to grip the windowsill. Her knuckles were white. "I'd have to disappear, like Sadie and Addie. Or I'd have to let them figure out what I've become. Can your vegetarian friends explain how I'm supposed to live like that?"

Lucy bit her lip. She didn't have long to consider her response. It was getting darker. It was only a matter of time before Mila came looking for her—and before Vanya noticed that Whitney was gone.

On top of that, she didn't have an answer. She'd been considering the same things since the moment Laurentius offered to make her a vampire. She had no idea where she would go. What would she eat. Whether she would pretend to be normal for Jillian for a little while, or if she would let her believe that her worst nightmare came true.

But this wasn't about her. She had a choice—or at least, she had a choice for now. Whitney hadn't had a choice at all.

"I don't know," Lucy said. "I *wish* I knew what to tell you. But right now, I think there's only one question that you need to answer. Are you willing to live this way, or not?"

Whitney didn't hesitate. There was a ferocity in her eyes that Lucy recognized down to her bones. She'd felt it often enough over the past few days. "I want to live."

Lucy was smiling as she shut off the water. "Good answer," she said. "I'm going to call for Mila now. Don't go anywhere."

Whitney made an odd face at that. A kind of startled frown. "I know you probably don't like her," Lucy said, "but she has to be involved. If we want to get up to the library alive . . ."

Lucy trailed off. That strange look was still fixed on Whitney's face. Her mouth was slightly open. Her stare was fixed on the opposite wall. If she were objecting to Mila, she would have said so by now. But she hadn't said anything.

Whitney staggered forward a half step, her forehead

brushing the windowpane. Then, finally, she looked down. Lucy, frozen, followed her gaze.

Whitney was wearing a ratty old academic decathlon shirt, probably the same one she'd been wearing the night she fled Quincey Hall. There were a few prominent holes worn in the fabric. It took Lucy a moment to notice that one of the holes had something protruding through it. A sharp wooden point, directly in the center of Whitney's chest.

Whitney's mouth opened wide, as if to scream. And then she began to melt.

Maybe *melt* wasn't right. But in Lucy's horror, she couldn't think of another word to describe it. Whitney's eyes dissolved into white, then gushed down her cheeks like tears. Skin melted to muscle; muscle melted to bone; her hair thinned and then crumbled away. She vanished layer by layer. Like a horrible time-lapse of rot. Like a corpse.

And the whole time, Whitney's jaw was open wide in that terrible silent scream. Lucy's mouth was open, too, but her scream wouldn't come, either. There was weight against her wrists, her ankles, her throat. She strained against it. It pressed her still.

Whitney's bones were dust by the time they hit the ground. And as the last of her crumbled away, Lucy could finally see who was standing behind her.

There was something so normal about the way he was looking at her. It was one of the first things Athena had told her, back at the chapels. That he relied on that normalcy to move beneath notice. But she understood then, for the first time, why she had walked into that kitchen and paid him no mind. His sandy-blond hair was kept in a neat, modern cut. His blue eyes could have been curious, even friendly. He had blandly symmetrical features and cookie-cutter handsomeness, and as he smiled, he could have been anyone. Lucy didn't see the monster there on first glance. She didn't even see the Russian aristocrat. She could have passed him dozens of times on the Rollins campus, in another life. She never would have guessed what he was.

She tried to scream again. This time she saw how he stopped her: that he lifted a hand, curled his fingers into a fist. She could feel the ghost of those fingers against her throat.

"Quiet, now," he said. He must have had a Russian accent at one time. Now his accent was broad, nondescript American. The same voice from the kitchen. The same voice that had told her to *hold still.*

Tears coursed helplessly down Lucy's face as she tried to force out a few words. He lifted his hand with a flourish, performatively relaxed his fingers. A little more air slipped down her throat, and he inclined his head. An obliging gesture.

She gasped. He hadn't given her much room to breathe. He'd barely given her an opening to repeat what she'd tried to say. "Why are you doing this?"

He looked confused. And in that confusion, his smile

slipped. Lucy saw the monster then. It was just beyond that polite, smiling mask. It waited in the absolute blankness that existed underneath.

"I was bored," he said. "And you were there."

And for a long moment, he held her there. The handcuffs hung uselessly off her wrist. It was well secured to the radiator. The only way to pull free would have been to pull the radiator from the floor. But she couldn't even try. Couldn't even move. She was pinned. Useless. Useless as she'd been this entire time.

There was a soft knock at the door. "Lucy?"

Vanya's eyes lifted, and Lucy stopped breathing. The faint flicker of interest sent adrenaline howling through her. "Stay away from her," she whispered. As if that would do anything. As if he'd stay away from any of them now.

He arched one perfect eyebrow. Then, with the same flourish as before, he raised his hand. He made a show of loosening his fingers one by one. And he released her.

Lucy couldn't tell which pain hit her first: her knees against the floor, or the tug of the handcuffs against her wrist. She didn't recognize her own voice when she cried out. It was a cracked and ragged sound. Far more animal than human.

She'd faintly heard the door flung open, but she flinched nonetheless when Mila hit the ground next to her. "Lucy." Frantic hands smoothed the hair out of her face. She'd probably never get to wash it now. "Lucy, talk to me. Where is he?"

She knew the answer to that question, of course. She knew it even before she brought herself to look up at the empty window, where he'd been standing until just seconds ago. She'd probably known it that first morning, when she woke up in her blinding white dorm room after Natalie's party.

He was everywhere.

He had always been everywhere.

They left for the radio station at dawn. They waited until the sunrise was midway into the sky, until most of the mountain was bathed in early fall gold. Mila's question last night had been answered in the worst possible way. There had still been a little light left in the sky when Vanya killed Whitney.

Lucy wondered if that light had hurt him the way it had hurt Whitney. But she doubted it. Whitney had looked so small and miserable and afraid. Vanya had looked perfectly pleasant the entire time. Even with the last of Whitney on his shoes.

These were some of the details Lucy left out as she recounted the story to Athena. It was horrible enough to say. She didn't want anyone else to see it, even in their mind's eye.

Athena didn't need much description, though. She looked as if she was imagining it well enough.

"Lucy, I can't imagine how hard this is," she said. It was her radio-host voice, that calm and gentle curtain. "But think one more time. Was there anything Whitney said that could help us?"

Lucy rubbed her eyes. The conversation should have been burned into her mind. But seeing Vanya, seeing Whitney dissolve into his hands, had scattered the order of it in her mind. She'd already told Athena the most important part—that Vanya planned to kill her as soon as she graduated.

"I don't know," she finally said. "All she said was that Vanya was hiding them in the tunnels, which we already knew. And it's not like we can go find them there, unless we'd like to die even faster."

Athena's flinch was soft, but Lucy felt it. Loud, useless infection. Telling her everything except what she needed to know. "And him? What did he say?"

That was the most useless information of all. *I was bored. And you were there.* She wasn't Athena, the Holmes to his Moriarty, the object of his fascination. She wasn't even a rabbit in the grip of a fox. She was an inanimate object. She was a half-eaten box of crackers.

"He didn't say anything," Lucy said. "He just killed her."

Athena studied the floor for a long time. "I know it doesn't feel this way," she said. "But there was nothing you could have done for Whitney. She's not suffering anymore. It . . . might have been for the best."

There had been plenty of words, in Lucy's life, that had knocked her feet right out from under her. Her grandmother's diagnosis, then her grandfather's. The bloodlessly polite email she'd received when she was eighteen, after she canceled her first college matriculation. Jillian telling her that she must have been glad that her grandfather was dead.

Athena's words landed somewhere central. Somewhere load-bearing in the depths of her chest. She felt it crack. And then altogether give.

"You don't believe that," she said. "I'm sorry, but you don't fucking believe that."

Athena rocked back as if she'd been shoved. Lucy could feel Mila shift behind her, maybe to take her by the arm—but Lucy stepped out of her reach.

"You gave your whole life up to stay here," Lucy said. "Sacrificed every single thing you came here for, just because you didn't want to leave your classmates to be hunted. You were nineteen. You must have been so scared, and you did it anyway. You can't tell me that you, of all people, think it's for the best that a girl is dead. I don't believe you. I don't."

"Lucy," Athena said. Lucy had never heard her voice shake like this. "She was already dead."

"Maybe she was!" Lucy was pacing now. Her own voice was shaking, too. When she spoke, she could feel the dents of Vanya's fingers in the dip of her throat. "But she wanted to live. She wanted to study at the Bodleian, or the Sorbonne, or somewhere with a bigger library than here. She wanted to know what to tell her family. If you're right, if becoming a vampire changes who you are completely, why would she still want those things?"

"And where does that get us?" There was no soft, calm curtain over Athena's voice now. Everything about her had gone rigid. Her anger at Dr. Horne the day before had restraint, but her face now held neither of those things. "Maybe you're right. Maybe she wasn't gone. Maybe Sadie Grainger and Addison Greene aren't gone. So then what? Do we let them do what they want? Do we let them have our classmates?"

"I don't know!" Lucy slammed her open palm against the wall next to her. She barely felt the sting of it. "I don't know any better than you do! But you told me that you didn't want to run, no matter how scared you were. On that first broadcast I listened to, you said we need to be Addison's family now. If you decide—if you decide that you can't save them without even trying—"

Then you're already running was what she wanted to say. It was what she tried to say, too. But it was as if hitting the wall had released some valve in her, and she couldn't close it. When she tried to step back, she stumbled.

"Hey." A pair of hands were instantly at her shoulders. Mila's. "I've got you. Why don't we sit down."

"I don't . . ." *Need to.* But it was possible that she did. Her mouth felt full and clumsy—the words were coming out slurred. Her head was spinning worse than it had the day before, with Laurentius of Rome's offer whipping through her mind. Except it wasn't only spinning this time. The room was looking a little fuzzy, a little dark at the edges.

She raised a hand, ignoring Mila's noise of protest, and tried to brace herself on the wall. But it didn't feel right. There was a deep fissure under her fingers.

Lucy turned her head, even as it sent another spike of nausea through her. There was a large, splintered dent in the wall, right where her palm had struck.

It was a kind of strength she didn't possess. A kind of strength she especially didn't possess now, when she was weaker than she'd ever been.

But it was the kind of strength that a vampire had.

Athena was looking at her with open horror. Her hands were no longer empty. The stake from her desk drawer was clutched tight in one hand.

Lucy opened her mouth to say something—maybe *No, it's not like that,* even though she didn't know what it was like. Something sharp brushed the inside of her lip. Instinctively, she ran her tongue across it. But there wasn't just one sharp point. There were two. Right where her canines should have been.

The haze at the edges of her vision crept inward, blanketing everything in gray. "Maybe I will sit down," she mumbled.

She remembered very little after that.

TRANSCRIPT OF ROLLINS UNIVERSITY STUDENT RADIO STATION WVBS ("PALLAS RADIO")

Broadcast number: 112

PALLAS (HOST): Caller number fourteen, you're on the air.

CALLER #14: Is this line safe? You never know who's listening.

PALLAS: A fair question. You'll notice that I'm referring to you as caller number fourteen. I strongly recommend that you not use your name, or the names of any others, at any point while we're on the air. And if you still have your radio turned on, you'll hear that I've disguised your voice.

CALLER #14: That's considerate of you. [pause] I want to report an incident. Do I just start talking?

PALLAS: Please do. But take your time.

CALLER #14: I saw a man tonight. Maybe you're going to think this sounds foolish. But I sat across from him for maybe half an hour, and he caught my attention. It was something in the way he watched people. Do you know what I mean?

PALLAS: I don't know that I do. Can you describe it?

CALLER #14: I thought you might be able to put your finger on it better. I've listened to you speak of meeting him. You said you got a bad feeling, and you ran. What did you notice, do you think?

PALLAS: Let's focus on your experience for now. You said you sat across from him. Where was that?

CALLER #14: Holden Student Center. He's already gone from there, though. I even followed him for a while.

PALLAS: Caller number fourteen, I don't think you should—

CALLER #14: Oh, it's okay. He lost me a while back. Moves so fast, you know. But he wasn't headed for the dorms. I don't think anyone has anything to worry about. The last I saw, he was headed in the direction of the multimedia center. Although . . . that's where you are right now, isn't it?

PALLAS: . . . When was this?

CALLER #14: He'd probably be reaching you now, Ms. Pallas.

That's an interesting name to pick for yourself—Pallas. You must think you're very smart.

[Four seconds of silence.]

PALLAS: Who is this?

[CALLER #14's line disconnects. A brief dial tone can be heard on the air.]

Editor's note: WVBS ("Pallas Radio") ended its broadcast at the conclusion of this call, two hours and four minutes before the end of its scheduled time slot. No further audio was recorded for Broadcast 112.

Eighteen

Click-click.

Lucy clawed her way out of a murky half dream. She wasn't where she last remembered. The broadcasting studio had been bright with the morning light—wherever she was now, the blinds were drawn. But she didn't have time to get her bearings yet. *What's easier than locking a door?* Laurentius had said. As if he'd ever had to imagine a door like his life depended on it.

But she did imagine it, even as the room spun. She pressed the lock, flipped the deadbolt. And her mind was so quiet, in the wake of it, that she knew he wasn't there.

Maybe he'd been too slow. Maybe she'd dreamed it. Or maybe he just wanted her to know that he was paying attention.

Something touched the side of her head. She flinched away from it, at first. But the voice that followed it was one she knew.

"It's okay," it said. "Can you sit up a little? Let's get you some water."

Lucy blinked away that locked door in her mind and finally began to register where she was. She was tucked into a creaky twin bed. The blinds above her, those were Mila's blinds. And sitting beside her, stroking her hair, was Natalie Baker.

"Natalie." Lucy's voice was a rasp. When she tried to move, she found her arms secured over her head, the way they had been for the past two nights. She was restrained again, she realized. In broad daylight.

"Sorry about those, by the way." Natalie helped ease her head up to take a sip of water. "Mila thought you might feel safer this way. But she's out for a bit, so if you want those untied, just say the word. No offense, but I'm pretty sure I could take you right now."

"Natalie," Lucy said again, clearer now after the water. She was faintly aware that she'd started crying. "I thought you left. You should have left."

"Oh. Oh, honey." A sunbeam fell across Natalie's face as she wiped at Lucy's cheeks, obscuring her expression. Her voice sounded thick. "Of course I didn't leave you. Didn't I tell you I just needed some sleep? I'm so sorry I took so long."

Lucy closed her eyes, dislodging a few more tears that Natalie hurriedly dried away. "You needed it."

"Not as badly as you need it right now," Natalie said. "We're, um . . . trying to figure out what's going on. But whatever it is, it's doing a number on you. Just try to rest."

She was probably right about that. Lucy felt delirious. She probably *was* delirious. But she felt a strange, feverish clarity, too. She could hear the sounds of Natalie's vitals, as usual. But she felt like she understood the emotions behind the heartbeat now. It was clear enough, if she listened closely. Under that breezy bravado, Natalie's body was singing with fear.

And yet it hadn't occurred to her not to come back. Or if it had, there was no trace of that, looking at her now.

If she lived long enough to speak to her mother again, Lucy needed to tell her that she was both right and wrong about the world. It had teeth. But it also had Natalie Bakers.

"The infection is progressing," Lucy mumbled. "I punched a hole in Athena's wall. I don't think I should be able to do that."

"That's what Mila said, too." Natalie had moved on to anxiously rubbing at her arm. "It's still too bright in here, isn't it? Sorry, we tried to make it as dark as we could. Here, I'll put this back on."

A cool cloth settled over Lucy's forehead and eyes, and the relief was so immediate, she could have cried all over again. The itchy sunlight faded into a damp cool, sending the occasional shiver through her. It wasn't wholly unpleasant. There was something almost grounding about the ripple of goose bumps down her arms.

"You said Mila left," Lucy said. "Where did she go?"

"Not sure." Lucy heard the grimace in Natalie's voice. "She said she had an idea, and she'd be back before sunset. Hopefully it's a really good idea."

Lucy made a small, affirmative sound. She was glad Mila wasn't here, seeing her like this. It was probably how Jon had looked before he died. At least Mila hadn't been there back then. Even if she had to watch it happen to Lucy, she hadn't had to watch it happen to someone she loved.

She willed herself to believe she wasn't there yet. If nothing else, she couldn't die on Natalie's watch.

"And Athena?" Lucy said.

Natalie paused. "That Provost woman wants her out of her suite by tomorrow," she said. "She's packing up over there now, I think."

"They can't shut her down," Lucy said, although it didn't sound convincing, even to her. They could shut her down. They *had*. She wondered if Athena would come see her, too. But no. That wasn't safe. If Vanya asked Lucy, right now, to hand Athena over—Lucy didn't know what she'd do.

Maybe they'd at least get to talk one more time, if this was the end. It would be nice to tell Athena that there were some things it was okay to run away from.

Not that Athena would listen. She wasn't going to run. Not from Rollins, not from Vanya. She didn't have it in her to fail. It was why Dr. Horne knew she'd reflect well on Rollins one day.

Maybe Athena could rid this place of Vanya before graduation. And maybe, if that happened, she could be convinced to try to get through to Sadie and Addison. To see if they were suffering like Whitney had suffered. Mila could convince her to try, probably. If Mila believed it herself.

"They offered to turn me," Lucy blurted out. All at once,

she could no longer keep it to herself. "Laurentius of Rome. He said he could turn me into a vampire."

Even with her eyes covered, Lucy could hear the change in Natalie's breath, the shift of her posture. Fair enough—Lucy hadn't exactly eased her into it. But she hadn't seen Natalie since Laurentius made her the offer. And now that she was giving it some thought, she realized Natalie was the only one she wanted to talk to about it.

"Oh," Natalie said. It was a supremely restrained response. But she sounded more curious than afraid. "Are you, um. How do you feel about that?"

Lucy laughed. She'd been feeling every possible emotion about it since the second Laurentius asked. But that wasn't really Natalie's question. The question was *Are you considering it?*

"Sometimes, when I think about it, it makes so much sense to me." Lucy was quiet as she spoke. As if making her voice softer would make the words softer. "More sense than anything has ever made. And that's the entire reason I came here, right? To find something I really wanted from my life?"

In the pause that followed, Lucy waited for Natalie to shut her down. It was the only smart thing to do at a declaration like that. But Natalie took one of Lucy's bound hands and squeezed it. "Well," she said. "You'd have to find somewhere with a nightlife, of course. The mountain doesn't have much of that to speak of, unless you count coyotes and possums."

"Natalie," Lucy said. "I'm serious."

“So am I,” Natalie said. And she was. She was using the voice she used for her orientation week library tours, the one that gently pulled everyone into line. “Athena and Mila aren’t here. It’s just us. And—and I don’t know how much longer this is going to last.” *This* could have meant any number of applicable things. Vanya’s game. Lucy herself. Probably both. “So, if you’re seriously considering it, you should tell me. I’ll bring him here myself if I have to.”

Lucy was thankful for the cool cloth—it caught her fresh round of tears. She really didn’t know what she’d do without Natalie. “Athena thinks that when you become a vampire, the person you are is gone,” she said. “Or at least, she thinks that if our instincts make us what we are, then new instincts make us something different. That we can’t truly love the people we used to love if we come to see them as prey.”

“Hmm,” Natalie said. “And is that why you’re hesitating?”

Of course she was hesitating. “I don’t know. I don’t know if I believe that, exactly. But . . . I *am* hesitating. And there’s no reason why I should. I’m dying anyway—what do I have to lose?”

Suddenly cold, Lucy shook her head to dislodge the washcloth. “There are things I was supposed to do,” she said, as Natalie dutifully pushed the cold cloth aside. “Live somewhere with public transportation. Pay too much for an apartment with people I barely know. Eat a meal at a restaurant with multiple courses. Work at a job that isn’t retail. Maybe in an office. And I’d hate my boss and complain constantly and dream about quitting, but I'd stay anyway, because I'd be able to afford the apartment and the train pass and the prix fixe meal."

Natalie laughed softly. "You can dream a bit bigger than that, you know."

"That already feels like a pretty big dream sometimes." The sun glittered against the ceiling. Lucy watched the shifting light. It still hurt her eyes. But if she wasn't going to be able to look at it for much longer, she should take it in. "Doesn't feel very big now, next to the promise of civilizations living and dying at my feet. But it's still enough. Enough that I don't know what to do."

"Oh, Lucy," Natalie said, barely audible. And looking up at her, Lucy knew that, for once, her friend had no idea what to say.

"It's okay." Lucy squeezed their joined hands, then untangled them. She'd gotten it off her chest. That was enough. "I think I should sleep."

"Of course," Natalie said. "Get some rest."

Rest was a tall order, though. It wasn't long before Lucy fell back into fitful dreams. She was faintly aware that in the dream, she was climbing the steep hill to Johnson Library.

And ahead of her, walking in a daylight they could never survive, were Sadie Grainger and Addison Greene. Addison kept looking back expectantly, as if to confirm Lucy was still behind them. Sadie resolutely faced ahead.

They had nearly reached the top when Addison raised a hand to stop them, her long hair swinging as she spun. "Home is right here, under our feet. You'll see it for yourself soon." She tapped the toe of her heeled boot against the ground. "I don't know why Whitney was so upset. The library's right over there."

Addison seemed to see something in Lucy's face then. Though Lucy didn't know what it was. She wasn't sure she even had a face, in this dream. "I miss her, too," Addison said. Her smile didn't flicker. The light behind her eyes did. "I wish she hadn't left us. But now we have you."

Sadie finally turned as well. She looked different in the full light than she had on her missing poster. Her freckles were a sunny, toasted brown. Her hair had threads of gold. The only thing about her that didn't radiate warmth was the blank curve of her mouth.

Lucy watched them, and they watched her in return—Addison smiling, Sadie staring. *What can I do for us?* Lucy wanted to ask. But the words didn't come together through the fog of her mind.

"It's not so bad," Sadie said. Her voice was soft enough to be toneless. "If you close your eyes, it's just like slipping into a bath."

Click-click.

Lucy jerked awake. But after a few seconds of panicked disorientation, it became clear that the sound that had woken her was the sound of a real door. Her wrists were still tied, and when she tugged them, the headboard creaked against her ear. The light through the blinds was orange and angled low. And in the doorway, a little out of her view, she heard two hushed voices.

"I can stay if you want." That one was Natalie.

"No. You should head back while it's still light." *Ah.* Mila was back. "She doesn't have much longer. Which means he'll probably make a move tonight."

"All the more reason to have an extra pair of hands, right?" Natalie again. Lucy wished she could steal a little of that bravery right now. "Just give me something to throw. Maybe something actively on fire."

Lucy wondered if Natalie, too, heard that odd note of finality in Mila's laugh. "Good night, Natalie."

There was a beat of silence. "Tell her she can call me if she needs to talk. I don't think I'll be sleeping, anyway."

Lucy heard some shuffling, the opening and closing of the door. But it was another long few seconds before Mila rounded the corner. She had a small bundle of papers clutched to her chest, and there was a new depth of grimness in her eyes. *Whatever I have to do?* she'd said, just a few nights ago. *Don't hold it against me.* Maybe she had decided what that was.

Lucy's smile cracked as she arranged it in place. At least one of them had made a decision.

"You're back," she said.

"I am." Mila crossed the room and took up Natalie's abandoned seat, laying her pile of papers on the bedside table to rest a hand against Lucy's forehead. "Do you need another blanket? You're still cold."

“I don’t feel that cold,” Lucy said. Her temperature wasn’t even in the top ten of her concerns at the moment.

Mila brushed her hair back, just once, before she pulled away. It wasn’t that firm, assured touch that she used to tie knots or nock an arrow. Her fingers against Lucy’s forehead were gentle and awkward, as if unsure of how hard to press or how long to linger. As if she’d never touched anyone like this before.

Poor Mila, Lucy thought. *Poor lonely Mila.* “Did you find what you were looking for?” she said.

“I think I did.” Mila glanced, once again, at the papers flipped face down on the night table. “I’m sorry. I know you must be exhausted. But I need to tell you something.”

Well. One thing Lucy could always say about Mila: She did know how to make a girl curious. “I’m listening.”

“Okay,” Mila said. No beating around the bush, then. Though Lucy supposed time was of the essence at this point. “This morning, I took the shuttle down the mountain. I had to walk like two miles from the stop in town to this shitty little office building. And I went to see this doctor there. Dr. Harris Thornton.”

Lucy couldn’t sit up very well, not with her wrists tied. But she propped herself up onto her elbows as best she could. “Not for me, right? I assume there’s not a lot a doctor can do for me at the moment.”

“Not for you,” Mila confirmed. “I went because Harris Thornton is one of the only certified medical examiners in town. I wanted to see if he did the autopsy on Jon when he died."

Whatever Lucy had been expecting to hear, it wasn't that. "Did he?"

"Well," Mila said with a grimace, "I had a lot of thinking to do on that two-mile walk. I realized, maybe Jon didn't even die in the town hospital. Maybe they medevaced him somewhere way down the mountain, and maybe I just wasted half a day when we don't have any time to waste to begin with."

"I thought you told me they didn't know how he died," Lucy said.

"Jon's parents told me the autopsy was inconclusive," Mila said. "But this week—being with you—I've been wondering. Was it that they didn't know? Or was it that the answer they got didn't make any sense to them?"

Lucy wasn't sure she'd ever been so scared to ask a question. "And did you find that out?"

"I found out that if you ever need to get information out of the front desk admin at Dr. Thornton's office, she's not above a good sob story. I told her that my childhood sweetheart died and no one ever told me why. All she asked for was a bit of proof that I knew Jon. Just to be sure it wasn't a prank. I showed her a few pictures and emails, a few texts I had saved . . ." Mila said. "It turned out Dr. Thornton did do the autopsy. He did list a cause of death. It *was* inconclusive. But only because it made no biological sense."

Mila paused, then. As if tripping on the information that

she knew Lucy wouldn't want to hear. But Lucy locked eyes with her, and she nodded. What she wanted wasn't their primary concern. It never had been.

"Jon's body showed signs of severe malnutrition," Mila said. "He starved to death, Lucy. On a campus full of people. With a stomach full of food."

Lucy struggled to leverage her body farther up—she didn't want to be lying down for this conversation. Mila leaned forward and moved to untie one, but Lucy flinched. "Leave it," she said.

"No," Mila said, slipping the right wrist out of the binding. "I'll put them back on later, if we need to."

"I'm not starving, Mila," Lucy said. "I've been eating, you made sure of that. Nothing has exactly been *tasting* good, but Laurentius said Hiro's clients just crave some red meat for a while."

"Didn't Laurentius say that he's never met anyone like you before?" Mila said. "He's probably never met anyone like Jon, either. He was eating. He was getting regular meals in the hospital. But he died. So . . . maybe it wasn't food that he needed to live."

Mila freed Lucy's other hand, and Lucy tucked the duvet against her chest, suddenly very cold. "What are you telling me?"

"Just like Laurentius said. All of the weaknesses, none of the strengths," Mila said. "Lucy—I think what you need is blood."

Nineteen

"No." Lucy didn't feel like standing, but suddenly, she had to. Her legs shook dangerously under her. "This is insane."

But Mila's jaw was set. Lucy had learned that when Mila made that face, she was not interested in listening to counterarguments. "*Insane* would be letting you die in my dorm room."

"Just a few nights ago you told me to try to understand if you had to kill me," Lucy said. "Is this not the line you were waiting for me to cross? Hurting someone?"

"It was. It was when I said it then," Mila said. "But a few hours ago, you told us that you believed Whitney wasn't totally gone. You begged us to consider that Sadie and Addison might not be lost causes, either."

"I was angry." Lucy started to pace. "And apparently, I was starving! Maybe I had no idea what I was talking about."

"I hope you did," Mila said. "You convinced me."

Lucy gripped the bed frame for support. Mila looked up

with that usual evenness. That controlled calm that made Lucy want to cling to her and throttle her in equal measure.

"Then I'll get a bird," Lucy said. "Or a squirrel, or something."

"It's getting dark," Mila said. "Neither of us should be outside."

"Mila," Lucy said. "You can't be suggesting that I drink from you."

"I didn't get to that yet," Mila said. Lucy wanted to reach out and shake her until she sounded as frenzied as Lucy felt. "But I guess you've come to the same conclusion I have."

"You could end up with the infection, too," Lucy said. "Then what?"

"I don't think so. You're not a vampire yet. And if it happened anyway . . ." She shrugged. "It wouldn't be so bad, being your thrall."

"I swear to God, if you don't take this seriously—"

"Who's not taking it seriously?" Mila said. "I'm being completely sincere. I'm conveniently available. I'm not going to run from you. And not to brag, but I take iron pills every morning with breakfast. I'm your best option. Your only option, if I'm being frank."

"And you're the only one of us who doesn't care if she lives or dies!"

The realization was barely formed in Lucy's mind even as it left her mouth, but as soon as she said it out loud, she knew it was true. *You promised me no more of this,* Athena had said.

Mila had probably meant that promise, or tried to mean it. But Mila had never really learned caution the way she tried to. The second Vanya was finally in her reach, she was right back to the old strategy: Stick her neck out and see if he'd bite.

Lucy knew what fear of dying was. She'd seen it in Athena and in Natalie. She'd lived with it all her life. That composure that Mila carried like a cloak was only shaken when someone else was in danger. Mila never lost her composure for herself.

"I . . ." Mila said. She looked a little stunned. "I don't *not* care."

Lucy sank onto the bed next to her. Just a few short minutes of pacing had her exhausted. Maybe Natalie had a point about being able to take her right now.

"I worry that your best-case scenario isn't that all of us survive," she said. "I specifically worry that your best-case scenario is that you're the only one who dies."

"I mean, maybe a little," Mila said faintly. "But only because I'm a realist."

"God, you really don't know when to quit sometimes," Lucy said. She could barely summon any heat to it. "If you hadn't met Athena, you probably would have died long before you meant to."

"Lucy," Mila said. And now, finally, she looked a little angry. "I'm not suicidal."

"I never said you were," Lucy said. "I said that you don't care, and right now that's not any different to me. You're asking me to do something that I may not be able to stop when I start.

If I—if you want me to do this, then you have to promise me that you're going to fight me off if I lose control. I have to trust that you'll fucking care if I kill you."

Mila let out a sigh and folded her long legs onto the bed.

"It's not my *best*-case scenario," she said. "I'd love to live, actually. Be really pleasantly surprised if I did. I'd have liked a year and a half left to actually fuck around in college. Get some failing grades for fun reasons. Maybe go off campus, for once. Did you know there's an entire mountain out there? I've never gone hiking. Every moment I'm at Rollins, I'm waiting for something to happen. When I decided that I was going to come here, I didn't know I'd spend most of my time waiting.

"So if it helps," she said, "I care most of the time. At least ninety percent of the time. And for the other ten . . . I care about being here for the end of it. You can trust that."

Lucy sat back as she looked at Mila. The bed was starting to feel so familiar under her. It smelled more like her now than it smelled like Mila. "That's not really what I was hoping to hear."

Mila's mouth twisted into a smile. "Sorry, babe," she said. "Tonight, that's what you get."

"You're such a pain in the ass," Lucy said softly. "Have I told you that yet?"

"In words, no." Some of the tension eased out of Mila. Probably because she knew she'd won. "In little side glances that you think are subtle . . ."

Lucy treated her to one of those side glances, which were never intended to be subtle in the first place. But the crook of

Mila's arm caught her eye, and then her attention. She had a prominent vein there. Cool blue, like her sheets.

Lucy's mouth parted. When she ran her tongue along her teeth, she felt the same two sharp points she'd felt that morning. She tried not to be afraid of them this time.

Mila had followed her gaze. And slowly she rotated her arm and extended it to Lucy. She had a little tattoo near the crook of her elbow. Orion the hunter. Of course.

"Right there?" Lucy whispered. The blood had a sound, when she was this close. A low and inviting hum.

"If it's good enough for phlebotomists," Mila said.

Lucy let out a short laugh. "I hope this isn't what phlebotomists do."

"Well. Maybe it's less awkward if you think of yourself like one," Mila said. "You're not doing anything wrong. You're just doing something necessary."

But as Lucy drew closer, there was nothing rote about it. Mila's pulse was loud enough to fill the room—it was in the cords of her neck, the tips of her fingers. It sounded as strong and assured as she was. It didn't even sound all that fast until Lucy opened her mouth.

Hunger had been an uneasy thing, since the bite. The strangeness of it had been so quiet that she'd barely noticed it until now. Vanya had been breathing down her neck—there hadn't been anything unusual about losing her appetite, or about choking down the rare meat she thought her body wanted. But holding Mila's arm in her hand, she thought of the dry, sinewy mouthfuls of the dining hall steak. The queasy, gnawing allure of the raw steak in the Falls Quad Café: not the steak itself, she realized now, but the bloody butcher paper it lay on. It wasn't that she didn't have an appetite. It was that there was only one thing for her. And now, finally, she was close enough to taste it.

She lifted Mila's arm to her mouth and pressed her lips against the waiting crook of her elbow. It should have felt unnatural. But the infection knew what to do. She just had to follow it.

She bit down. And gradually, the skin gave under her teeth, and Mila's blood filled her mouth.

It didn't taste like she thought it would. Though it wasn't as if she had a frame of reference. She'd tried one of her mother's iron gummies once, and it had tasted like fruit with a spike of metal, like biting into an apple and losing a tooth. Mila's blood tasted like something deep and savory, garnished with a ribbon of honey. It was so hot, pouring down her throat. She hadn't realized how cold she'd been until she felt how body temperature should taste.

She gasped, and it spread her mouth wider, her bite deeper. Instinctively, she jerked back, but Mila's hand settled between her shoulder blades. "It's okay," she said.

Lucy would have questioned that, if she'd had the ability. But that ability was so far beyond her now. Every starving cell was blanketed with warmth, and suddenly she was alive. Her thoughts were connecting, her body was moving without the pain or fatigue that had clung to her these past few days, and she drank, deeply. She didn't know the half of it before, when she'd wondered whether or not she could stop. She knew now, with a certainty as cold as she was, that she would live her whole life at the crook of Mila's elbow if given the chance.

But Mila's heartbeat was labored, her body quietly protesting under Lucy's teeth. Her free arm spasmed, grasping at Lucy's side for purchase, and the euphoria shifted. She could feel Mila's nails through her shirt, little pinpricks against her ribs that jolted her with little snaps of electricity.

Lucy gasped again, and this time it dislodged her mouth from Mila's skin. She wouldn't have called herself starved for touch. She was busy, was all: She was graduating, then she was breaking up with her high school girlfriend, then she was on deathbed duty, and then she was a vampire's thrall. It had been a while since she'd been so close to anyone. She'd been able to ignore it pretty well.

But hunger was hunger, she realized. You could starve without knowing it, if you didn't know what starving felt like.

"I'm okay," said Mila, misunderstanding her hesitance. "Keep going."

But Mila's pulse didn't sound as okay as her voice did. And when Lucy hung back, she found it wasn't hard to do so. The desperation of the first few mouthfuls was gone. It left her head a clear and lonely place: no red voice, no Vanya or Laurentius.

And the movement of time had slowed to the pour of syrup. There was nothing for her to do right now. Nowhere to go. No rattling door to lock.

She bent to Mila's arm again, and she drank down the blood pooling in the crook of her elbow. She ran her tongue across it until she exposed the skin underneath. The punctures seeped as she pulled back, but only a little. The bleeding had started to slow.

Lucy pressed her mouth to the wound. She didn't drink this time. She just marveled at the warmth of it. And if it felt like a kiss? If it *was* a kiss? Then good. What was there to be embarrassed about anymore? She'd already made herself clear.

She withdrew, and sat up. And as she locked eyes with Mila—then and only then did Mila's pulse finally speed up.

Mila's eyes were wide and dark in the low light. Lucy's own eyes must have looked black in the shadows falling across the bed. When she wiped at her mouth, a smear of blood came away on her hand. But Mila didn't look scared. She just watched her.

"You said that I always look good," Lucy said.

Mila barely moved. "I said that."

Lucy sat back to fully look at her. Mila's swishy shoulder-length cut was disheveled. Her skin was paler, nearly white. She was rubbing the wound at her elbow with her thumb, but she was looking only at Lucy. She wasn't something to eat or not eat. She was just Mila.

Lucy let that potential energy thrum between them. And

when she got her fill of it, she said, "Are you going to do anything about that?"

Mila surged forward and took her into her arms, so forcefully that Lucy was lifted to her knees. And their lips finally met.

When Laurentius had told her what it would feel like to be a vampire, he should have mentioned this. This, Lucy thought dizzily, should have been a key selling point. Or maybe this was just how it felt, after so many days, to experience something that didn't hurt. If Mila's touch had been sparks, her body against Lucy's was a live wire. The last time Lucy had touched anyone like this had been after graduation, when Jo Seward had her so gloriously overstimulated that she'd been laughing and shrieking protests into her pillow.

Jo was sweet. But Jo had never kissed her like this.

Lucy's hands slid up the outside of Mila's thighs, and Mila made a little sound directly into her mouth. Lucy reeled back, grinning. She felt drunk. Maybe she was. "You're cute."

That brought a bit of blood back to Mila's cheeks. "It's been a while."

Lucy ran a hand down her side again, a soothing gesture this time. "We can stop," she said.

"Don't you dare," Mila said. And as Lucy adjusted her grip to cup her face, an overwhelming fondness cut through the hunger. That was her hunter. Laying her head in the wolf's mouth.

Lucy leaned in, nudging past Mila's hair, and pressed her

lips to Mila's neck. "A classic for a reason," Mila murmured. Lucy felt the vibrations of it more than she heard the words, but she shook her head. She wasn't going to drink again. She took the skin into her mouth, running the borders of it against her teeth. Mila's pulse fluttered against her breath, but she was careful not to bite down, or break the skin. She just let it roll against her tongue.

Mila held her lower back with one hand. The other brushed the inside of her thigh, at the juncture of her leg, and Lucy chased the pressure of her fingers until they were flush together. Lucy was shaking—her tremors were jolting the both of them, but the harder she shook, the harder she held on. Mila was saying something to her, something soft. But with her face pressed into the crook of Mila's neck, the sound of her blood was all there was.

Lucy reeled back to take in a lungful of air. And as the cool air of the room hit her face, the euphoria broke like a fever, leaving only blissful blankness in its place. She dropped her head onto Mila's shoulder, breathing heavily, and for a while, she reveled in thinking of nothing at all.

Mila eased her back down to the bed. Lucy started to protest, until she realized this was more of a controlled fall. All the life Mila's blood had given her had settled into her body. The exhaustion on its heels didn't feel like the heaviness of the past few days. It was decadent. Like something she was getting away with.

"Are you okay?" Lucy giggled at the sound of her own voice. She was slurring a little.

"I'm fine. A little dizzy." Mila stretched out along Lucy's side, draping an arm across her chest. "We should both get some rest."

Lucy nodded, her eyes already closing. She was going to sleep easy this time.

"Do you need anything?" Mila asked. Lucy, already half-gone, could barely turn to kiss the side of her jaw.

"Just stay," she mumbled. And she let herself drift.

The crawl back to consciousness was slow and delicious. Lucy allowed herself the luxury of keeping her eyes shut. It was still dark, she could tell that much. Which meant that all she needed to do was go back to sleep.

But sometime while she'd been out, Mila's arm had disappeared from across her collarbone. She hadn't left the bed—Lucy could feel the pressure of her hip—but she was sitting up, speaking softly. Which probably meant that Lucy should be paying attention.

The sounds swam too slowly through her mind to make much sense at first. But eventually, they formed into words.

". . . realize this is going to sound like an excuse," Mila was saying. "But you saw her. She wasn't going to last much longer. I think that if you looked at Jon's autopsy report, you would have done the same. I know you're probably listening to this like, *The hell I would.* But I know you, boss. You'd have wondered if it was the right thing to do, but you wouldn't be able to stop yourself, either. Even if you were ninety-nine percent sure she was beyond saving. You'd do it for the one percent of doubt."

Lucy crawled a little closer to wakefulness, but not quite close enough to open her eyes. Mila was saying something important. Mila was usually saying something important. But Lucy's thoughts moved like a pleasant sludge. She could have rolled over and pressed her face into Mila's side and buried herself there for the foreseeable future. But if she moved, Mila might hang up. So she feigned sleep, and she continued to listen.

"I just didn't want this to go on without you knowing," Mila said. "I've kept a few secrets from you. Since we found Lucy. From the beginning, I guess. I thought you'd be disappointed in me if you knew I'd never really gotten more patient. But I don't want to lie anymore, even by omission. You're the closest thing to a friend that I have. Maybe I should actually let myself be a friend to you, instead of whatever the hell I've been doing."

She paused long enough that for a second, Lucy thought she was done. "Anyway," she said. "This is getting long, and it's late. Maybe you're actually sleeping through the night for once now that you're off the air, though I doubt it. But I guess I've got good news and bad news. The bad news is, I think Lucy might be right. She just drank my blood, and she's still herself. And I know that makes things more complicated. Believe me, I already kind of miss when I thought my bow was all I needed to end this. But—the good news is that maybe there's something we can do to help those girls. And that maybe it's not too late for Lucy."

She let out a long exhalation. "I know you think about Sadie and Addison every day. I know how badly you wish that you could have helped them. Even if it makes things hard—even if it makes things complicated—I think this might be the best news we've gotten in three years."

There was a pause. And then Mila said, "Good night, Athena."

Lucy sank into the silence that followed. Her thoughts were still moving too slow to parse everything Mila had said. But good news was a good thing. Maybe Athena would even let herself believe in it.

"And"—Mila pushed a lock of hair off Lucy's face—"good morning to you."

Lucy blinked owlishly. Mila laughed at that, for some reason. "How did you know I was awake?" Lucy said.

"Heard your breathing change," Mila said.

"Hey." She scowled. Mila laughed at that, too. "That's my trick."

Mila tucked Lucy back into her arms. "How are you feeling?"

"Hmmm." It might have been a bit easier to think without the gentle expand-contract of Mila's diaphragm threatening to rock her back to sleep. But she would just have to power through it. "Good, on one hand. On the other hand . . . weird. Good-weird."

Mila grinned, and Lucy felt it. Not through the movements of her body—she felt it cut the air. "You look like I felt after my first Seder with real wine."

"Yeah," Lucy said, with another heavy blink. Her mind was slowly starting to come back online. Online enough, at least, to notice the massive bruise she'd left on Mila's neck. "Oops," she said softly.

"Yeah, *oops* is right," Mila said with a smile. "You mauled me, you maniac."

"Sorry," Lucy said. Though she wasn't feeling particularly repentant. "Are you okay?"

"A little tired. But otherwise, pretty human," Mila said. "We'll see for sure when the sun comes up. But I think as you are, you're probably not capable of turning me into anything."

"Well, don't say it like that," Lucy mumbled. "That just makes me sound inept."

"You'd be a very fearsome and dangerous vampire." The hair-stroking resumed. "But you're not there yet." Mila's hand kept moving as she asked, "So. How much did you hear?"

Lucy winced, though any guilt she felt didn't prevent her from continuing to angle her head into Mila's hand. "I was trying to be quiet."

"You were. But I still knew you were listening," Mila said. "Don't worry. It wasn't a secret or anything. If I really didn't want you to hear it, I could have gotten up."

"But you told her," Lucy said. "What I did."

"Hey. What *we* did," Mila said. "I told her it was my idea, too. She knows me too well to doubt that."

Mila had stopped stroking her hair and started gently scratching at the crown of Lucy's head. Lucy's thoughts had finally started to come back together, but she figured she could enjoy this for a bit longer. "I'm sorry," she said again. "I made things more complicated between you."

"Unfortunately, complicated was inevitable," Mila said. "We spent so much time waiting before you came. Researching, keeping an eye on the students, waiting to act. But I think we both knew from the start that once the time came, we weren't going to be in total lockstep on everything. We were just able to ignore it until now."

"Mm." Lucy rolled over so that she could look at Mila fully. Poor Mila. Even now, doing what she fully believed was right, she wouldn't let herself off the hook. "You don't have to keep apologizing, you know."

Mila's hand stilled. "For what?"

"For not being the person you think people want," Lucy said. "You didn't betray Athena by not agreeing with her on everything. And you didn't betray Jon by not loving him as much as he loved you. Just because something hurts someone doesn't mean it was wrong for you to feel in the first place."

Mila stared down at her with a look on her face that Lucy had never seen before. And in that moment, Lucy finally climbed far enough out of her haze to feel proper panic.

"Oh my God," Lucy said. "Please ignore me. That was

overstepping, right? I think the starvation killed off a few brain cells responsible for common sense. Also, I might still just be high as sin. I'm so sorry."

Mila blinked. And when she spoke, she didn't *sound* mad. "High as sin?" she said. "All right, Miss Southern Belle."

"Jacksonville is the South. Culturally Georgia, basically." Lucy eased herself to a sitting position. Mila rose up to do the same. "It's a Jillianism, actually. My mother."

"Right, Jillian. We spoke on the phone." Mila extended an arm, inviting Lucy to slide in. Which, of course, she did. "Have you called her back, by the way?"

Lucy winced into Mila's shoulder. "Touché," she said. "Serves me right for prying."

"It wasn't meant to be a touché," Mila said. "I just mean... we could have a busy few days ahead. If you want to call her back, you should call her back."

Lucy rested her cheek against Mila's shoulder. A "busy" couple of days. She was fairly sure that Mila was trying to tell her she should say what she wanted to say now, while she still could. Though she still didn't know what she'd say. *You were right?* No matter how much they'd fought, she was pretty sure her mother would not be happy to be vindicated on that particular point.

She felt a pang in her chest, thinking about that half conversation in the Quincey lobby. *Oh, Mom,* she thought. *I just wanted some time. I didn't want that to be the last conversation we ever had.*

Mila squeezed her arm and didn't pry. God. She really, really liked Mila. "Do you want to go back to sleep?"

"I'm pretty awake," Lucy said. "I feel . . . good, actually. I hope that's not a bad sign."

"I think it's the opposite, actually," Mila said. At Lucy's questioning sound, she added, "I just keep thinking. If Vanya is keeping Sadie and Addison hungry, then that must give him an advantage somehow. Maybe keeping you fed will make you less vulnerable to him."

Lucy straightened. "Less vulnerable how?"

Mila opened her mouth. But she didn't get a chance to answer. There was a soft knock at the door, startling them both.

"It's okay," Mila said. Her heartbeat hadn't quite caught up to her words, though. "I'm still an RA, remember?"

"At this hour?" Lucy said. "And didn't they send out an email about you being on leave?" The only thing Mila had done for her job since she started watching Lucy was have that call with her boss about Whitney. And surely it wasn't her boss out there in the middle of the night.

"Yeah, but they neglected to make my door invisible." Mila looked a little shaky on her feet as she transferred her weight to the floor. "Someone probably just forgot."

Mila snatched up her green cardigan as she moved to the end of the bed. Lucy watched, still a little enraptured, as the rising bruise in the crook of Mila's elbow disappeared into the fabric. "Should I hide here?"

"Please," Mila said wryly. "If you'd really like me to think about the future, I should plan to have a job when this is all over."

Lucy sat back on the bed, listening to Mila flip the deadbolt, unlock the door, and take the doorknob in her palm. Though as Lucy sat there, she thought she heard a second, softer sound overlaid with Mila's movements. A sound like whoever was on the other side of the door had gripped the doorknob in return.

Click-click.

"Mila!" Lucy leapt out of bed and made for the other side of the room. "Mila, don't—"

But as she rounded the corner to the short corridor, the door was already standing open. Mila was facing forward, her back rigid. And ahead, in the fluorescents of the Quincey hallway, stood an unfamiliar young man, flanked by three people whose faces Lucy now knew very well. Sadie. Addison.

And Vanya.

Twenty

"Connor" was the first thing Mila said. It took Lucy a moment to realize that Mila was addressing the stranger in the center of the group. "I need you to get back to your room and shut your door, now."

"No, Mila, it's totally okay," the boy said. As Lucy took a step closer, she could see that flat, dull look in his eyes. The same look Natalie had in Lower Alton. "I'm sorry. I know you said not to invite anyone in because of someone having a bad boyfriend. But this guy says it's totally a misunderstanding."

"It's totally a misunderstanding," echoed Vanya. "And just to make sure there aren't any further misunderstandings, Connor here can wait with us until you invite us into the room. Isn't that right, Connor?"

"Yeah, man, of course." Connor laughed as he swayed on his feet. "Glad it's all gonna work out."

"Mila," Lucy said quietly.

"I know," Mila said. The threat was clear enough. Invite them in, or that was the end of Connor.

Screw it. Lucy wasn't about to watch some poor kid get slaughtered. "Come in," she said.

"Lucy," Mila snapped.

"Ah, well, Lucy, that won't do." Vanya's smile was so relaxed. Like he was giving her some tips on campus life. "You can't invite me in. You don't live here. I'm afraid playing house isn't good enough," he added, his eyes flicking to Mila's arm.

Mila's next words were in Russian—and Lucy could tell they weren't particularly polite. Vanya laughed, like they'd just shared an inside joke. "I feel like I'm meeting a celebrity," he said. "Jon's cute little girlfriend. Not very cute or little anymore, are you?"

Mila's body screamed with sheer superhuman restraint. Lucy could feel how badly her fingers itched for her bow. But Connor was still staring ahead with his flat, dull eyes. Addison's painted nails rested on one of his shoulders, and Sadie was whispering a soft litany over the other. He was trapped. Which meant they were trapped, too.

"Connor," Mila said. "Go back to your room. The rest of you . . . come in."

Sadie had to lift herself onto her tiptoes to whisper into Connor's ear. "You did such a good job, Connor. Go on back home now."

Connor blinked hazily as Addison rotated him by the shoulders and gave him a gentle push down the hall. By the time Vanya, Sadie, and Addison had filed into the room, Lucy could only just hear the slight stumbling of his footsteps.

Vanya shut the door behind him.

The rest happened quickly.

Sadie and Addison flanked Mila almost too fast for Lucy to see. Mila was already in motion, too—she elbowed Addison in the chest, then rounded on Sadie. But she was breathing heavily, from exertion that should have been nothing for her. Lucy's stomach dropped like a stone as she realized: Mila had lost too much blood.

Lucy lunged to get between them. She only made it a single step. One hand clamped down on her shoulder, and the other gripped her jaw, wrenching her around.

She found herself eye to eye with Ivan Volkov.

There were no blinds between them this time, no window glass. If she'd had a stake in her hand, she'd barely have had to extend her arm to drive it through his crisp white button-down and into his heart. But Lucy's fists were empty. She didn't have a weapon. She didn't have anything.

She fruitlessly clawed for his eyes, even knowing it wouldn't land. And it didn't. Vanya's hand left her shoulder and stopped her wrist cold in the air, with a grip nearly tight enough to break it.

And behind her, she heard Sadie's toneless whisper. "Aren't you exhausted, Mila?" she said. "You've lost so much blood. Why don't you sleep for a while?"

Vanya swiveled Lucy's head to look at the two of them,

clamping her jaw tight enough to stifle her scream. Sadie had sunk to her knees, and Mila was spread across her lap, her face slack and her eyes closed. Sadie gently tilted her head to let her hair fall away from her neck. The bruise Lucy had left stood out like a brand.

Addison's face crumpled with sympathy as Lucy began to struggle harder. "Don't worry, sister," she said. "We won't take her without you. Whatever we have, we share."

"Please," Lucy whispered. Vanya's grip was so tight that she could barely force the words out. "Please, Sadie, Addison—we want to help you."

Sadie traced the bruise on Mila's neck and watched Lucy without a word. Addison just smiled that beatific smile. "We're trying to help you, too," she said. "You must be suffering so much. You won't be in pain anymore, not when we bring you home." She turned to Vanya. "Can we bring her home now, Mr. Volkov, sir?"

"Well said, Addie." Vanya was so gentle when he turned Lucy to face him that time. As gentle as her single faint memory of her father, comforting her during a summer storm. "But we can't bring Lucy home with us just yet. There's something I'd like to ask of her first."

He looked back at Lucy. And she remembered, then, something Laurentius had said to her. Vanya wasn't a complicated specimen. Lucy looked at the barely concealed enthusiasm in his eyes, and she didn't have to guess what it was for. There were two things she knew he wanted. To have Athena. And to hurt Lucy.

So she anticipated the *click-click* a second before she heard it. She pictured her door. Clicked the lock, flipped the deadbolt. And when she felt the door of her mind catch, and not open, a thrill of victory broke through her fear. Laurentius was right. It was the easiest thing in the world.

"I won't be doing you any favors tonight," Lucy bit out. "And now I see why you have Sadie doing all the work. Seems like you're not very convincing to people who aren't starving."

Vanya's smile had dropped. And in its place, that terrible blankness had returned. "And the night I met you?" he said. "Were you starving then?"

In a way, of course, she had been. "I didn't see you coming then," she said. "I see you now."

Her words landed. She saw them flicker behind his wide, dark pupils. Maybe he'd kill her. But at least if he did, she'd die having gotten under his skin.

"Are you proud of yourself?" he said. "You must feel strong right now. But it's not your strength, is it? If you hadn't stolen it, your Mila would have put up a much better fight."

The truth of it burned. But Lucy held on to her ferocity for dear life. "She would have put up more than a fight," she said. "She would have put one of those arrows over there through your heart. You're right. I was selfish. But even if you kill us both tonight, you're not going to get Athena."

Vanya considered her. And as he did, his good cheer seemed to return. "Oh, I'm well aware that she's a handful," he said. "Why do you think I came to ask your help? But it looks like I need to take care of that borrowed strength of yours first."

He pulled her in and held her horrifyingly close. She felt his breath before she felt his teeth.

It was the third time Ivan Volkov had bitten her, but the first she remembered. He'd swept the first two out of her mind—or maybe it was her mind that had been trying to protect her from this, from the feeling of her own life being wrenched out of her.

She screamed. She was faintly aware that she shouldn't have been screaming, not when anyone who came to help would just die too, but once it tore its way out of her there was no stopping it. And no one answered her, anyway. One of the girls, Sadie or Addison, was playing music, drowning her out. Even if they weren't, there were so many reasons for people to scream on a college campus. No one thought anything of it. No one was going to come save her.

Lucy felt it, in excruciating detail, as everything left her. Mila's strength. Mila's warmth. The steady pillar of rage that had been keeping her upright. Nothing remained but ice and weight. She was taking on water, and she was sinking.

Vanya pulled off her neck and leaned in close. There was something so comforting about his voice when he whispered. So reasonable.

"I don't think I want to wait until graduation anymore," he said. "I think you should bring Athena Barnes to me before sunrise. Do that for me, and I can give you the two things you want most in the world right now. I'll give you your girlfriend. And I'll give you the life you deserve."

He released her. And as her legs buckled, as her vision tunneled and Mila's dorm room washed away, she was aware of a faint sound. The sound she had trained herself, for the past few days, to listen for, even in her sleep. The sound of a hand on a doorknob.

But in her last moments of consciousness, she couldn't find a door to lock. All the doors she could imagine were wide open.

Bring her to me.

The voice was what woke her, but the pain was quick to follow. She rolled onto her side with a soft cry, then tried to lever herself up—her neck was throbbing, her head splitting, but she needed to move.

The room swam into place, and there was no one to move for. There was no Vanya or Sadie or Addison, no Mila. And she had no idea how long she had been out.

Lucy used the wall to haul herself to her feet, closing her eyes against the wave of nausea it brought on. Her phone. She needed to call Athena.

Her hands shook wildly as she pulled up her contacts. She'd need to tell Athena that Mila was gone, and it was her fault. She needed to tell Athena to run.

She needed to bring Athena home.

The phone dropped from Lucy's nerveless fingers. She pressed at her throbbing temple, as if the pain were something she could smother. But the pulse had a rhythm. A voice that lived only in her ears.

Bring her to me. Bring her to me.

In a wash of horror, Lucy pieced together the last events she could remember. Vanya had fed from her again. He had undone everything Mila had risked her life to give Lucy. She remembered trying to lock the door, the way she had been taught. But that door was wide open. He was inside now. She could feel his fingerprints everywhere.

She remembered his voice, telling her to bring Athena.

And she wanted to.

Of course she wanted to.

Lucy lunged for the dresser, where her purse was tucked neatly against the wall. She'd been messing up Mila's neatly ordered bedside those past few days. Her allergy medications were in one corner, her ChapStick in another. She gathered them up quickly, nearly knocking Mila's dorm telephone to the floor. She didn't need any of these things, none of them. But she wasn't coming back here, so she had to leave Mila's dorm the way she found it. She shouldn't have to deal with Lucy's things when she came back.

She scooped up her phone, flung it into her purse, and ran.

It was still full dark on the mountain. So many things had happened that it felt as if morning should have come hours ago. But the big, backlit clock in the quad courtyard read three thirty a.m. Almost two hours to sunrise.

She kept her head angled toward the ground as she walked. She didn't want to risk meeting anyone's eyes, didn't want to risk turning the red voice's hunger on anyone else. There was nothing to risk, though. No one else was out this late. There were no footsteps around her, no foggy breaths in the cold night air. It felt as if no one else on the Rollins campus was awake.

Though someone was awake. Lucy could feel her, pacing in her broadcast studio.

Bring her to me, said the red voice.

Lucy broke into a run, toward the woods. All the way there, she didn't encounter a single soul, wandering late. It was good, of course. It was a relief. But it would have been nice, she thought, if she could have seen one last friendly face. It wouldn't have been smart. It just would have been nice.

Dead leaves crunched under her feet as she pushed herself up the steep hill a few yards from the tree line. Her footsteps were slowing. The wave of adrenaline that had carried her out here was waning, and without it, the cold weight of her body had started to pull her down. Her legs shook as she reached the top of the hill.

As she slowed to a stop, she studied the other side of the hill a few feet ahead. It would have been a long way down. It was a much steeper drop on this side than the side she'd climbed, lined with rocks and jutting tree roots. The distance probably wouldn't be lethal if she fell. But if she hit one of those rocks or one of those tree roots the wrong way— Well. All of this would be over.

The sound that escaped her then was one she'd never heard from her own mouth before. A jagged sound, like the way her mother had cried at her own mother's funeral. How was it that after all this, she still didn't want to die?

She lowered herself to the ground, and she huddled tight to herself. The cold in her was too deep to reach, or to warm. But it felt good to sit. It eased the nausea a little. Maybe now that she'd caught her breath, she could think more clearly.

So she tried again. Pulled her phone out of her purse and opened her text thread with Athena. Her fingers froze halfway. Why was it her responsibility to warn Athena about any of this? All of it, from the moment she started that radio show, *had been her choice. This was only the natural conclusion.*

Lucy locked her phone while she still could. It was no use. She could barely think Athena's name without letting the red voice in. And if she went back to campus—

And if she didn't? Even if she was able to keep Athena safe, that left Mila alone, unarmed. Lucy thought about Natalie, about the way she'd calmly walked into Sadie and Addison's arms. And Natalie hadn't been drained of her blood just hours beforehand.

Lucy's ragged breaths fogged up the lock-screen photo on her phone. She ran a finger across it, clearing the image of her smiling face next to Jillian's. Their cheeks were pressed together for a selfie. Lucy's fingers were raised in a peace sign. Jillian's fingers were barely visible at the bottom of the image, resting against Lucy's shoulder. Lucy had meant to change the lock screen after they fought. But when the thought of it had been unbearable, she'd left it as it was.

If you want to call her back, you should call her back, Mila had said. She hadn't said *while you still can,* but Lucy had known exactly what she meant. Lucy just hadn't thought that her last chance would come so soon.

It was 3:45. She knew it would scare her mother to hear the phone at this hour. But it couldn't be helped.

The phone rang two and a half times. Probably just long enough for Jillian to jolt awake, look at the caller ID, and pick up. "What's wrong?" she said. Her voice was still thick with sleep. "Are you okay?"

Lucy's heart broke to hear it. It broke in a way that she thought it had stopped breaking for Jillian a long time ago. She was so scared, all the time. Lucy understood that it wasn't her responsibility that her mother was scared. But now, when she had no more energy for resentment, it just hurt.

"I'm okay, Mom." She shifted. The damp leaves were soaking into the fabric of her leggings. "I'm sorry it's so late. I just—I feel bad about where we left off. I'm sorry. Go back to sleep."

"No." She could hear movement on the other end of the line. Her mother sitting up, maybe. "No, we can talk now. I wasn't sure if you . . . Well. How's your stomach?"

She smiled into the line. Right. Mila had made up some

stomach bug in the name of parental intervention. "Much better," she lied. "Just a twenty-four-hour thing."

In the brief silence that followed, Lucy could almost see her mother's face, trying to figure out what to say. Lucy knew the feeling. "I'm sorry" was what her mother finally said. "I've been horrible. Of course I know you weren't waiting for your grandfather to die. That was a terrible thing for me to say."

"Oh," Lucy said, a little taken aback. Right. That text that had upset her so much, that day of the party. She'd completely forgotten it. "It's okay. I mean . . . not okay, but . . . don't worry about it anymore. I know you didn't mean it."

"But I have been worrying about it," Jillian said. "My dad—he said something to me, before he died. He said you were going to fly the nest one way or another, and I could choose how far. He knew I was going to drive you away. And he was right."

"That's the thing though, Mom," Lucy said. Yesterday she wasn't sure if she would have been able to put any of this into words. Now it was pouring out of her. "I guess what I've been trying to explain to you is that the distance isn't a punishment. I wasn't looking at a map thinking, *What's the farthest away I could possibly be from my mother?* But . . . I *did* need to be somewhere away. I just thought the best place for me to be away was here."

"I get that. I heard you, I swear. I just don't understand it." Her voice was still a little sleep-blurred. Maybe that was why she sounded confused instead of hurt. "I don't understand what you can get there that you couldn't get here. There are other schools that you'd like. Schools closer to your aunts and uncles, or friends of mine. Places where someone could look out for you."

Lucy closed her eyes. Her head was starting to throb again, making it that much harder to get the words right. But she had to get them right. She wasn't going to get another try.

"There are things I've never done, Mom. Until I got here last week, I'd never seen mountains in person. And according to a Californian I talked to the other day, the Appalachians are 'barely mountains anyway,' so apparently I could go see even bigger mountains, if I wanted to. I've never been in a place without cell phone signal, I've—" She laughed wryly as she shivered. "I've been cold before, but I've never seen snow. I know there's a lot of sadness in our home. But I didn't just want to get away. I wanted to be somewhere where I could see past it. I wanted to know what might make me happy. Not knowing what I wanted . . . it felt like being dead."

The next throb was the sharpest yet. Enough to draw a little gasp out of her. "Lucy?" Jillian asked.

"Sorry." Lucy breathed slowly. Whatever respite the woods had given her was quickly evaporating. "I just wanted to tell you—I want this for you too. You know? I want you to see beyond the sadness in that house. You're allowed to figure out what you want. You're not leaving Grandma or Grandpa or Dad behind if you figure out what you want."

Her chest clenched. It felt so strange, so surreal to explain a hope that she was watching shrink away in real time. She wished she'd taken Laurentius's offer while it was still her choice to make. Although even now, she couldn't say if she wanted it.

It took her by surprise when her mother spoke again. There was a firmness in her voice that Lucy barely recognized. "Lucy, I'm getting online and buying a plane ticket now. Can you tell me how I can get to campus from the airport?"

"Mom?" Lucy's heart jolted. "I just told you—"

"I heard you. I promise I did." It really wasn't Lucy's imagination. Jillian sounded nothing like the scared woman who had answered the phone. It had always been so much easier for Jillian to be *in* a crisis than to be anticipating one. "But something is wrong. I can hear it in your voice. I know you, sweetheart. You didn't call me at this hour just to talk."

Lucy was breathing fast enough now that the cold air stung her chest. She'd made a mistake. Of course Jillian knew something was wrong.

"Mom," Lucy said. "I'll call you tomorrow, when I have more time to talk. Please don't buy a plane ticket until then. Please just wait for me."

But she was lying. Of course she was. And her mother always knew when she was lying. "It looks like the earliest I can get there is tomorrow night," she said. "But I *will* get there. Lucy, please don't hang up. Please tell me what's wrong."

The pain in Lucy's skull felt like a knifepoint now. It was almost over. She wouldn't make Jillian listen to it ending. "I have to go," she said. "Goodbye, Mom."

The woods were so quiet when she hung up. Quiet enough, for a moment, that Lucy risked scrolling through her texts once again. She dismissed Jillian's return call, though she felt the red voice's longing to answer it. *There would be more food, after all, if her mother came. And her sisters were so hungry.*

She could feel herself crumbling by the time she opened her text threads again. But this time, she didn't try Athena's name. In one final burst of inspiration, she scrolled to Natalie.

Vanya has Mila, she typed. *Tell Athena get out of studio. IF YOU SEE ME, RUN.*

After she hit the send button, Lucy started to throw her phone out of reach, in the direction of the nearest tree. But when her arm was halfway through the air, she stopped. Lowered it. Very neatly tucked her phone back into her purse.

And then Lucy Easting was gone.

The thing that was not Lucy Easting walked out of the woods.

The campus was as empty as it had been before. Only the lamplight was there to greet her. It didn't hurt her eyes this time. Everything was so much harder when one was fighting their own nature. Lucy had gotten so close to understanding that.

It was just past four a.m. now. In less than two hours, the first light would start to touch the sky. As she wound her way through the arteries of Rollins University, little signs of life tugged at her hearing. Low voices in the science building, babysitting their experiments. The slow, syrupy heartbeat of someone in the student center, fast asleep over his studying. His blood was sluggish in his sleep. It could have been enough to make Lucy hungry again. But that wouldn't do. Her sisters hadn't eaten yet tonight. Nor had her maker.

Lucy turned past the student center, onto the path that would take her downhill. And she followed the path to the radio station.

Athena would still be there. Natalie said she had to be moved out by morning, and she didn't have the courage to leave in the dark. Even off the air, the studio was still the safest place in the world for her. It must have been hard for her to let Lucy into that place, knowing what would happen. She should have listened to her own instincts.

The thing that wasn't Lucy Easting reached into her purse and withdrew her ID card. Then she swiped into the building and walked, languidly, down the now-familiar halls. She was in no rush. Two hours was an abundance of time. Though the quicker she finished, the quicker she could eat.

Mila would be upset. The thing that wasn't Lucy Easting found, to her irritation, that this bothered her a little. But there was only so much she could do. When she brought him Athena Barnes, her maker would let Mila go free. The thing that wasn't Lucy Easting couldn't ask for any more kindness from him than that. Maybe Mila would come to understand that, in time.

She swung open the door to Athena's suite.

And the room was silent.

The thing that wasn't Lucy Easting stared at the scene ahead, uncomprehending. The cushions were still piled in their corner, as was the sleeping bag. The recording equipment sat waiting on the desk. But the drawers looked as if they'd been hurriedly, haphazardly emptied out. The only thing left, as she drew close, was a single stake, left behind in the top left drawer. It shivered a little from the force of her footsteps. Rocked from side to side, as if someone had just let go of it.

In all the years since she met Ivan Volkov, Athena Barnes hadn't once left the safety of her studio before sunrise. Until tonight.

Which was the keenest relief Lucy had ever felt.

And it *was* her feeling it. The red voice had faltered. There was no obvious place for the compulsion to drive her now. Natalie had gotten the message. And Athena was gone. Hopefully safe.

Lucy breathed out heavily as she reached into the desk drawer. She had time. She didn't know how much. Which meant no more hesitating. No more clinging to a life that, it seemed, she was never meant to have.

As she lifted the stake, she ran through a litany of mental apologies. To Natalie, for being such a high-maintenance party guest. To Athena, for driving her to wherever she was now. To her mother, for proving her right. To Mila, for not being able to collect her personally.

But Athena and Natalie would find a way to save her. Lucy hoped, as hard as she could, that they'd all make it out alive. She hoped Mila would get the chance to rethink her best-case scenario.

She lined the stake up against her chest—but something made her pause. A soft footstep against the floorboards. Lucy faltered, and turned.

The last thing she saw was Athena, swinging something directly at her head.

Twenty-One

Lucy's eyelids twitched but stuck. Someone was talking, very high up and very loudly, and whoever it was, Lucy needed to tell them to run. She didn't hear the red voice yet, but it wouldn't stay away forever.

"She still isn't waking up," the voice said. "What if I gave her a concussion on top of everything else?"

"Not to speak for Lucy," a second voice chimed in, not unkindly. "But if you happened to give her a concussion while saving her life, that might be the best thing to happen to her this week."

There was a rustling, and then the second voice was much closer to her ear. "Lucy?" it said. "I know you must be exhausted, babe. But we need you to open your eyes."

Oh. Lucy shifted, and despite the roaring pain in her head, she managed to pry her eyes open. Natalie was kneeling next to her—Athena a little farther away, closer to the door.

She was still in the studio. She recognized the feel of the cushions she was lying on.

Maybe she did have a concussion. She was surprised to see Athena there, but she couldn't quite put her finger on why. If she did have a concussion, though, that was *not* the best thing to happen to her that week. The best thing was kissing Mila.

Mila.

Clarity hit like an anvil. She snapped upright, but she didn't get far: One of her wrists was bound to the radiator next to her. And she'd finally gotten her wish, it seemed. Whoever had tied her up had used a length of rope.

"It's okay, honey." Natalie, still on her knees, scooted a bit closer. "You're safe here. But before we do anything else, we need you to drink."

Natalie lifted her henna-red hair off her shoulders, revealing her neck, and Lucy crawled back as far as she could manage. No. No, no, no, this was a nightmare. The red voice was almost certainly coming back any minute, and there Natalie was, flashing her aorta. "Natalie," she said. "you need to take Athena and go."

"Mila said that her blood made you stronger." Athena's voice was much smaller than Lucy had ever heard it before—and she, too, was staring at Natalie's neck with something like dread. She didn't run, though. Even though she categorically should. "It could help you stay in control."

"It *did* help." Lucy had pushed herself far enough that her bindings had begun to strain. "And then Vanya took Mila, and she was too weak to fight back."

"Do you think I'm fighting anything?" Natalie asked. "I'm not the muscle of this operation. Come on. Drink up."

Lucy shut her eyes, as if not looking at Natalie would do anything for the ferocious hunger that had just returned to her. If they stalled much longer, it wouldn't be the only thing that returned. "What if I can't stop?" she said.

"If you can't stop," said a third voice, "then I'll make you stop."

Lucy's bindings made it very difficult to twist in the direction of the sound. But once she managed it, she found herself face-to-face with two of the last people she would expect to see in Athena's sanctuary. Hiro Minamoto, and Laurentius of Rome.

"Poor thing." Hiro was perched in Athena's desk chair, his face swimming with pity. "Your lovely little friend there is right. You'll need a full stomach if you're going to shake his compulsion."

Lucy, still shocked to see them at all, barely took in the words. "How are you—"

"I went to them. Last night, after Mila sent me home," Natalie said. "I thought we should, like . . . exchange numbers in case of emergency. And then lo and behold, we had an emergency."

For a long moment, Lucy felt a bit dizzy with wonder. What were the odds that her first college friend was the kind of person who would make a phone tree with two elderly vampires?

She'd clearly missed a lot tonight. But if Athena and Natalie had been willing to take all these risks, she should do the same. "Natalie, are you sure?"

"Of course I am. My last phlebotomist told me I had the best veins she'd seen all day," Natalie said. It was not an answer, nor was it really a comfort. "Here. From the neck?"

Natalie's pulse rabbited under her exposed skin. Lucy felt the red voice rising in her like bile. "Crook of the elbow," she managed. "Like giving blood." Over her shoulder, she added, "Do not let me hurt her."

Laurentius clicked his tongue as he moved beside her. "I've already said that I won't."

Feeding from Natalie was nothing like feeding from Mila. Mila's blood was rich and slightly sweet—Natalie's was as smooth and bright as white wine. She wasn't as stoic as Mila, either. She gasped when Lucy bit down, squirmed as she drank deeply. Lucy was grateful for it. It meant she never forgot who was under her tongue, even as the red voice filtered through the edges of her consciousness. *Why hold back?* it asked her. *It would be so easy to finish her.*

But as promised, Laurentius tugged her back. Gently, at first, then more forcefully when she resisted. "All right, enough," he said. "She's not as robust as your hunter."

"Yeah," Natalie said, slumped against Athena's desk. "Remember what I told you before? No manual labor."

Hiro smiled as he eyed her. "You'll want to take it easy for a moment, Red."

"No argument here." Natalie waved a single weak hand. "I'm comfortable."

Lucy moved to lie down herself, shifting to allow Laurentius to untie her so she could do so more comfortably. She caught Natalie out of the corner of her eye, squinting with concern, and Lucy was suddenly awash in how much she loved her. Beautiful Natalie. Brave Natalie. Natalie who looked so nice in green and smelled like something expensive.

"Natalie," Lucy mumbled to the ceiling. "You were born in the wrong era. You should have been a prophet. Or like that Hollywood starlet who invented Wi-Fi."

There was a rustle of movement, and the next thing Lucy knew, Athena was kneeling next to her. "Is she all right?"

"Feeding can bring on a kind of euphoria," Laurentius said. "The sensation can be intoxicating when you're young."

The sight of Athena so close to her was enough to jolt Lucy back to herself, if only a little. "You should keep your distance," Lucy said. "We don't know yet if it worked."

Athena's braids gently rocked around her shoulders as she shook her head. Her ever-present fear hadn't dimmed. But she sat calmly, legs folded under her, as if running away hadn't crossed her mind. "I've been close to two vampires tonight," she said. "What's one more?"

"Yeah," Lucy said. Her head was clearing faster than it had with Mila. Maybe because she'd taken less blood—or maybe she'd gotten slightly used to the taste of it. "I didn't expect that."

"You were right," Athena said. Though her forehead creased as she said it. "Well—I don't know whether or not you were right. But you nearly killed yourself trying to keep Natalie and me safe. If you could fight your instincts like that, then I need to consider the possibility that we could reach Sadie and Addison, too." Athena's dark eyes went grave as she added, "But we can talk about that later. Tell us what happened to Mila."

Lucy caught a glimpse under the window blinds as she levered herself upright. There was a blue tinge to the light. Not sunrise yet, but it would be before long. "She's alive," she said. "Or she should be. He said—he said that if I brought you to him by morning, he'd let her go."

Athena's fear calcified as she stood. "Then you need to take me there as soon as possible."

But she'd barely taken a step before Laurentius held up one hand. "Out of the question," he said. "He doesn't intend to let any of you go. Surely you see that."

It seemed that Athena welcoming vampires into her studio was one thing, but letting them tell her what to do was another. "What else can I do?" she said. "I can't let Lucy go in there alone. And you've been very clear that you won't be involved."

Lucy hadn't seen a crease that deep in Laurentius's forehead since the day she'd met him. "Yes," Laurentius said crisply. "I have been very clear about that from the start. We have that in common, don't we?"

That was the wrong thing to say. Though that was probably why Laurentius had said it. "I'm aware," Athena bit out. "And my inaction means that my friend might be dead. Are you comfortable with where your inaction is going to lead?"

"Stop that. Enough." Lucy had to cling to the desk to pull herself up. Hiro crossed the room in one elegant stride to help her. "Athena, what happened isn't your fault, and Mila is not dead. There's nothing you could have done tonight. If you'd been there, he just would have taken you, too.

"And you." Lucy was a bit too shaky to whirl on Laurentius the way she wanted to, but she gave it her best shot nonetheless. "How much longer are you going to tell yourself that you're only getting involved just to show Hiro that it's pointless?"

Lucy was wrong. *This* was the angriest she'd ever seen Laurentius. "Hold your tongue."

But his threat was useless. Hiro had already rounded on him, too. "What does she mean?"

"That's what he told me. While we were in my mind." It was probably some kind of vampire faux pas to reveal what someone said in the sanctity of a private mind conversation, but Lucy was beyond caring. "That's why he first agreed to this: because he thought maybe you'd see what terrible fate befell me, and then you'd leave here without a fuss. But I don't think that's why he's here now. I don't think you're any different from Hiro, Laurentius. I think you're still holding on to hope, if only a little, that you won't have to leave Rollins."

Hiro had gone very still, staring at him. Laurentius was determinedly looking at the wall. "You said you'd grown sick of this place," Hiro said.

"I've grown sick of every place," Laurentius said, a bit too forcefully. "I never pretended to be happy about leaving. You know I hate moving."

"But you've never admitted that you wanted to stay, either," Hiro shot back. "If you wanted to fight for this campus, then we should have fought for it."

"And let him tear you apart?" Laurentius said.

"Oh, beloved." The term of endearment held a heavy warning. "If after all that about how 'neither of us are a match for him,' if what you were worried about the whole time was *me*—"

"I wasn't saying anything that wasn't true," Laurentius said. "Neither of us *are* a match for him. But you're the one who insists on antagonizing him."

"Of course I do!" Hiro said, with an expansive gesture. "I agreed that I wouldn't physically fight him! I said I'd leave, if that's what you wanted! I never said I wouldn't make his life here hell on the way out! Rollins is ours. Even if we leave it. It'll never be his like it was ours."

It was faintly absurd, Lucy thought. The man who had outlived the divine rule of kings was at a loss for words. He opened his mouth. But if he even had a retort, he didn't share it.

So it fell to Lucy to be the next one to speak. If she didn't, she was fairly sure Athena was going to object to this idea of Rollins being *theirs*. "Listen," she said, "it'll be light outside soon. If you two are leaving, now's your chance. I appreciate your help, but I'm offering you an out. Are you taking it?"

"I am not," said Hiro, directly to Laurentius. "And you shouldn't, either. Unless you've grown so ancient that you've forgotten all your pride."

That was what finally cracked him. Though not in the way Lucy expected it to. Laurentius ran a slow hand across his face. When he dropped it again, she saw that he was laughing. It was a soft, controlled sound. But all the hard lines of his face vanished into it. "You're nearly as ancient as I am."

"You're only as young as you feel," Hiro said tartly.

Laurentius of Rome scowled. But there was something strangely warm in it. "Then I won't take the out, either," he said to Lucy. "But I'm warning you: I was not being modest about my chances against that brat."

"Oh, that's fine," Lucy said. "Because I don't want you near him. Any of you."

Lucy had finally achieved what she set out to do. Everyone in that room was suddenly on the same page. Even if that page was "utterly nonplussed."

"What do you mean by that?" Athena said.

Lucy smiled as she surveyed the room. Maybe it was Natalie's blood in her system, that *yes, and* mentality of hers. But a to-do list was starting to come together in her mind. One that she was fairly certain none of them would like.

"I'm going to do exactly as he asked," Lucy said. "I'll come home to him. And I'll go alone."

Disliking her plan was one thing. But the disagreement was so vehement, Lucy felt as if she was being heckled.

She waited out their protests with as much patience as she could muster. That patience had started to run low, though. She couldn't keep Mila waiting much longer.

"I don't understand why you're being stubborn *now*," Laurentius said. "You did it. You've convinced me. I'll go with you."

"And you've convinced *me* that if you try to fight him, it'll be a bloodbath," Lucy said. "Also, it's officially too light outside for you to leave this studio. There's no steam tunnel access in this building. You're here until sunset."

Laurentius gave her a look like he couldn't decide whether to pull out his own hair or hers. Even Hiro looked perturbed. "Then we'll wait until sunset," he said. "I don't think this is smart, Lucy. You can't fight him alone."

"We're going to need the light, if this all works out," Lucy said. "And if it helps, I never said I was going to fight him."

"So you're, what," Laurentius said, "just going to wander the tunnels until you find him?"

"I don't think I need to," Lucy said. When the red voice had been in her mind, she felt as if she'd known exactly where "home" was. But she'd known where it was even before that. "I had a dream yesterday. One where Sadie and Addison showed me a spot on that steep hill leading up to the library. I don't think it was entirely a dream. Which means that if there aren't any tunnels connecting to the library itself, the closest entrance is—"

"The Goldwell building," Athena said softly.

"Exactly," Lucy said. The same building where she'd first noticed the tunnels. She'd been so close that day. And she felt it, even if she hadn't quite understood it at the time.

"All that time, he was just feet away from the library?" Laurentius said.

"To be fair, beloved," Hiro said, "that sounds like something he would do."

Laurentius's glare could have withered a field of daisies. "All right, then. All of that aside. If we're not meant to fight, what *are* we meant to do?"

This, Lucy thought, might go over even worse than a battle royale with Vanya. She let the borrowed audacity from Natalie's blood carry her through. "It's like you told me. Someone is enabling Vanya to be here. It would be really helpful if someone could make sure she stays well out of our way today."

Lucy braced for the fight, but it seemed it had all gone out of Laurentius already. She saw the moment his disdain surrendered to resignation. "And by 'her,'" he said, "you mean that you'd like me to run interference with Isabella Horne? Because you should know that she's not aware that there's more than one vampire on her campus."

"I can make the call," Hiro said. "I don't mind making the introductions."

There was some kind of debate going on behind Laurentius's eyes as he watched his partner of centuries. Finally, he said, "You should feel free to be straight with her.

Tell her there's good news and bad news. She'll be losing a megadonor today. But she can expect to gain another."

There was something so young about the way Hiro's face lit up. It was the surprise, Lucy thought. People his age probably weren't surprised by much anymore. "I thought you wanted to keep that money for emergencies."

Laurentius had a funny smile. Reluctant, somehow. As if it was just one more thing he had to endure. "We're staying, aren't we? I suppose we can think of it as rent."

"And what about me?" Athena had been watching the whole exchange quietly. Lucy had felt the tension coming off her in waves as she waited to speak. "I'm ready now, Lucy."

For the first time since they'd met, Lucy did feel older than her. Only by a few insignificant years. But the realization softened her, in a way. It made her feel more human than she had in days.

"She's my best friend," Athena said. "I told her I'd keep her safe."

I guess we're best friends, Mila had said to her, just the other night. *Though I don't know if she sees it that way.*

Mila, Lucy thought, with a twist of her heart. *She does.*

"I'm going to bring her back to you," Lucy said. She hoped, from the bottom of her heart, that that was true. "I'm sorry. I know you don't want to feel as if you're running away. But your fear isn't something cowardly, Athena. It's not something you need to be ashamed of. You're afraid because you want to stay alive. Trust that instinct. Because if you go with me, I don't think you'll leave.

"And besides," Lucy added. "I have a different job for you. And I think I can give you something else you want."

Athena didn't look too sure about that. "Which is what?"

Lucy smiled. "The last word."

TRANSCRIPT OF ROLLINS UNIVERSITY STUDENT RADIO STATION WVBS ("PALLAS RADIO")

Broadcast number: 1

PALLAS (HOST): I don't really know what to say. Which I guess is a bit of an embarrassing way to open. All that time I spent applying for the grant, getting into this studio, learning how to use the equipment—and I never actually planned how I was going to open my first broadcast.

So . . . I guess I'll start here. I met a monster, here at Rollins.

I expected a lot of monsters from this place. Tuition bills. Roommates. Out-of-touch faculty. An exciting new host of weird microaggressions from rich white kids. But this monster, I didn't see coming. He wanted my life. He almost got it.

For a second, the night he and I crossed paths, he was close enough to touch me. He had the coldest hands I've ever felt in my life.

It's almost needless to say that no one believed me about my monster. It's not like anyone would have really listened to me about all those monsters I expected, either. My mom always said if those monsters got to me, I didn't have to let them get me. I could always come home.

I could go home right now, too. Mom would help me buy a ticket tomorrow, if I asked. It would be expensive. Way more expensive than she can afford. But she wouldn't ask me a single question. She'd just be happy to see me.

I could leave. But then the world would spin on, thoughtless and cruel as it always is. No one here believes me, and no one ever would. And if no one believes in this monster, then no one watches out for him, either. Going home means leaving this campus to be hunted.

So on this first broadcast, I'm going to ask you all for a favor. I don't plan on making a habit of that: This show is for you, not me. But if you could do something for me tonight, I would ask you to forget what you know to be true. Allow for the possibility that this place holds monsters that you never expected.

When you listen to my voice, try to believe what I'm telling you. One of these days, it might keep you alive.

My name is Pallas, and this is Pallas Radio. I hope you'll keep listening.

Twenty-Two

Athena and Natalie escorted Lucy to the basement of the Goldwell building. The astronomy lecture was in progress as they passed. Lucy had completely forgotten that there was class today. If she survived, she'd have a lot to catch up on.

She allowed herself the fantasy of catching up on missing homework. Cramming all the pages of reading she missed, probably sitting in for a makeup quiz or two, answering a few solicitous emails from professors and TAs. Waiting in a bus shelter that would never display a missing poster for her.

She thought of Sadie's missing poster then. And it struck her that she hadn't seen one for Addison. *We have to be her family now,* Athena had told her listeners on the radio.

Lucy adjusted the heavy burden in her arms as they made their way down the stairs. They'd stopped by Mila's dorm to pick up one thing: her bow, which was now nestled in its black carry bag. Mila wasn't usually without her bow for so long. She'd be missing it by now.

"Final chance to rethink me going with you," Athena said. "We could leave the last word to Natalie."

Lucy managed a smile. "Natalie doesn't do manual labor, remember?"

"Yeah, well. I could make an exception this one time," Natalie said. "But you seem pretty sure."

"Sure as I've ever been," Lucy said. She hoped that it was justified.

As they stopped in front of the entrance to the tunnels, Athena took Lucy's free hand. "I trust you."

Lucy squeezed before she let go. "What's important now is that you trust Hiro. He's going to be listening for my signal. And once he gets it, it'll be down to him and you."

She could feel Athena's eyes on her as she shifted Mila's bow to grab the doorknob. It was a little warm under her fingers, like someone had just been holding it. "How did *you* know to trust him?" Athena finally asked.

Lucy paused. The way ahead still sat in her palm, as warm as something alive. Athena had said earlier that she didn't know if Lucy had been right or not about vampires. By the cold light of day, Lucy didn't know, either. She'd felt so sure, in the wake of Whitney's death, but part of what Athena said rang true, too. Vanya, Laurentius and Hiro, Sadie and Addison, even Whitney in her short second life—none of them thought exactly the way people thought. It could have been their new instincts, like Athena theorized. Or maybe it just changed a person, when life had no end.

But there were also things their nature couldn't explain. Complications and contradictions and attachments. A selfishness that could only be human. So Lucy knew how to answer Athena's question. Probably not an answer that would satisfy her scientific mind. But an answer that satisfied Lucy now.

"The same way I knew to trust all of you," she said. "I didn't know. I just tried."

She opened the door, and allowed the sounds of the earth to envelop her completely. She took one look at the two of them before she turned the corner, out of sight. Their faces were already indistinct shapes in the hazy basement light.

The steam tunnel was dark enough that Lucy's eyes saw it in crisp detail. The pewter and bronze pipes ran in thick bundles along the wall, decked with yellow caution stickers. Everything else was bare, cold concrete: the walls around her, and the way ahead. It was the kind of place that might have been eerie, had Lucy not found much better things to scare her as of late.

She moved briskly, as if she'd think better of all this if she gave herself time to. But there was no going anywhere else now. There was just her, this tunnel, and Mila. And, of course, the vampires.

So she let down her guard, and let the world in. Natalie's blood had long drowned out the red voice. But if Lucy was quiet enough, she could hear the imprint of it on her mind. A subtler series of directions.

Holding Mila's bow tight to her chest, Lucy allowed herself to be guided home.

She could tell immediately when she was getting close, even before she noticed the tunnel was widening. Even before she felt Addison or Sadie, or the presence of the man who had brought them all there, she heard a single beating heart, slower and deeper than the hearts of the rats and the worms. Mila was there. Not far at all now.

Lucy wouldn't dream of keeping a pretty girl waiting.

She slung the bag over her shoulder, turned the corner, and held up both her hands to send the signal that she wasn't a threat.

They were gathered in an open space. A sort of atrium, where different pipes met and branched out: There were four different paths out of the room, probably leading all across the campus. Lucy saw Mila first. She stood as if at attention, staring ahead with the same horrible flat eyes as Natalie had in Lower Alton. Sadie was on one side, whispering in her ear. Addison was on the other, smiling like a child on Christmas.

And then, of course, there was Vanya. He looked to Lucy first. Then to the bag slung over her shoulder.

"Uh-oh." He laughed and raised his hands, like she'd just pointed a Nerf gun at him. "Don't shoot."

"I didn't bring it to shoot . . . Mr. Volkov, sir," she said. It was what Addison had called him back in the dorm. She could see the way it brightened his eyes a little to hear it. "It's not loaded.

I left the quiver back in her dorm, see? I just . . . wanted to give Mila a parting gift."

Vanya walked in a wide arc around her, as if to observe for himself. When he spoke, his voice was unconcerned. "Go ahead and take that, Addie."

"Of course, Mr. Volkov, sir." For someone who'd just crossed the room in the blink of an eye, Addison was so gentle when she took the bag from Lucy's shoulder. Lucy smiled at her as they made eye contact. And in response, Addison glowed.

"I knew you'd come," she said. "Sadie wasn't sure."

Next to Addison, the look on Vanya's face was all business. He sized up Lucy like he was taking inventory. "My voice is no longer in your ears," he said. "But you decided to come anyway?"

"Yes, sir," Lucy said.

"And yet you come here empty-handed." The casual, modern cadence of his voice shifted into something colder. This, Lucy imagined, was the aristocrat. He was probably never far below the surface. "You call that bow a parting gift. So without holding up your end of the bargain, you expect me to let the girl go? I imagine you didn't get into such a good school without learning how to do your homework, did you?"

She looked at him calmly, even as she choked on her own rage. All that he had done to her. All that he had done to all of them, and he was making a little joke. He had torn her life apart out of boredom. He still had a spot of Lucy's blood on his collar. And he thought he was funny.

She was going to kill him.

But not yet.

"I tried to find her for you." This part, Lucy had practiced with the others in the studio. She wanted to make sure she sounded as pathetic as Vanya already thought she was. "I went to the studio, but she was already gone. My friend Natalie was there. I—I told her to just forget she'd seen me. I told her to go back to her normal life. But she was *screaming*. I couldn't get her to stop. And I . . ."

Sadie had stopped whispering into Mila's ear. Lucy didn't notice until she pretended to look away, pretended the next part was too much for her to say out loud. Mila's eyes looked a little clearer now, without Sadie's perpetual instructions. But she didn't move, or speak. And if she understood what Lucy was implying, she didn't react.

"Ohhh," Vanya said. "So you fed from her."

There it was: the bit that Lucy needed to sell above all else. She knew that every vampire in the room could hear her hammering heart even better than she could. But she had lived a week with a vampire's senses. She understood the information the body could give—and the information it couldn't.

She pretended to hesitate. It gave her a moment to close her eyes, take a breath, and think of the door that Laurentius had taught her to imagine. She clicked the lock. Flipped the deadbolt. Her heart could tell them that she was scared. But as long as this door stayed closed, it couldn't tell them why.

"I killed her," Lucy said. "And . . . I think I enjoyed it."

There was a small intake of breath, drawing Lucy's attention back to Mila. She seemed aware of her surroundings now—and she definitely understood exactly what Lucy just said. Mila had that evaluating look as they locked eyes. The one that had always reminded Lucy of a cat. Lucy had never figured out how to read that look.

"Sadie," he said. He was looking at Mila, too. "I asked you to keep her calm."

"I've been keeping her calm since dawn." It was the first time Lucy had heard Sadie's voice exceed a whisper. Vanya's face barely darkened. But Sadie shrank like she'd been chastened. "I'm sorry," she said. "If I had something to eat—"

"I know that I'm asking a lot." Vanya's face rearranged itself into something that was probably meant to be sympathy. "But if you can hold on just a little longer, there'll be plenty to eat."

Lucy took a quiet breath. "Sir, Mila is stronger than she looks. If Sadie is tired, then maybe Addie could help hold on to her."

Addison looked absolutely delighted to be assigned a job. "I can help Sadie, sir," she said. "I'd be happy to."

There was something horribly indulgent about Vanya's smile. "All right, then," he said. "Go ahead, Addie. If it'll make everyone feel better."

"Of course, sir." Addison returned to her original position on Mila's other side, the bow's bag swinging from her free arm. Mila's unreadable stare narrowed.

Suddenly, Addison's voice was in her head. *I hope you know what you're doing,* she said, directly to Lucy.

Lucy maintained eye contact just a second longer. She hoped it looked as cold as it needed to look. She didn't have Hiro's gift for slipping into people's thoughts, and she didn't have an opening to give Mila any sort of signal. So for now, she needed to keep to the act. Even at the risk of tricking Mila, too. *I'm trying to stay alive,* she said. *You should try to do the same.*

She looked away from Mila, back to Vanya. And as she did, she heard another voice—one that she thought she would have to call out to first. Unlike Vanya's voice in her ear, it was a whisper. Not obtrusive. Not even red. It was so quiet, so subtle, it blended with her thoughts like it belonged there. Lucy could see immediately why it was so good at slipping into the cracks of people's minds.

Why are you lying? it said. *Natalie Baker isn't dead. I can hear her thinking all the way from Goldwell.*

Somehow, Lucy suppressed her smile. *Sadie,* she said. *You were just the person I was hoping to talk to.*

"All right, all right, now," Vanya said. "Let's take a step back here, Lucy. You didn't bring me Athena Barnes. And not to put too fine a point on it, but that is the one thing I asked you to do."

"I realize that. And that's my fault." Lucy knew, without looking, that she'd just stepped into the cold ring of light filtering down from the manhole cover. The light settled over her like a fever. "But if you turn me right now, I can still help you find her. I've spent more time with her than any of you."

Vanya clapped his hands as he laughed. "Whitney told me you hadn't decided your major yet. I certainly hope you didn't have Business in mind. You'd like me to hold up my end of the deal for nothing more than a promise on your end?"

Lucy paused, as if to gather her thoughts. As she'd hoped, Sadie slipped right into them. *If you wanted to talk to me, there were easier ways to go about it,* she said. *You've delivered yourself right into his hands. And if you think he'll let your girlfriend go, you're as naive as he is.*

It felt strange to laugh only in her mind. *Naive, huh? I'm not hearing the undying respect he clearly thinks he has from you.*

You said it yourself. That placid expression remained on Sadie's face, even as her voice went bitter. *I'm trying to stay alive. Whatever that means now.*

This part, more than anything else, had been a gamble. Lucy had come into this tunnel knowing just a handful of things about Sadie Grainger. That she had a family who loved her enough to hang all those posters. That she was talented in a way that Vanya relied on. And that when she'd spoken to Lucy in her dream, the ambivalence had struck her, even in her delirium. Lucy knew the sound of resignation when she heard it.

So she said, *Then I have a proposition for you. Watch this, and say nothing.*

Watch what? Sadie asked. But Lucy had already started to speak.

"I just wanted to tell you," she said, "that I appreciate what you've done for me so much, Mr. Volkov, sir. Whitney told me you saw through me, at that party, and you really did. You were right. I did want everything you offered. It just took me a while to figure that out.

"That said . . ." And here, she finally did smile. She couldn't help it. "I do have a competing offer on the table. So . . . don't you need to convince me, as well?"

Vanya's laugh curdled in his throat. *"Offer?"* he said. "From those fossils in the library?"

"I wasn't going to make this personal," Lucy said mildly. "But yes, if you insist on asking. They've got their quirks, but they really seem like they'd be good with boundaries. And Mr. Minamoto makes this delicious herbal-blend tea. You've gotten me this far—and did I tell you how much I appreciate that? I just think they might be the better fit, emotionally speaking. Unless, of course, you're open to some renegotiation. You let Mila go, and I'll join you."

Vanya closed the distance between them in seconds. "Ingrate," he snapped. "You've overestimated your position here."

"I *am* an ingrate," she agreed easily. "You should know this already. I left my home. I left my mother alone in her grief for a chance at being happy. So why should I not look for the best deal? I have things that you need. I'm not that impressed at the accommodations here. And I don't think I'm going to like the taste of rats. So if you'd like me in this family, perhaps you should sweeten the deal."

"You think I need you?" he said.

"Of course you do," Lucy said. "You know Athena is smarter than you. It's why her existence still burns you, even after all these years. Do you think if you kill me, the person here who knows her best, that you'll be able to get the better of her? Because I don't think that you will. I think she'll escape you. And then I think you'll never see her again."

Vanya yanked her close, the smell of her blood still on his breath. On the other side of the room, Lucy could hear Mila struggling, but even as Sadie held her back, she didn't resume her whispering. All she did was watch.

"Did you really come here to negotiate?" Vanya said. "Because I'm starting to think you came here just to insult me."

"Of course I came to negotiate." Lucy's voice was hoarse. She could feel herself shaking in his grip. "I like Laurentius and Hiro. But my sisters are here. I want to know them, if I can. I wonder if you knew this, when you decided to come here, but this school has some of the most interesting people I've ever met. I'm sure they're no exception. Why did the two of you come here? What did you love, Addison? What was your major, Sadie?"

One of Vanya's hands moved to Lucy's jaw, forcing her mouth shut. *What are you doing?* Sadie called into her mind. *All you're doing is making him angry. He's going to kill you long before you get what you want.*

"Hold your tongue," Vanya growled.

Lucy would have laughed, if she could. *Unless what I want isn't what I've asked him for.*

Which means? Sadie said.

We'll get to that, Lucy said. *I'm more interested in what you want. You and Addison.*

"I think I'm finished hearing out your requests," Vanya said, in the same moment.

"That's fine," Lucy gritted out, against the pressure of his grip. "It was worth a try."

Sadie's thoughts had begun to move faster, as though she were aware they no longer had much time. *Addie just wants to be here,* she said. *With him, and with me. If she wants anything else, she doesn't say, not even in the privacy of her own mind. She was lonely, and now she's not.*

And you? Lucy asked.

I wish I had the opportunity to be lonely, Sadie said. *I know what your friend Athena thinks of us. I can hear it in your mind. I did become something different, after he turned me. I became nothing. He hasn't let me be anything. Not even the monster you must think I am.*

Lucy struggled, though she had no hope of getting free. It was a calculated move. One designed to make him angrier.

"How about a counterproposal?" Vanya said. "I'll forgive everything you've said. I'll let you join this family. And then I'll feed your girlfriend to your sisters."

Lucy bared her teeth as she smiled. Surely Vanya could hear the fear in her pounding heart. Surely he couldn't differentiate it from the anticipation.

"Laurentius was right," she said. "You really aren't that complicated."

As Vanya released her throat, raked her hair back from her neck, Lucy wondered if she sounded shaky even in her mind. *What if you could find out?* she asked Sadie. *What you are without him.*

Then I'd think you're desperate and you're bargaining, Sadie said. *I couldn't help you right now if I tried.*

Vanya's teeth pressed lightly against her neck, as if feeling out the boundaries of her vein. When he held her like this, he couldn't see Lucy. He couldn't see the look on her face as she steeled herself.

I'm not asking for your help, Sadie, she said. *I'm just asking you to keep watching.*

Vanya's bite made its way through the bruising and scabbing, and Lucy felt the *pop* of her skin giving way once more. He had fed from her gently before. He was very far from gentle now.

You said that before. There was impatience in Sadie's flat voice. *You've got moments left. What am I supposed to watch?*

Lucy tightened her grip on Vanya as he drank deeper. Her vision flickered. The warmth of Natalie's blood was leaving her. It would be all down to her adrenaline now.

Well, she said. *Natalie Baker isn't dead. Athena Barnes didn't run away. And there's one more thing.*

Lucy could feel in Vanya's posture the moment he was about to break away from her. He straightened, leaning his cheek against the top of her head, and it seemed his good cheer was back: He laughed as the tension drained from his body, laughed again as Lucy held on to him to keep them both upright. The euphoria Laurentius had talked about was rushing in. It seemed he was still young enough for it to go to his head.

Go now, Lucy thought.

What? Sadie said.

Lucy didn't dare take her attention away from Sadie or Vanya too long. But as she turned to look at Sadie, she caught Mila's eye in the process. And she winked. *I wasn't talking to you,* she replied.

"Mmm." Vanya reeled back in her grip with the soft eyes of a drunk man. "Your turn."

Lucy smiled, and looped another arm around his neck. She imagined the chain of events that must have been playing out above her head. Hiro, back in the broadcast studio, listening for her signal. Hiro picking up his phone to send Athena a message of his own. Athena preparing the last word.

Lucy held tight to Vanya. "Yes," she said. "It is."

There was a deafening scrape overhead, metal dragging against metal. The halo of light that Lucy had stepped into, that Vanya had met her in, shuddered with the sound. And somewhere aboveground, Athena pulled back the manhole cover above their heads. Lucy felt the sunlight cascade over them, but her eyes remained on Vanya. She wanted to see the moment he realized.

And he did. He jerked back, away from her, but Lucy was ready for him: She clenched around him like a jaw, both arms around his back, one of his legs between both of hers. She was exhausted, but as she'd hoped, the euphoria made Vanya slow and clumsy. He twisted and clawed as his skin bubbled beneath her hands, but he couldn't break her grip.

Addison was screaming. She took a few steps toward them, but there was no way for her to make it, not without leaping into the sunlight herself. The black bag with Mila's bow had dropped from her nerveless fingers. Mila, now completely unrestrained, watched it happen.

That last thing, Sadie? Lucy said. *Is that your sister just gave my girlfriend her bow back.*

Mila broke away from Sadie and Addison. Addison was still screaming, still darting from side to side as if there was some safe angle to save her maker. Sadie was as still as she'd been asked to be. So when Mila picked up the bag—the bag where she always kept a spare arrow or two in case of emergencies—no one stopped her.

"Lucy!" Mila bellowed as she nocked her arrow. "Out of the way!"

Lucy released Vanya and flung herself to the side, rolling twice and landing on her back. She levered herself upright just in time to see Mila's arrow hit home. Straight through Vanya's heart.

He was so much older than Whitney. But it seemed age didn't slow the inevitable. He had enough time to look down to where Mila's arrow was lodged in his chest before his skin sloughed from his muscles like wet clay. His eyes burst, coursed down his cheeks, and when he opened his jaw to scream, it detached, landing on the ground with a soft *thud.* His hair, the sandy blond that Lucy had first noticed standing there in the kitchen, thinned and crumbled. And finally, his bones broke down to dust and scattered. The thing that had killed Jon, had turned Sadie and Addison and Whitney, had terrorized Athena for nearly her entire adult life—he made for a surprisingly small pile on the concrete.

Addison bolted. If she was fast before, she was beyond human eyesight now: there one moment, down a tunnel the next. Sadie faltered long enough to look at Lucy, just long enough for Lucy to see that her ever-dull eyes were lit with curiosity. Then she too was gone before Mila could nock another arrow.

Lucy saw Mila consider chasing them. But she was barely upright. Even the exertion from that single shot had her shaking badly. She ran for Lucy instead. She was shaking—or Lucy was, or they both were. They had to lean hard against each other to get Lucy to her feet.

But when Mila pulled Lucy into her arms, there was no strength missing from her grip. Lucy clung to her in return. The bruise she'd left on Mila's neck was right next to her cheek. Lucy turned to press her lips against it.

"Sorry to keep you waiting," Lucy said.

"Yeah, well." Mila kissed Lucy's forehead in turn. "If you were working on that performance, I'll forgive you."

As they stood there, holding on to each other, a voice

entered Lucy's head one more time. Not a whisper this time. Not slipping through the cracks of her mind as smoothly as her own thoughts. It was just a voice. Just Sadie herself.

Addie got ahead of me, Sadie said. *But I don't think you'll have to worry about her, once I catch up. She'll miss him, for a while. But she'll still have me.*

Lucy gripped Mila tight as she said, *And do I have to worry about you?*

Well, Sadie said. And Lucy thought she heard the smile from that missing poster, breaking through at last. *That's for both of us to find out.*

Twenty-Three

"Is that mold?"

Lucy paused halfway to the next step so she could reach back and give Jillian Easting's arm a gentle tug. "There is no mold in this library, Mom. It's a black scuff."

"It *smells* like mold." Jillian gave the wall, which in Lucy's opinion was quite definitively scuffed, a narrow-eyed look as she passed. "Do you remember when we moved into the apartment on Hodges? It smelled exactly like this."

Lucy frowned over her shoulder. "Was that moldy? I thought it was just wet."

Jillian sighed as she stepped onto the landing of Johnson Library, B2, reaching back to sweep a stray cowlick from Lucy's face. "Yes, darling daughter," she said. "The wetness was the entire issue."

Lucy sighed back, though she allowed it. It was Jillian's second day at Rollins, and now that she was reasonably confident that nothing was fatally wrong in her daughter's life, she'd consented to a tour. Lucy, in turn, wasn't sure she had consented to a comprehensive rundown of all the dangers of the Rollins campus. But to know Jillian Easting was to understand all the different ways that life could kill you. And strangely enough, it was a little comforting to think of all the much more normal ways she could die.

Jillian, for her part, was settling back into the typical spectrum of worrying as well. Lucy still wasn't entirely sure that Jillian had bought the "panic attack" cover story. But Jillian had, at great length, accepted that everything seemed fine, at least for now. Of course, the long conversation she'd had with Lucy's extremely competent and devastatingly ripped RA had gone a long way toward all that.

All of that was likely to change when Jillian knew that her daughter's roommate had disappeared just before classes began. But even if it was inevitable that she'd find that out eventually, she wasn't going to find out that day.

And speaking of which . . . "You're okay with waiting here while I get my books?" she said. "I just need to have a quick meeting with the reference librarian."

"I'll entertain myself, don't you worry. Although . . ." The ever-present crease in Jillian's forehead smoothed as she saw a tall blond figure disappear into the office in the back. "I'd be much more entertained if he stuck around."

"He's married," Lucy called over her shoulder as she made her way across the floor. "And ew, by the way."

Jillian's laugh was always quick when it came over her. Like a fish skimming the top of deep water: just a flicker of scales, and then gone. "Your mom is old, Luce. She's not dead."

Lucy turned her own smile forward as she crossed the room, then stepped into that office herself. Laurentius and Hiro watched her shut the door as if they had long heard her coming. But then again, she was sure they had.

"Your mother?" Hiro said.

Lucy didn't quite feel the faint strain in her legs until she collapsed into the chair opposite Hiro. She was still a bit shaky from Vanya's final drink—and dragging Jillian up and down the mountain wasn't exactly helping matters. "She wants to see that I'm okay," she said. "I'm trying to demonstrate with visual aids."

Laurentius, standing just a little behind Hiro's perch on the tufted velvet stool, made a faintly judgmental sound at that. "Nearly fifty years working in higher education," he said dryly. "And the only thing that never changes is children lying to their parents."

"You realize that's a little parental of you to say yourself, darling," Hiro said sweetly.

"Oh, hush," Laurentius said, to which Hiro threw his head back and cackled.

"I'm not lying so much as excluding distracting details," Lucy said. "There's just a lot of distracting details in this particular instance." Which was partially why she'd stopped by the library in the first place. "Have you worked out your terms with Dr. Horne?"

"Indeed. As you guessed, it seems that I set those terms now—or my money does, at the very least," he said. "I've convinced her to think of a story for Whitney Fielding's family. Not the usual runaway story, as you specified."

"She didn't say what the story would be?" Lucy said. At Laurentius's raised eyebrow, she said, "Whitney was close to her family. She . . . didn't want to leave them without any answers."

Lucy knew that there would never be a way to give them full closure. It was one of the things that had kept her awake in the nights since she'd killed Vanya. But they deserved to know that she was gone, in whatever way Dr. Horne could convince them.

"She said she would think of something," Laurentius said. "I don't envy her the task. To say a child ran away is easy. That's what children do. To say a child is dead, and yet have no body to show . . . It will be difficult to convince her parents of that."

The thought settled hard in her stomach. "She'd better think of something," she said. "She gave Sadie's and Addison's loved ones false hope. This is the least of what she owes."

"Speaking of Sadie and Addison," Hiro said. "Are you still feeling hopeful about them?"

Lucy scoffed. "Depends on the day,"

Granted, it had only been two days. Two days wasn't much time to cause a lot of chaos. But Sadie and Addison had been starved for years. They had to be out there looking for food. Wherever they were looking for it, though, it wasn't Rollins—not yet.

Maybe Sadie was still looking for Addison. Or maybe they'd found each other, and they were biding their time. Or maybe . . . Well. As Sadie had said, in her parting words, she didn't know what it was she planned to do. Maybe she still didn't know.

"That aside," Laurentius said. "When you said you wanted to meet . . . I thought it would be for the other reason."

Ah, Lucy thought. There was also that. "The other reason was also on my mind," she said. "But I wasn't sure whether to bring it up."

"As I told you, I've only made that offer before once," Laurentius said. "I wasn't expecting to be 'left hanging.'"

"Not all of that was my fault," Lucy said. "I told you I'd think about it. I got interrupted halfway through thinking about it."

Laurentius was characteristically unimpressed by that. Hiro reached up to pat at his arm. "You can't expect her to decide as quickly as I did," he said. "She's not in love with you."

"Yes, well." Laurentius cleared his throat loudly. "I suppose if you'd like to keep thinking about it, that's all right. I just imagined that you'd like to complete the transformation quickly, with those two girls on the loose."

"That's the thing." Lucy paused. Not because she wasn't sure of her decision. She'd talked Mila's ear off about it all night. But the one thing she hadn't considered was how to say it to them. "I was hoping I could keep thinking about it . . . indefinitely."

". . . Beg pardon?" Laurentius said.

"I mean, not forever, obviously," Lucy said. "But I just don't know yet, so—I'd like to extend my decision timeline a bit. And stay like this, for now."

Lucy would have thought it impossible, a few days ago, that Laurentius's usual scowl could hold a touch of concern. "I don't think I need to remind you that 'like this' means all the weaknesses of a vampire and none of the strengths. The sunlight will still be a burden to you. You'll continue to need blood to live, though perhaps not as often as a true vampire would. And considering the number of times Ivan fed from you, the infection will be slow to fade. It may take months."

"Well," Lucy said. "Good. That gives me plenty of time to weigh the options." At Laurentius's sharpened stare, she said, "Sadie said something interesting, back in the tunnels. She was curious about what kind of monster she'd be without Vanya. I guess I'd like to figure out what kind of monster I am, too. And now that you two are staying, there's no more rush for me to decide."

Hiro lightly nudged Laurentius with his elbow. "That's a lovely idea, Lucy."

"It's wishy-washy nonsense," Laurentius said. Though Lucy knew him well enough by now to know that she'd won.

"But . . . my offer will remain on the table. As you said, I'm not going anywhere. And neither, it seems, are you."

"What a shame for Rollins, though," Hiro said with a sly smile. "Your appetite likely won't be normal for quite some time. Does that mean they've traded one bloodsucking fiend for another?"

"Oh, don't worry about that." For the first time in days, Lucy felt a warmth that seemed to come from herself. From her own blood. "I only terrorize a select group of people."

By the time Lucy put her mother back on the shuttle to return to her hotel, she was already running late. She took her time, though, walking the now-familiar path to the campus radio station. The quicker she reached the studio, the more she would have to pack.

She swiped in, and even all the way at the door, she could hear laughter coming from Athena's suite. "—think we're just going to have to carry the cushions," she caught Natalie saying. "They're not going to fit in a box. Why are these so big?"

"I got them from some Swiss site," Athena said. "Maybe that's why? Like how different continents have different standard paper sizes? Ah, maybe we should leave them here, though. Just in case—"

"Just in case of what?" Mila's voice. It was enough to make Lucy finally pick up her pace. "I hope you're not thinking of studying in here. Terrible environment for concentration."

“I wasn’t thinking I’d work in here . . . exactly,” Athena said. “I just thought . . .”

Lucy took pity on her and peeked around the door. “What’s going on now?”

“She’s trying to go back on her decision,” Mila said.

“I’m not going back on anything,” Athena shot back. “What I was *going* to say was that, now that Dr. Horne’s let us back on the air, maybe I should stay on for a few days, just to help with the transition.”

“Ah, yes.” Lucy grinned. “And if those few days turn into a few weeks—”

“Exactly what I said,” Natalie declared as Lucy hugged her from behind. “Hello, my love.”

“Hi, babe.” Lucy’s smile broke open as she looked to Mila. “Hi to you, too, I guess.” Mila smirked, and bowed her head in a faux-courtly gesture.

“Anyway,” Natalie said as Lucy released her. “She’s trying to give us the slip. Except instead of trying to escape, she’s trying to stay forever.”

“Not forever,” Athena said weakly. Mila knocked their shoulders together—a tiny, bolstering gesture. It made Lucy smile wider to see it. “I just . . . don’t feel as if I’ve done enough.”

“Thena,” Natalie said. The nickname was new, and Athena still seemed pleased by it. “You lifted that manhole cover and you burned him up like a little ant. And then Mila shot him.”

Mila saluted at that.

"I know. I do know he's gone, I swear, I just..." Even through all her fear and doubt, Athena had never once looked helpless to Lucy. She looked helpless now. "Sadie and Addison are still out there. And... who knows who else. I'm not sure I know how to believe that the worst might be over."

Lucy nodded. That wasn't dissimilar to how she felt herself. "Well. I think my mother would remind us here that we're never actually safe."

"Oh," Athena said flatly. "Thank you."

Lucy laughed. "What I was trying to get at is—this campus had dangers before you. It'll have dangers after you. But that doesn't mean you're the one who has to be on duty all the time. Go live your life. We'll be here."

"If we need you, it's not like we're not going to see you just about every other day," Mila said. "And if we need you sooner than that, we know where you live. Which I gather is actually a real dorm now, right?"

Athena cast a heavy look around the studio. Maybe the other day, in the height of her infection, Lucy would have looked at Athena and known exactly what she was feeling. But a few days of rest later, that clarity was gone. She couldn't reach it anymore. She was back to listening to the beats of Athena's heart, and taking a guess.

"Well," Athena finally said. "Maybe Dr. Horne was right. Maybe there's still time to do a thesis."

"Thena," Natalie said fondly. "Beautiful Thena. If you use your newfound free time to take on another project, I'll kill you myself."

Athena laughed, and bent to pick up an armful of her too-big floor cushions. "Then in that case . . . I guess I'll see you all at dinner."

"I'll help you with your stuff. Lucy and Mila can hold down the fort, can't they?" With a big, wicked grin, Natalie blew a knowing *mwah* to the room—and then she and Athena were gone, shutting the door behind them.

Lucy laughed as she turned back to Mila. *So* subtle. "Hi."

"Hi," Mila said. She was wearing that green cardigan again. The one that made her look softer, more unassuming. "How's your mom?"

"Beset by the horrors," Lucy said. "But good."

"How are *you*?" Mila said.

"Good," Lucy said. But even without Vanya there, Mila was still the hunter. Lucy couldn't hide anything from that searching stare. "Maybe a *little* hungry."

Lucy had been hesitant to say it. It had only been a couple of days since she fed from Mila last, and she knew she'd taken too much then—she was wary of doing it again. But an odd gleam hit Mila as she said it. An anticipation.

And Lucy thought, *Oh*. Maybe in this case, the euphoria went both ways.

"I'm sorry to hear it," Mila said, closing the distance

between them. Even when they weren't touching, she was so warm. "Can I do anything about that?"

Lucy lifted herself onto her tiptoes to kiss her. And as she smiled, she felt the points of her own fangs against her lips. "Come to me."

And, laughing, they fell together.

TRANSCRIPT OF ROLLINS UNIVERSITY STUDENT RADIO STATION WVBS ("PALLAS RADIO")

Broadcast number: 456

UNKNOWN SPEAKER: My mother always said I'd get eaten alive, out here in the world.

Of course, every time she said it, "the world" meant a different thing. The bus stop. The crosswalk. College, eventually. When I was little, I always thought reassuring her was just a matter of proving that I was capable of navigating the wicked snares of the grocery store parking lot. But what my mother was holding on to was deeper, like it so often is. What she was afraid of was never bus stops, or crosswalks, or campuses. To her, they were all the same: a lottery wheel, always turning. And every time she or I left the house, it turned again and again.

I was never afraid of the wheel. Maybe it was the fact that she'd raised me in a layer of Bubble Wrap, but I've always found it romantic that there's no real life without chance. And if all the terrible things waiting for me—in the grocery store, at the crosswalk, or here, on our campus—if all of them came down to bad luck, then that was more comforting than scary. There's no real malice in that. Whatever could happen to me, it would never be personal.

I tried to tell her that, once. But that was never how she saw it. To her, the wheel had intention. It had teeth.

Maybe you're thinking, *Bet you wish you'd listened to her now.* But I think we were both right. There was something waiting for me, out here in the world. It *was* by chance. It wasn't my fault. And it was never personal.

But it had teeth all the same.

Well. Let me back up a little bit. We're back on the air, after our brief suspension. Our beloved Pallas is taking a little break—I'll be filling in until her return, whenever that might be. And I know she would want me to lead with the good news. Our friend with the cold hands is no more. And a big part of that is down to all of you.

I'll give you a moment to celebrate. Raise a beverage of your choice. I'll wait.

That said, Rollins, not all the news tonight is good. This place may be safer than it was just a few nights ago. But as my mother would remind you, the teeth still remain. There are people who claim to protect us who allowed our campus to become a more dangerous place. People who failed Sadie and Addison. Our classmates are still out there, listeners. And they have cold hands of their own now. And where they're planning to go from here—I think only they could tell us that. If they even know yet.

So. *Is it worth it?* you might think. *To step out the door and into whatever hungry mouth is waiting? Is it worth it to defeat one danger and find a couple more in its place?*

I don't have the answer to that. But if it helps, here are two things I do know. That not everything with teeth is a danger. And that there's a whole world out there. If my mother knew everything, she might disagree that it was worth it, for me to go through there just to get here. But my mother isn't hosting this show.

Go see that world. Climb over those hungry mouths to get here, if you have to. Chances are, those teeth will leave you alone.

And if you get bitten nonetheless? Call me.

And, oh. Speaking of which. Now, how do I put this through . . . ?

Ah. There we go.

Good evening and welcome, caller number thirty-three. You're on the air.

Acknowledgments

As a lifelong horror fan, getting to write a vampire book was a childhood dream come true. To begin, I'd like to thank all the brilliant writers, filmmakers, and other creators in this genre who have inspired me since I was a kid, and who inspire me still. You are far too numerous to name, but I hope you feel the love anyway!

To Olivia Zavitson, my editor, thank you for your keen insights, your brilliant ideas, and for helping shepherd my radio children through their long dark night. To Kari Sutherland, thank you for shaping the world of Rollins with me, and for finding it such a wonderful home at Hyperion Avenue. And to Mike Whatnall, thank you for joining me across the finish line and on the journey ahead.

I'd also like to thank the team at Hyperion Avenue: Adam Wilson, Meredith Jones, Guy Cunningham, Sara Liebling, Daniela Escobar, Crystal McCoy, Amy King, Greta Shull, Daneen Goodwin, and everyone else who helped make this book what it is. Thank you as well to Katie Anderson for your perfect cover design.

To the team at the Highlights Foundation, and to all the incredible people I met there, thank you for making my retreat one of the best writing experiences I've ever had. *Thrall* would not exist without the time I spent in the Jane Yolen cabin, revising the night away. Thank you as well to all the critters that kept me company that week . . . even the spiders.

Thank you as well to Sewanee: the University of the South, for hosting me at their Young Writers' Conference a very long time ago. Not only did that workshop teach me how to push harder and dig deeper in my revisions, but your gorgeous, moody, mountainous campus lit the spark in my brain that became Rollins University over twenty years later. (I should say, though, that Sewanee does not currently host any vampires. At least, not that I'm aware of.)

To my friends, thank you for always keeping me moving forward even when I can't see the way ahead myself. Thank you to my compatriots in the book community, including but not limited to: Ivy Fang, Nina Varela, Annie Cardi, Alex Brown, Courtney Gould, Karuna Riazi, Grace Li, Chloe Maron, Nicole Lesperance, and Mike Lasagna. Thank you to the incredible Boston booksellers for always making me feel like I belong, especially the staff at Porter Square Books, the Silver Unicorn, and All She Wrote for your kindness and support over the years.

To my community, for whom no thanks is strong enough. To Kate and Alexander, for making a room of our own. To Rob, for helping me keep this publishing adventure more fun than frightening. To Hannah and Christine, for the laughter, the sage advice, and the salt. To the Murkwood crew, for the all-you-can-eat sushi and for testing the limits of *Yes, and.* To Susan, Rebecca, and Martin, for the queer movie double features and for talking about anything and everything over a cozy dinner. To Shannon, for pork belly bao and all the hot goss. To Sarah and Miranda, who have always been there, and always will be if I have any say. To LP, my family in my pocket, for always holding my hands, and for letting me hold yours in return. And to BLCZ house, for making a home with me.

And finally, to Dad, Mom, Keenan, Sara, and all the rest of my family. Thank you for celebrating every victory like it's the first.